TRUEISH CRIME

A Kat Makris Novel

Alex A. King

Also by Alex A. King:

The Kat Makris Series

Disorganized Crime (Kat Makris #1)

The Women of Greece Series

Seven Days of Friday (Women of Greece #1)

One and Only Sunday (Women of Greece #2)

Freedom the Impossible (Women of Greece #3)

Light is the Shadow (Women of Greece #4)

Pride and All This Prejudice

Paint: A Short Love Story

As Alex King:

Lambs

For Bill and Corinne, who don't mind eating leftovers. I love you. Guess what's for dinner ...

1

If you tilted a map of Europe sideways, Greece looked like a wonky Tyrannosaurus rex. Athens was the tip of one of its stumpy arms. Kalamata was its beady eye. And the city where my father was born was near the base of what was, unmistakably, the male dinosaur's wang.

When my seventeen-year-old self pointed this out to my parents, my mother had immediately begun to rumble like Krakatoa. Laughter poured out her, until she was drowning in her own lava flow of tears.

Dad wasn't cackling with her.

He sat at the kitchen table, picking at his Greek salad (onions, tomatoes, olives, olive oil, vinegar, and enough salt to send a monk's blood pressure skyrocketing toward the stroke zone) his mouth sagging in an exaggerated frown.

"You mock Greece now," he said, "but if Alexander the Great had not died so soon, he would have eventually conquered America, and you would both be speaking Greek right now."

Dad had a sense of humor, but not about Greece.

"First he would have had to discover the Americas," Mom said.

"Greeks already knew, trust me." He tapped a finger on his temple. "They knew. It was the other countries that took their time discovering the rest of the world. I don't call them civilizations because no one was civilized before the Greeks."

That had launched a playful argument between my parents about whose country was better. Normally Dad won their mock battles because of his tendency to become morose when dwelling on Greece for too long. Mom felt sorry for him. That and she could only take so much of his wallowing.

"Kat, walk away from the sad man," she would often say. "No sudden moves, or he might start singing folks songs."

The singing of the Greek folk songs was something to be avoided, preferably at a run. When he told stories they were fantastical, elaborate, and horrifying tales about Greece's boogeyman, a creature named Baboulas. When he sang, his lyrics turned strange corners, winding up in dark alleys and atop high peaks, often with nothing but a sheep or goat for company. And he packed those lyrics into the whining style of *Rembetika*, a popular Greece folk genre that shares a common ancestor with the screech of a handsaw when it scrapes green wood. One of his most popular compositions was a grating ditty he called *I Have a Sheep and a Gun, Now Where is My Souvlaki*? Another favorite was *I Left Her Foot in a Box and Carried With Me Her Shoe.*

That night, he launched into the second one at the dinner table, mid-bickering.

Mom had clamped her hands over her ears. "Let's make a run for it!" she yelled at me. I was ready to rocket out of the room to get escape the noise when the singing—if you could call it that—stopped. Dad's face split into a grimace.

"If he puts your foot in a box, you cannot run—trust me. You will hobble, hobble, hobble to your grave."

I remembered gripping the curved rim of the chair's back, as I hovered between running and staying. "Who?"

This was a story I didn't know. Oh, I'd heard the song, but his songs had a tendency to be isolated incidents. They were self-contained; his stories about Baboulas never bled into the verse. This was the first time he'd referred to the *song* outside of the song.

"They called him the Rabbit, because he was quick! And he delivered messages for Baboulas in puzzle boxes. Sometimes words, sometimes gold, sometimes a foot or an ear."

My butt slid back onto the chair. I leaned forward on the table, elbows pressing into the wood. "Where did the feet and ears come from?"

He made a face. "Sometimes Baboulas supplied them. Other times, he cut them fresh himself."

Mom stopped to gawp at him. "Seriously? That's what you're going to tell her?"

His gaze had flicked to me then snapped back to Mom. The grin died, as grins do, when they run headlong into an unhappy woman.

"What?" he said, two palms up. "It's a story. She sees worse at school and on the TV."

"We dissected frogs once …" I started.

"See?"

I had been about to say that going to public school in Portland, Oregon, frog dissection was as violent as things got outside the school gymnasium.

"No more talk of body parts shoved into boxes." Mom underlined her meaning with the swish of the fork she'd snatched up off her plate. "Ease up on the stories, okay, Mike? I don't want Kat thinking its normal to chop off body parts and post them to your enemies."

"These are the same stories I have always told her!"

"I haven't heard this one," I chimed in.

"And you won't," Mom said. She gave Dad a look loaded with shrapnel.

Dad stabbed a chunk of pale feta, trapped it on the fork with a curl of raw purple onion. "Have I told you the one about the wife who defied her husband?" He shoveled the food into his mouth.

"No," I said.

Mom rolled her eyes at me. "This I've got to hear."

"Because that never happened in Greece," Dad said, his mouth full. "Only in America." A slice of whole wheat bread flew at him frisbee-style. Mom had been the queen of frisbee golf, so the bread nailed him, despite a decent feint on his part.

He swallowed, shook his head. "You both laugh now, but Greek wives respect their husbands." He winked and went back to eating.

Not Mom, though. She had a funny look on her face. Normally lightly tanned in summer, the color had suddenly bled out of her skin.

"You okay, Mom?"

"Yeah, I'm fine. Tired, that's all"

She was lying, I knew it. Up until then, bullshit had been Dad's domain. A simple lie slipping out of my mother's mouth had the emotional impact of the San Andreas Fault cracking up for California's finale.

Change was coming. It was two years away, but even back then I could feel the static as the malignant storm began mustering its anomalous army.

I wasn't a fan of change. I'd never tasted more than a spoonful before.

~ ~ ~

Sweat poked its damp head out of my pores to see if it was safe to roll away, and was immediately sucked out of my skin by a thirsty sun scraping its hot tongue across Greece.

July was a mean girl, and she was showing off. My epidermis was sloughing like a leper's back because I'd recently left it in July's oven too long. Now here I was baking it again, for a good cause.

The Family had swarmed the roads of Mount Pelion to do their biannual litter pickup, because Grandma believed one should always balance organized crime with acts of benevolence and civic duty. People flocked to the mountain for the vistas, and when they mounted their buses and prepared to ride off into the sunset they had to have somewhere to stuff all those souvenirs, so their litter had to stay. The locals weren't much better. One man's trash was another man's trash, and so nobody got around to picking it up.

The spike in my hand jabbed the ground … and missed. I went at it again, this time nailing the sheet of newspaper.

"You need a new tradition," I said. "Maybe something indoors, with air conditioning."

There was a pause. A big one. The kind a granddaughter could fall into. And my grandmother wasn't the kind of person who did ladders if she'd pushed you into the hole to begin with.

After a short eternity had passed she said, "This is the tradition. If we did something new it would not be a tradition."

"Eventually it would be. Traditions have to start somewhere, you know."

"Pick up the garbage, Katerina. Put it in the bag."

My name is Katerina Makris, I'm twenty-eight, and recently I discovered my grandmother—the grandmother I didn't know existed until a week or so ago—is the head of a crime syndicate in Greece. My mother is dead—cancer; my father is presumed kidnapped—crooked-nosed men; and my uncle's name is Rita.

All the twitching I was currently doing wasn't because of my family situation. I'd punctured the front page of yesterday's newspaper, and I was on it, in black and off-white.

"Hey, I'm on the front page," I said, waving the spike under Grandma's nose. I had to aim low, because for a larger-than-life character she was built short. My paternal grandmother was me, if we were identical sweaters, but I'd been saved for special occasions, while she'd been worn nonstop for fifty years by a slightly overweight homeless person. Gravity'd had its way with her repeatedly, then stuffed her into a black dress, hoping the cotton blend would contain the fallout. Looking at her reminded me that at five-four I had nowhere to go but down.

She squinted at my mug on the crumpled newspaper. "Are you sure?"

I plucked the paper off the spike and smoothed it on my chest to show her.

The headline read, *Greek Mafia Princess Returns Home.* A puff piece, filled with baseless speculation about why I was in Greece after living my first twenty-eight years in the United States. They'd published pictures of Grandma's main henchman, the silent but deadly Xander, carrying me like a handbag, moments after a psycho ex-cop called dibs on my head. And they had a photo of me dining al fresco in one of the coastal villages with Detective Nikos Melas, the local hot cop. Not a date, more like a business proposition. He had wanted me to be bait.

She made a noncommittal sound.

"Did you know about this?"

She shrugged. "Yes. I asked them not to run it, but they refused. I will be having words with this reporter."

"Define words." Words, to Grandma, could mean bullets or knives or poison.

"Words. They come out of my mouth, Katerina."

"Is any of that a euphemism for torture or murder?"

Behind us, laughter burst out of a pie hole. The mouth that found this all so amusing belonged to my cousin's cousin's cousin, Takis. If a wizard came along and breathed life into a short stick figure, then dipped it in grease, it would be Takis. Personality-wise, the thirty-something henchman was the result of an unfortunate coupling between a Jack Russell Terrier and an asshole.

Until Takis and my second cousin Stavros, who resembled a mangy, dark-haired Pooh Bear, snatched me from my Portland home I hadn't even known my Greek family existed. Prior to that they'd been fodder for occasional speculation, like leprechauns and their pots of gold.

"Poor Katerina, she's worried you'll whack the reporter," he said.

He was right. With this family I had every reason to be concerned.

"I mean … it's one article," I said. "I guess the pictures don't even look that bad …"

Grandma said, "We do not kill reporters, Katerina."

"There was that one …" Takis started, but Grandma blasted him in the face with a withering glare. "Maybe there was no reporter," he muttered. "Heh. I was mistaken. It happens sometimes. But don't tell Marika that, eh? Already she makes my life miserable."

Marika was his wife. She was too good for him, but so was most of humanity.

None of the wives were with us today. The only women standing in the weeds at the side of the road were Grandma, Aunt Rita, and me. Earlier, when I'd asked Grandma why it was the three of us amidst a sea of men, she told me the wives had their hands full wiping their husbands' butts. The last thing they needed was to pick up more garbage.

I pocketed the front page. "Let it go," I said, gathering my hair into a damp ponytail. Like the rest of my family I had dark hair, and a lot of it—most of it on my head. Genetics had kept the mustache and given me the Greek hips. An unimaginative person might comment that I had curves in all the right places. A clever person would point out that everyone has curves in the right places, because that's the way the human body is put together. So what I had was nothing special.

Takis was winding up for another smart-ass remark when our heads all turned. Something with a powerful internal combustion engine was rumbling our way.

We all gravitated deeper into the weeds, waited for the vehicle to swerve around the tight twist in the road. Mount Pelion's roads were steep and even more crooked than my family. Take the corners too quickly, you'd fly the rest of the way home.

A bus nosed around the curve. It rattled past, blasting smut from its tailpipe in a thick, chewable cloud. The bus had barely gasped around the next corner when an SUV sailed up the incline, using the bits of the road that weren't filled up with bus. The gas-guzzler crunched to a stop on the … Well, it wasn't really a shoulder. It was more like the guy painting lines on the road sneezed, creating an extra couple of inches of what wasn't technically road. Anyway, that's where the SUV stopped. The driver's side door opened and one of the lesser Greek gods climbed out and planted himself in front of me.

Xander. Grandma's go-to henchman. He had been with her since he was a baby, after something went terribly wrong and his whole family was killed on her command. He was tall, dark-haired, with skin the color of burnt caramel. Walls wished they were built as tough as Xander. Maybe ten years ago, he'd been a pretty-boy, but today, in his early 30s, his edges were too hard and too lived-in to be beautiful. Most of the time he schlepped around in casual wear, which was good. He was intimidating at the best of times, but dressed up he was deadly. Today he was doing me a favor: Hawaiian shirt and jeans.

"Do you have a last name?" I asked him, suddenly curious. "Or is Xander like a Madonna or Cher thing?"

He didn't say anything. He never did. But he looked good while he wasn't doing it. He took the garbage bag from Grandma, the litter spike from my hand, and passed them off to one of the cousins.

"Time to go," Grandma said. "I have an appointment I cannot miss."

Xander turned around and reached for something in the glove box. He drew out a small, square package. It was wrapped in brown paper and tied with jute twine. The sender was either profoundly lazy, or moderately clever, because there was no return address, or any address, unless it was in invisible ink. Nothing on it but Grandma's name, penned with a flamboyant hand. If I was mildly envious it's because my handwriting hadn't evolved past middle school.

It wasn't until Xander didn't hand over the package that synapses twanged in my head. Something wicked had come this way, and it had arrived in this box.

Although I knew better, my mouth said, "What is it? Is it a bomb?" My brain face-palmed. The question had slipped out without its permission. The box was sealed, therefore there's no conceivable way anyone standing here could know what was in it.

Grandma gawked at me like I was several animals short of a zoo. Under the circumstances, I couldn't disagree with her.

"All the mail is checked," she told me. "Everything comes through security and it is tested for metal and explosives." She reached for the box, but Xander pulled his hand away. If he was worried, I was worried.

Did I say worried? I meant I was freaking the hell out. Now that the bomb possibility had been swept away, my brain was spitting out other nightmare scenarios. Dad was still missing, presumed kidnapped. Ten days had passed without so much as a whisper from my father or his abductors. Not even the authorities—Greek or American—had coughed up a shred of information about his disappearance. If anyone knew anything they weren't singing.

The good news was that the box in Xander's hands was too small to hold a human head. The bad news was that it was the right size to hold a quarter of a human head—maybe even a third. Or any number of smaller body parts, some of them vital organs.

"What's going on?" Aunt Rita called out.

My father had two brothers. The middle child, my uncle Kostas, lived in Germany, where he ran what was about to become his own Family. The youngest was Aunt Rita. Grandma called her a *travesti*, but I still wasn't clear whether Aunt Rita was a cross-dresser or transgendered. She'd told me to call her Aunt Rita, so that cleared up the whole pronoun situation. Today she was as close to *au natural* as she got, picking her way over to where we were standing, in short overalls, combat boots, and a blond wig styled in a high ponytail. She had mastered the art of no-makeup makeup. Her chin said it was five o'clock somewhere, but not here.

"Someone sent a package," Grandma said.

Aunt Rita's gaze flitted from the box, to me, and then back to the box. I knew what she was thinking because I was thinking it, too.

"Michail," she said in a blunt tone.

"Katerina?"

My grandmother could pack a lot of meaning into one itty-bitty word. For instance, now, when she said my name, what she really meant was, '*Katerina, it's entirely probable that your father's body parts are in this box, therefore you need to go and stand waaaaay over there so you don't go Brad Pitt in* Se7en *when we open this box.*'

To which I replied, "Grandma," knowing full well she understood what I meant was, '*Over any number of dead—well, not dead, because killing is bad, but let's go with critically injured, with the possibility of a full recovery—bodies am I going anywhere except right here. Now somebody open the box.*'

Xander was still holding the box, only now he was holding it in the air, where neither Grandma nor I had a chance in hell of reaching it.

"My Virgin Mary!" Aunt Rita rolled her eyes and tickled Xander. He folded, leaving me to pick the low-hanging fruit out of his hand.

I stood there slightly stunned for a moment, shocked that I'd won. Aunt Rita took advantage of the blip in my programming and snatched the box. In seconds she sawed through the twine with her teeth and threw aside the brown paper.

Grandma glared at her youngest child.

Aunt Rita looked at her. "What?"

"We are here to pick up garbage," Grandma said, "not make more."

I picked it up and folded the paper carefully, in case we needed it later for clues. Meanwhile my aunt was inspecting a plain white gift box. It had been fastened together here and there with bits of tape. She hacked through those in a jiffy with her manicured nails.

"Huh," she said, peering into the flimsy cardboard box.

We all craned our necks—except for Xander—to take a look.

It was a wooden puzzle box, with a combination reel. Letters, not numbers. Eight across. The entire English alphabet on each reel. Right now they were spelling out *gobbledygook*. Or rather, *gobbledy*.

"That looks German," my aunt said, reading the reels. She pulled out her smartphone and began Googling the letters.

"English," I said, saving her the trouble. "It's part of a word. Gobbledygook."

"Gobbledygook?"

"Gibberish."

"Gibberish?"

I hunted around for the right Greek word. "*Anoisies*." Nonsense.

"I do not know what is inside, but I know who made it," Grandma called out. She had lost interest in the box's contents and wandered off, which was weird, because it was now about five hundred percent more interesting. Anyway, she was showing her disinterest by climbing into the SUV, and Xander was holding open one of the back doors, waiting on me to join her.

It was a no-brainer: There was a cold wind blowing, and I intended to shove my face in front of the vent to catch it, so I climbed into the backseat. Aunt Rita jumped in the other side.

"Who?" I asked.

Grandma sniffed. "An old bastard I used to know."

"Why did he make you a puzzle box?"

"I think this is his way of telling me he knows who has Michail."

My heart began to boogie. It was a lead—our first real lead since Dad had been *escorted* from our Portland, Oregon home. My inner child kicked the driver's seat. She could be kind of a problem child, which was weird, because aside from a rash of underage drinking, I had been the good girl all my life.

"What are we waiting for? Saddle up!"

Grandma glanced back. "We cannot go to see him."

"Why not?"

"Because he is in a maximum security prison."

2

Ten minutes later I was tugging open the screen door to Grandma's house. If you could call it a house—and I wasn't sure I could. It had all the prerequisites of a house: walls, roof, floor, rooms, but with fifty or so years of neglect tacked onto its life sentence. Grandma's house was going places, and the places it was going were all city dumps. It was a dog leg-shaped hovel, a one-story death trap, a throwback to the days before building codes were implemented. The garden was approaching jungle status, an amazing feat for a garden that existed entirely in red pots. This hovel was the centerpiece of a palatial compound, one of those family heirlooms that was passed down from eldest child to eldest child, in the Makris family. Which meant I was in the inheritance zone, whether I liked it or not.

But the compound …

My family's compound could have kicked the Kennedy compound in the misshapen consonants.

The air was coolish in Grandma's house. The shutters were hugging the windows, keeping the sun out. The gloom was punctured here and there by the occasional ray squeezing through a gap. The kitchen had one table, several chairs, and a plastic tablecloth, which was apparently a Greek thing. Cloth tablecloths were only trotted out for good company. According to my aunt, family couldn't be trusted not to spill food, while guests knew their reputations hinged on whether on not they were sloppy eaters. The appliances were old school, old-fashioned, and—in the case of the refrigerator, which had a lift-and-pull handle—just plain old. The painted windowsill was peeling. The ceiling wore oil stains from a half-dozen generations of Makris. Nothing below waist level could be called a cupboard. Grandma kept her pots and pans behind flowery curtains.

Grandma's kitchen currently had two occupants.

Papou, who despite being called "Grandfather" was no one around here's grandfather, was at the kitchen table, peeling an apple with a pocketknife. Papou's face suggested that it used to be a planet, but had experienced an unfortunate collision with a meteor shower and lost. He was so old it was a wonder Lord Elgin hadn't hauled him back to England with the rest of Greece's marbles. He rode around in a wheelchair with a mounted rack for his shotgun. Fortunately, no one would give him any shells. Papou was Grandma's advisor, what the mob back home called a consigliere.

There was a man seated across from him. A stranger. He was olive-skinned, mid-thirties and reminded me of barbed wire. He wore a wife-beater with dress pants. His elbows were on the table, his head in his hands. He looked like a man with one problem too many. Like, say, my family.

"You have a visitor," Papou said to Grandma, who was right behind me. "Did you know Katerina was in the newspaper?"

I pulled the front page out of my pocket, flattened it on the table. "It's true."

"I knew," Grandma said. "Who is this?"

"A dead man with a pulse," Papou said. "He's here because of the newspaper. Everybody knows she is here, and now certain parties are not happy. They want her to leave or die, so one of them hired this *vlakas*."

A *vlakas* is a Greek idiot. It's a special Hellenic brand of stupidity.

My hands and feet went icy cold. "To make me leave or make me die? Because there's a difference …"

Grandma was staring at me, as though she wasn't so sure I was her blood.

"Really?" Aunt Rita asked. "That's what you wear to an assassination?"

The man looked up at my aunt. "What are you? Because I don't talk to whatever it is you are. What if it's catching? I could wind up in Mykonos, dancing in a cabaret, selling my *kolos* to sailors."

My aunt flicked his ear. "Oww," he howled.

"Should we call the police?" I asked.

"No," everyone said in unison. They all went diving for the nearest red object, which was an apple in the fruit bowl. Greeks have superstitions out the wahzoo. Touching red cancelled out the bad juju that came with two or more people saying the same thing at the same time.

After everything died down, Grandma spoke.

"Today you are a lucky man. Do you know why?" She settled into the wood-and-straw chair at the head of the table. She didn't wait for his answer. "Listen and I will tell you. Today, here at my table, you are a man with choices. You can tell me who you work for, or you can stay quiet. They are both valid choices."

"I choose quiet," he said.

"Are you sure? Because that is the bad choice."

He shot us all nervous glances. "Why? What happens if I don't tell you?"

"One door leads to the castle." I leaned against the kitchen counter, squelching the desire to sit on it and swing my feet. "And one leads to certain death."

"Castle?" He looked confused. "What castle?"

"There is no castle," Grandma said. "But there is certain death."

His gaze bounced between us. "And telling you who my employer is, which one is that?"

"Castle," I said. "Although that should be obvious."

"What happens if I give you the name?"

"Certain death," Grandma said.

"Wait." I looked at her. "They can't both be certain death. That's not right or fair."

"The death is certain," she said. "The hand dealing the death is different. When his employer discovers his treachery he will be killed."

The man began to blubber. "I don't want to die."

"Assassins," my aunt said. "They don't make them like they used to."

"How did they use to make them?" I asked her.

"Clever and better dressed."

"It's not fair," the wannabe assassin wept. "I'm a guy trying to make a living. Time are hard, you know?"

No one said, '*Hey, there are other jobs*,' because there weren't. Greece was starting down the barrel of a twenty-six-percent unemployment rate.

"What's with the outfit?" I asked.

"This?" He tugged at the white wife-beater. "I was trying to fit in."

"With who?"

"The farmers."

"We have farmers?" I asked Grandma.

Papou scoffed, but there was humor behind the sound. A laughing *at* me, not a laughing *with* me. "Who do you think picks all the fruit and raises the sheep you eat?"

"Kindly elves?" I wasn't serious, but this was me trying to cope with the knowledge that I was on yet another hit list. It was the second time in as many weeks. I wondered if I could expect fifty more.

Grandma shook her head. "You are your father."

Except not a former mobster or a current giant question mark. When Grandma had drugged me and shot me back to America—a temporary problem; I boomeranged right back on a commercial flight—I had discovered a cache of, well, cash, alternate identities, and a gun. All the passports had Dad's face but different names. He was Alessandro, he was Pierre, he was Ivan, he was a lot of people I'd never met. So far I hadn't said a word to Grandma. It was a Dad and me problem. A father-daughter failure to communicate. And I didn't know who I could trust here. Worse, I didn't know who I couldn't trust.

"Think of this as an opportunity," I said, ignoring her observation. "If you tell Grandma who hired you, then you get to extend your life, for …" I glanced at the others, hoping someone else would supply the answer.

Aunt Rita was the benefactor. "For as long as he can run very fast."

"See? If you're a good runner then you might get to live another fifty or so years. Cheer up," I said. "It's not all bad news."

"I can't run fast. I took a bullet in the knee."

We all made *Yikes, that's too bad* faces. His blubbering gained momentum. I reached over to where Grandma kept a box of tissues and dumped them in front of him. Watching a grown man cry is never pretty. They do it even uglier than women because they have so little practice after the age of four.

"There has to be a middle ground," I said. "A way he can keep his life and tell us what he knows." I wasn't saint material, but I liked to think I was a fundamentally decent human being. I had never committed a crime, other than the underage drinking. Well, there was the time, about a week ago, when I stole Xander's car, but it was more like borrowing than stealing, seeing as I had every intention of forking out for a carwash before returning it. And there was the whole leaving America, entering Greece, then reentering America illegally, but that wasn't my fault either. At the time I was incapacitated by something Grandma had brewed up. When I left the America the second time, the TSA had treated me to a groping, an interrogation, and they'd made everyone empty out their pockets. But they wore badges that said they were allowed to be the bad guys, so I did the legal thing and played along. And I had come *this* close to being a murderer, but Xander saved me the trouble by blowing the bad guy's head off at the last second. In my defense—and Xander's—the man had been about to kill me.

Bottom line: I wasn't cut out to be a criminal, especially not a career criminal. Grandma had revealed plans for me that included catapulting me into her seat when she went to have a sit-down with God, but there was no way. Once Dad was safe and sound I was going home, back to a new job that I didn't have yet. It would be a cool winter day in hell before I became the head of a criminal organization.

Crime was in my blood but it wasn't in my hands, where it really counted.

"What would you do, Katerina?" Grandma asked.

Every head swiveled my way. She'd dumped me in the hot seat.

Think. Try not to go full-on deer in the headlights.

"He could …" I look to them for confirmation that wasn't coming. "… give us his employers name, then he could pretend to be hunting me?"

"I could do that," the guy said quickly. "I always wanted to be an actor."

I nodded enthusiastically. "See? Then while he's creeping around, pretending to hunt me, we could send someone to negotiate with his employer."

Grandma looked dubious. "Negotiate."

"Sure," I said. "Look at how Don Corleone did it. He was a diplomat first and foremost."

"You want me to be like a character in a movie?"

"It was a book before it was a movie."

"Yes, but the movie was superior."

She had me there. "It doesn't matter which was better. But you should negotiate first."

"This person wants to kill my only granddaughter, and you expect me to negotiate?"

Aunt Rita, Papou, and the hitman were bouncing back and forth, watching us.

"It's a starting point," I told her. "If it doesn't work you can do it your way."

We both looked at the hitman.

"Is death certain?" he asked.

"Eventually," I said.

~ ~ ~

The hitman, whose name turned out to be Elias, worked for a tinpot gangster named Fatmir the Poor, an Albanian who had fled his country when their economy collapsed in the early 1990s. No longer poor, Fatmir kept the name as a reminder of what he had once been.

"Do you know him?" I asked Grandma, when we were alone in the kitchen. She was moving things around behind the counter, staying busy without accomplishing anything tangible. It wasn't like her to avoid baking in these situations. Normally baking was her go-to method of thinking, dealing, and procrastinating. What was she really up to?

"I have heard of him. He is a …" She pointed to her head.

"A king? Balding? A headless horseman? A Pez dispenser? Wait—is he a patient at a psychiatric facility? Because that would explain why he wants me killed." I expected charades from Xander, not Grandma.

"A muslim." She spoke the word as if it were a hand grenade wedged in her mouth.

"So?"

"He wants to build one of his churches in Athens."

"So?"

"Greece has no room for a mosque."

Grandma was part of a generation that clung to its -isms. If it wasn't Greek-born, and Greek Orthodox, it was immediately suspect. If the golden oldies released their grip the whole country might unravel. All those Turkish and Persian invasions throughout history had made them twitchy about which sorts belonged and which sorts should get back on their boats and paddle.

"Okay," I said. "But I wouldn't say it to Fatmir's face when you speak to him. Not if you want me to live."

She didn't look up from her task, which seemed to be a ritualistic form of dithering. "I will not be going to speak with him."

My brain flopped around, hunting for the right question. What it came back with was, "Huh?"

"Rita and Takis will be going as my emissaries."

I crunched the numbers. The total was in the negatives. "So you want me to die?"

"This is not the first time either of them have negotiated on my behalf. Takis looks like an idiot, yes, but he is a good tool."

I couldn't argue with that. Takis was a tool.

"Why don't I go?"

"No."

Subject closed. Sealed with wax. Chained shut. Good thing my personality came with a crowbar, for emergencies.

"It's my life. I should be allowed to bargain for it."

"No."

Okay, so I had the crowbar, she had the sledgehammer.

"What about the puzzle box?"

"I will deal with that later."

"But it's our only clue."

Xander knocked on the screen door and entered. He said nothing, just stood there, but the kitchen was suddenly too small. I had a sudden premonition, an inkling of where he and Grandma were going. When the Baptist was holding me captive, he had mentioned Grandma had cancer, something she was keeping secret from us all. Except … Xander knew. Someone had to be ferrying her to and from her appointments, and it was no secret that Xander was one of her most trusted confidantes.

Grandma lifted her head. She nodded to Xander and he vanished into her bedroom. He returned a moment later holding a small travel bag.

"We will talk when I get back." Her words were cool but she touched my face with a warm hand.

"When will that be?"

"Soon."

~ ~ ~

In the old days—a couple of weeks back—I would have been content to sit around the compound, watch TV, swim, and generally maintain my status as a couch potato. But times had changed.

I had a clue. I didn't know what it was—true—but I had one. Grandma had left the puzzle box at the bottom of her stocking drawer for anyone to find.

Aunt Rita and Takis were gone. Grandma and Xander were gone. Which left me with Papou and the rest of the Family. If Grandma knew who had sent the box, maybe her advisor did, too, seeing as how they were from the same geologic period.

I found him at the back of the compound, between the building and the wall, blowing smoke like the Little Engine That Could. When he saw me he dropped the cigarette on the ground, then he burst into curse words, most of them involving unnatural acts with animals.

"I saw that on the internet once," I told him. "I was looking for a pot roast recipe. What are you doing back here?"

"Not smoking, that's what I'm doing."

The ground in the compound was a neat arrangement of flagstones. It was interrupted here and there for the gardens Grandma tended herself. Each was an explosion of color and scent and green stuff, some of it pointy. Papou had planted himself by a sprawling oleander, and judging from the small nest of cigarette butts at its base he did that a lot.

"I don't care if you smoke, and I'm not going to squeal. It's your funeral."

"I hate cigarettes," he said. "They stink and they taste like a Turkish hooker's ass. I smoke to die."

Papou had a half-hearted death wish. He was taking the long, slow, scenic route to Hades.

"If Grandma sees all those cigarette butts you're a dead man."

"Pick them up," he said.

"You want me to pick up your mess?"

"That's the idea."

I leaned against the wall, folded my arms. The wall surrounding the compound was a tall stack of stone slabs, held together with tough mortar. Jericho wished it had a wall this strong. An army could blast trumpets here for a thousand years and it wouldn't budge. Although, someone in the Family was bound to open fire on them after the first five minutes of tuneless trumpet-blowing.

"I'll pick them up if you help me with something."

He stared at me. Hard. It was easy to picture his head orbiting a sun somewhere before meteors knocked it out of rotation. His face split into a big smile.

"All right. I will help you. But only because you remind me of your grandmother before this life had its way with her."

I nodded once. "Someone sent Grandma a puzzle box. Wood, with a combination reel. English alphabet. Grandma said she knew who it was from, and that the sender was telling her they had information about Dad's disappearance."

A lie skittered across his eyes. "I don't know who that could be."

"Grandma also said the sender was in a maximum security prison."

"The Family knows a lot of people in prison. Could be any of them."

"Lying."

"Who is lying? No one, that is who."

"Still lying."

He slapped the air. "Bah. Show me your box."

~ ~ ~

Papou blinked at the box. Granted, things were dim in Grandma's kitchen.

"Is it jogging your memory?"

"I can't remember what I ate for breakfast. How am I supposed to remember someone I have not seen in fifteen years?"

I hung him on my sharply raised eyebrow.

"*Fila to kolo mou*!" he swore, which translated to *kiss my ass*. He pointed at me. "You are tricky. I will have to watch you."

"So who is he?"

"An animal and an idiot." A satisfied smirk made itself cozy on his face. "If you can open it I will tell you who sent it."

"That's not fair."

"You made me a deal, I make you a deal. Figure out the combination. After you do that, and pick up the cigarette butts like you promised, I will tell you."

The old guy had snookered me.

"How am I supposed to figure out the combination? I need context, a place to start."

He rolled out the front door, chair clanking as it maneuvered the single step. "You can do it. I have faith in you. Okay, maybe not faith, but something like faith, only smaller."

Over by the fountain a man was pretending to prune a tree that didn't need pruning, mostly because it wasn't there. I faked not seeing him and he faked not seeing me. Already Elias the Assassin and I had a functional—even amicable—relationship.

I sat under one of the wide-brimmed umbrellas scattered around the courtyard. Each came with a table and chairs, and it was here that the family—and the Family—spent their evenings after siesta. The courtyard was also home to overhead trellises with grape and other vines slowly clambering across the wooden frames, but underneath the light was filtered and patchy. I wanted full blackout. It was slouching toward noon so the place was deserted. Time for lunch and a nap. Not for me; I wasn't Greek enough to snooze in the afternoons, guilt-free.

I plonked the puzzle box on the table and scratched my head. Without context it would be close to impossible to figure out the combination. I spun the dials and contemplated how many eight-letter words were in the English dictionary. That's if it was even a word. For all I knew it was a random combination, designed to foil Scrabble pros.

It was a game.

My goat wandered over with his canine posse. The lop-eared ruminant had appeared by magic on my borrowed bed a couple of days after I'd arrived in Greece. Nobody recognized him, and I hadn't discounted the idea that he was some kind of Trojan goat; although, you'd be hard pressed to fit even a sixteenth of a soldier in its four stomachs. That's without armor. Even a goat would balk at bronze. He was brown-and-white, and so far he'd decided to stick around. Who could blame him? The menu here was varied and plentiful. He had quickly bonded with the compound's pack of dogs, primarily lurchers, with a penchant for long naps, dropped food, and cuddles.

He nuzzled my hand, looking for crumbs, and then went to work on a nearby bush.

"Does it have a name?" Elias called out.

I shook my head. "No name."

"You should give it a name. Everybody will be less inclined to cook him if he has a name."

"Really?"

"Sure. It's always harder to kill someone you know by name."

He would know. "I'll think about," I said.

He saluted me and went back to his mime.

I slumped on the table, both eyes on the box. It mocked me silently.

"Know what I would do if I were you?"

Elias again.

"About what?"

"The box."

"What would you do?"

"Kids," he said. "They can open anything, even if it doesn't want to be opened."

His thought was in the right place, but he was stabbing it from the wrong angle. Kids can open anything, *especially* if it doesn't want to be opened.

~ ~ ~

It seemed impossible that Takis had caught Marika and conned her finger all the way into a gold ring. On the outside they were a mismatched pair, and probably on the inside, too. If he was a tool, she was a soft, comfortable sofa in flowery prints. They occupied the roomy apartment on the top left corner of the compound.

Takis' wife had long hair she normally kept caged in a tight bun. It was black with a natural hint of blue. When she rushed toward me, it brought to mind the inevitability an oncoming train, when your shoe is caught in the tracks and you've had ten swigs too many from the Boone's Farm bottle.

"Katerina!" she said, pulling me into her arms. We exchanged hugs and continental kisses, as was customary around these parts. All the kissing Greeks did, they'd be the first to fall if there was a worldwide pandemic.

Marika was a woman who sprinkled her sentences with exclamation points. She used up her yearly quota in every conversation. "You have come to visit! Let me make coffee!"

My mission would be temporarily interrupted if I let her navigate me into the living room. One didn't drink coffee and go; there would be food, there would be gossip, there would be two hours gone.

"I'd love to sit here and drink coffee with you, but I can't." I held up the puzzle box. "It's a clue about Dad. I think. I was wondering if your kids might be able to work it out."

Marika looked dubious. "My boys?" She and Takis had a handful of boys, semi-wild, part simian, with a dash of mad professor. They were good-natured kids who'd either rule the universe some day, or lay waste to the whole shebang. "The way they open a box is with fire or an axe."

I was afraid of that.

"You should ask Litsa." Her hands engaged in a simple form of flagless semaphores. "Her Tomas can break into anything. He has a bright career ahead of him as a safecracker."

In some families—decent ones—that would be considered a minus, but in this one it was a huge plus. The criminal gene was filtering down through the generations. The other genes didn't stand a chance—not when they were mugged and supplanted in utero.

I tried to smile, but my face got stuck on the way there.

"It will be okay," Marika said, beaming. "This family … it takes time to get used to how they are. No one in my family has ever committed a crime. Not so much as a stolen piece of fruit, yet look what I married. You get used to it. Here." She reached into her apron pocket, retrieved what looked like a Twinkie's Greek cousin, pushed the plastic-wrapped cake into my hand. "Don't tell Baboulas I gave you a store-bought cake, okay? She would flip."

Her secret was safe with me, and I told her so. After pocketing my cake, and asking for directions to Litsa's and Tomas' apartment, I was on my way.

I stepped sideways.

Litsa's door flew open. I looked at her; looked back at the fist I hadn't had a chance to use yet.

"Katerina! Could be I heard what Marika told you."

Could be. "Is Tomas in?"

She nodded and ushered me inside, while simultaneously screeching, "Tomas!"

Litsa was in her late thirties. She and her husband, whose name I couldn't recall with her voice stabbing my eardrums, had three boys. She was the kind of woman who worked hard at looking cheap, and she succeeded beautifully. Her nails were real acrylic, her ponytail was clip-on, and her boobs had arrived in individually wrapped containers, before the surgeon stuffed them into her chest. The apartment was almost as spacious as the one next-door, but there was more fake gold and less good taste.

"Sit," she said, steering me into the living room. Litsa didn't do things old school. Unlike generations before her, she didn't keep a room for entertaining visitors. But then Grandma didn't either. Her house didn't have the space … or a toilet in her bathroom.

Tomas Makris wandered into the room in Spiderman underwear and Transformers slippers. He had the family nose and black hair shaved close to the scalp. In his slippers he was about three-and-a-half-feet-tall, which seemed normal for a five-year-old. He looked at me with wide, dark eyes.

"What's it like being a foreigner?"

My brain spluttered, but my mouth made up for it. "Foreign."

He nodded. "I figured."

"Are you in school yet?"

"No. Kindergarten is keeping me back. I failed finger painting."

"Really?"

"No."

I looked at his mother. "Does he know he's thirty?"

She shrugged somewhat helplessly.

"What's that?" His eyes were glued to the box in my hand. "Is that for me?"

To crouch or not crouch, that was the question. On the one hand, he was five. On the other, he was thirty. I crouched, hoping it was the right move.

"It's not for either of us, but I was hoping you might be able to open it."

"English alphabet," he said, inspecting the puzzle box. "Eight letters."

"Do you know English?"

"I know puzzles and combinations. I can open anything."

"So I heard."

"I can also burp the alphabet. Want to hear it?"

"Maybe later. It's a pretty big achievement, though. I know grown men who can't do it."

"It's all in here." He pointed to his diaphragm. "And you have to gulp a lot of air between letters." He gave me a quick *alpha, beta, gamma* to demonstrate.

I won't lie: I was pretty impressed.

"Let's go," he said. "I think better when I'm in my fort."

"I will bring coffee," Litsa called after us.

The boy's fort was made of pillows, sheets, and a couple of traditional Greek chairs. It was a good fort, and he beamed when I told him so. He ducked under the sheet and held it up for me to join him.

"Is it true you're going to be Baboulas someday?" he asked once we'd both settled beneath the fort's cotton roof. He dropped the "door." Instant comfort. Nothing bad could touch me here. Not even the Goblin King or the boogeyman.

"Not if I can help it."

You will be," he said, with absolute certainty. "If Baboulas wants you to be, you will be."

"If I don't want to be, then I don't have to be."

He considered my words. "That's not how it works."

"That's how it works in my world, unless you have a tiger mother."

"What's a tiger mother?"

When I explained about tiger mothers, and how they'd claw out your heart if you got less than an A-plus in a test, he frowned. "Greek mothers are more like sea turtles. Except Baboulas. She's more like an elephant." He twiddled the dials. There was a small click. He handed it back to me.

"Baboulas," I said, reading the word.

"They weren't even trying." The poor kid sounded disappointed. He brightened up. "What's inside? Is it chocolate?"

I lifted the lid and peeked inside. "YOWZA!" I slammed it shut. "Definitely not chocolate."

3

"That's not a finger," Papou said.

"Usually they send a finger," Stavros said. He had joined Papou in his smoking nook, but he wasn't smoking. He was sitting on the ground cross-legged, doing cross-stitch. It was an eerily accurate recreation of Theophanes the Greek's *Transfiguration of Jesus* … in teeny, tiny x's.

"It's definitely not a finger," I said. I wadded up my fear and nausea, shunted them to the side. Unfortunately, I couldn't quit glancing sideways at the emotional mess. If what was in the box was part of Dad, I was going to implode. There would be a burst of tears, a loud *pop*, then I'd vanish. "Grandma told me you guys don't send body parts."

"As proof of life." Papou scraped a match on the wall. It burst into flame. Greeks didn't believe in safety matches. They figured they went to the trouble of stealing fire from the gods, so why take the red phosphorus out of matches and stick it on the side of the box? Fire, they believed, shouldn't be smothered with rules. "But we'll send anything as proof of death."

"I remember one time we sent an ear," Stavros added.

"That's no ear," I said.

Papou cackled around the damp end of his cigarette. "I know what it is, eh? I have one myself." He made a V with his hands, pointed at his crotch. It was an obscene Greek hand gesture that he'd toned down to merely informative. "And like this one, it doesn't work."

I pulled out my phone, dialed Aunt Rita, who was on her way to Athens with Takis.

"Ela," she said, answering the phone the way Greeks did, with a 'Come' instead of a 'Hello.'

"I have a penis," I said.

"Me too," she answered.

"This one's in a wooden box."

There was a long pause, but not a silent one. Music and howling stuffed itself into the gap in our conversation. Wherever she was, someone was in pain.

"Jesus," I said, "is that Takis?"

She made an affirmative noise. "He calls that singing. I would threaten to shoot him in the face but he's driving."

A death sentence for both of them, for sure, if she fired. Greeks don't know the meaning of *drive slowly*. They hurtle from one location to the next, pictures of saints propped up on the dashboard, crucifix dangling from the rearview mirror. God is their insurance company.

"He'll have to stop eventually," I said.

The baying quit abruptly. "I heard that!"

"Is the *poutsa* in the puzzle box?" my aunt asked.

"Yeah, in the puzzle box. Litsa's youngest opened it for me."

"That boy is going places," she said. "With luck none of them will be prison."

"I doubt they'd be able to keep him inside for long."

I could feel her nodding. "Whose is it?"

"I don't know."

"Is it Michail's?"

Papou was looking at me. Stavros was looking at me. Although there were miles between us, I could feel my aunt looking at me.

"How should I know?" I squeaked. "He's my father. I shouldn't know what his Oscar Meyer Wiener looks like!"

"What is an Oscar Meyer Wiener?" Stavros asked.

"It's a sausage," I explained. "A hot dog."

"Ah, a *xot donk*! We have those here, too."

My stomach growled. The two men looked at me in horror.

"My belly is stupid," I said. "All it heard was 'hot dog.' "

I moved past the hunger. An idea was beginning to unfurl in my head. "There's someone who might know," I said slowly.

"Who?" Papou asked.

"Dina," Aunt Rita and I said at the same time.

She gasped. "Touch red!" There was a squeal of tires, and Takis yelled, "*Gamo ti putana*, you stupid *skeela!*"

Which loosely translated to: *Engage in intercourse with a woman of negotiable affections, you stupid she-dog.*

I closed my eyes. "What did you touch?"

"*Vromoskeelo*!" Aunt Rita screamed back at him. Huh. As far as insults went 'dirty dog' wasn't too bad. "I touched the pimple on his nose. That thing needs its own area code. Go see Dina," she told me. "She will know."

I ended the call. Stavros and Papou were watching me.

"Anyone want to come for a ride?"

Stavros raised his hand. "Me. Pick me."

"What about me?" the old man said.

"I guess you could come, too."

"Forget it." Papou flipped his hand at me. "You drive too slow. How is that going to kill me?"

"Are you going to tell me who sent the box?"

"Are you going to pick up the cigarette butts so your grandmother doesn't find out I have been smoking?"

"Later," I said.

"Then I will tell you later."

Damn it, he had me.

~ ~ ~

Dina was Dad's former girlfriend, the woman he'd been with before he jumped ship to America and married my mother. Thirty years later she was still devoted to Dad. Her entire home was a shrine to his awesomeness. Only her bathroom was exempt from the Dad-worship, because who wants their deity to watch them poop? She lived on a steep hill, where the houses were as stubborn as Greece's people. If an earthquake came, a storm, the Turks, they weren't going anywhere. They would stay right here on their incline, hugging Greek soil and rock for eternity.

Halfway there, I spotted company in the rearview mirror—company that wasn't my assassin, Elias.

A cop car.

Detective Melas.

My mouth groaned, but my body yelled "Yay!" without a shred of sarcasm.

Big showoff, he flashed his lights and indicated for me to pull over. Defying law enforcement didn't come naturally to me, despite the patterns in my DNA, so I snugged up to the next bare patch of curb, hopped out of the Beetle, tried to look like I wasn't carrying around a severed wang in a box.

Stavros slapped the leather seat I'd vacated. "Are you okay?"

"Great." Delivered with a side of sarcasm Stavros didn't get. How could I be okay when I was possibly in possession of one of Dad's body parts, without the rest of Dad?

"Because you're standing the way I had to stand the time I pissed my pants."

I had a comeback curled at the back of my throat, but had to swallow it when Melas swaggered over to me. He did it on purpose, walking the bad-boy walk. He was wearing jeans and a button-down shirt with the sleeves folded to his elbows. In another week his dark, wavy hair was going to need one-on-one time with clippers and a pair of scissors. His body was hard and trim. I'd seen glimpses of what was underneath, and it was delicious. Part of his face was hidden behind sunglasses, but I knew his eyes were warm, dark chocolate, and when he looked at me I felt like the only woman in the world … this week. I had discretely asked around. Melas had the kind of reputation that sunk a Greek woman, but elevated a Greek man to living-legend status.

He grinned. My stomach tied itself into damp knots. "Do you know you're being followed?"

"Yes."

"Who is he? I don't recognize him."

He was talking about Elias, who had cruised to a stop several car-lengths back. He was poised behind the wheel, waiting.

"Oh, he's not one of Grandma's. That's Elias. He's an assassin working for Fatmir the Poor. Do you know him?"

"Fatmir? Only by reputation." He shook his head. "Jesus. Who's his target?"

"You're looking at her."

"What did you do to him?"

"I guess he doesn't like Americans."

Melas looked at me like I was speaking French. My joke must have flown over his head and splattered on the hot road.

"I was in the newspaper," I said, taking pity on him. "Apparently Fatmir isn't happy Grandma thinks she's got an heir."

"In the newspaper?"

"Front page."

"What were you doing on the front page?"

"Among other things, eating dinner with you. It was a fluff piece."

"Slow news day."

"Maybe the Greek mafia is a more cheerful topic than the economy."

He nodded to the box in my hands. "What's in the box?"

"A clue."

"What kind of clue?"

"A penis-shaped clue."

"Penis-shaped? What's penis-shaped?"

"A penis."

His skin had seen a lot of sun this summer, turning him to a deep, burnished gold, but as my words sank in all that color washed away.

"A real one?" I nodded. He glanced around. "There's a severed …" The correct anatomical word stuck in this throat. "… In that box?" I nodded again. "Lady, you've got problems."

"Hey," I said. "It's not like I chopped it off and sent it to myself."

His color wasn't looking any better. "Where are you taking it?"

I told him and he stared at me, blinking.

"Jesus Christ," he said. "This I've got to see."

"You can't come with us!"

"Why not?"

"It's … It's official family business."

"Your family is the Greek mafia and I'm a policeman. That means your business is my business. Either I come with you, or we can take that … that box back to my office."

"You don't have an office."

"My boss does."

He climbed back into his police car, and I jumped back into my Beetle, zipping away before he'd had a chance to buckle his belt.

Stavros shook his head, clearly impressed. "The way he does blackmail, he could be one of us."

The mercury had to be pushing a hundred. I parked at the foot of the narrow street in a patch of shade. When I stepped into the sunlight, the heat caved in on me like a cheaply built roof. The Beetle had air conditioning, but I hated to use it now that I was driving a convertible. I relied on fresh air and low speed. Back home I had a ten-year-old Jeep with air conditioning I ran all summer long.

A pang of longing crept up on me and tapped me on the shoulder. Home. My car. Dad. Part of him could be in this box. And if it was, where was the rest of him?

My gut clenched. There was a small balloon in my diaphragm that expanded and contracted as my fear levels rose and fell.

Melas crunched to a stop behind us. I took a deep breath and somehow —by the power of sorcery—managed to put on a smile that wasn't wobbling.

"Let's do this," I told the two men.

Dina's house was one white cake box set in two parallel lines of nearly identical cake boxes. The roofs were all flat, topped by TV antennas and washing lines. Unlike all the other yards in the neighborhood, Dina's fenced-in space was a barren slab of concrete that she swept constantly, when she wasn't inside paying homage to the memory of my father. If anyone who could tell me whether this was one of Dad's bits it was Dina.

We found her in her yard—surprise, surprise—sweeping. Briefly, I wondered if she'd ever sought professional help for her issues. Last week she sent a tray of tulle-wrapped, poop-filled wedding favors to the local police department to show her appreciation for their complete failure to stop a serial killer from conning her. With a little help, she and I had ended his career in crime ourselves.

Dad's former girlfriend had the kind of figure one could use to prop up a load-bearing wall. She was a lot of woman packed into a smallish container. Density had trumped mass.

"You." She made a sniffing sound. "What do you want?"

I didn't waste time—hers or mine. "I need you to identify a penis."

"Are you calling me a *putana*? What makes you think I can identify it? You should ask your aunt."

If Aunt Rita were here she'd zip off a smart comment about how Dina had become a born-again virgin after Dad split Greece. According to my aunt, the sugar had been licked off that candy repeatedly, and by dozens of different tongues, long before Dina and Dad became a thing.

"Ain't nobody got time for this," I muttered in English. Three faces looked at me. "Heh," I said. "It's an urban American prayer." I held up the box, showed it to Dina. "See this box? There's a penis in it. It might be Dad's."

"Why would it be in that box?"

I looked at her—hard—until the light bulb in her head exploded.

She gasped and clutched her chest. It took a while—the woman had a lot of acreage to cover. "My Virgin Mary, Michail!" Her brain and heart went to battle over her face. They fought long and hard for control of the muscles. In the end her head won. She blinked away any potential tears and put on her no-bullshit expression.

"Show me," she commanded, fanning her face with her hands.

Everyone crowded around me. I lifted the lid, revealing the male appendage in all its glory—and gory.

Clonk.

That was the sound of local law enforcement fainting. Melas had collapsed in a manly heap.

"It's not that big," I said.

"It's pretty big," Stavros said. "And that's not fully extended."

Stavros knew a lot about other guy's dicks, on account of how he watched so much porn. Not all of it human, I suspected.

"It's not Michail's," Dina breathed. "It's not Michail's."

The bucket of relief was poised over my head, but I wasn't about to let it splash Flashdance-style over me yet.

"Are you sure?" I prompted her.

"I would know it anywhere. His is bigger and it's different." She leaned in and poked at it with one sharp fingernail. "See this?"

"See what?" To be honest I wasn't inspecting it too hard. If it was Dad's, ogling his private part was horrifying, wrong, and upsetting. If it was someone else's, then it was still wrong, horrifying and upsetting. A severed penis is a severed penis—ask Melas, who was still spread out on the concrete, groaning.

"Wait there. I will show you." Dina vanished into her house.

I crouched down beside the detective. "Are you okay?"

"No."

"Can you sit up?"

"Make it go away."

To the best of my abilities, I pulled him into the sitting position, back against the fence. One at a time, I bent his legs. "Head between your knees," I said. "It should help."

"Don't tell anyone I fainted. Please."

"I won't. But Stavros will."

"It's true." Stavros bobbed his head. "I will tell Takis, and he will tell everyone."

"How about you don't tell Takis?" I asked.

"I can't help myself," he said sadly.

Dina reappeared, waving a Polaroid photo. "Look! This is Michail. He let me measure it and take a picture."

It was a primal reflex the way my hands jumped up to cover my eyes. "This is so wrong."

"Isn't it magnificent?" Dina asked, waiting on a round of approval that wasn't going to happen. Not with this audience.

I didn't want to. I really didn't want to.

"You do it," I told Stavros.

"I don't want to look at it."

I peeked. He was looking at it.

"Okay," he said, after a long, hard look. "It's not the same one."

The lid fell back into place. My brain took several pinches of relief, a handful of question marks, and tossed them into a blender. What it came back with was: "So then whom does it belong to?"

"I don't know," Dina said. "It's not Michail's, that's all I care about."

We left the Queen of Empathy to her sweeping and trudged back down the street. I followed Melas to his police car to make sure he was going to make it. His color was slowly coming back. He had worked his way up to the shade of whipped honey.

He stared off into the distance, where there were ponies, and rainbows, and no dismembered members. "Who sent you that thing?"

"Nobody. They sent it to Grandma."

"Who sent it to her?"

"She didn't say, but she knows them, whoever it is. It's someone in prison. That's all she told me before she left. Papou said he'd tell me who it was if I could open the box."

He gnawed on that a moment. "Where's Baboulas?"

"Away."

Both eyebrows crept higher.

"I don't know," I said. No mention of the fact that I could guess. Grandma hadn't shared her health status with me. No way was I going to share it with Melas.

He lounged against the car. A hundred degrees and the man was in jeans—and he looked cool wearing them. Detective Nikos Melas was an impossible situation. We were attracted to each other, yeah, but he was a lawman and I was the offspring of a former hitman—amongst Dad's many other talents—and the granddaughter of one of Greece's most notorious women.

He already had a bad habit of turning me on when I'd rather snipe at him. My body's memory had perfect recall when it came to The Kiss he'd stamped on my mouth last week. Those stupid hormones of mine wanted a rematch.

Well, they weren't getting one. I was the one in control of my moving parts, and where I wanted to move was far away from Detective Melas—effective right now.

Too bad he had a look on his face that said he wanted to converse, now that his color was returning to normal.

Here it came—the bad boy grin. Followed by that move where his eyes slowly raked over my body, digging up all kinds of feelings I didn't want, most of them in my underwear. I hadn't seen him since the day after he'd been one of a four-man rescue team who'd saved my bacon from the Baptist.

"I've been thinking about taking you out again," he said.

"We're out right now."

"Are you snippy because I haven't called?"

He wished. "Why would I? Our date wasn't a date. It was business."

He blew out a long stream of hot air. "Maybe I wanted it to be a date."

"Did you?"

"It's complicated."

You're telling me. "It's complicated because you're making it complicated. All you have to do is quit bringing it up and—voila! —uncomplicated."

"That's not how it works."

"Denial solves a lot of problems." I thought about it. "Maybe not *solves*, but denial definitely has its place."

He changed the subject. "How are you?"

"So hot and sweaty that either my sweat glands shut down or the heat is sucking it up faster than I can make it."

"I meant to check on you, see how you were doing after the Baptist thing."

"You didn't."

"But I wanted to."

A cold spider clambered up my spine. The former cop was dead but the horror lived on. Fear was like a zombie: reanimate that sucker and it would stump around after you forever, moaning for its share of your brain.

"I'm fine," I said. Was I fine? Not really. More like fine-ish. Except for the part where a serial killer almost snuffed my lights out, where my family was the mob, and where my father was still missing and maybe dead.

"I have to go," I said. "I have a thing."

"I know. I saw it. I'm coming with you."

"No, you're not."

"It's evidence of a crime."

"For all you know it fell off." He looked at me so pointedly he could have poked out my eye. "Or it could be from one of those medical corpses."

"Which would make it stolen property."

"You suck, Melas."

He grinned. It was the slow, lazy expression of a man who had me where he wanted me. "Not even once, honey."

I jumped back into my yellow car, revved the engine, cranked the radio's volume button until the speakers blew my hair back. Then Stavros and I blasted back toward Mount Pelion with Melas on our tail.

By the time we reached the compound, and I killed the engine outside the garage, I'd already come up with a dozen different identities for the man with the missing frank. He was a medical corpse, like I suggested to Melas. Or some poor homeless guy who'd been in the wrong place at the wrong time. He was the sender's enemy—or a friend who really screwed up. The sender had delivered a message, but where the heck was I going to find an interpreter, and what did any of this have to do with Dad? Without Grandma around I'd have to figure out who sent the box, then go to the source itself.

A big voice in the front of my head began hammering on about how it wasn't like me to go running off to a prison, demanding answers from inmates. I mean, look at *The Silence of the Lambs*. Things almost ended Very Badly for Clarice Starling, and she was a professional. Me, I was a former bill collector. Former because Grandma razed my workplace and broke my boss's legs. Now he was being eyed for arson and investigated for tax issues—the issue being that he hadn't paid them properly. This is no way qualified me to waltz into a prison with empty pockets and a mouthful of questions.

My stomach churned audibly.

"Hey!"

Melas. He was stuck on the wrong side of the gate. Oops.

"Can I come in?" He seemed so sad standing there, gripping the bars, handsome face smushed between them.

I looked at the guard. The guard looked at me, request poised on his lips.

"No," I said.

"Katerina ..."

"Go home, Melas." I blew him a kiss and trotted under the arch into the courtyard. As always, it was like walking into Eden—minus the serpent and the naked people. Grandma had fountains, fig trees, a conservatory, an enormous pool where Xander did late-night laps, and pockets of gardens arranged in pretty patterns.

Papou still owed me a name. Now it was time to pony up the goods.

But first I scooped up every last cigarette butt, stashing them in a paper bag I'd rustled up in Grandma's kitchen, and took them with me.

His apartment was on the second floor at the far right end of the compound, Stavros had told me, facing the family orchard.

Papou hollered, "Come!" when I knocked. The door was unlocked, so I went right in.

"Why aren't you on the ground floor?" I asked.

"Nobody expects the cripple to live on the second floor."

He didn't explain further. To my ears it sounded like a Zen saying. *Only the hand that erases can write the true thing; it is the power of the mind to be unconquerable; do not seek for the truth, only stop having an opinion; nobody expects the cripple to live on the second floor.*

I nodded because what else could I do? He sounded like a legit Greek philosopher, and I knew my Greek philosophers. After my mother died I quit looking to God for answers and took up philosophy instead. Regular history had a better track record than biblical history. They say there's wisdom in the Bible, but it's a long slog through the begetting and incest.

The old man's apartment was cluttered in an orderly way. The living room walls were barely visible behind the shelves, each of them filled with an arrangement of doohickeys and figurines and books. The hall closet was open, but I couldn't see inside from where I stood.

"I was a collector of life's mysteries," he said. "I am waiting now to collect the final one, but the delivery man is late, that *malakas*."

"Before he gets here do you suppose you could tell me who sent Grandma the box?"

He rolled over to the closet door, pushed it shut. "I was trying to go out like that guy from *Kung Fu*, but I couldn't find rope or a blue pill, so here I am talking to you. The man you want, they call him Rabbit."

A hot, invisible needle shoved itself in my eye. An old memory was the hand behind the needle. It wanted to be remembered, and it wanted to be remembered now.

I winced. "Why do they call him Rabbit?"

"Because he has a hundred children. What's wrong with your eye?"

"Nothing's wrong with my eye. Does he have a real name?"

"Stelios Dogas is his name. There's something wrong with your eye or your head."

"I'm fine—really. Where have they got him locked up?"

"Larissa's prison. It's a big yellow building, the color of piss." He chuckled. "You are going to see him, aren't you? Before you do, see about that eye or they will keep you there."

"There's nothing wrong with my eye. Someone has to talk to him. Grandma isn't here. He sent a clue and I have to find out what it means."

"I think you are mental." He drew little air circles on one temple. "Going there is the worst thing you could do. If you think it's a clever idea you have problems."

No, I knew it was stupid. Worse than stupid. It was *totally* stupid. Sometimes a woman needed an adverb to underscore how idiotic something was. This was one of those times.

"Sometimes clever and right are the same thing, sometimes they're not."

"That's a good answer. I didn't think you were capable of it."

I grinned at him, but it was window dressing. Inside, my nerves were firing off messages. *Can you believe this chick? All balls and no brain. Rabbit … Rabbit … Rabbit …* "I got lucky."

"Must be your grandmother's genes."

I asked him something I hadn't had a chance to ask anyone else yet. "What was my grandfather like?"

"Yiannis?" He shrugged. "Imagine a rock sitting on the ground, doing nothing. That was your grandfather."

That was … unexpected. "How did he die?"

"He walked into an ambush. He was looking for a sofa so he could sit."

"My other grandfather died when a dog crapped on his lawn." Mom's dad had famously blown an artery screaming at the neighbor's Great Dane.

"Must have been some crap."

"It was on his newspaper."

He nodded like he knew about dog crap and newspapers. I guess some things were universal.

"You go to see Rabbit, you be careful. He has charmed the pants off virgins, nuns, married women, and the occasional Turk."

"He's in prison."

"Bah! Bars mean nothing to a man like that. If there is a crack he will fill it. Don't show him anything he can put his *poutsa* in."

Suddenly, the earth vanished beneath my feet. That sharp, pointy memory had conjured up a battering ram. It slammed into the barrier between past and present, flooding my head with an old tune Dad used to sing.

"*I Left Her Foot in a Box and Carried With Me Her Shoe …*" I sang.

"That is a song we used to sing about Rabbit," he said sharply. "Where did you hear it?"

"In a kitchen."

"We used to sing it the bar and at parties. Always there was ouzo involved. Rivers of ouzo."

"There wasn't any ouzo when I heard it, just Greek salad." And the cold tolling of an early warning bell that none of us had recognized as the beginning of an end.

"Things have really changed if that song was served with salad."

"I hate change," I said.

"Funny, because that is all you have done since you got here. And there is more coming—an avalanche of change, I think." He rolled over to the shelves on the north-facing wall, grabbed a leather and metal contraption that looked like ancient horse-wear. He tossed it to me. "Put this on before you go."

"What is it?"

"A chastity belt."

I threw it back, trying not to let the "Ewww" escape. "It's a maximum security prison."

"That doesn't mean the security is good. All it means is that it has the maximum security the prison can afford."

~ ~ ~

As Papou said, Larissa's prison building was the color of stale morning urine. With its razor wire hairdo atop the fence, it was impossible to mistake the prison for anything other than a correctional facility. What it was correcting I wasn't sure, but it didn't look like it could make honest men out of anything, let alone crooked human beings.

"Want me to come with you?"

That was Stavros. He'd tagged along for the forty-five minute drive, after I told him where I was headed. Elias was with us, too, discreetly parked several spaces away.

"I should be fine," I told him. "How hard can it be?"

"When my friend Rikki was in here I used to bring muffins every month. He really liked muffins."

"Is he still here?"

Stavros lifted his chin then lowered it. That's what passed for a headshake around here. "Someone shanked him for the muffins. They were good muffins."

"What kind?"

"Apple cinnamon."

"Those are good," I said. "Okay, here goes."

My wardrobe was limited. Most of what I owned was in my closet back home, the one in Mom and Dad's house, where I still technically lived because it made Dad woozy to think about cutting the cord. I'd leased an apartment a couple of weeks ago, but Grandma had it burned down before I could move in … or tell Dad. Anyway, clothes. I went with jeans and a fitted T-shirt. It was the closest thing I had to business casual.

Getting into a Greek prison turned out to be easy. I showed them my passport, signed the sign-in sheet, followed a rolling boulder made of a Greek mother's baklava. Maybe I'd seen too many movies, but I expected to wind up on the good-guy side of one of those booths with a Plexiglas window and an archaic handset. When the guard led me to a cramped room with a metal table, complete with a loop for cuffs, and two metal chairs, I asked about the booths.

"Sold them," he told me. "It was that or toilet paper."

"I bet the prisoners appreciated the paper."

"Wasn't for them."

He left me alone in the room. Before long, I began wondering if I should sing prison songs. The only one I knew was that Sam Cooke song, but everything except the chorus was hazy. I tried to recall inspiring lines from *The Shawshank Redemption*, but nothing was happening except boredom.

After too much time had passed, the blob rolled back in with a coworker and a lanky old man wearing handcuffs and a uniform straight off a zebra's back. He had a complexion like the Grand Canyon, thinning gray hair, and a pair of rubber slip-on shoes that were two sizes too big.

His gaze felt me up. His mouth settled into a leer.

"Who are you?" he asked as the guards shoved him at the chair on the far side of the table, and chained him to the table's loop. Then the guards made a big production of leaving the room.

Ha! I wasn't fooled. They were listening in, guaranteed.

"Katerina Makris."

"I know Katerina Makri. You are not her."

"Little old lady?" I held my hand up to my chin. "About this tall?"

"She was not so old the last time I saw her."

That was the thing about prison: Put a man behind a wall and the rest of the world marches on without him—sometimes all the way to a cliff. A lot had changed in Greece during the past fifteen years. When they'd tossed him inside, Greece was saving up for an Olympics it couldn't afford. The government had still been faking a happy marriage to the European Union. People were collecting money that was scheduled to evaporate in a few short years.

"That was a long time ago. Sometimes people go for years without looking older, then—BAM—the years gang-bang them. Maybe that's what happened to Grandma."

"You are Michail's girl." He shifted in his seat. The leer didn't quit. "Now I see it. What do you want? A little …" There was nothing ambiguous about his hand gesture.

"Dream on, old man," I said. "Papou warned me about you."

He spat on the ground. "That *malakas*. I shit on his head."

That was going to be tricky from prison, unless his aim was stellar and he had rocket-fueled bowels. I sat in the chair the guard had left for me, and hoped he wouldn't spit in my direction. I wasn't programmed with the kind of disrespect required to slap an elderly man, who was only several naps away from the big sleep.

"You sent Grandma a puzzle box."

"Did I? What was inside?"

"You don't know?"

His face was blank. "Who knows? I don't know."

4

"Wait—what? How can you not know? You sent Grandma the box."

"I made the box, yes, but I did not send it. I'm not responsible for what's inside." He leaned forward, winked. "What was inside, my baby?"

Ugh. "Grandma said it was a clue. A message."

"What message?"

"Now would be a great time to quit playing dumb."

"You could show me what's under that shirt. What happened to dresses? In my day women used to wear dresses."

"I could leave," I said.

"But you won't. Because you want something from me, or you wouldn't be here." He swished his hand through the air. "Forget it. I'm too old and tired for games. I don't know anything. All I did was make the box. I had no choice." He did a little head wag as he weighed his words against the fate of what was possibly his eternal soul. "Okay, I had a choice, but I wanted a *tsibouki* and a carton of cigarettes. You don't know what it's like in here. No women. Not enough men who look like women from the back if you squint until everything is blurry."

The thought of him on either end of a blowjob was horrifying. Where was the mind bleach when I needed it?

"Who did you make it for?"

"I don't know. A guy. I have made many boxes for many people—ask your Grandmother. I made many for her so she could send messages to her enemies"

Questions balled up at the back of my throat, but I only let the pertinent one pass. "What guy?"

"A guy."

"Did he have a name?"

"Everybody in Greece over the age of three months has a name."

That was true enough. Up until a Greek Orthodox baptism at three months, every baby was named *Moro*—Baby. Never mind that there are no surprises what the child's name will be. Every kid gets a hand-me-down name from one grandparent or another. Only risk-taking parents, who are obviously cruising for disinheritance, veer off the beaten-to-death path.

"So what was it?"

He leaned back. His smile had the illicit gleam of an ivory dagger. "If I tell you, if I do you this favor, then you owe me a favor, yes?"

My debts were stacking up. First Baby Dimitri, the Godfather of the Night and Cheap Souvenirs, had coughed up an item in his store in exchange for a, thus far unredeemed, favor. Now Rabbit wanted to swap my something for his something. An even trade? Somehow I doubted it. But he had me over the figurative barrel. He had information—information I needed. Somebody had commissioned him to make that box, and that somebody wanted to send a message to Grandma.

"A comparable favor. One of equal value. Nothing more, nothing less."

The ivory dagger unsheathed itself another inch. "Deal." He tapped the table between us with flat palms. "The name you want is Eagle."

"That's not a name, it's a nickname."

Two palms up. "That's what I have."

"What does he look like?"

"What does any man look like? That's how he looks."

A vein throbbed in my temple. "Can you be more specific?"

"Not without some kind of restitution."

"What do you want?"

His fingers tapped out a rhythm on the tabletop. His eyes wiped their smutty selves all over the top half of my body like he wanted something of a sexual nature. Which meant I'd be leaving here without a description.

"Souvlaki," he said after he'd spent way too much time trying to engage his x-ray vision for a peek under my shirt.

My breath whooshed out in a relieved stream.

"Sure," I said. "I can do that. If the guards are okay with me bringing in food."

The door opened. The human meatball stuck his head in. "The charitable thing to do would be to bring some for everyone."

"The whole prison?"

"No. Who cares about the prisoners? Most of them are on a hunger strike anyway. I'm talking about us." He glanced at Rabbit. "And that guy, I suppose."

My nest egg shuddered. "How many?"

"On this shift, twenty."

I tried not to gawk. "Twenty for this whole place?"

"Times are hard." He pulled me aside, out of Rabbit's hearing range. "See these guns?" He patted what on a smaller person would have been a hip. "No ammo."

"What if you need to shoot somebody?"

He shrugged. "This is why we fry fish on their lips, so they do not have strength to revolt."

To fry fish on someone's lips was the charming Greek way of saying they got their kicks tormenting prisoners.

"There a souvlaki place around here?"

"Down the street."

I went back to Rabbit. "You want anything to go with that souvlaki?"

"*Patates tiganites*!" the guard called out from the other side of the door. Fried potatoes. French fries.

"You heard the man," Rabbit said. "Hey, do you know why they call me Rabbit?"

"Papou said it's because you've got a hundred kids."

He wagged his eyebrows at me. "We could make it a hundred and one."

Ugh.

'Down the street' wasn't down the street. At least that's what my phone said. And I believed the latest technology over the hungry guard. It was down the street, two over, and down five more streets.

Stavros was backing out of the parking spot when I heard something rumbling in the distance. I squinted.

"That sounds like a helicopter," I said.

"It is a helicopter."

Definitely a helicopter. A nimble black one.

"Think they're bringing in a new prisoner?"

Stavros shrugged. "Could be."

"We should watch," I said. "The souvlaki can wait, right?"

The bird buzzed closer, lower.

In the pilot's seat was a horrifyingly familiar figure. Wearing black wasn't a fashion statement to Grandma—it was a billboard. She was devoted to my grandfather, despite his premature departure some thirty years earlier, and she made sure the whole world knew it. Nowadays his remains lived in an olive oil can in the kitchen.

I said, "That looks like Grandma flying it."

"That is Baboulas flying it."

A cable slithered out the side, its end tumbling to the prison roof. A second figure zipped down the cable.

"And that guy jumping out of it looks like Xander," I said.

"They could be twins."

"What are they doing?"

"If I had to say, I would guess that they are attempting a prison break." Stavros had his phone out in a flash. "Takis will want to see this."

"You're recording it?"

"Sure," he said. "Why not?"

"Evidence of a crime?"

He shrugged. "It's not the worst crime I've recorded."

I was suddenly curious. "What was the worst?"

He opened his mouth to tell me, but then all hell broke loose. Sirens began to howl. They knocked the other four senses out of whack. Guards who'd trained for this stumbled around with their combat gear. Inmates, who'd been hoping for some excitement in their day, tore around like chickens.

Xander had acquired a guard uniform from somewhere. He scaled down a drainpipe, cut through the unruly crowd—easy when you're part wall—barged in through front doors.

My breath caught. Grandma and the helicopter were hovering above the building, line dangling. My gaze slid all over the place, hunting for predators. The guard towers were—miraculously—unmanned.

When I mentioned it to Stavros he said, "Austerity measures. They cut funding and jobs. The prisoners are lucky to get food. There is a rumor that the kitchen cooks rats. In Korydallos there are two hundred inmates for every guard. They say it's standing room only in some of the cells."

"Jesus," I said. "Our prison system stinks, too, but it's not that bad. Yet."

I watched with a fascinated sort of horror as guards battled the prisoners. The meatball hadn't been lying about the bullets. One guard hurled his handgun like a boomerang. It came back when a burly prisoner snatched it up and beat him with his own weapon.

A rope ladder unraveled over the side of the helicopter. Xander appeared on the roof with a slight, graying figure.

Rabbit.

He shoved Rabbit up the first few rungs, boosted himself up behind the old man. They scrambled up and into the helicopter.

Then Grandma buzzed off in what I assumed was a borrowed bird.

I slumped in the passenger seat. My heart didn't know what to do with itself. Skip beats? Run laps? It looked to my head for help, but my thoughts were jangled. We had witnessed a prison break, conducted by Grandma and Xander, which had to be some kind of major league felony.

Stavros was still recording.

"Did you get all that?" I asked him.

He pushed the red button. "Uploading to YouTube right now, then I will send Takis the link."

"You can't do that!"

He looked puzzled. "Why not? The file is too big to email."

"Because the cops will see who did it!"

A pause happened. Stavros's head did some slow addition. "I didn't think of that."

We both looked at his phone.

"Oh," he said. "It finished uploading." A moment later he said, "It has five hundred views already."

"Take it down!"

"Okay, okay." He fiddled with the phone some more. "I took it down." More diddling and face-making. "Too late. Somebody already copied it and put it on Reddit."

"Maybe you can't see their faces."

He perked up. "Maybe my hand was shaking and it's too blurry to incriminate anyone."

I grabbed his phone, found the video, hit the triangle to make it play.

Our chatter crackled out of the speaker. It was the perfect accompaniment to Grandma and Xander's prison break.

"Dippy doodles shit on a stick," I breathed. Grandma was screwed, Xander was screwed, and Curly and I were bent over the hood of this car, getting screwed. Stavros had handed the police everything they needed to nail my family through the forehead for this crime.

An argument could be made that we only recognized Grandma and Xander in the video because we knew them, but it was thin and wheezing. The police could probably zoom in on their faces, swivel the bird around onscreen and nab the license plate number.

"Do helicopters have license plates?"

"In Greece sometimes even cars don't have them."

My phone rang. We both looked at it. There was wild fear on Stavros's face, and I knew mine was its mirror.

"Don't answer that," he said.

"I have to. It's Grandma.

"She's going to kill us and have Takis bury us in Turkey."

"You recorded it—not me!"

"She won't care," he said mournfully. He buried his head in his hands.

I answered the call. "Hello?"

The silence wasn't completely empty. There was crackling, the sound of Grandma's hellfire under our feet.

"Katerina?"

"Grandma?"

"Tell Stavros I want to see him as soon as you get back to the house."

"Okay."

"When I am done with Stavros I will deal with you."

Gulp.

Stavros didn't lift his head. "What did she say?"

"I think you're right about Turkey."

~ ~ ~

We drove back toward Volos in a horrified silence. I wondered if she'd let us have a last meal.

"Does Grandma let people have a last meal?"

"No. No last meal. Whatever you ate last, that's it."

I was afraid of that. "What did you have?"

"A croissant with Camembert, roast turkey, red onions, and cranberry sauce. I roasted the turkey breast myself, and I baked the croissants."

Even though I was about to be killed, that sounded great. "You cook a lot?"

"I took a course."

"I had a piece of Grandma's spanakopita."

"That's a good last meal."

"Yeah, but I don't want to die on an empty stomach. Do you?"

"No," he said slowly. "I don't."

5

"Have another *dolmada*," I told Stavros.

"It won't fit." He shoved it into his mouth anyway.

This was potentially our last meal and we were taking it seriously. That meant we had picked a seaside *taverna* with a reputation for excellent food. Not that it was difficult to find good food in Greece. Throw a small rock and you were bound to hit a plate fully loaded with delicious eats.

Only a generous blue umbrella stood between us and the sun; it kept knocking on the canvas, trying to find a way in. We were alone. Well, unless you counted the German couple sitting two tables away. They had first-degree burns but they looked happy about their situation. All the other pansies had retreated to their cloistered bedrooms, snoozing the afternoon away because they lacked the fortitude to handle the blistering heat.

Did I say pansies? I meant the smart people, who probably weren't in danger of winding up at the bottom of a deep hole on Turkish soil.

I sucked down another *frappe*. Greece had cornered the market on iced coffee. They tossed instant coffee, sugar (or not, if that was your thing) cold water, and ice cubes into a cocktail shaker, then shook until the whole thing was dense foam. Then they poured it into a tall glass, stuck a straw in, and changed your life.

"I was thinking we could stay here forever," I said. "We've got food, drink, the beach, and a bathroom directly across the street. Grandma wouldn't kill us in front of all of these people."

We looked at the German couple.

"In front of all these two people," I said.

Stavros thought about it for a moment. "Or we could run away."

"Where would we go?"

"Las Vegas. I hear you can get anything in Las Vegas."

True, but did you really want it?

The more I thought about it, the more the idea had merit. We could run away. It had worked for Dad—

Oh. Yeah. His mother had known where he was the whole time. She'd even come to visit me, with Mom's help. I had no recollection of the time we spent playing together at the park, but apparently Xander had been there, too.

Maybe we could run farther. New Zealand sounded promising, or … what was that nugget on Australia's foot called? Tasmania.

"How about Antarctica?" I said.

"I like polar bears," Stavros said. "We should do that, right after I go drain the snake."

"Wrong pole."

"I like penguins," he said, switching hemispheres. "They are cute in their little tuxedos."

He jogged across the street to the *taverna*'s storefront. The cooking happened inside the building, but the tables and chairs were mostly outside along the waterfront, with a few inside for people waiting to take their food to go.

I dragged my gaze up and down the deserted beachfront road. Nobody but us and the Germans and a couple of stragglers down the far end of the promenade, knocking back *frappes*. The sun was at its highest point, shooting for a top-down assault. The heat was coiling into one massive, overstuffed feather duvet, and it had plans to smother those of us dumb enough to be outside.

Stavros jogged back, his fly half mast. His face was pale, his eyes wild.

"Get up! I hear a helicopter!"

Now that he mentioned it, I did hear the faint buzz of an incoming bird.

"Probably a police helicopter. Or a news helicopter."

"No, the local police cannot afford a helicopter. Baboulas bought it from them!" he said urgently. "We have to run. Or hide. Or run and hide."

"What about the check?"

He dumped a wad of euros on the table. "Happy? Let's go!"

The whirring was moving closer. It sounded like a swarm of furious giant hornets.

I stood and stepped out from under the umbrella, my belly loaded with good Greek eats. When I moved it was how I imagined wading through quicksand, which, so far, hadn't been a real problem. The dangers of quicksand had been overhyped in my childhood.

What I needed was a good nap, but the caffeine surging through my system wouldn't give me permission. The coffee wanted to dance, the food wanted to nap, and so they struggled for dominance while I watched the sky, a hand shielding my eyes from the glare.

There was a helicopter, all right, and it was moving our way.

Inside my head I started running, but my feet hadn't received the message. All the food in my gut was blocking the transmission. If running was going to happen I wouldn't be the one doing it.

"Argh! It's coming right for us!" I said lamely.

"That's what I said!"

"What are we going to do? I can't run! Not with all this food in me."

"Too bad we are not Ancient Romans," Stavros said as the helicopter lowered its belly to the road. The Germans had their phones out, capturing footage of the most unexpected part of their vacation. "They used to vomit their food before the next course started."

Now that he mentioned it, throwing up sounded like an inevitable evolutionary step. But it would have to wait, because Xander jumped out of the chopper and landed on the ground with a visual thud.

"The good news," I yelled, nodding to the front of Stavros's pants, "is that you already got rid of your coffee. Again."

6

"Sit."

I pulled out the kitchen chair, sat, tried not to freak out. The sight of Grandma measuring ingredients into a bowl made me want to hurl.

Grandma's baking meant one of two things: either she was trying to cope or trying not to explode. Hopefully, if she exploded it wouldn't be in my direction.

"Somebody had to go see Rabbit," I said. "You were gone! I had no choice! Okay, I had two choices, but that was the better one. So don't even think about reprimanding me. If you'd told me what you were up to then I wouldn't have been there with Stavros and his camera. Also, not to be judgmental, but you broke a man out of prison. That's not exactly sound decision-making."

I'd made the mistake of standing mid-rant, after Grandma had commanded me to sit. Grandma wasn't a woman you defied unless you wanted to wind up standing at the bottom of that hole in Turkey, with a lot of dirt taking a nap on your head.

"And you thought it was best for you to go see him?"

"Who else was there?"

"The whole Family," Grandma said quietly. "Did it not occur to you that I would not wander off, who knows where, when there might be a clue at last about my son's whereabouts?"

"You didn't tell me anything. You left."

"I do not have to explain myself to you, Katerina. You have one foot out of the cradle. And now thanks to your … zeal, I will have the police asking difficult questions."

"I told Stavros not to record it."

"So he told me. I will deal with him later." She put an uncomfortable amount of weight on the word *deal.* The range, with Grandma, was impossible to gauge. On the one end was baking, on the other … execution.

I didn't have the ovaries to ask where on the spectrum this particular *deal* fell. I was worried she might tell me, and then I'd be forced to do something crazy to plead for my second cousin's life.

"Go easy on him," I said. "He was there because of me."

"You can leave now."

"Okay …" Where were the threats to send me back home or lock me in the dungeon? Unease hoisted itself onto my shoulders. It wanted a piggyback ride. It *expected* one.

"I have a lot of baking to do."

"Okay."

"And many decisions to make."

That unease wrapped its hands around my throat and squeezed as it tried to get a better foothold on my spine. Panic pulled out its billows and began to huff and puff at my adrenal glands. I could almost feel the cool breeze above my kidneys as it fanned. Decisions about what?

Then I remembered she had Rabbit here somewhere. Possibly in the dungeon.

"What about Rabbit?"

"What about him?"

"He didn't send you that box."

"I never said he did," Grandma told me. "I told you I knew who made the box."

The wily old bat was at least one square ahead of me on the chessboard, once again.

"He told me who sent it."

"Oh, he told you, did he? What name did he give you?"

"The Eagle."

"The Eagle." She made a face. Not a very impressed face. Somehow I'd pictured her more excited than this. "You do not think that is strange?"

"Why would it be?"

"You walked in there, a stranger, and he gives up the name."

"He did ask for a favor."

"A favor." The question mark had been hammered flat until it was more like a long, uncomfortable period.

"Don't worry," I said. "I wrapped it up in conditions. The name for an equal favor."

"An equal favor." Her obsidian eyes degraded to flint. "Oh, well, that is different. An equal favor."

"I did what I thought had to be done to find Dad. If it was the wrong thing … sorry, but you weren't there. It was my call to make."

""There is nobody named the Eagle that I know of—not in this business. And I know the people Stelios Dogas knows. We go all the way back to the beginning, Rabbit and I."

"Could be someone new."

"No."

"Could be someone old with a new name."

"No."

"Why would he give me that name then?"

She smiled. Grandma was a little old lady, but that smile make my innards wobble.

"It is a dangerous thing to owe a favor. The people who come to me to ask for my help, they know this. Never do a favor unless you are certain of the other person's loyalty. A gift is different." She shrugged over the bowl as her hand worked. "You can give anybody a gift. If they choose to repay you someday … then it is a good surprise. If not, then you are not disappointed. But favors … favors are dangerous. You asked for a name and promised an equal payment in return, and now I will have to take that favor upon myself to fulfill, when he asks it of me."

"I didn't ask you to—" I started.

"It is my responsibility as the head of this Family and as your grandmother."

I inched toward the screen door that separated the kitchen from the front yard. Outside held fresh air, and freedom, and also the outhouse. In here there was a grouchy munchkin-sized ogre with a compulsion to bake.

"I'm going to check on my goat."

She looked up from the bowl. "Before you go, what was in the box?"

"You don't know?"

She shrugged. "Why else would I ask?"

"I figured you'd opened it before leaving."

"No."

"It was … uh … a man's penis."

"Not a woman's?"

Oh God, was she kidding? I checked. There it was, the twinkle in her eyes.

"It wasn't Aunt Rita's," I said carefully, "if that's what you're asking."

The pause that followed was so long that I couldn't be sure it was technically a pause. For all I knew the conversation had ended, and on a deadly note.

Well done, Kat. Insult the Godmother's youngest child, the one she's sore about anyway.

"It wasn't Dad's," I said, eager to wedge something other than my own foot into the silence. "I figured you'd want to know."

"I do not want to know how you know."

"Dina," I said. "She identified it for us. She kept pictures."

We both made faces.

"That woman …" she said

~ ~ ~

I wanted to hunt down the name Rabbit had given me, but finding out there was no such person had lopped off that plan's head. The twerp had tricked me.

I left Grandma's house and trotted over to one of the courtyard's tables, with Googling on my mind. I pulled up the Crooked Noses Message Board, a forum dedicated to organized crime of every flavor. The top thread in the Greek Mafia sub forum was all about Rabbit's prison breakout. Stavros's video had gone viral. He'd killed the original but the Internet's memory was long.

The Crooked Nosers were filled with speculation, most of it about who had shot the video. They had managed to uncover the news about my visit with Rabbit, and now they were pooping out a million and one scenarios about what I could have been doing there.

It's got to be connected to her father's disappearance, they said.

Stelios Dogas has been in prison fifteen years. What would she want with him?

Child support, someone suggested.

My mouth fell open. Where did they get this stuff? I couldn't even defend myself without leaping out of the virtual closet.

I was checking my email—I'd won the Irish lottery again—when Detective Melas swaggered through the archway. His face was hard and grim. Whatever was scheduled to come out of his mouth, I didn't want to hear it.

"I didn't do it," I said as he planted himself in front of me like a statue. All that was missing from this art installation was Zeus's thunderbolt. Also, Melas was wearing too many clothes to be an actual Greek statue, but it was probably better this way. For both of us.

"I know, I saw the video. Know what else I saw?"

"Why don't you tell me." I rubbed my stomach. No more last meals for me. Next time I'd prepare to die on an empty stomach. "I ate a huge lunch and now I'm too tired to play guessing game."

"You and Stavros chatting, that's what I saw."

"Technically you didn't *see* that, you heard it."

His eye twitched. "What I also saw was the hood of your yellow car."

"Lots of yellow cars in Greece. It's a happy color."

"Do those people sound like you?"

"A lot of people sound like me."

"Were their names on the visitors' list at the Larissa prison?"

"Maybe. Who can say?"

"I'm thinking you can."

"If the wind changes direction," I said, "your face could be stuck like that."

He pulled the stick out of his ass and sat in the chair directly across from me.

"That looked like Baboulas flying that helicopter," he said.

"Pretty much every Greek woman over the age of seventy wears black."

"And the guy on the ground looked like Xander."

"Lots of guys look like Xander."

"He's a walking boulder. Almost nobody looks like him."

"*Almost* nobody isn't the same thing as nobody."

I fiddled with my phone and tried to play cool, which was harder than it sounded when it was this hot. The pool and fountains were tormenting me with their lapping and splashing. Yes, I could have jumped in the pool, but under this sun I'd fry. I'd already lost an anaconda's worth of skin.

"I think Stelios Dogas is here somewhere," Melas said.

"If he is nobody's told me about it."

"Think he's got something to do with your father's abduction and that box with the … the …?"

"Severed penis?"

He looked slightly relieved that I'd wrenched out the word stuck in his throat. "With that."

It was sympathy that made me sigh and say, "Okay, I talked to Rabbit—Dogas—but I had nothing to do with the prison break. No, I don't think he's got anything to do with my father's kidnapping. No, he hasn't got anything to do with the box. He made it, that's all."

"Made it?"

"I guess the guy's hobby is making puzzle boxes."

"So you're saying he made it for someone else?"

I nodded. "Someone offered him a trade."

"What did he get in return?"

I told him and he grinned. "Sounds like a good trade."

"Oink."

The grin sprawled wider. "Guilty. So who commissioned the box?"

"A guy called the Eagle."

He chewed on that a moment. "Never heard of him."

"That's what Grandma said. She thinks he was bullshitting to get me out of there."

"I hate to say it, but she's probably right. We're not talking a good person here. The man was in prison for a reason."

"What did he do?"

"They nailed him on public indecency, but that was an excuse. Name every crime there is, he's done it."

I wondered if Greece had crazy laws like we had back home in some states. In Oregon we weren't allowed to pump our own gas or use canned corn as fishing bait.

"Fifteen years for public indecency, isn't that extreme?"

"Thirty years. There was a donkey involved."

Eww.

My brain was quietly working through mental Pilates. Rabbit had thrown this Eagle person's name out there with confidence. If he was a liar he was unflinching. I'd bet a very small amount of real money, or a large amount of Monopoly money, that the Eagle was a real person. Just because Grandma and Melas hadn't heard of him, didn't mean he didn't exist.

As soon as I could untangle Melas from my hair I was going back to the Crooked Noses Message Board to see if they knew of any references to this Eagle.

If that failed, well, I wasn't exactly without friends in the Greek underworld.

Okay, friend. Singular.

And not exactly a friend. Penka was more like a Bulgarian drug dealer who traded prescription drugs for thick wads of cash. She worked for Baby Dimitri, Godfather of the Night and Trinkets. We kind of bonded while she was chained to a bench at the police station. Last week I went with her to a funeral for her friend Tasha, a Russian dealer and prostitute, who'd been murdered by the Baptist for the crime of being a police informant.

Melas stared at me. "What are you thinking?"

"I'm not thinking. Ask around, it happens a lot."

"Liar. You're always thinking."

"How can you tell?"

"Smoke coming out your ears."

"You don't know anything about me."

"I know you want me."

"I don't want you or anything like you."

"Sure you do," he said. "You're afraid to admit it."

"That's date-rape logic."

His eye was this close to twitching. I brought out his inner neurotic. Luckily for one of us—maybe both of us—his phone buzzed. He picked it up, scrolled one-fingered. Then he stood.

"Leaving so soon?"

He blew a sigh. The hair flopping over his eyes fluttered. He shoved it back into place with an impatient hand.

"Got to go. But I'm not done with you yet." It was almost awkward, the way he stood there, like he couldn't figure out what to do with me. Behind his eyes a solo round of kiss-kill-marry was taking place.

I decided to toss the poor guy a bone. Probably not the same bone he wanted to toss me, judging from the decision that had finally happened in his head, and that had now worked its way into his eyes and settled on his mouth. He was smirking. Definitely smirking. My underwear was a wall he wanted to blast through. My continent was something he intended to conquer. He wanted to go Alexander the Great on my ass.

"Fire!" I shrieked.

He cocked his head. "What?"

I waved my hand at his phone. "It's an emergency, whatever it is. Hurry. You know where to find me when you're done."

He shook his head and wandered back the way he'd come, bewildered. A moment later I heard the roar of his wheels spinning dust and stones.

With Melas out of the way I went on an intelligence hunt. The Crooked Noses didn't have anything for me in their archives. I could have started a new topic but what if someone in the Family was keeping tabs? An inquiry about this Eagle, on today of all days, might backfire.

There was no other choice: I had to take my investigation to the streets of Greece. They weren't particularly mean, but they were throwing up sheets of skin-melting heat.

~ ~ ~

I found Penka on her usual stoop. She wasn't alone. Sitting next to her was a scrawny kid, more bantam rooster than human. He was dripping in gold chains with chunky euro sign pendants. His oversized tank top revealed his distant relationship, twice removed, with the gym. The back of his saggy, baggy pants wasn't visible from the street, but I instinctively knew there would be a mile of boxers when he stood.

Penka had perched her significant-sized self on the far end of the stoop. She was wearing red shorts and an off-the-shoulder top that didn't want to be there. Her hair had been recently re-dipped in a bucket of bleach and styled with a blender. Her customers liked her to look cheap. It made them feel better about their habits. The stoop was attached to an empty beach house, built in the fifties and, by the looks of it, abandoned not too long after. The house stuck out like a recently whacked digit in the row of apartments and motels that had sprung up in the 80s and 90s.

"You want to buy asshole?" She hooked her thumb at the kid, who was still at least a couple of years away from his twenties. "Here, I have one. I give it to you cheap."

"Wow, thanks. Too bad there's only room for one in my underwear."

"You keep laughing, fatty," the kid told Penka. "You'd be sucking my dick if my uncle told you to."

"Who's his uncle?" I asked.

She rolled her eyes. "Baby Dimitri. This is internship."

"Wow, drug dealers have interns?" The things you learn.

The kid nodded at me. "Who's the bitch?"

"The bitch," I told him, "is going to punch you in the throat if you're not careful."

He scoffed at that. "Nobody hits the Donk."

"Donk?"

"You don't know the word donk?"

I exchanged glances with Penka. She rolled her eyes. I knew how she felt. "No."

"It's like thees," he said in the worst American accent I'd ever heard. "Yo, donk, wats app?"

My eyes went big and round. I felt my mouth sag in horror. The douche on the step mistook my reaction for ignorance.

"You never heard of Snoop Donky Donk? Man, you are old." He zeroed in on my chest. "Nice tits though."

It was without regret that I punctured his hot-air balloon. "Haven't you heard: he's Snoop Lion now."

His arrogance bottomed out. "What?"

"Snoop Lion. Google it."

"Matherfacker," he said, snatching up his phone.

"Some intern," I told Penka.

"Most drug dealers no have interns. Only me. I am lucky." Her face said, *No, not lucky at all.* "What you want?"

"Came to ask you if you know a guy. How's business?"

"Business stinks. Nobody wants good drugs—they all want cheap sisa now. This economy is eating my paycheck."

Sisa was Greek meth. It was currently chowing its way through the drug-using population, due to its affordable street price.

"You could get another job," I suggested.

"Who would hire her," Donk said, "except the circus?"

Penka whacked him upside the head with a packet of Ambien.

"This job is okay. Gives me plenty of time to read." Penka always had a magazine handy. She had a penchant for the fashion and gossip rags. "So tell me who is this man you look for?"

"Calls himself the Eagle. Or maybe other people call him the Eagle. Whatever. Eagle. Does that mean anything to you?"

Donk flapped his arms. "Caw, caw."

"That's a crow," I told him.

"Eagle."

"Crow."

"Eagle."

"Have you thought about killing him?" I asked Penka.

"Donk." Penka opened the cooler behind her. She tossed him a bottle of cola. "Have a drink."

"That's right," he said, grinning. "Bitches bringing me drinks. Where's the Cristal?" He popped the lid, chug-a-lugged half the bottle.

"No Cristal," Penka said dryly, which was the only way she ever said anything. "What you think this is? You want champagne, go intern for cocaine dealer."

"Maybe I will," he said. Then he slumped over.

We both looked at him. He was out cold.

"Uh," I said. "Did you know Baby Dimitri's nephew passed out?"

"I don't know how that happened. Maybe something in his drink."

"Like drugs?"

"Could be drugs, could be he was tired. Very tired."

"Let's go with tired," I said. "Funny, he still looks like a loser when he's sleeping."

"Is the open mouth and the drooling." And the ridiculous outfit that was cool in certain circles, ten years ago. "I heard the name Eagle," she went on. "Maybe a place. Where, I don't know. I am Bulgarian, not Greek. Why you ask?"

"It's a potential lead in my father's disappearance."

"Maybe he is there."

"Sounds high up."

"Americans are soft."

"I don't mind heights," I said. I didn't mind heights, except the high ones. It wasn't a phobia per se, but it could become one, say, if I fell.

"Is maybe not too high," she said, back-peddling.

"Too late. My mind is already contemplating the worst."

"If you were Bulgarian you would always contemplate worst."

~ ~ ~

Baby Dimitri was my next port of call. I couldn't peg Baby Dimitri. On one hand he and Grandma were enemies and business competitors, but the way he spoke he had a lot of respect for her. The Godfather of the Night and Souvenirs was Dad's generation, but he dressed for Florida in the 1960s. His shoes were white, his pants were sharply creased, and his shirtsleeves were folded high on his wannabe biceps. He had the look of a man who invested heavily in Brylcreem.

I found Baby Dimitri and his henchman Laki sitting outside, under the cover of his shop's striped awning. It was one in a chain of stores catering to tourists and locals. A narrow road separated the string of shops from the beach. The storefronts were done up in colors that had clashed so often they were flaking and peeling. Baby Dimitri sold a colorful mixture of shoes and souvenirs.

"Katerina, Katerina," Laki said. "Here is Katerina Makris."

"With an S," Baby Dimitri added. They both chuckled.

Laugh it up, sleaze-balls.

"Hey, Laki," I said. "Burn anything lately?"

Baby Dimitri's decrepit flunky flashed his gold tooth. It was the only thing in his mouth that wasn't gum or tongue. "Business is slow. You need anything burned?"

"Not today." His face collapsed like a soufflé. Oh, man. "But if I do I'll let you know."

He perked back up again.

What kind of person hates to make a mobster feel bad? A person like me, that's who.

"I met your nephew," I said to Baby Dimitri. "Interesting internship you gave him."

"How is my worthless nephew?"

"Sleeping on the job."

"*Gamo ti Panayia mou*," he swore. "That boy! Lazy! All he wants to do is wear gold chains, listen to the rap music, and fuck my prostitutes for free." He shook his finger at me. "I would not let him touch them even if he paid top dollar. As lazy as he is, it could be contagious. What can I do with lazy prostitutes? Nothing"

"He calls himself Donk. That's not his real name, is it?"

He shook his hands at the sky. "Donk! His real name is Yiorgos—George—but that is not good enough for him."

"Not 'kanksta' enough," Laki said.

The things Greeks could do to a G were interesting. They forced it out the nose and tacked on a K.

"Kanksta! Thuks! That's why I sent him out with one of my dealers. Give him a taste of reality."

"He's slumped over on a stoop, sleeping. Before that he was complaining about boredom."

He shook a finger at me. "That's the idea. There is nothing tough about selling drugs. Nobody thinks you are cool. They will say you are cool to your face, but only because they want your product for cheap or free."

"Maybe you should throw him in the deep end of the pool, show him how bad it can get."

He squinted at me like I was laying a trap. "Why?"

"If he's that lazy he'll probably think selling drugs is easy money he doesn't have to work too hard for. Give him something that will scare the wits out of him."

"Hmm …" He made a '*Keep talking'* circle in the air with his finger.

"That was kind of my entire sales pitch."

"Maybe I need to send him outside the Family."

"Great idea," I said. "You should do that." Then I noticed he was looking at me thoughtfully. "No. No, no, no. My Family won't want him."

"Not them—you."

"I definitely don't want him. He called me old, so I had to crush his hopes and dreams."

"See? You can teach him respect."

"What do I know about respect? Nothing. Ask my grandmother."

The rotten jerk, he pulled out the big guns, aimed them at the part of my head responsible for honor, duty, and promise keeping. "You owe me a favor."

"I …" My mouth dropped open. When I recovered I said, "This is worth more than a cheap bag of marbles!" A week or so back Baby Dimitri had gifted me a bag of marbles that I used as ammo for my Dad's old slingshot—the only weapon my grandmother would let me have. He'd told me they were a favor, and that I owed him one in return. Now he was calling it in.

"I don't recall putting a euro value on the favor—" He looked at Laki. "—Do you?"

"Nothing, that's what I remember," Laki said.

"Fine," I said. "But I want something else besides the marbles. Something bigger."

"You want a ball?" Baby Dimitri turned to his sidekick. "Do we sell balls?"

I blinked. "No, I don't want a ball. I don't mean physically bigger."

"Okay, what do you want?"

"Information."

"What kind of information?"

"I need to find a place or a person."

"And you think I know?"

"Don't you know everything?"

He nudged Laki. "I like this one. She has fire and she knows when to give me compliments."

Laki's shoulders shook with silent mirth. "You should hire her. Snatch her out from under the old woman's nose."

Given that you could hurl a rock in Grandma's birth decade and hit Laki, he had some nerve.

Baby Dimitri leaned back, folded his arms, made himself comfortable. "Okay, tell me."

"Eagle. That's all I've got to go on. Maybe it's a person. Penka thought it might be a place."

He chuckled. "Too easy. If you're talking a place, it's Meteora."

Meteora. Middle of the Sky. Towers of sandstone with monasteries gripping the tops and sides. Meteora had been home to monastics since the 1300s, now six monasteries remained out of more than twenty. Today they were inhabited by fewer than ten monks and nuns apiece, operating primarily as tourist attractions.

"Meteora?" I nibbled on a hangnail.

"Meteora," he said. "The eagle's nest is one of the old monasteries nobody uses. If you're asking about a person, they say that's where the Eagle lives. But my guess is there is nothing there but the bones of monks and some bricks. What about it?"

"So the Eagle *is* a person?"

"He is a rumor, and one I haven't heard in several years. Sometimes rumors are true, other times they are wishful thinking on the part of people who like to believe in things. Why you ask?"

"It's probably nothing," I said. "I was curious, that's all."

"Where did you hear about the Eagle?"

"Nowhere."

He gave me a sly look. "Does this have anything to do with Rabbit? A little mouse told me you went to see him, minutes before a mysterious man busted him out of prison."

"No."

"It is a mystery." His fingers tapped out a rhythm on his knee. Lights flickered in his eyes. He was enjoying this. "Why would a pretty girl go to see an old fossil like Stelios Dogas?"

Laki left his seat, sauntered down the sidewalk. From the back I saw him dive into his pocket and pull out a packet of tobacco and rolling papers.

"Where's he going?" I asked the Godfather of the Night and Cheap Shoes.

"Laki? Who knows?" He zeroed in on me. "Why did you go to see Rabbit?"

"I wanted to make new friends."

He laughed. "New friends! You are making a lot of new friends in Greece. Not always good ones. Look at us."

"We're not friends."

"But we could be, someday."

Out of the corner of my eye I saw Laki throw something that looked suspiciously like a bottle with a rag sticking out of the top. A bottle with a rag on fire.

"Jesus," I screeched.

Laki grinned back at me. "Watch this," he called out, pointing to the bottle in his hand. He threw the bottle into the open window of a small, black SUV.

Somebody screamed, girlish and thin. A man bolted across the street, fire licking his clothes and hair. He leaped off the cement dock, into the water. Then the vehicle exploded in a blinding halo of flames

Like a tide retreating before a tsunami hits, the beach emptied and poured into the street. Everyone wanted to gawk at the burning car. Never mind that it could spit hot metal at any moment.

"That was Elias!" I shouted. "You set my assassin on fire!"

"So Laki did you a favor."

Speaking of Laki, he was back. "Did you see that? That was a good one."

As if we could miss the giant fireball.

"That's my assassin. He's with me!"

"He was following you, watching you through binoculars. A creeper," Laki said. "That's why I make fire."

"He's supposed to be watching me! That's the idea!" I stopped for a moment. "Where do you keep the bottles?"

"It is a secret." He flashed the gold stash in his mouth.

After abandoning shop, I jogged over to the water's edge, peered into the water. Elias was standing there, steaming. The fire had fizzled most of his hair, and his eyebrows were singed. He smelled like a burning voodoo doll.

"You okay?" I asked.

He shrugged. "I think so. How is my hair?"

"You could be a trendsetter," I said. "I bet there's some weirdo in Paris right now dying to make burnt hair the hot new thing."

"My car?"

I glanced back at the burning automobile. It was beyond help. A few blocks from here a fire truck was howling for traffic to get out of its way.

"*Gamo ti maimou*," he said, as I helped him out of the water. "Now I'll have to steal another one, and I hate stealing cars."

I wasn't sure relations with a monkey weren't illegal in Greece. There was that whole alleged "monkey bite" that supposedly killed King Alexander in the early 1900s, so I didn't comment on the first part.

"You can't steal a car!"

His forehead scrunched. "Why not? Other assassins do it."

"Why don't you rent one?"

"I don't have a license. The plan was to get one after Fatmir paid me for killing you."

A thought crept across my mind. "Wait—I'm your first contract?"

He nodded.

Shit.

Damn it.

I felt sorry for the guy. I rubbed a hand across my forehead. A headache was coming, I knew it.

"You want to ride back to the compound with me?"

"What for?"

"Maybe Grandma will let you borrow one of our cars."

He brightened. "You think she'd be okay with that?"

"As long as you don't kill me."

He thought about it. "Okay."

~ ~ ~

My grandmother was standing by the fountain when we eased up to the compound gates. With her was Xander, dressed down in baggy cargo shorts and a T-shirt. A third person was with them, a face I didn't recognize. In her hands the woman held a handkerchief. They worked constantly, twisting the cotton, wringing its wretched neck. Her face was stricken, her posture desperate and defeated. I put her in her mid sixties, not a widow judging from the colorful geometric print dress she wore. Her heels hung slightly over the backs of her sandals.

I pulled through the gates, parked. Grandma waved me over.

"Wait there," I told Elias, nodding to the garage. I couldn't leave him sitting in the sun.

"This is my granddaughter," Grandma was saying as I walked over. "Katerina, this is Kyria Koufo. She has come to me with a problem." She gestured for her guest to speak. "Tell Katerina what you have told me."

"But she's a girl—"

"She is my granddaughter," Grandma said, a steel blade under the velvet cushion of her words.

The other woman didn't look convinced. Her eyes darted from Grandma to me, and back again, as though seeking a loophole. If there had been one I'd have tossed it to her. Something about her demeanor suggested that her story wasn't only sad, but humiliating.

"It is my husband," she said, lying down under Grandma's steamroller. "He sleeps with my friend. Both of them betraying me, those snakes. That I could have lived with, but yesterday I discovered they have concocted a plan to kill me. My husband will inherit everything, and he and my friend will live a pretty life together while I rot in the ground with worms gnawing on my lips."

I wasn't sure worms gnawed, but what did I know about worm physiology?

"He cannot be allowed to get away with this," she went on.

"Kyria Koufo is a woman of considerable wealth," Grandma said. "Wealth she has earned. We have known each other for many years."

The scorned woman bobbed her fashionably coiffed head. "I know your grandmother is wise in these matters, so I have come to her for counsel."

Grandma looked up at me. "I want to know, Katerina, what would you do?"

My brain blew a gasket. "Excuse me?"

"How would you handle this problem?"

'*I don't know*' probably wasn't the answer Grandma was looking for, or one she'd accept. I chewed on the inside of my cheek while I considered the angles.

"What outcome do you want?" I asked Kyria Koufo. "Do you want to keep your husband? Divorce him?"

"I told her not to marry him," Grandma said. "I knew he would be a problem. Is that not true?"

Kyria Koufo bowed her head. "I was weak. Blind."

"Love has a funny way of making you its bitch," I said. They looked at me blankly. "It's an American saying. It means love can make you do what it wants."

"I never loved him," Kyria Koufo said. "But he is hung like a bull."

Yikes. There was a visual I didn't need. "So … what do you want to do?"

"He is my husband, she cannot have him."

"You want to keep him?" I asked.

She shrugged. "I want her not to have him."

That seemed fair-ish. "If you tell them you know about their plan, they'll deny it. If you try to end it first, he'll … uh … *talk* you out of it—if it's the money he wants." Think, think, think. "How did you find out?"

Grandma spoke. "They tried to hire a contractor."

That was a pretty way of saying the couple tried to hire a hitman.

"One you know, I presume?" I asked her.

Grandma gave a one-shouldered shrug.

Kyria Koufo closed her eyes. "If he had come to me like a man and asked for a divorce, I would have been fair. He was a good, attentive husband, until this. Five percent of my fortune could have been his."

Five percent, eh? The epitome of generosity.

"Why don't you ask him for a divorce and offer him that five percent settlement?"

"And let her have him?" She stabbed her chest with one finger. "Never!"

What was I supposed to suggest? The woman was the architect of her own problems.

"You could push her down some stairs," I said, joking.

Kyria Koufo looked at Grandma. "Clever girl. That idea I like."

"I was joking," I yelped. "For the record, it wasn't a suggestion."

She stuck a hand in her pocket and pulled out an old-fashioned change purse, stiff satin with a silver clasp. She snapped it open, retrieved some coins, pressed them into my hand, folding my fingers around the cool metal. "Buy yourself something nice, eh?"

"You can go now, Katerina," Grandma said.

When I looked back, Kyria Koufo was spitting out words in a thick stream, while Grandma stared at some distant point, far beyond the iron gates.

~ ~ ~

It still didn't seem possible that I, Katerina Makris, who had never been anywhere outside of the United States, was in Greece. At home, places like the Grand Canyon and Yellowstone were old, but they lacked a certain weathering that crossed the line between old and ancient. Greece was a heap of ancient things built on top of something antediluvian, stacked on the very beginning of time itself. Greece felt like God's starting point and, at times, His first draft.

What was Meteora if it wasn't a blip in the blueprint, the result of a hand not yet used to the drafting pencil?

The sandstone towers stood isolated between the Pindos Mountains and the Plain of Thessaly. The towers that were still occupied by monasteries and their religious guardians were often speckled with tourists traipsing up the hundreds of steps thoughtfully cut into the steps, now that hauling people up via basket or rope was considered a safety issue.

~ ~ ~

The next morning I was loading up my car for a road trip I hadn't told Grandma about, when Donk rolled up to the gatehouse on his scooter.

"Yiorgos," I said.

His mouth drooped. "Donk. I don't get why I'm stuck with you."

"You misunderstood. I'm stuck with you."

"Are you kanksta?"

"No."

"You got a gun?"

I retrieved Dad's old slingshot from my bag. "This is so much better than a gun."

"Says who?"

"Says me."

His gaze wiped itself across my Beetle. "This is a girl's car."

"Don't like it? You can ride in the trunk."

Soft chuffing broke out behind me. I whirled around to see Xander laughing. He was soaping up his motorcycle. It was big and black and he rode it hard.

"He's a gangster," I said to the brat. "You should go with him."

Xander's laughter died suddenly. Donk had that effect on people.

"Can't," Donk said. "My uncle said I've got to go with you or he's going to cut my mother's allowance."

"Your mother gets an allowance?"

"She doesn't work."

"Why not?"

He gave me a look like I was clearly Greece's biggest idiot. I wasn't—not while Greek Eminem was standing in front of me in his saggy pants. "Because she's a mobster's sister," he said. Then he looked me up and down. It made me feel like slapping him. "I'm the nephew of a powerful man. You want to give me *tsibouki*?"

"How old are you?"

"Sixteen. I heard you old ladies like them young. Coukar."

"I'm twenty-eight and I'm too old for your crap," I said. "Get in the car."

"Where are we going?"

"Road trip."

It was ninety or so miles to Meteora. We could be there and back in a day—easy—me and my sidekick, Donk. Too bad the idea of being alone with this schmuck made me want to barf. I needed company, solidarity, someone who knew how to wear pants.

"What if I don't want to go on a road trip?" he said.

"It's not optional."

"I don't have a permission slip."

"Do I look like I care?" I trotted over to Xander, who was busy with a sponge. "Is Stavros around?"

He shook his head.

Damn. I didn't want to go it alone with Snoop Amoeba here.

"Come on," I said. Donk rolled his eyes, muttered something under his breath. But he followed me through the arch, into the courtyard.

He blew out a whistle. "Cool creeb," he said in English, doing a hatchet job on my mother tongue. "What's with the crack house in the middle?"

It was one thing for me to insult Grandma's dilapidated shack. It was quite another for someone with droopy drawers and a stick-on tattoo of knuckle-dusters on his … I was going to say bicep, but it looked more like his arm swallowed a mouse. Anyway, this kid wasn't going to insult Grandma's hovel. The end.

I stopped. Looked him dead in the eye. "That's where the wicked witch lives. She eats disobedient children."

"Are you on your period?"

"Don't make me hurt you, Yiorgos."

He winced. "Okay, okay. Don't have to be a bitch about it."

It was all I could do not to grab him by the ear and drag him upstairs. I settled for stomping. Stomping was for angry people and giants—and I was no giant.

I knocked on Marika and Takis' front door. It flew open a moment later.

"Katerina!" She looked past me to the scowling Donk, lurking in my shadow. "Who is this?"

"Yiorgos. He's Baby Dimitri's nephew. I'm giving him lessons."

"Don't say that name," Donk said.

Marika shot him a warning glance. "What kind of lessons?"

"He's learning how not to be a *kolotripos*." I mouthed the last word, which was Greek for asshole, in case her kids were within earshot.

"Donk," the boy said. "My name is Donk."

She squelched a smile. "Come in, eat, drink. Are you hungry? You look hungry."

I shook my head. "Thanks, but I was kind of hoping you might want to go for a drive."

"A drive?"

"In my car."

"On …" Her eyes lit up. "… An adventure?"

"On a small adventure." I held up my fingers to show her how small. My finger and thumb weren't even an inch apart. But Marika didn't look like she minded. An adventure was an adventure was an adventure.

"Takis never takes me on adventures, only Walt Disney World. And that was not an adventure. He ate and drank and looked at girls while I dealt with the boys."

"So you deserve an adventure."

"I think," she said slowly, "I would like an adventure."

"It might be dangerous," I warned her.

"No problem. I will bring supplies."

~ ~ ~

Fifteen minutes later, Marika was done mustering supplies. She had changed from her housedress into another nearly identical flowery dress. Her hair was like mine, up in a no-nonsense ponytail. She was carrying a cooler in one hand and a big, black handbag over one shoulder.

No food necessary, I'd told her before Donk and I had come downstairs to wait, and her eyes widened. "You mean we are going to … eat out?"

"Scout's honor," I said, although I'd never been a Boy Scout and Marika had no idea what I was talking about anyway. All she knew was that it was a solemn promise, and that we were going to eat food she didn't have to cook. I was going to have words with Takis when he and Aunt Rita returned from their powwow with Fatmir the Poor. There was no actual law about taking your wife out for dinner once in a while, but it was bad manners not to.

So Marika had forgone the food, but she brought out a cooler anyway.

"What's in the cooler?"

"Insurance," she said. She handed it to Donk.

He folded his arms. "Homie don't carry nothink," he said in mangled English.

"Carry the cooler," I said.

"No. You can't make me."

I looked at Marika.

"I have got this," she said, and clobbered his ear.

"Ow!" he wailed. He snatched up the cooler and trudged to the Beetle.

"Put it in the backseat," she called out.

Xander was still sponging down his motorcycle.

"We'll be back tonight," I told him.

He gave me a look like I was supposed to tell him where I was going, and I gave him a look right back that said no way, wasn't happening. Grandma wasn't the FTA; I wasn't required to file a flight plan. Anyway, I was sure they had a transmitter on my car.

"What are you doing?" I asked Donk. He'd tossed the cooler in the backseat and grabbed shotgun for himself.

"Nobody puts Donk in the backseat."

Marika slapped the back of his head. "Get in the back," she said.

"What's wrong with you?" he howled.

I grinned. "She's got a bunch of sons and her husband's a henchman. She's not about to tolerate bad manners from Snoop Pipsqueak."

His head tilted, shaving several points off his IQ. "What is 'pipsqueak'?"

"Google it," I said.

Marika and I fastened our seat belts and blasted out of the compound.

7

We ran out of city, then we ran out of villages, and soon we were on a thin road to the middle of Nowhere, Greece. Nowhere, Greece is somehow more charming and picturesque than Nowhere, USA. Pockets of wildflowers had spilled onto hillsides. The silver-green olive trees snarled at beeches, both of them wrestling for the same thimble of water. In places, the road seemed to be on the endangered species list: its edges had giant bite marks where the earth had been shaken away, leaving the blacktop nothing to sit on.

"This is boring," Donk said from the backseat, where he was slouched with one arm draped over the door. "You bitches are boring. I want to stop at a strip club. Are there strip clubs wherever we're going?"

"Sure," I said. "They dress up like nuns."

"I plowed a nun once. That's how good I am. Even a nun wanted a piece of the Donk."

This one was an eye-roll a minute.

"Kid," I said, "I don't even know how you can say that with a straight face."

"You don't believe me? Who wouldn't want a piece of this?"

I made the mistake of glancing back. He was manhandling his mortadella—with enthusiasm and vigor.

Oh, God. "You'll go blind," I said.

"You'll go blind when I shoot it in your eye."

Marika peered in the rearview mirror. "That? My youngest was bigger than that when he was born."

Mr. Happy got a sudden sad-on. "Bitches," Donk said. "Always keeping men down."

"You are not a man," Marika told him. The kid sank into the backseat like punched dough.

I grinned at her. "You're good."

"He's nothing compared to Takis."

"Who's Takis?" Donk asked.

"My husband. And he does bad things."

Donk unclipped his seatbelt, scooted closer. "What sort of bad things?"

"I do not ask, but I pray. Every day I go to church to pray for him."

Takis was a weasel but he got the job done. I was about ninety-nine percent certain he chopped off the Baptist's head with an axe and stuffed it in a jute sack after Xander blasted the former cop's cerebellum out of his skull. But I wasn't about to tell his wife or the kid in the backseat. Takis didn't seem like he was down with the whole caring and sharing thing. Mobsters, in their own way, were like cops. There were parts of the job they couldn't take home.

"Prayer." The kid scoffed.

For a moment I thought Marika was going to reach back and slap his head again, but she settled into the seat.

After a while she said, "There's someone following us in one of Baboulas' cars."

"That's Elias, my assassin. Grandma let him have one of ours."

Donk scooted forward again. "You've got an assassin? What does he want?"

"Not too bright this one," Marika said.

"To kill me, mostly."

"Why doesn't he shoot your tires out or something?"

"Because he's not going to kill me. He's following me around, making it look like he wants to kill me."

"Why?"

"To placate his boss while negotiators talk him out of the contract."

"He's a double-agent?" The kid flopped back. "Cool," he said in English.

Marika's head swiveled on its stalk, in my direction. "Who did Baboulas send to negotiate?"

My brain stuttered. I couldn't *not* tell her the truth, could I? Marika and I were on our way to being friends. We were on an adventure together—an adventure that might be dangerous. You have to be honest when you're on a dangerous adventure together. It's in the unofficial rulebook.

"Aunt Rita," I said.

"Who else?"

"Maybe Grandma sent Takis, too."

"To negotiate? My Virgin Mary! He can't even discipline our children, how can he negotiate for your life?"

"I kind of wondered the same thing," I said. "He's not exactly subtle."

"He is as subtle as an avalanche of minotaurs."

"As subtle as a swimming pool filled with spiders."

"As a bag of Zeus's thunderbolts," she said.

Donk tossed his two cents in. "As subtle as triple-D tits."

"Nobody asked you," I said.

"You're boring. Even that fat Bulgarian drug dealer was more fun."

"Going on an adventure is good." Marika adjusted her sunglasses and rested her arm on the open window. We had the top down, breeze blowing back our hair. "It's about time someone else in my family had some fun. This is a new beginning, I can feel it."

The village of Kalabaka was a white and red rug thrown over Meteora's feet. It was quaint, charming, and all of those adjectives that suggested this was a place that liked to look good on a postcard but hated unwed mothers. Towering over the village, a pudgy gargoyle on its stone perch, was the Monastery of the Holy Trinity.

Marika clutched her chest. "Meteora! When we were courting Takis promised to bring me here, but we never came. The minute we were married —bam!—the babies came and the romance was dead."

"There was romance?"

"In the beginning. He used to steal flowers from Baboulas' garden, until she threatened to chop off his hand for stealing."

We cruised through the streets of Kalabaka. I'd come here with nothing but a vague reference to a place that may or may not exist.

"How are we going to find this place?" I mumbled.

"You're worse than boring," Donk said. "You're a boring idiot."

I stopped the car. Beside us, dozens of pairs of shoes were lined up on the sidewalk. Alongside them, on metal racks, cute handmade bags and jewelry caught the sunlight and flung it in my eyes. A wrinkled leather sack in a black dress zoomed in on us.

"You want new shoes? For you, cheap!"

"Thank you," I called out, "but I don't need new shoes."

"Everybody needs new shoes," the old woman said.

"Except me."

"What about them?" She nodded to my passengers. "They look like they need new shoes."

"They don't need new shoes either, but thank you."

"Take your 'thank you' to the devil! And move that car before I call the police."

"Wow, you really know how to make friends," Donk said from the backseat.

I hooked a thumb in his direction. "He needs new shoes."

"Fuck you," he said. "I don't want some old goat's shoes! I wear Air Chordans."

The old woman slammed her hands down on her hips. Her chin and chest went into defense mode. "What's wrong with my shoes, eh? You don't like?"

"Your shoes stink. They're for girls and *poustis*." Girls and gays.

"What you say?"

Aaaaand … the old woman went straight from defense to offense in under five seconds. She hefted the whiskbroom leaning against the rack.

"Donk," I said.

The kid didn't know a warning when he heard one.

"I said your shoes smell like ass, old lady. Do I look like a *pousti*?" Mr. Puniverse beat both fists on his chest. "I'm the Donk! I'm all about the *mouni*!" He stood as best he could in the backseat of the Beetle and grabbed his crotch. I didn't have the heart, or the inclination, to tell him that he had his reproductive organs mixed up.

"*Mouni*, eh? Who teach you to talk like that?" She looked at me.

"Hey!" I squeaked. "He's not mine. Or hers."

"No," Marika assured her, "he does not belong to either of us."

The old woman's scowl sagged another inch. "Disgusting! What is wrong with you women? Why can't you find a man your own age, eh?"

Marika elbowed me. I hit the gas.

"I could have taken her," Donk said. He was puffed up like a twig.

"She's an old woman."

"So?"

"Respect your elders."

"Old people," he muttered and slouched back down. "What's in the cooler?" He tapped his fingers on the lid. "Any snacks?"

"Nothing for you," Marika said.

"Stop somewhere, eh? I'm hungry."

What the heck, I needed directions anyway. My cellphone connection kept flaking out and there was no public Wi-Fi that I could find. So I pulled over outside a row of shops and darted into a souvenir shop for a map of the nature-made towers.

~ ~ ~

We drove a while. The pillars seemed close on a map but the proximity was a lie. And I couldn't get a bead on which one was this Eagle character's home base. Asking around the village hadn't helped.

I said, "I didn't expect them to be so spread out. They look more … clustered in photographs."

We drove some more.

"Are we there yet?" Donk asked.

"No," Marika and I said at the same time. We both scrambled to grab the first red thing. Only we were all out of red things.

"Great," Marika said. "Now we will fight. Do you think we should do it now to get it out of the way?"

"That's probably a good idea."

"What should we fight about?"

We mulled it over and came up empty-handed.

"Got any food?" Donk asked.

"Are you hungry again?" I said, incredulous. The kid was a walking garbage can.

"What do you mean again? That was an hour ago!"

Damn it, the little weasel was right. We were driving and driving and getting nowhere, except lost and confused.

I pulled over. Turned in my seat to look at Donk. "Call your uncle. I need to know where I'm going."

"Why would I do that?"

"Because I'll buy you lunch if you do."

He made faces as he crunched the data and worked his way toward a decision.

"Okay. Deal. But I want a *xambookar*."

His English made me wish for an icepick to drive through my eardrum.

"Make the call."

~ ~ ~

Baby Dimitri came to the rescue. He knew a guy who knew a guy who thought he knew which tower was the eagle's nest. The Godfather of the Night and Espadrilles made sure I knew I owed him. My intangible debts were racking up.

Anyway, we were on the move again, this time toward a definite blip on the map. It wasn't long before I was parking at the foot of the shortest tower. You'd never know it from the bottom. It rose into the air like a giant wiener. This was where Greece overcompensated for being a smallish country.

We emptied out of the car.

Hand shielding my eyes, I stated the obvious. "I don't see any steps. Do you see any steps?"

"No steps," Marika said. "Footholds, yes, but no steps."

"Aren't there supposed to be steps?"

"Maybe the monastery was abandoned before they built steps."

Probably that was it.

I stood there scratching my head. "There has to be a way up."

Marika said, "If only we had a helicopter."

"Grandma has a helicopter. We should have brought that."

"Whoa," Donk said, clearly impressed. "You've got a helicopter?"

"My grandmother does."

"That's kanksta. You should see this," he said, wrestling with his phone. "There was a prison break yesterday. They used a helicopter."

Crap … "Huh. Interesting."

"It's amazing. Watch." He thrust the phone under my nose. Marika and I stood there and watched Grandma maneuver the bird into position over the prison roof.

"You know it is funny," she said, eyeing me sideways, "that sounds like Stavros."

"You think so?"

"And the woman, she sounds like you."

"She sounds like a woman."

"And the car is yellow."

"Huh."

"The same yellow as your car. And you and Stavros were gone yesterday afternoon."

"We were at the beach."

"Then where is your sunburn?"

"Okay," I said. "Maybe we were there."

"And that man on the ladder, he looks like Xander."

"That's what Detective Melas said."

"You were at the Larissa prison?" Donk asked.

"Only if you're not recording this," I said.

He raised his hand. "Xi fife!"

Marika smacked his head. "Put your hand down. You know better than that."

"But it's an American thing. Xi fife!"

"This is Greece," she said. "No *moutsa*!"

The *mousta* was one of the Greece's favorite obscene hand signals. The flat palm, fingers spread, the upright hand, all combined that meant either you were rubbing poop in the recipient's face, or calling them a frequent visitor to Rosie Palmer's house to pay a sticky visit to her five daughters.

"What were you doing at the prison?" Donk asked. "Visiting all your friends?"

"Checking out your future home," I said. "Animal control won't take you."

"Really?"

"No. I was following up on a clue."

"What clue?"

I looked him in the eye. "A severed penis."

He turned white, passed out on the dusty ground.

"Detective Melas did the same thing." I nudged him with my foot.

Marika scrunched up her nose. "Men are weak. Imagine if they had to push babies out."

We stood there contemplating the horrifying logistics while Donk groaned on the ground. "I need a drink," he said.

I popped the cooler open, expecting to find drinks, then slammed the lid back down. "There's no drinks in there," I said.

Marika had packed supplies, all right, but not the food and beverage kind. All the Greek necessities: jackets, in case it got cold—in July!—slippers, in case we lost our shoes, various icons of saints I couldn't name, and guns.

Did I say guns? I meant submachine guns or assault rifles—I didn't know the difference. Those small, wonky, T-shaped weapons that spit projectiles and had the ability to kill a lot of people, and fast.

Drinks, though? Nope.

I tried not to whimper.

"Figures," he said. "Good thing I scored some from the Bulgarian. She gave me a dozen bottles." He waved a bottle at me and popped the lid before taking a long swallow.

"Jesus," I said. "You sure you want to drink that?"

He looked at the plastic bottle. "Why?"

My head shook. "No reason."

Ten seconds later he keeled over a second time.

This time Marika nudged him. "What's wrong with him?"

"A Bulgarian drug dealer happened to him."

"What did she give him?"

"I don't know. Something Bulgarian?"

"My Virgin Mary!"

"He'll be fine," I said. "It's nothing he can't sleep off."

We looked up at the stone tower. It was easy to imagine it toppling over, crushing us to death. A way up hadn't materialized.

A throat cleared behind us. Elias had parked behind me in the black sedan. He'd stuck his head out the window. "There's a rope ladder around the other side," he called out.

I waved. "Thanks." With my elbow I nudged Marika. "Let's go."

Elias was right, there was a ladder made of what looked like newish rope. Someone had been up here, and recently.

"I'm going up," I said. "You should stay down here." In case I needed a medevac, which out here could be a donkey. "If the rope breaks I don't want your children to grow up without a mother." I knew what that was like and it sucked, although Dad had done his best to fill in the gaps.

There could be a clue at the top of that rope ladder. There was no way I wasn't going up.

8

It was five minutes later.

"You need help?" Elias called out.

I shook my head. "We're good."

"You don't look so good," he said.

Don't look down, Kat. Don't look down.

I looked down. So far I was only about six feet up the ladder. Huh. It felt higher.

Don't look up, Kat. Don't look up.

I looked up.

The sandstone glared down at me. Was it my imagination or was it looming?

"I think this rock is alive," I said.

"Rocks are not alive," Marika said. "That is a children's story."

"There's a children's story about rocks coming alive?"

"My mother told it to me, and now I tell it to my boys."

"Does anything good happen in the story?"

She shrugged. "Only to the rocks."

That figured.

One at a time, I boosted myself to the next rung, then the next. They were floppy and they shifted as I adjusted my weight. What I'd taken for a gentle breeze was becoming a serious death threat as the ladder swayed.

I glanced down. Marika was hauling herself up behind me.

"You don't have to come up," I said.

"This is an adventure, yes?"

"Yes."

"Then I am coming up! I am tired of sitting in the car while everyone else has fun."

"If we fall?"

"Your assassin can call the ambulance."

That seemed fair. Elias was turning out to be a helpful sort of guy.

My travel guide—aka: the Internet—told me the tower was close to two hundred feet. Wrong. It was at least ten thousand. That's how it felt. My muscles burned. My gut churned. The wind was doing its best to blow my eyeballs out of their sockets. I imagined Dad's old crony, Jimmy Pants, who was now a high school gym teacher, laughing at my lame level of fitness. I wasn't sure there was a level of fitness this low. My level was subterranean.

Not Marika's though. She was hauling significant ass up the ladder.

"It's the boys," she puffed as she passed me. "All day I run, run, run. Children are suicidal. It's my job every day to stop them from killing themselves."

There's a scene in *The Chronicles of Riddick*, where the deadly sun sweeps across the planet and cremates every living thing in its path. Our sun had watched that movie, and now it had ambition and goals.

The good news was that the remainder of my peeling skin had evaporated. The bad news was that Sol was now blowtorching what was left of me.

I was nearly at the top. Marika had made it up a few minutes ago, and now she was tossing inspirational quotes at me.

You can do it. Don't look down or you'll die. How do you feel about wheelchairs? Never mind, if you fall you will die instantly—or close enough to instantly. Are you wearing clean underwear?

That sort of thing.

As I reached for the final rung I had a primal urge to scream, *Khaaaaaan!* What I lacked was ability. My breathing was ragged, my voice hit-or-miss.

"I didn't die," I said in loosely connected, randomly spaced fragments. Then I put my head between my knees and waited to feel human again.

When I lifted my head I was in Dresden, post World War II. What had once been a monastery was now a pile of haphazardly tossed blocks, resting on a foundation of tougher blocks. There were a few standing walls but they were slowly getting around to the business of sitting. A light rash of greenery had crept up the tower and spread itself over the ragged landscape. The sun was trying to burn it off but mountains do longevity better than anyone, and that's where the roots were, deep in the shaded cracks.

Marika was turning in a tight circle, hand shielding her eyes. "The view," she said, "it never stops."

I took a deep breath. Tried to picture myself standing on flat ground, within inches of sea level. The edge was something I was determined to avoid until it was time to leave. But even sitting I could see the world was infinite here. It went on and on and on and on, a bit like the recently converted.

"What are we looking for?" she asked me.

"A clue." I dragged myself up off the ground.

"What does a clue look like?"

No idea. Which was why I was inching around the rocks, squinting at everything, and trying not to fall and die.

"Rabbit said the Eagle commissioned the box with the penis."

She crossed herself. "I thought you said that to scare Donk."

"No, there really was a severed penis. Someone sent it to Grandma. I traced it to a man named Rabbit in Larissa's prison, and he told me he made it for the Eagle."

"Are you sure that is what he said?"

I thought about it. "Yes."

"And this Eagle person is here—are you sure?"

Good question. One I should have asked myself sooner, before zipping away on a road trip.

"No, I'm not sure. That's why I'm here."

Overhead, the sun was laughing at me. I plopped down on a rock. Sitting struck me as sturdier. You never read about a guy who fell off the ground and snapped his spine.

I brainstormed out loud. "That rope ladder was fairly new, so someone has been up here recently. All the TV I've watched, you'd think I'd know what to do next."

On TV there was always a clue, which lead to another clue, which lead to a solution. Up here we had rocks, blocks, a killer view, and all the fresh air we could swallow.

"Why do you believe there is a clue here? Maybe this Eagle was here, but now they are not. If I cut off a *poutsa* I would hide."

"Where?"

"Somewhere in the middle of nowhere."

I looked up at her, disbelieving. "We are in the middle of nowhere, on a tower of rock."

"Oh," she said. "I forgot."

I wanted answers and I wanted at least one of them to be here and now. Dad's trail was cold and only growing colder.

I stood. Brushed myself off. "Okay, let's go."

But I wasn't going, was I? My feet were taking me on one last look around the jagged rooftop. Old bricks, outlines of rooms ascetic people used to fill. Lots of bird crap. Nothing fresher than the ladder. It had been tied to the deepest roots.

"We should go," I said.

"Home?"

"There's nothing here."

"We could visit the monasteries," she suggested slyly.

"Don't we have to be covered up?"

We both looked down at the white town. From up here it looked like spilled milk.

"I guess we could go shopping."

"An adventure in between adventures!"

Marika's enthusiasm for life was catchier than crabs at a 70s key party. We returned to the ladder, which was where Marika ran into a big problem: herself.

"My Virgin Mary," she wailed. "I cannot climb down there."

I patted her shoulder. "It'll be okay. Do the same thing you did to climb up, only do it backwards, and try not to fall. Be Ginger Rogers!"

"Who?"

"She was a movie star and dancer."

"You are not helping!"

"I don't get it," I said. "You scrambled up like a mountain goat."

"Up is different. Down is the problem. Look how far away the ground is!" she cried.

It was pretty far.

"Okay," I said, "let's troubleshoot this. We're up here and the ground is down there. We need to get from here to there, and all we have is this ladder. So the ladder is it—our only way down. Troubleshot. Bam!"

She shook her head so hard the flyaways from her bun lashed her round cheeks. "I think I will stay here. It's not so bad, and the view is wonderful. Do you think someone can airlift food up, and maybe some television?"

She must have missed the part where there were no electrical outlets. "What about your boys? Don't you want to climb down and see them?"

"They will survive without me."

"What about Takis? Who'll make his fries and pray for him?"

"His mother is dead, but he has a father. Let him do it."

"Takis has a father?" It seemed more likely that he'd sprung out of a carbuncle on someone's butt, kind of like Athena did with Zeus's head.

"His father is a jackal."

That made sense. Takis *was* kind of a watered-down Antichrist, but less evil and more douche.

"Okay," I said. "I guess I could call Grandma and have her bring the helicopter."

"No! You cannot call Baboulas! She'll be angry."

"She'll get over it." I pulled out my phone.

"No, I'll climb down!"

~ ~ ~

Five minutes later, Marika was on the ground, shouting inspirational messages, once again. I could do it, she told me, the woman who'd been a shivering mess ten minutes earlier.

She was right: I could do it. And I could do it a lot faster if she'd shut up and let me climb down.

Finally, I was able to let go and fall the last couple of feet. I landed with a gymnast's flourish.

Elias was still there, but now he had a friend. The new guy was more beard than man. His eyes were jet beads peering out over a humpbacked nose. A dense, black forest surrounded it all. His build was slight, his height average, and he was wearing Jesus sandals.

My assassin hooked a thumb at him. "This is Mo."

"Mo." I nodded. "Nice to meet you."

"Do not talk to me," he said, "Yankee female dog."

I looked at Elias. "Friendly guy."

"Mo is shit—Iranian shit. But he's a good assassin."

"Persian," Mo barked. "The best subset of Iranian."

So, Mo was Persian, and he had the rug tucked under his arm to prove it.

"Wait," I said, double-taking. "You're an assassin, too?"

Mo said nothing.

Elias turned to him. "She's asking if you're an assassin, too."

"Tell her I am the best assassin in Greece."

"But—" Elias started.

"Tell her."

Elias rolled his eyes and looked at me. "Mo says he is the best assassin in Greece, but that is not—"

"Silence!" Mo shouted. "Infidel. Tell the Yankee dog she must kneel while I cut off her head."

"You're not cutting—" I started.

Mo looked up at the sky. "Tell her!"

Elias sighed. "Mo would like you to kneel while he—"

"I would not *like* it," Mo said. "It was not a request, it was a command. Kneel."

"A-ha," I said. "You spoke to me."

"Tell her I did not speak to her."

Elias said, "He did not—"

I held up one hand, careful not to make a *mousta* out of it. "I got it. Tell him I won't kneel."

"She won't kneel," he told Mo.

Mo pulled a big, scary sword out of thin air. It had curves like a banana. "Ask her if she will kneel now."

"Cool," I said. "It's an Aladdin sword!"

He looked horrified. "It is a shamshir. Excellent for cutting off heads and hands. It was my father's father's father's father's great-great-grandfather's sword."

"Was his name Xerxes?"

He looked at Elias. "Why is she speaking to me?"

I let out a long, exasperated sigh. "Why is he trying to kill me?"

"Don't take it personally," Elias said. "It's work. It's not like we do this for fun."

"It is a little bit fun," Mo said. "Especially when their heads bounce and a hawk swoops in and steals it."

We all looked at him in horror.

He slapped his belly, laughing. "It happened one time, the funniest thing I have witnessed in my life. The hawk came down and carried the head away, seconds after I cut it off." Tears streamed down his cheeks and went missing in his shrubbery. "We never did find that head."

"Who was he?" I asked.

"A thief. I was supposed to cut off his hand, but I missed. Memories!" Then he paled. "Shit," he said. "I talked to you again, unclean woman!" He unrolled his carpet, dropped it on the ground, and faced what I presumed was east. He dropped down on the carpet and began to chant.

"Who does he work for?" I asked Elias.

"Don't you tell her," Mo called out, before resuming his chant.

"A Pontic Greek named Harry Harry."

A Pontic Greek was a Greek who hailed from Pontus, now a part of northeastern Anatolian Turkey.

"Harry Harry is not the boss of me," Mo flung over his shoulder. "But yes, he wants her to die."

"And he wants me dead … why?"

"Tell her I do not ask why. It is my job to cut, that is all, and take her face back on ice so he can make mask for his gallery."

"You can't kill her," Elias said. "She's my kill. This could make me."

My stomach turned. "My face? Jesus."

"Jesus was a prophet, nothing more," Mo said casually.

People have wanted to bust my kneecaps, rip off my head and shit down my neck—their words, not mine—anything to get out of paying their debts. But back home those threats had been limited to baseless gauntlets thrown down the phone line. In Greece people legitimately wanted me dead, and they had the means to hire assassins to do it. Other people I knew who had visited Greece never had these kinds of problems. But then their families weren't Greek mafia, were they?

"Here's the thing," I said. "I don't want you to kill me."

Mo didn't look up from his carpet. "Tell her that is too bad."

"He said it's too bad," Elias said.

"I got that part. In fact, I'm getting all the parts. Tell him I want to talk to his employer."

Mo sat back on his haunches. "What did she say?"

"She wants to talk to your employer."

"Harry Harry does not talk to Yankee pigs."

I snatched the phone out of his back pocket, turned it on, began scrolling through recent calls.

"You cannot do that!" Mo wailed.

Marika folded her arms. "Funny, because it looks to me like she's doing it."

I hit dial, dancing out of the way as Mo swung his Aladdin sword.

"Smiling Panda Massage," a woman's answered. "You will leave with a smile, guaranteed."

I hung up, dialed the next number.

"Happy Happy Massage."

End call. Next on the list.

It rang and rang as I leaped around, staying one swing away from the blade.

Donk sat up, rubbing the sleep from his eyes. "I had a dr—ARGH!" He rolled under the Beetle. "There's a crazy Arab with a knife!"

"I am not an Arab! And it is a shamshir," Mo screamed. He hurled the sword at the ground in a snit worthy of a toddler. "Not a knife. Not an Aladdin sword. A shamshir. It is the best sword in history!"

"That is why Persia conquered Greece," Marika said. She slapped her forehead. "Oh, I was mistaken. That happened in a different universe."

I threw the phone back to Mo. "Nobody's home." I raised my hands in a T. "Timeout," I said. "I need to make a call." Everybody stopped, even Aladdin. I dialed Aunt Rita.

"Come," she said, the way she always did.

"Do you know a Pontic Greek named Harry Harry?"

"I know him," she said. "Why?"

"He sent a guy with an Aladdin sword to cut off my head."

"Tell the infidel I will smite her if she says Aladdin one more time," Mo shouted.

"Where are you?" my aunt asked.

I looked up at the stone tower. "Meteora."

"Meteora? What's in Meteora except rocks, virgins, and tourists?"

Marika said something behind me, and then I heard Takis say, "Is that my wife?"

"Tell him we're on an adventure," I said.

Aunt Rita told him. His voice went Chernobyl. "On an adventure? She is supposed to be home with our children, not out having adventures!"

"Did you get that?" I asked Marika. She nodded.

"Put me on speakerphone," Takis barked at me.

"No."

"Put me on the speakerphone now."

"Can you do telekinesis?" I asked him.

"What? No."

"Then you won't be going on speakerphone."

"*Gamo ti Panayia mou*," he swore. Then he yelped.

"What did you do to him?" I asked my aunt.

"Flicked his ear." Her voice became deep, serious. "Who did Harry Harry send?"

"Some Persian named Mo. Skinny, wearing sandals, more hair on his face than a dog's butt."

"That sounds like most of his guys." She lowered her voice. "Is the other assassin still with you?"

"He's here. Why?"

"Look, we went to see Fatmir the Poor, but someone else got to him first. He's dead."

That wasn't all; I could hear it in her voice. "What aren't you telling me?"

"Somebody cut out his heart. Leave Harry Harry to Takis and me. We'll go see him next."

"Thanks." My voice wobbled out on unsteady legs. Fatmir the Poor had wanted me dead, but that didn't meant the feeling was reciprocal. I would have been satisfied if he had agreed to forget about Elias killing me.

"Anything for my niece." She blew me a kiss and disconnected.

"Do you want the good news or the bad news first?" I asked Elias.

He looked dubious. "Good news."

"Fatmir is dead."

He looked stricken. "If that is what you call good news, I don't want to know the bad."

"That was both," I admitted. "Bad for you, good for me."

He sat on the rocky ground, elbows on his knees. "What will I do now?" he said in pathetic voice that tugged at my empathy strings. In a way, I was responsible for his financial situation. If I'd let him kill me maybe he could have collected his moolah before Fatmir lost heart—literally.

I thought about it a moment. An idea popped into my head. "You could make sure Mo doesn't kill me, and I'll make sure you get paid."

"Be your bodyguard?"

"Kind of."

"I could do that," he said, perking up.

"Traitor," Mo cried. "Yankee pig clicks her fingers and what do you do? You lift your skirt and jump! In my village *you* make *her* jump. Then you take her home and force her to have your babies and never let her drive again."

"You—" I stabbed at the air with my finger. "—My aunt and cousin's cousin's cousin are going to have a sit-down with your boss."

"Harry Harry is not the boss of me."

"You said that already. I mean your employer. And in the meantime, don't even think about killing me."

"You are the Thought Police, but you cannot control what is in here." He tapped on his head like it was a ripe watermelon. "In my head I will be cutting off your head fifty different ways, then violating your dead body."

Marika slapped the back of his head. "Who raised you, eh? Your mother would cry if she could see you."

"She has no eyes, how can she cry or see what I am doing?" We all looked at him in horror. "My father plucked them out for looking too long at a man. Unfortunately, he acted rashly. The man was her optometrist."

Ugh.

I trotted over to where Donk was still shivering under my car, hauled him out by the leg. He flailed and struggled, but I wasn't about to let some brat get the best of me.

"Get in the car," I said.

"Fack you!" he said in English. Obviously he was buddies with the guys who enjoyed decorating walls and overpasses. The facks were rampant there.

I reached into the backseat, flipped the lid on Marika's "supplies", pulled out a gun that was about the size of a bread loaf.

Everyone hit the deck.

"Want to hear something frightening?" I said. "I have no idea how to use this. I know which end goes where, but that's it. Marika and I are going to check out the monasteries, but first we're going shopping. Donk, get in the car. Elias, you're in charge of making sure Xerxes doesn't kill me—"

"Xerxes was a sissy mama's boy!" Mo cried.

"—Marika, you're in charge of making sure I don't kill Donk."

We jumped into my yellow car and sped away, whipping the ancient dirt into a sepia tornado.

"If anyone kills Donk it will be me," she said.

9

The best thing about all the steps was that they eventually ran out. We had hauled ourselves up the approximately three million steps that led to the Great Meteoron Monastery, and we'd done it in long, flowing skirts that had done their best snag our feet and snap our necks. We'd left the menfolk at the foot of the tower with the cars. Elias was in charge of making sure no one got their mitts on Marika's guns.

The low hum of tourists using their best indoor voices outside washed over us. It was the sound of people confused about whether the monastery was a church or a sedate theme park. People stopped to look at us as they contemplated one all-important question: Could they get to their phones without seeming rude? Some didn't care. They snapped away, loud and proud.

"Greek Amish," one guy said like they knew. The words were English, the accent American.

"Give me a break," I said, rolling my eyes. "Amish are from Pennsylvania."

"I didn't know you people flew in planes," the big guy said. He was red-nosed and seven months pregnant, the kind of guy who yelled at his television during football season. Beer was his poison and hot wings were his remedy.

"Flying horse buggies," I said, wearing my best deadpan. "We borrowed the spell from Santa Claus."

His mouth opened, closed, opened. He muttered something about " 'Murica" before shuffling away.

I looked down at my dress, then Marika's similar outfit. She looked like a sofa, which meant I probably resembled a loveseat. "I guess we overdressed."

"They said long skirts, we bought long skirts."

The other female tourists were in mid-calf-length skirts that didn't make them look like they were part of a technology-free society or religious cult.

"Looks like long means mid-calf, not scraping the ground."

"I like it," Marika said. "I feel pretty."

Not me. I felt like I was this close to snapping an ankle.

~ ~ ~

We were standing in front of a skull case. Interesting choice in decor. Personally, I would have gone for books, but maybe the monks were phrenologists.

Marika leaned sideways into my personal space. "There is somebody following us, and it is not your assassin." She pushed the words out of the corner of her mouth.

I went to turn around.

"Do not turn around!" She dived into her bag and pulled out her cell phone. One push of the button later, she flipped the camera and pulled me into a cheek squeezing hug. "Selfie. Smile!" Then she let me go. "See?" She tapped the screen, zooming in on a woman two bodies back.

"Never seen her before. You?"

Marika jerked her head up. "No."

In the photograph the woman's gaze was stuck to the back of my head. Her hair was big, terrorized recently by a fine-toothed comb. Her makeup was inspired by 1980s MTV. She was sin—the cheap kind, found at the bottom of a bottle of Keystone Light.

"Okay," I whispered to Marika. "We're going to back out of here and see the rest of the monastery. Let's see if she follows."

Sure enough, the woman followed, always several bodies back. She was in a modest dress that was in direct conflict with her head and knee-high boots. The boots were black, flat-heeled, and laced, like combat boots that forgot to quit growing.

That's when I spotted the man with the eagle on his shoulder. Not a tattoo, but a real eagle, its talons biting into the man's leather vest. He was inside the monastery gates, gaze scanning the thin crowd. I grabbed Marika and pulled her into an alcove.

"What is it?"

"A man with an eagle."

"A real eagle?"

"It's on his shoulder, like a pirate with a parrot."

She peered out. "That is the short-toed snake eagle."

"You know birds?"

"Who do you think does my boys' homework? You think they do it? No, I do it. And now I know my eagles."

I was impressed and I told her so. She beamed, but it dimmed quickly.

"What are you thinking?" she asked me.

"That could be the Eagle."

The man was so shady he probably cast a shadow on a moonless night. There are two kinds of men who wear leather vests. One discards his clothes for money; the other one takes money and keeps the clothes on. Both types are known for zooming away on motorcycles, often with your belongings. He was tall and a hungry kind of thin. His mirrored sunglasses were shooting lasers at passersby. The bird moved its head this way and that, missing nothing except, hopefully, us.

"Shouldn't it be wearing one of those hoods?"

"Maybe," she said. "My boys didn't get to that part, yet."

Cleopatra moved into the frame. I watched to see if her gaze snagged on Eagle Guy, but the transition from left to right seemed smooth. She turned around, hands on hips, mouth like a murder scene.

"Keep an eye on them both," I said. I zoomed in on the selfie again, cropped her face, and texted it to Aunt Rita.

Five seconds later, my phone shivered.

Who is that?

I was hoping you knew.

No, but I want that lipstick. If you get a chance, ask her.

My aunt had priorities. Lipstick was one of them.

"Maybe she's another assassin," Marika said. "You do seem to be collecting them."

"I wonder what happens when I get the whole set? I wouldn't mind exchanging them for a cool prize."

We got lucky. That's all I could say about what happened next. Latex Lucy flubbed her super-stealthy tailing moves and backed up to the alcove. Marika grabbed her in a headlock and dragged her in. The woman was quicker than a cobra. Takis' wife had mad skills.

"Okay," Marika said, pushing her catch against the wall. "Tell us what you know."

"That was pretty good," I said. "Takis give you some tips?"

She scoffed. "This is how I get the truth out of the boys."

Latex Lucy's face twisted. She made a sound like a cat about to hawk up a dead mouse. Then she spat in Marika's face. The clear mass stuck to Marika's forehead, then began a slow slide down her nose.

Marika gasped. Her tan skin flashed red.

"Tell me this *vromoskeela* did not spit on me."

Vromoskeela was right. Spitting in someone's face makes you a dirty female dog. Even I knew that.

"It could have been bird poop, but I don't think so."

"Bird *kaka* would be better, because the bird doesn't know what it is doing."

Latex Lucy's head swiveled. Her gaze latched onto Marika's. "You must be a terrible wife. I feel sorry for your children that they have to tolerate you."

"Who are you?" I demanded.

"Cleopatra."

Marika's eyes narrowed. "What did you say?"

I touched her arm, the one pinning Cleopatra's neck to the ancient wall. If I didn't diffuse the situation it was entirely possible she'd send Cleopatra to the afterlife without all the proper burial customs. What if the monastery didn't have enough bandages?

"Before you kill her, let's find out what she wants, okay?"

"What I want," the wannabe Queen of the Nile said, "is for this donkey to let me go."

"Her name is Marika," I said. "She's with me. And my name is Katerina Makris."

"I know who you are," she said, "and I know what that is."

Marika said, "Let me kill her."

"We still don't know who you are," I said. "But so you know, in my head I'm calling you Latex Lucy."

"My real name is a queen's name."

"Yeah, she was a queen. Right up until she got dead. Why are you following us?"

"I'm not following you, I'm walking behind you. That's not a crime."

I thought about that a moment. "Probably it is somewhere. Maybe North Korea. Who are you?"

She flashed an expensive smile. She looked cheap but her dental work was top dollar. "Nobody."

Marika stepped on her foot.

"Okay, okay, I'm following you."

"Why?" I rolled my eyes. "Oh, God, are you trying to kill me, too? Because I have to say, that's getting old."

The real Cleopatra's low-rent sister shrugged. "We're looking for the same person. I can't find him but I found you. I figured I'd stick close, see what you dig up."

"Who? My father?"

"Why should I tell you? My boss thinks you're stupid, and I'm inclined to agree, but you're all we've got."

"Who is 'we'?"

Her lips pressed together. They were morbidly fascinating, like slugs this close to exploding.

"Fine," I said. "Get out of here and stop following me."

"I can if I want to." She winked and slithered away.

Eagle Guy was sitting on a bench with his bird. He was giving me the willies.

“Are you going to talk to him?” Marika wanted to know.

Was I? Emotions swam around inside me. Eagle Guy’s whole package was intimidating enough without the bird. The eagle was hard liquor icing on a moonshine cake. But I’d come to Meteora for a good reason. I wasn’t about to walk away from a lead, no matter how sharp its talons were. This could be Dad’s life or death.

“On it,” I said.

As I trotted over, I tried to look like I wasn’t recruiting for a cult. Without looking at me he stood and began to wander away, headed toward the monastery gardens. Even the bird was ignoring me.

“Excuse me,” I said.

He didn’t stop.

I picked up the pace. So did he. I followed him down a short flight of steps, lined with shrubs potted in terra cotta, then he jagged right and vanished through an arched doorway. I hoisted my skirt up several inches and slipped through, plunging into darkness. The light behind me was close to useless. Most of it had been filtered out by a giant fig tree, its limbs leaning over the small courtyard. So my pupils had to pick up the slack and dilate, but they were moving slowly.

By the time I could see I was out of luck. Eagle Guy was gone.

I hiked back to where Marika was waiting, eyeing postcards in the tiny souvenir shop.

“Let’s get out of here,” I said to Marika.

“All this old stuff is creepy anyway,” she said. “I thought it would be different.”

“Different how?”

“Not so old.”

~ ~ ~

On solid ground there was another new guy. He had the kind of face that was easy to forget and difficult to describe to a police sketch artist. He was what they had in mind when they invented the word *beige*.

"This is Lefty," Elias said. Somewhere along the way he'd found a bag of sunflower seeds. He chewed, spat, tossed another seed into his mouth. "He says he's here from Cyprus to kill you."

"Of course he is," I said. I nodded to the new guy, whose real name was probably Lefteris. "Join the club. Who's your employer?"

"I freelance," he told me. "It changes. This job is for some asshole from Delphi."

"How do you do taxes on something like that?"

"Private contractor."

"Okay, well, Elias is in charge of you two—" I swung my finger from Lefty to Mo. "—not killing me until my family's had a sit down with your employers. Can you handle that?"

Lefty's face said he couldn't. "Don't kill the target, don't get paid. I like getting paid."

"And I like being alive."

He planted himself on the ground, legs apart, arms folded. "I'm here to get paid."

My eyes rolled so hard I came this close to spraining something. I turned to Mo. His loose hinges were about to become useful. "Are you going to let him scam you out of your paycheck?"

"Never! Cypriot pig!" Then he dropped his carpet on the ground, followed it down there. "Allah, a million apologies, I did not mean to speak to the unclean Yankee woman."

Who watches the watchers? The other watchers, of course.

Speaking of …

I pulled out my phone, opened the selfie Marika snapped, and showed it to the men. Elias and Lefty shook their heads. Donk's eyeballs popped out of his skull, then he hoofed it back to the car, hands clasped in front of his groin.

"I cannot look at that," Mo said. "She is unclean. That woman wants men to do perversions upon her." He opened one eye and took a good gander. "Is it too much to ask that she is a virgin?"

I know we're not supposed to judge books by their covers, but I was sure Cleopatra had hopped onto the train to Pound Town years ago.

"Probably she's still a virgin at something," I said.

"Like reading," Marika said, then she pointed. "What is that?" It was veering into late afternoon and the sun was gearing up for one obnoxious last gasp before conceding its throne. There was a speck falling out of the sky, and it was coming right for us.

"Eagle," Mo said. "When I was a child we had one as a pet. It would hunt rats for our breakfast."

He was right: It was an eagle. An eagle that looked suspiciously like the one on Eagle Guy's shoulder. And it was holding something in its talons.

It swooped past, and as it did it dropped its payload.

"Bomb," Elias hollered. I threw myself onto the package.

Everyone else scattered.

10

No booms, no bangs, no fireballs.

I peeled myself off the ground and picked up the package. It was wrapped in the same plain brown paper as the puzzle box. I brushed myself off. "I thought you said it was a bomb."

"Bomb detection is not an exact science," Elias said, checking the label. "I think this is for you."

It wasn't for me. Once again, it was for Katerina Makri—no s.

"Grandma," I said, and began ripping into the paper.

"You cannot open someone else's mail, infidel!" Mo said.

"It's not technically mail if it fell out of the sky," I told him.

"Carrier eagle is what they used to use in my country in the old days."

"In your country it's still the old days," Lefty said.

Mo turned on him. "Shut up, Cypriot pig. Are you Greek, are you Turkish, who knows?"

"Could be worse." Lefty spat on the ground. "Could be Persian."

"You wish you were Persian. We are the chosen people!"

"Chosen by who? Garbage collectors?"

The two men went round in circles until Marika cut in. "I thought Jews were the chosen people."

"Nobody listen to the woman," Mo said. "She is unclean. All women do is bleed and steal a man's money."

Chuck a handful of wheat into my mouth I could grind it to flour between my teeth, thanks to this mob—no pun intended.

"Enough!" Under the paper was another box, this one square, where the other was rectangular. Set into the front was an identical combination wheel.

"Here we go again," I muttered.

"Here we go where?" Mo glanced around. "Where are we going?"

"The last one had a *poutsa* inside," Donk shouted from the backseat of my Beetle.

"A *poutsa*?" Lefty asked.

I nodded. My heart was flipping out as I speculated what was hiding in this box. Once again, the combination was eight letters. I spelled out B-a-b-o-u-l-a-s hoping for a pattern, but the lock wouldn't budge.

"Of course it did," Mo said. "What else would you send a Yankee whore? Everybody knows you all collect dicks and stick them to your walls."

A long, pained sigh escaped my throat. "Do you think we should wait to see if Eagle Guy comes back down?"

"I have to do laundry," she said.

That was that. I got in my car. Dumped the box in Marika's lap. Turned the key. If the others wanted to follow, they could.

"This was a good adventure," Marika said. "What are we doing next?"
"Is it me or does he look pale?"

"Imagine if we were really gangsters," I told Marika.

We were back at the compound, watching Donk wobble away on his scooter. The assassins and Cleopatra had installed themselves at the mouth of the compound, outside the gates. The guard ducked out and exchanged words with them, then they all rolled back toward the trees. Grandma couldn't have assassins clogging the works—not if they weren't hers.

Cleopatra rolled down her window, stuck out her big flashy 'do. "Are you going out tonight? Because if you're not I'm going home."

"Say the word and I'll shoot up her car," Marika told me.

"What would Takis have to say about that?"

"Nothing, if he knows what is good for him."

"I don't think Takis knows what's good for him," I said.

~ ~ ~

I didn't waste time telling Grandma about the box. Instead, I went straight to the guy who could open the thing. Litsa wasn't around, but Tomas was at the pool with his brothers and cousins. He waved when he saw me, and raced over when he spotted the box in my hands. The five-year-old was dry by the time he reached me, pool water sucked up by the great wet-vac in the sky.

"Is that for me?"

"Just the puzzle part," I said.

"Did you try *Baboulas*?"

"Yes."

He flopped into a deck chair, box in his lap, legs dangling.

"Can I look inside this time?"

"Probably not."

Five years old, yet he took it like a cheerful, fully-grown man. "Okay." He twiddled the knobs. "Have you ever been to the dentist?"

"Lots of times. Why?"

"Mama says I have to go to the dentist. I've only been once before and I don't really remember it. Were you scared?"

"Maybe the first time, but not since then. They gave me a bumblebee made of dental cotton."

He nodded as he worked the puzzle. "That's a good strategy. Maybe they'll give me some stickers or something. Can you come with me?"

"Isn't your mother taking you?"

"She has a thing."

"What kind of thing?"

"I don't know. She said a thing. So you can you take me?" His little face was pinched, his eyes hopeful. Saying 'No' would be like kicking a kitten.

"Wouldn't miss it for anything," I said.

He flashed me a grin. "I like you." He handed me the box. "It's unlocked, but I didn't open it because you said not to."

The kid was something else. My ovaries gave me a poke, said, '*Tick tock. You could have a few like him if you could hurry up and find a man who doesn't prefer penis.*'

"You're a genius," I said.

"I know." No gloating about the fact, only serene honesty.

"Let me know about the dentist, okay?"

He nodded.

~ ~ ~

I hoofed it back to Grandma's hovel. She wasn't around, but the yard was occupied. Xander and Papou were playing a game of backgammon. Xander's gaze latched onto me and didn't let up until I was standing beside them.

"Who's losing?" I asked, trying to stay cool. Xander's intensity could crush a woman.

Papou flipped his hand at Xander. "Even when he wins, this *malaka* loses." He nodded to my hand. "What's in the box?"

"I don't know yet. I haven't looked."

"If it is another *poutsa* this one is smaller."

I set the box on the table, taking care not to disturb the board.

"Go make us some *frappe*," he said, "then we will look in the box."

The feminist movement took one step back as I turned on one heel, but it rebounded, and then some, when Xander's hand curled around my wrist and reeled me back in. He sat me down in his chair, then disappeared inside, presumably, to make the iced coffee.

"Xander is not nice to anyone unless he feels they deserve it, or he wants to do *nee-noo nee-noo* with them." The old man gave me a pointed look.

"I deserve it," I said. "I am pretty awesome."

He snorted. "I am sure that is it."

Five minutes later, Xander was back and all three of us were peering into the box. Inside, on a bed of black satin, was a heart. A potentially human love muscle.

"Whoever this person is, he is a romantic," Papou said.

Couldn't be romantic. Romance usually gave me butterflies; the only things circling in my stomach were sharks.

"Oh boy," I said, feeling nauseated. "Aunt Rita said they found Fatmir the Poor dead, and someone had cut out his heart. That could be it."

"Maybe. Maybe not." Papou had gone back to his game. Obviously internal organs didn't bother him too much.

"Why not? How many guys do you know who are missing a heart right now?"

"In politics and crime? All of them. I only know I have one because the doctor tells me it's no good."

"I think it's Fatmir's heart."

Grandma chose that moment to waddle back into her yard, dirt sprinkled on her knees. She'd been tending to the compound's gardens. "What have you three got there?"

"A heart," I called out.

"A real one?" She took a gander at the box's contents. "Human," she said. "Maybe it belongs to Fatmir the Poor."

Rocky-style, I raised my hands above my head. "That's what I said."

Grandma looked up at me. Somehow she always managed to make it feel like looking down. "Where did you get this?"

"An eagle."

"An eagle?"

"Hooked beak, big talons, goes squawk-squawk."

Papou cupped a hand to his ear. "How does it go?"

"Squawk-squawk."

"What?"

"Can I push him in the swimming pool?" I asked my grandmother.

She was too busy frowning to answer. Whatever she was thinking she was working hard at it. The gears were really grinding.

"A bird … it gave you this? It fell out of the sky?"

"That's pretty much exactly how it happened. I was standing there with Marika, Donk, and my three assassins and—"

"Three assassins?"

This was going to take a while if she kept asking obvious questions. "Elias, who is now on my payroll on account of how Fatmir is dead. He's making sure Mo doesn't kill me. And Mo's making sure Lefty doesn't sneak a bullet in first."

"Which one is Lefty?" Papou asked.

"He's a freelancer. He's from Cyprus."

Grandma looked at Xander, who nodded.

"What is a Donk?" Grandma asked.

"Baby Dimitri's nephew," I explained.

They looked at me.

Grandma shook her hands at the sky. "I am afraid to ask."

"It's kind of like an internship," I said. "Baby Dimitri had him out with one of his dealers, but that wasn't 'gangsta' enough for the boy."

Grandma said, "Take him nowhere. Show him nothing."

"I didn't." Except that I took him to Meteora, but it wasn't like I'd had a choice. It was take him with me or leave him to roam the compound.

She wagged a finger at the box. "This does not look like nothing."

"Didn't open it until he was gone."

"Hmm," she said in a judgmental tone that suggested I was to blame for something, but she didn't know what yet.

I said, "Why isn't anybody asking *why* some sicko is sending us body parts?"

"They are not sending *us* anything," she said. "They are sending them to me."

"The eagle gave *me* the package."

"And whose name was on the wrapping, eh?"

"Yours." And mine-ish. But I'd be pushing my luck off a cliff if I said that.

"It is a message," Grandma said.

"So I figured. But what's the message? I thought you said it was a message about Dad."

"I like to chop up people," Papou said.

I glanced at him. "The sad part is that I'm not sure if that's the message or if you like chopping up people."

Grandma's face twisted. Between the wrinkles and the slow grinding of her facial muscles she was downright igneous. She was a woman struggling. She didn't want to admit she didn't know. At least that's how I read it. I could have been wrong, but I suspected any minute now she'd go to the mixing bowls.

"We will find out in time," she said.

"Let's look at the facts," I said, pulling over a chair and helping myself to its wooden comfort. "We have a penis that's not Dad's, but no body missing a penis."

"That's called a woman," Papou said. Grandma shot him in the face with her stink-eye.

I went on. "And we have a heart, and there's a dead mobster out there with a hole in his chest." I did some math. It wasn't pretty. "Maybe Harry Harry the Pontic Greek is missing a penis."

Grandma raised an eyebrow. Good thing she'd never been Botoxed because she raised her eyebrow at me a lot. "Tell me you have not met Harry Harry."

"That's who Mo works for. He's one of the other assassins. Skinny little Persian guy? Carries a rug around with him? Calls me a Yankee pig?"

"That's all Persians," Papou said.

"Harry Harry, too." Grandma shook her head. "A lot of people want you gone, my girl."

As previously mentioned, seeing as she was Greek, what she said was *girl my*. But that's not the sort of thing you can put in a story without confusing people.

My hands did one of those magicians' flourishes. "That's why I've got the assassins watching the assassins."

"That's not too bad," Papou said. "This one can think on her feet."

"I do think better lying down," I admitted.

"Everybody thinks better lying down, but usually about embarrassing things that happened decades ago. When I can't sleep my brain always wanders back to the time when I was eight and my mama caught me making love to a chicken." He looked at us, shrugged, not a shred of shame or regret on his face. "It was in the icebox, dead. I was sleep-walking, okay?"

I winced. Grandma stared at him. Xander was busy studying the heart. Maybe he was thinking about shifting from organized crime to medicine. Maybe, like me, he was trying not to think about the old guy in a compromising position with a future entrée.

Grandma spoke up. "These assassins are not my men, I cannot trust them. So from now on I want you here in the compound."

Here we go again. "No. We've been through this before, and the answer is no."

"I am trying to keep you alive."

"And I'm trying to find my father."

"So am I."

It was a stare-off. She'd had almost a century longer to practice, so the odds were against me, but I couldn't not try.

She heaved a massive sigh. "At least let me give you a bodyguard. One of my men."

"Marika's a pretty great bodyguard." Except for the bit where she'd flipped out at the top of the rock. But we've all got our quirks and fears.

"Marika is Takis' wife and the mother of his sons. She cannot be your bodyguard."

That was probably for the best. "Who?"

Her head swiveled to Xander.

"No," I said quickly. Then I felt bad. "It's not that you're not a fantastic bodyguard, but I'm a problem you don't need." Plus, there was the part where he was Grandma's snitch. "And you need Xander," I told Grandma.

Xander leaned back in his chair, folded his muscle-roped arms. My thoughts flashed to the waterfall of silver and gold scars down his back. The man lived a life of danger, and something inside me didn't want to dunk him in more.

My phone pinged. Text message from Aunt Rita.

Harry Harry is dead.

Is he missing a penis?

No, both eyes. Why?

I quickly texted and told her about the heart.

Coming home, she wrote.

"Aunt Rita and Takis are on their way back. The bad news is that Harry Harry can't see as well as he used to. The good news is that he's dead, so the vision thing won't be a problem."

"Xander," Grandma said. "Check and see who else—if anyone—is dead. There is a pattern here and I do not like it. Harry Harry, Fatmir, and who else? The bodies do not match the body parts."

"I guess now we sit and wait for eyes and a body to go with that …" Papou wiggled his little finger.

~ ~ ~

The family descended upon the courtyard as the sun began to slouch out of the sky. The courtyard was wired with strings of fairy lights, invisible by day, delightful by night.

While the children played—at least I thought they were playing; from the sounds it was possible they were killing each other—their parents and other adults slow-walked around the compound, not unlike the way people did at the promenade.

Rabbit was there. Already less gaunt, he'd rustled up civilian clothes and managed not to look like he was a former inmate. He was sitting in Grandma's front yard, arms folded, spinning a bullshit story about another prison break at the Korydallos prison that had also involved a helicopter.

"True story," he said. "Only they caught the *malakas*. It was his second botched prison break."

Papou was there, too. He was ignoring Rabbit as hard as he could. His back was to the man, which was the less damp way of spitting in a Greek's face.

"Bad planning," Grandma said. "And stupid friends." Then she turned the tables on him. "How many boxes?"

"Eh?"

"The boxes. How many did you make?"

"I have made hundreds, Katerina. You know this as well as I do."

"Playing stupid does not suit you."

Papou lobbed some words over his shoulder. "Who says he's playing?"

Rabbit jumped up. When he grabbed his crotch, it was with a velocity that suggested he'd woken suddenly from a bad dream and wanted to make sure his bits hadn't been relocated to a sizzling skillet. "Eat it," he said to Papou.

"Did someone offer me a toothpick?" Papou said without turning around. Bitchy was something he did better than a closet full of swishy men.

Grandma had a look on her face like she wanted to shove them into separate corners and spray them with bullets. "In recent history, Stelios."

Rabbit sat. "One. Why?"

"We have two."

"Impossible!" He blasted out of his seat, hovered momentarily, then crash landed back onto the wood and varnished straw.

"Oh, then if you say so it must be true," Grandma said.

He didn't relax. He knew the axe was coming, and from the droop of his mouth it seemed as if he'd decided that being born wasn't his best idea.

"I made one box. One." He scurried around in his own head, hunting for excuses. "Maybe someone else made the second box."

"The box was identical, except for the size."

He tugged on the hem of his new shirt. "Let me see."

"Katerina, bring the box."

I didn't want to touch the thing. Too bad Grandma didn't look like she was in a negotiating mood. I got the box from the kitchen, set it on the table. The contents of both boxes had been stashed in the fridge in plastic containers.

Rabbit eyed it suspiciously. "What was inside the second one?"

Grandma told him. His face stayed passive, unreadable.

"Hmm," he said. He shuffled his chair closer to the table, examining the box from every available angle without touching a single surface. Maybe he was afraid of catching death cooties. He leaned back, arms folded. "Not one of mine."

"Are you certain?" She said it in the kind of voice that suggested her real words were, *Is that your final answer*?

"Of course! I know my own boxes."

Papou grunted. "Looks like one of your boxes to me, but what do I know?"

"*Skasmos*, old man," Rabbit said.

"Why are you here? You don't belong in this place."

Rabbit settled back in his seat. A smile hoisted the edges of his lips so that it was a pale parody of mirth. "I have an invitation. Ask Katerina."

My mouth opened to deny everything, until I realized he was talking about the other Katerina—Grandma.

"He is my guest," Grandma confirmed. "For now."

There was a death knell if ever I'd heard one. Only Grandma could make two normal words sound like an impending air embolism.

"Looking at your face make me want to vomit," Papou said.

"So go."

"No," Papou said. "I do not trust you." He touched his eye. "My eyes fourteen."

Which was the Greek way of saying: *I'm watching you.*

I was starting to get the feeling these two had history. History like Henry VIII and Anne Boleyn; Leonidas and Xerxes; Zeus and everybody.

"If you want to fight, do it in your own time," Grandma said. "Are you sure about the box?"

Rabbit slapped his fake-o smile back into place. "I would bet my life on it."

"You might have to."

The smile died. "I am telling you, it's not mine. The work is shoddy, unprofessional. Look at the edges? Rough. The varnish is not perfect. You can see the brush strokes. See?" He pointed to the side. "A bristle. I would rather die than leave a bristle on one of my boxes. Whoever made this, he had no pride."

"Who ordered the first box?"

"I told her, it was the Eagle."

Grandma looked at me. "You said this box was delivered by an eagle."

I nodded. "There was a guy with an eagle at the monastery. When we got back to the car the eagle swooped down and dropped the box." I watched Rabbit as I spoke. No reaction. He was good or he was ignorant. Money wasn't something I'd bet either way.

"You did not say there was a man," she said.

"You didn't ask. He was a creepy guy with an eagle on his shoulder and mirrored sunglasses."

"Did he say anything?"

"No. He was busy hanging out with his bird. And I didn't see a box."

"Would you recognize him if you saw him again?"

"If he had an eagle on his shoulder and those sunglasses, sure." Because the bird was one hell of a distraction. A parrot, I could have seen past that, but eagles ... That's not something you see every day, even in Greece where old women tote chickens in sacks onto buses.

"Katerina," she said, shaking her head. Then she zeroed in on Rabbit again. "When did he come for the box?"

Arms folded high and tight on his chest, he shrugged. "I don't remember the date. There are two dates that matter in prison. The day you arrive and the day they let you leave. In between, the days are all the same day."

She kept her gaze cool and level. "You know I can find out who came to visit you, eh? Every person for fifteen years."

"Do your fingers still stretch that far, Inspector Gadget?" He laughed at his own joke—which made one of us. A joke needs breathing room to be funny. There was none here. Grandma had filled the atmosphere with her chilly countenance.

Nobody moved. Nobody spoke.

Nobody wanted Smaug to think they were going to lunge at the gold.

Suddenly, the wind changed direction. Grandma's face melted until she was any other old lady with a complexion like a fast food bag.

"Would anyone like spanakopita? I have some fresh."

~ ~ ~

Aunt Rita and Takis slouched home close to midnight. Takis splintered off at the fountain, dragging himself up to the apartment he shared with Marika. My aunt sagged into one of the yard's chairs.

"Tell me something good," she said to me. It was the two of us now. Grandma had wandered off to bed an hour ago. Papou and Rabbit had skulked back to their respective corners; and I could hear the slow splashing in the pool as Xander did laps. It was all I could do not to shove my nose up to the fence behind the outhouse and gawk.

"Grandma made *kourabiedes,*" I said.

"That *is* good." She vanished inside, returned two minutes later with a couple of Greek butter cookies doused in powdered sugar. She plopped down beside me, looking every day of fifty.

"You okay?"

"Today I feel old," she said. "Have you ever seen a man with his heart cut out?"

"Only in the second Indiana Jones movie, and that was more like snatched out."

"How about eyes gouged out of their sockets?"

"Not recently. Or ever."

She nodded slowly as she broke off a chunk of cookie. Powdered sugar drifted through the air.

"I have seen things," she said. "Terrible things. Seeing someone with body parts removed is more ugly than normal murder. It's perverted—not sexually, but in the head." She listened for a moment. "Is that Xander in the pool? Never mind, I am too tired to look at him. What happened to the assassins?"

"Elias is working for us now. He's watching Mo, who is watching Lefty. And there's a woman following me."

"The one from the photograph?"

I nodded. "I forgot to ask about the lipstick."

"Eh, we can always have someone snatch her purse." Her lips lifted at the edges. She was pulling my leg. Maybe. "Does the Persian know his boss is dead?"

"Not yet—not that I know of."

"With luck that will be one fewer pair of eyes on you." She stood with the plate, kissed the top of my head. "If you decide to go back to America, I will miss you."

"Don't worry, I'm not going anywhere yet."

"When the time comes, if you want to go—go. Don't let Mama force you to be someone you don't want to be."

Grandma's voice wafted out between the shutters. "I heard that, Rita."

Aunt Rita winked at me. "Ears like a dog."

"That I heard, too."

~ ~ ~

On the other side of midnight I crawled between the sheets in my tiny, temporary room. Grandma's second bedroom no longer seemed strange to me. I was used to the cramped space and the fifty-year-old furniture. This space was becoming more mine every day. My clothes were in the drawers. My suitcase had been banished under the bed. On the small dresser sat the wooden statue Baby Dimitri had given me. The little guy had a dick that was reaching for the stars. It had made it as far as his chin.

Before clocking out for the day I checked on the Crooked Noses, to see if there was anything new. Mafia activity was their meat and potatoes, but the Greek sub forum was small enough that they welcomed reports of potentially related crime. Sure enough, they'd picked up the Fatmir and Harry Harry threads, and now they were trying to determine if, and how, they were connected. So far none of them pointed back to me. With luck it would stay that way. I didn't want to be involved.

I checked email, scrolled through Facebook's feed, but everyone's updates seemed bland, surreal, as though they were fabricated: Here is an advertisement for how the average newsfeed should look. Day by day it was becoming less relevant. *They* were becoming less relevant.

Or maybe I was the one drifting away. The lone balloon cut away from the bunch.

I thought about what Baby Dimitri had said about the kind of friends I was making here. I didn't want my only friends to be the kind of people I might have to visit in prison someday. I didn't want to bring muffins to be people who'd be shanked over apple and cinnamon. Normal was what I needed. People who would ground me. People who couldn't buy and sell cops, who didn't think Ambien was something you should be able to buy at the beach.

Soon—I hoped—I'd be home. Back to normal. Back to where my friends were paying for cable and refilling their prescriptions at Rite Aid and Walgreens.

But for now I had to dig deeper into the weirdness.

Eagle Guy. He was the one. His bird dropped the package, after he'd all but run away from me.

Had he followed us up to the monastery, or had we unwittingly followed him?

How could I find him again?

Grandma must have been reading my brain waves from the next room, because next thing I knew she was tapping on my door. I cast the sheet aside, peered out through the door. She was in a black, billowing nightgown, all her bits untethered. Gravity and time had had one hell of a party at Grandma's place. Looking at her I saw my future, if I didn't invest in good foundation underwear.

"Are you okay?" I asked her.

She waved my concern away. "I am sending men to Meteora to see if they can locate this man with the eagle."

"What happens if they find him?"

"They will bring him here."

"And if they don't?"

She gave me a funny look. "Then they will not bring him here." She shook her head at me and shuffled back to her room. I flopped back on the bed.

If Grandma's men came back empty-handed I had some ideas. That bird of Eagle Guy's had to come from somewhere.

What I knew about eagles was limited to the correct spelling of eagle and their penchant for rodents, but there had to be places out there that accommodated those who had to have a cool and unusual pet. Maybe he'd read too much Harry Potter and couldn't score an owl. Maybe he had an unhealthy attachment to his character in a computer game. Regardless, he had to ply his bird with an eagle-sanctioned diet and provide it with healthcare. What I needed was a professional bird nerd, someone who could tap a few keys and spit out a list of individuals who regularly purchased an unusual number of mice.

I scrounged up the name of a nearby vet who knew birds. Tomorrow morning I'd go see him, see if he could point me in the right direction.

~ ~ ~

Cleopatra was sitting around in a white Renault. She wasn't even trying to hide.

Not far from where she was parked were Elias, Mo, and Lefty, in their respective vehicles. It was a weird tableau, all of them in what was basically Grandma's front yard, but right now my issue was with the wannabe queen of the Nile.

"You can't park here," I said.

"Apparently I can."

"This is trespassing."

"So call the police. All I'm doing is sitting here, enjoying the Greek sunshine."

I glared at her. "I don't think you are."

Cleopatra rolled her windows down. "Take a look. Do you see anything other than a glamorous, beautiful woman enjoying the day?"

"I see a fossil from the 80s done up like a dog's dinner."

She blew me a kiss.

"You're a creep!"

"I'm not creepy. You're jealous." She dry-spat several times to shoo away the evil eye. The evil eye is what wafts around Greece, latching into babies and attractive, accomplished people. Compliments are generally served with a side of spit—fake or real—because the evil eye, like sane people, hates being spat on. I kind of wanted to spit on her, too, but not for the safety of her soul.

If she even had one.

I stomped back to my car, where Marika was leaning against the side, a big shoulder bag obscuring most of her middle.

"Is that Cleopatra?

"Yes."

"Why is Baboulas letting her sit there on her property?"

"That's a good question." The three assassins I understood. Grandma knew the score and she was tolerating them for my sake. But Cleopatra? I wondered if she had some kind of in.

We trotted over to the guardhouse, where the day guy was leafing through a paperback novel.

"Why is she out there?"

"She who?"

I pointed. He stared at the car. "Oh. Her. I don't mind her being here. Brightens up the scenery."

Yeah, the way glitter brightens up a stripper.

"I need my slingshot," I said.

Marika lit up. "Are you going to shoot them?"

"Just her. She's a pain in my butt."

"No." She hoisted up her big bag. "I will speak with her."

"Are you sure that's a good idea?"

"I have five children—four sons and a husband. I can handle the Queen of Egypt."

Marika stormed over to the car, bag swinging.

I'd seen how Marika handled her menfolk. With a loud voice and the kind of hand waving that could command a large orchestra. "It's okay," I called out. "I'll get rid of her myself."

She pulled one of those fun-sized machine guns from that huge bag of hers and opened fire on the hood of the Renault. BAM! BAM! BAM!

The three assassins leaped out of their cars, weapons waving. They exchanged embarrassed glances when they realized they were witnessing a very short catfight. Inside the guardhouse the guard answered his phone. He fired off a few words and hung up.

"Baboulas wanted to know about the gunfire," he said, "so I told her."

I trotted out to where the gun was still smoking.

Cleopatra stuck her head out the window, bared her teeth in an approximation of a grin. "Your friend is stupid. The engine is in the back."

"Stupid, eh?" Marika stomped around the back and unleashed another deafening volley. "Who is stupid now?" she yelled. "Who? You are stupid, that is who!"

"You shot my car!"

Marika dropped the gun in her bag. "I did nothing. I was standing here, enjoying the day." She strolled back through the gates to the Beetle.

"You shot up her car," I said.

"It was an accident. My finger slipped and her car was in the way when it happened."

"That's a pretty good story," I said.

"Every one of my sons, and Takis, has told me that story when I caught them picking their noses and eating the boogers. Always it is an accident, their finger slipped."

The TMI (Too Much Information) was strong in this family.

"Where are you going today?" Marika asked me.

"I have to pick up Donk, then I'm going to see a veterinarian."

"What happened to his scooter?"

"He didn't say."

"I have never met a veterinarian before."

I looked at her.

"Maybe he will use some big Greek words you don't know." She gave me a meaningful look.

"I … guess you could come with me?"

"Today is your lucky day because I am free. Come." She climbed into the Beetle's passenger seat.

"It's not really an adventure," I said.

"I am a stay-at-home mother. Everything that does not involve snot or *skata* is an adventure."

"You won't need the gun."

"Okay, but I will bring it anyway. Takis says you never know when you will need insurance."

~ ~ ~

Donk glared at Marika. "When do I get to sit in the front seat?"

"Never, that is when. We should see about getting him a car seat," she said to me. She turned around to face the teenager. "You look young enough to still need a car seat."

"I'll sit in a car seat when you go on a diet."

Marika turned back around. "I think he is going bald. Does it look to you like he is going bald?"

I glanced in the rearview mirror. "Hard to say with that hat on."

"Hats make you bald," she said with absolute conviction.

"I'm not going bald!" He swiveled the brim around to its intended position, slouched in the seat, defeated. Poor kid, Marika had likely set up a new neurosis. It made me wonder which way she made her offspring twitch.

My phone jangled. Melas was on the other end.

"Find any body parts lately?" he asked me.

"I bet you say that to all the girls."

"Only the crazy ones."

This from a guy who had boned a mobster's wife and knocked her up.

"Hanging up now," I said.

"Okay. I won't tell you what I know."

"I'm listening."

"We found a dead guy behind one of those roadside shrines on Pelion. A sheepherder called it in. He's missing a … a body part."

"Which body part?"

"The one you found."

"Which one?" I said on automatic. What could I say; my brain was busy processing the part about a dead body.

He launched immediately into cop-mode. "You found another one?"

Oh boy. Why hadn't I kept my mouth shut?

"I didn't find anything." I lowered my voice. "It … fell out of the sky. In a manner of speaking."

"Fell out of the sky."

"An eagle dropped it."

There was a pause. A long one, during which I fancied he debated the merits of dumping me on the next America-bound boat.

"Meet me at the Volos morgue," he said.

"Do I have to?"

The line was already dead.

"Change of plans," I told my passengers. "We're going to the morgue." A moment passed. "Where exactly is the morgue?"

11

The Volos morgue was in the belly of the hospital, and it was close to overflowing. I had left Donk in Marika's custody. She was circling the block because parking was non-existent. My assassins couldn't find parking either, so they were following in her tire prints, chomping at the bit because I'd told her to drive at the speed of snow melting in February. By some feat of magic (I suspected she'd used sexual favors) Cleopatra had nabbed a disabled parking space by the front doors.

"Don't worry," I had told her on the way past, "the moment they look at you they'll know you belong there."

Back in the morgue, with its walls the exact ghostly shade of green they use to paint phosphorescent star and planet decals, I was listening to the morgue attendant bitch about the guests who wouldn't leave. He was a little schnauzer of a guy, whose expression teetered on the edge between laughter and tears.

"It's the economy," Melas told me. "People can't afford to bury their dead, so they dump them here."

Yikes. "What happens to them?"

"Prison food." The attendant glanced back at me. "Joking. Sorry, morgue humor. Some we have to keep indefinitely. Others … we manage to get permission from the government to bury them. Did you bring the organ?"

"I didn't realize I was supposed to. Nobody—" I glanced pointedly at Melas. "—asked me to."

"Where is it?" the detective asked.

"Refrigerator." They looked at me. "What? Where else would you put it? In this weather it's the fridge or the freezer, and I figured you wouldn't want it to get freezer burn. I was being considerate."

They were somewhere between horrified and entertained.

"Let's go look at your guy," the attendant said.

It was wall-to-wall meat lockers like on TV. The place reeked of disinfectant and broken dreams. Probably the latter belonged to the attendant. He looked like he'd rather be at the beach, knocking back *frappes*, instead of sliding a dead man out of a vault.

The body was covered in a sheet.

I wondered where it had begun, this ritual of covering the deceased. Were we hiding our dead from the boogeyman by stashing them under bedclothes?

The attendant to the dead said, "You okay with this?"

I nodded. It was that or pass out in a puddle of my own puke.

Melas moved closer so that his words brushed my ear. "All you have to do is say if you recognize him or not."

Deep breath. Let it out slowly. "I'm fine. Show me."

Down went the sheet.

Dark hair. Olive skin. Pre-death he'd been cultivating stubble. Average build. Maybe forty-something. Spider tattoo on his neck.

I shivered.

"Don't know him."

Up went the sheet. Slam went the locker.

I excused myself and slid out the door. Melas followed.

Gastric acid was making noises about how it wanted to see the light. I closed my mouth, tried to think. Out there somewhere was a Frankenstein, chopping bits off bad guys and sending them to me.

Well, Grandma. But I was taking it personally.

"I'm sick of Greece," I said to Melas. "Greeks probably kidnapped my father. Someone is always trying to kill me. Everyone I know except you is a criminal of one kind of another. And I'm slowly getting used to that. Now, it's not so weird that I'm surrounded by killers and dealers and money launderers. It should be weird. It should be horrifying."

His hard cop face softened. "It *is* horrifying. But right now your brain is trying to cope. It's pushing all the weirdness aside so you can do what needs doing to find your father."

"You think so?"

He leaned against the wall and slung an arm—his, thankfully—around my shoulder, and snugged me up to him. "I think about it a lot. He who fights with monsters should look to it that he himself does not become a monster."

"Nietzsche. Look into the abyss long enough, the abyss looks into you."

"I don't do this job for the monsters," he said. "Locking them up is a byproduct. What I do is help people. That's what I concentrate on when the darkness gets too thick and deep. You're not getting accustomed to the darkness—you're doing what has to be done to find your father."

That—I wanted that to be my truth.

"Do you guys have any leads about the body in there?"

He shook his head. "We're spread thin—and getting thinner. We're down a bunch of informants after Pistof blazed through them. Others are either afraid to come forward or they want to be paid. The department doesn't have spare cash. That … thing from the box is the only lead I've got. I don't suppose you guys took fingerprints?"

"I don't think they do that."

Notice the clever way I changed *we* to *they*? I wasn't one of them. I didn't want to be. Once I found Dad I was out of here, back to where the biggest crime happening in my vicinity was a speeding ticket, maybe shoplifting. I wanted to be around people who could honestly say they'd never killed anyone.

That wasn't too much to ask, was it?

And here came the now-predictable tsunami of guilt. The Family was the only family I had besides Dad, and I wasn't sure I had him anymore. The voice noodling around inside my head told me he was still alive, but there was another voice in there, too, and it had a 'glass is half-empty' kind of personality. It said Dad was dead and this family was all the family I'd ever have, so I'd better not screw it up.

"You'll let me know if any more body parts show up, right?"

"Sure," I said. "Why did you call me?"

"He had a picture of you in his pocket. One from the newspaper."

Melas walked me out of the hospital. He was parked in the emergency bay; being a cop came with perks. Not many, if you were a Greek cop, but some.

Cleopatra jumped when she saw me. She had been slapping some more paint on her face.

Melas stopped to gawk at her car. "Are those bullet holes?"

I squinted. Shrugged. "Could be. Who can say?"

He shook his head. "Where's your car?"

"No parking. Marika had to drive it around the block a few times. Sure enough, here came Marika, my Beetle screaming to a stop as she hit the brakes. Behind her, several sets of brakes squealed as the assassins tried not to plow into one another.

Obviously snow melted fast here in February.

"Circus?" Melas asked.

"Entourage."

"You have an entourage?"

"I have Marika, Donk, the walking blowup doll back there, and three assassins."

"That's some entourage. All three trying to kill you?"

"It's complicated."

"Something tells me with you it always is."

"The only thing complicating my life is Greece. I used to be a couch potato." Judging by the look on his face, something got lost in the translation. "Lazy," I said. "I like TV and potato chips."

His face went through the motions of processing my words, then he nodded.

"I'll follow you."

"Wait—follow me where?"

"Your place. Those organs are evidence."

~ ~ ~

Another day, other party. When I pulled up outside the garage the bouzouki music was already going. A bouzouki is the bastard offspring of an acoustic guitar and a banjo. It's downright twangy.

These bouzouki players were live and they were family, so there was no switching them off. Rembetika—Greek folk music—and I don't get along. It's like listening to twenty cats expressing ennui over a sardine.

"I did not know Baboulas was making a party today," Marika said. "If I had known I would have stayed behind." The way she said it I knew she knew, and she'd had no intention of staying behind. She was digging the adventure too much.

Donk brightened up. "Party?"

"Don't get excited," I said. "It's not your idea of a good party."

"Can't you drop me off at a strip club?"

"No. For starters, I don't know where one is."

"I do."

Marika shut him up with a look.

My phone rang. The second I answered, Takis barked, "Is my wife with you?"

"Sure she is, Booger Eater."

"Heh," he said. "Who eats boogers? Pigs, that's who."

I oinked.

"I cannot believe she told you those lies! She is a monster!" He went silent for a minute. "Tell her to come home, or I will change your lights."

Translation: I'd better send his wife home or he was going to put the hurt on me.

"Already there," I said and disconnected. "That was your husband," I told Marika. "He wants you to come home."

"Poor little Takis," she said. "Nobody to wipe his *kolos*."

I wasn't entirely sure that was a metaphor, so I left it alone.

"Come on," I told her and Donk. "My nose says there's good food happening."

My nose was right. Once again they'd trotted out the giant rotisseries, and now a sheep was busy rotating over glowing coals. I tried not to look deeply into its dead eyes.

Unlike Harry Harry, it still had both of them.

Long tables had been set up with chairs. Not a formal sit-down lunch, but more of a buffet and choose-your-own-seat when you get hungry. Aside from the meats, every Greek side dish and appetizer ever had been magicked onto a couple of tables. It was a miracle the legs didn't buckle under the weight of all the food.

"*Kokoretsi*! All right!"

Melas had caught up to us, and he sounded way too excited about Greece's most deceptive dish. *Kokoretsi* looked like the best thing you could put in your mouth. The meat crisped to a golden crust as the hot coals worked their food voodoo, and it smelled like the kitchen of a five-star steakhouse. But under the hood it was lungs, kidneys, hearts, and other gross things tied onto the spit with intestines.

You couldn't pay me to eat it, but I was happy to sit here and breathe.

"You're a sick man, Melas."

He rubbed his flat belly. "What I am is a hungry man." He grabbed a plate and began constructing a skyscraper of food.

My stomach was making noises like it could eat, but I kept having flashbacks to the morgue. I left Melas and the others to their party and went back out to where the three assassins and Cleopatra were parked.

"You guys can come and eat, if you like. Looks like there's plenty for everyone."

"Is that *kokoretsi*?" Elias asked. I nodded and he jumped out of his car, reeled in by the scent of cooking organs. Lefty followed.

But not Mo. He stood there, staring at some point beyond my left ear. As far as I knew he still didn't know his employer was dead.

"Tell the Yankee pig I do not want her food."

Nobody told me anything, on account of how there was nobody there to tell him anything. Except Cleopatra, and she was busy picking at her teeth in the rearview mirror.

"It's not my food," I said.

His gaze fixed itself to a point beyond my left ear. "Ask the pig if there is pork."

"No pork," I said, mostly sure that was true.

He slouched off after the other guys. Which left me and Cleopatra.

She got out of the car and stretched, revealing an ocean of bare midriff.

"I guess I could eat," she said.

I stopped her with my hand. "No. No food for you. You can stay here."

Jaws grinned. "I don't think so. I was invited."

The guard. I was going to kill him. Okay, maybe not kill, but we'd be having words, and most of mine were scheduled to be loud.

I hoofed it back to Grandma's house with every intention of curling up with a book. After the morgue I wasn't in the mood for fun or socializing. As soon as the chilled body parts were in Melas' custody, I'd excuse myself without excusing myself, that way no one would have chance at talking me out of it.

That was the plan.

The kitchen was empty. The countertops were clean. I lifted the fridge's handle, yanked open the door.

Blinked.

Two somethings were missing. The penis and heart were gone. Not a sign of the plastic containers Grandma had put them in.

I checked the freezer. Nothing except ice cream and some regular meat. Checked the garbage. No Mr. Winky. No heart.

Ohmigod. We had been robbed.

I called Melas, wailed, "We've been robbed!"

12

Outside the refrigerator, that no longer held organs of the human kind, Melas was balancing his plate of food on one hand. He was picking at the meat with a fork, contemplating the situation.

"Maybe someone threw it out," he said.

"Why would they do that?"

"Was anything else taken?"

A quick jaunt to the bedrooms said no, this was an isolated incident.

"I wouldn't know where to start," he said. "Everyone in your family is a criminal, so they're all suspects."

"What kind of sicko steals a heart and—"

"Organ," he said. "Please say *organ*."

"You're weak."

"I'm male."

Yes, yes he was. It took most of my willpower not to notice. The rest of my willpower went into avoiding seconds and thirds of my grandmother's pastries. If I let down my guard right now I'd be torn between tossing myself at Melas and stuffing the baklava on the counter down my throat.

"As I was saying, who would steal organs?" I thought about it—hard. My gaze traveled around the kitchen, up his legs, down his arm, back up his arm to his wide shoulders, down again—reluctantly—to the food in his hand. "Oh God," I gasped. "The *kokoretsi*!"

The color drained out of Melas' face. The plate clattered to the floor.

"Ugh," he said. Then he bolted for the bathroom.

Boy, was he about to be surprised. The toilet was—

"Outside," I said, as he ran back into the room.

He flung the kitchen door open and vanished. Seconds later I heard the sound of him heaving.

This was one of the many reasons I avoided organ meat. You never *knew*.

I cleaned the food off the floor, dumped it in the garbage, poured a tall glass of refrigerated water and carried it out to him. He was pale, shaking, leaning one-handed against the outhouse wall.

"I ate a dick," he mumbled. "I ate a dick."

"Maybe it was in a different part. The spit is pretty long and the … you know … wasn't that big. It can't have stretched far."

He dry heaved again.

Grandma hobbled into the yard a few moments later. She stopped inside the gate, hands pressed to the small of her back.

"What's wrong with you, Nikos?"

He shook his head. "Nothing."

"Are you sick? You look sick."

I clued her in. It took a moment, but then a grin broke out on her face. "*Po-po*! I told the men to get the rest of the meat out of the refrigerator. They must have taken it."

"It's evidence, they can't eat it!" I said.

We looked out at the people carrying their plates over to the *kokoretsi* for refills.

"Too late," Grandma said. "Better we do not tell them."

"But … evidence."

"Do you want to see Greek people panic and stampede?"

"My God," I said, horrified. "Now we'll never know if it was that poor man's penis."

"What man?" Grandma asked.

Melas took a long sip of the water I'd poured. He pulled out his phone, tapped on the gallery. He handed the phone to my grandmother.

"You can't show her pictures of dead people," I said.

"I'd wager she's seen a body or two before," he said.

Grandma nodded. "Maybe one or two." She passed the phone back. "I know him. He is in sex trafficking." Her face said she didn't approve. Grandma was not, according to Dad's former—and now dead—best friend, a fan of the exploitation of women. "His name … I do not remember."

"Harry Harry is dead. Fatmir the Poor is dead," I said.

"Fatmir and Harry Harry are dead?" Melas asked.

I ignored him. "And now we've got another body in the morgue, one missing his penis." It was simple math, but Greece made my brain sticky, like hot chewing gum. I had three assassins, one of whom was still working for a dead man, one who was working for the family …

The answer practically wrote itself down.

"Geez." I slapped myself on the forehead. "Lefty? Hey, Lefty!" I called into the compound.

Lefty wandered over, plate in hand. "Thanks for the food," he said. "Usually my targets don't feed me, but you're okay. I hate to kill anyone who gives me food, but the job's the job. It's not personal."

Yeah, yeah, yeah. "Show him the picture," I told Melas.

"What?"

"Humor me, okay?"

Melas pulled up the picture of the dead guy.

"Is this your employer?" I asked Lefty. He took a long look and jerked his head up. *Tst.* "No."

Disappointment spiraled in my head, alongside a smallish whirlwind of fear. This meant someone out there still wanted me dead, and for now they still had all their body parts.

"Who's your employer?" Melas asked.

"You think I'm going to tell a cop?"

Melas folded his arms. He looked big and bad, and if I'd known the guy's name I would have sung like a bird.

Lefty deflated. "I don't know his name. All I know is his money is good and he doesn't look like the guy in the picture."

"Can you describe him?" Melas asked.

"He looked like a man. Head, body, arms, two legs. Brown hair. I didn't look closer. You don't in this business."

That was most of the world, outside of Scandinavia.

"I could haul you in for questioning," Melas said.

"You could try, but it won't help. I don't know what I don't know." He sauntered away, eating.

"If another box shows up," Melas told us, "call me and don't touch it."

Takis wandered over. He was carrying a plate and fork, too. "What's going on?" he asked, mouth stuffed with kokoretsi.

"Keep doing that," I told him.

"What?" Flecks of food flew.

"Chewing. I'm enjoying watching you eat a dick."

"What are you talking about?"

I shook my head. "Nothing."

~ ~ ~

Before Melas left I had one request. "If someone claims the body, can you let me know?"

"Why do you want to get mixed up in this?"

"I don't. I want to know, okay? Can you do that?"

"Sure," he said. "And don't forget, my mother still wants you over for coffee."

Ugh. "I don't understand why."

He leaned against his cop car, arms folded. He was made of steel cables, strapped together with delicious man-candy.

"She wants to know you. And she wants her plate back."

"Fine, fine, I'll go."

"When?"

Never. "When I have time."

"What are you doing now? You could follow me over, I'll show you where my parents live."

"Can't right now," I said, lying my ass off. "I've got a thing."

"What kind of thing?"

"Uh …" I glanced around, looking for a suitable excuse. There was nothing, not even my goat. "Argh! I can't think of anything. Why, brain? Why?"

"Follow me," he said.

The Melas family lived in Makria, in a two-layered square box. Like most of its neighbors it was white, the roof was red, and the yard was hidden somewhere under a forest of greenery. The pots were—predictably—red. It was a wonder there was any red paint left for the rest of the world, the way Greece slapped it all over the place.

What this house had that its neighbors lacked was a helmet-haired lady warrior. She was slight. She was short. She wanted my head on the plate I was holding—I knew it.

She lowered the broom in her hand when she spotted me skulking along behind her son.

"Is that my plate?"

"Yes, Kyria Mela. Thank you. I washed it three times."

She took it from my hands. "I will wash it again, to be sure."

"Mama," Melas said.

"What? It could have picked up anything on the way here. Have you read about the Ebola in America? Terrible. People dying all over the place."

"Two," I said. "We had two Ebola deaths."

"Like I said, all over the place." She swiped her gaze across my everything and made a judgmental face. "Come inside. Nikos, are you hungry? I will fix you something."

"I already ate at Katerina's place."

"What did you eat?"

"Lamb, salad, bread. They were having a party."

She patted him on the arm. "That is not a meal. I will make you a plate."

"Lucky for you you've got one right there," I said, nodding to the plate I'd returned. Holy flying razor blades, my mouth was a runaway train.

"Yes," she said dryly. "Very lucky."

"What's her problem?" I asked Melas, after she'd vanished into the kitchen, leaving us in her special company room.

"What do you mean?"

My eyebrows lurched north. "Never mind."

I sat in that small, airless room, hands in my lap, ankles crossed, trying not to screw things up. Something told me Kyria Mela—no S on account of her second X chromosome—didn't approve of the sort of woman who crossed her legs. She was bound to see it as the move of a slut.

Only my eyes wandered around the room. Lots of photographs were cluttering the table—a dining room-sized behemoth elaborately carved out of dark wood. The frames were heavy and ornamental, most of them crystal or silver-plated. Most of the faces in the photos were a variation on Melas's theme.

"You have a brother?" I asked him.

"And two sisters," he said. "They smashed my mother's heart when they moved away."

"Let me guess," I said. "You're the baby of the family."

He laughed. "Eldest."

"Damn. I had you pegged for the youngest."

"Why?"

"It's the, uh, umbilical cord."

"What?"

"You're, uh ..."

"Jesus," he said, realization finally dawning. "You think I'm a mama's boy."

I opened my mouth to deny it, but then his mother swept back in, carrying a tray loaded with coffee, cold water, and some kind of sweets. She rested the tray on the table and divvied up the goods. The sweets were sticky preserved cherries. Diabetes was coming for me, and I'd go a willing victim.

"Drink the coffee," she commanded. "After, I will read the cup."

"You mean ... my future?"

"Your past, your present, your future. All of it is inside the cup."

"Mama, leave her alone. Katerina doesn't want her cup read."

Maybe her ears heard him, but her face didn't. "Everybody wants their cup read."

Normally I would have laughed it off. I'd visited my share of psychics over the years, usually arm-in-arm with one friend or another. Stick a bunch of teenage girls in a room, eventually one of them was going to suggest a clairvoyant or a Ouija board. We'd do anything to see if that hot guy likes us back. This seemed like a golden opportunity. Probably it was woo-woo hocus pocus, but what if it wasn't? Melas's mother was scary enough for me to believe she might have a direct line to the other side.

"It's okay," I told him. "Read my cup, please."

Did she approve? Disapprove? Who can say? Her face was a flat sheet of glass in a dark cave. The woman gave away nothing.

"Drink the coffee, not the grounds."

The coffee was thick enough that a spoon would have trouble leaning, and it was sweet enough to rot teeth in a flash, but I swilled it down until there was nothing left but grounds and a burning in my gut.

"Hmm," she said, eyeing me. "Turn it over on the saucer, twist clockwise three times, then push it to me."

I did as she said, then we sat and waited for a few minutes.

"You have a beautiful family." I waved my hand at the crowd of photographs, their heads of varying heights on the tabletop.

"Lucky will be the woman who marries into this family. Everyone in my family makes beautiful babies."

I swear to God—with whom my relationship is shaky, at best—Melas's mouth twitched, that rat bastard. He was getting a kick out of this. Maybe to him this was payback for the dick-eating incident.

"Do you have grandchildren?" I asked.

"Ten. Five girls, five boys. But do they live close? No. They smashed my heart when they moved away."

"Well, at least you've still got M—Nikos close."

"Yes, one out of four. He knows better than to leave his mama and shit in my heart."

Oh boy. Mommy issues in aisle three. The umbilical cord was more of a leash, short and tight around his neck.

What was I supposed to say?

Fortunately, she plucked the cup off its saucer and began to tilt it this way and that, absolving me of the need to say anything.

"Hmm," she said in an ominous tone. Was that aimed at my past, present, or future?

I leaned forward eagerly, like a little kid. "What is it?"

"Death."

Oh, was that all? My heart rolled a few paces forward, then clunked to a STOP. It looked both ways before resuming its dull *thud-thud*.

"Death in your past, death in your present, death in your future."

"Death is in everyone's future, eventually." I was trying not to freak out. "Unless they're a vampire or Keith Richards." I thought about it for a moment. "Come to think of it, Keith Richards could be a vampire, which would explain a lot."

She glanced up from the cup to gaze upon a babbling idiot. "There is no such thing as vampires."

"Don't say that too loud, you'll incite a riot. *Twilight* fans are merciless."

A sigh rose out of her throat like a submarine. "A lot of death in your cup. But I see children, too. You will have an easy time with those big hips."

My mouth dropped open. "Huh."

"And your father," she said, "is still alive."

13

"Mama," Melas said.

"He is?" I croaked.

"You be quiet," she told her son. "The cup knows."

"It's a cup. Don't get her hopes up."

She reached over, flicked his ear. He yelped.

Any other time I would have laughed, but my head was spinning on the inside. It was a big, old centrifuge in there, and in the center Dad was standing still, wondering what the hell was going on—but he was alive. He also resembled Harrison Ford, tied to the stake in *Raiders of the Lost Ark.*

I lifted my head. "Are you sure?"

"The cup knows," she said darkly.

"Does the cup ever get it wrong?"

"Sometimes it obscures the truth."

"So, it lies?"

"How can it lie? It is a cup."

How much of a know-it-all could an inanimate object be?

"Exactly. So how can it know?"

"Magic," she said, like that was completely reasonable. "Your grandmother always comes to me when she wants to know the future. If it is good enough for her …" She shrugged, face twisted like it was my own fault if I didn't buy into her party trick.

"Okay, so he's alive. Where is he?"

"Eh, the cups shows many things, but not maps."

Of course not.

~ ~ ~

The afternoon felt like it wanted to cut me.

Melas walked me to the edge of the village, where our cars were waiting. Before I knew it, he had me between a sheet of metal and a hard place. "My mother likes you," he said.

"See, now I didn't get *like* from that. Tolerate, maybe. Mostly I think she wants me dead. I'm kind of seeing a pattern when it comes to Greece."

"Trust me, she likes you. And I like you, too." His gaze moved to my mouth.

"Don't even think about."

"I can't stop thinking about it."

"Well, you need to, and so do I."

He lowered his mouth to my ear. "I knew you were thinking about me, too. Why don't you tell me some of your thoughts and I'll tell you some of mine."

My brain stuttered.

"Penis Guy," I said. "You'll let me know if someone claims him, right?"

"Tell me about the heart."

"What about it?"

"What's the real story?"

"I told you: An eagle dropped it."

"Dropped it?"

"I guess it was heavy," I said.

"Where did this … eagle drop happen?"

"Meteora."

"What were you doing in Meteora?"

"Following a lead." Of sorts.

He raised an eyebrow. "And?"

"Dead end."

"You scare me," he said.

"You scare easily."

He laughed. "No, I don't. The things I've seen … Anyway, you do scare me. It bothers me, you running around out there, no idea what you're doing."

Ugh. "Spare me the chauvinist spiel. Like you, I've got a job to do, and I'm doing it. Things would be smoother if people like you cooperated, but you're not. So I'm working with what I've got."

"Which is?"

"Next to nothing."

"How does Stelios Dogas fit into all this?"

It took me a second to realize he was talking about Rabbit.

"I'm not sure he does fit into this."

"Then why did your grandmother bust him out of prison?"

I pushed him away from my neck. "You're groping in the dark, Detective Melas."

"Speaking of groping in the dark, you want to go out tonight?"

"No."

"Good," he said. "One of us has to show restraint."

~ ~ ~

The party was over, the Family—and the family—gone to their afternoon beds. Because the eating stopped didn't mean Grandma's hands quit cooking, though. She was baking again, but her hands were working slowly, a cat tiring of its prey's lack of get-up-and-oh-god-run.

"Did Nikos leave already?"

I slumped into my usual chair at her table. "He had somewhere police-ish to be."

"I wonder who ate that man's *poutsa*?"

I wouldn't put in my hand on a Bible and swear to it, but I think she winked at me. "Hopefully your least favorite family member. Is it true, does Kyria Mela really read your coffee cup?"

She shrugged. "Everybody does it. Why do you ask?"

"She read my cup."

Her eyebrow twitched a silent 'And?'

"She told me Dad is still alive. Also, she said I had big hips."

"Your hips are good Greek hips."

Aunt Rita came slouching through the door. The kisses she blew did nothing to cut through the swirl of perfume. "My Virgin Mary, there is nothing wrong with your hips. I would kill for your hips."

It was true; Aunt Rita's hips were lean, probably because the infrastructure was male. But I had to hand it to her: she was rocking the Daisy Dukes and cowboy boots.

Grandma crossed herself. "Kyria Mela read this one's cup. She told the girl Michail is still alive."

"Then he is alive!" Aunt Rita said. "Kyria Mela's cups never lie."

"She said sometimes they obscure the truth."

"That's not a lie, it's …"

"Obscuring the truth," Grandma said.

Aunt Rita snapped her fingers. "Exactly. Obscuring the truth."

My eye twitched. "Explain to me how that's not lying or getting things wrong."

"Give her an analogy, Rita," Grandma said.

My aunt rubbed her hands together. "Let me warm up the brain machine. I'm supposed to be sleeping and my head knows it."

"Why are you up?" I asked.

"I was asleep, but then I had a dream I ate a *poutsa*."

We looked at her.

"Not a sex thing," she said quickly. "I was eating it as a food. It was weird and disturbing, so I woke up."

Did I look at Grandma? No. If we locked eyes right now the laugh would burst out of my mouth.

"That is weird," I said, trying not to let nature take over.

"And disturbing," Grandma added.

Aunt Rita's gaze flitted between us. "What's wrong with you two?"

"Analogy, Rita," Grandma reminded her.

"Okay, I've got one. There's a rug on the floor. A small, round, handmade rug that is worn thin in places. Under the rug is a child's small toy. I don't know what kind of toy because I can't see it. And you ask me what's under the rug. I tell you *something* is under the rug but because I can't see it I don't know. Then you ask me to guess, and I say my best guess is that it's a ball. The bump is ball-shaped, so it could be a ball, but it could also be a doll's head or something else close to spherical. Eventually we get tired of guessing and we pull the rug off. Underneath is a snow globe. See, the rug showed the shape of the thing, but that is all. The cup is the rug. What Kyria Mela sees in the cup, that is the snow globe."

"So … Dad is alive but he might be hiding under a rug?"

My heart was chilling out, refusing to pump faster, under the hazy circumstances. My head, like Fox Mulder, wanted to believe. The rest of me was involved in a tug-o-war between the two, so I felt jittery and out of sync with my body.

"Move over," I told Grandma. "I feel the need—the need to bake."

~ ~ ~

It was late when Melas texted. I'd been listening to the slow splash of the pool as Xander did his nightly laps. How the guy could float with body fat that low was a question for someone who hadn't dropped out of college when her mother died.

We have pickup.

Who?

Why?

Just curious.

A moment later, my phone buzzed. Melas.

"Don't think you can go looking for these guys. They buy and sell women like you every day."

"I'm not looking for anyone. I want to know who claimed his body. Was it family or …" I rifled around for the right word. "… coworkers?"

"Family," he said. "Wake is tomorrow."

"Where?"

"Sweet dreams," he said and ended the call.

That wasn't the end of that—not by a long shot. I swapped my T-shirt for a cotton knit sundress, shimmied out the window, and tiptoed out to the pool. My goat was there, nibbling on Xander's towel.

"Bad goat," I hissed. I tugged on the towel, then the goat, but neither of them showed any sign of cooperation. Finally I settled for reclining in one of the poolside chairs, my face suggesting that I knew n-o-t-h-i-n-g about a goat eating a towel.

Goat? What goat?

If Xander knew I was there, he made no indication until he climbed out of the pool, like a submarine rising silently out of the sea. Even after he was on dry land he didn't speak—not that he ever did. He relieved the goat of his towel, using what must have been magical goat-whispering powers, and locked onto my gaze with his, while he toweled himself off. My tongue glued itself to the roof of my mouth. He was peanut butter; I was bread. There was a joke there about spreading, but I wasn't going to make it.

"The dead guy, the one without the …" I waved in the general direction of his groin, trying not to look closely. "Do you know who he was?"

He nodded. To his credit he didn't go all shaky at the mention of a lopped off knob.

"I don't suppose …" I shook my head. "… you know where his family lives?"

He stared straight at me, unreadable. Then he threw the slightly chewed towel over one shoulder and stalked off.

I followed. What else was I gonna do? I trailed behind him, over to the main building that surrounded the courtyard, where I knew he had a ground floor apartment.

He stopped when he reached his door. Turned around, a '*Why me?*' expression on his face.

"Can I come in so we can discuss this?"

He opened the door, waved like he was saying '*Be my guest*,' but with a sarcastic edge.

Xander's place was bachelor chic. Sleek computer on his desk, black bedding, brushed aluminum appliances. In the bedroom floor, under a throw rug, a trapdoor had been cut, leading to the compound's control room. Grandma could run the world from down there. She had eyes and ears in area police departments, including Detective Melas's shabby building.

I didn't help myself to his couch or chairs, and he didn't offer. He vanished into his room, came back a moment later wearing a loose pair of shorts, so I was forced to keep staring at a mile of upper body muscle, all of it smooth and tan.

"I don't want to talk to them." Yet. "I want to scope them out without my tail. Two of the men who wanted me killed have shown up dead, missing body parts. And now we've got a dead gangster with a missing penis—a penis we no longer have, so nobody can check if it was his or not. But it has to be, right? How often does anybody in Greece end up with a dick whacked off? Not often, I bet."

He picked up a notepad and pen, scribbled a message.

What happened to the penis?

"The same thing that happened to the heart: *kokoretsi*."

What I expected was for him to turn pale, but he didn't. He leaned against the wall, laughing silently. Laughter suited him. It downgraded him from god to mere mortal—the kind of mortal a woman might want to know better.

"All I can say is I've been vindicated," I said. "There's a reason I don't eat *kokoretsi*, and this is it. You never know when someone is going to toss in some human organs."

He reached for the paper. *Don't like it either. Can't trust it.*

"I think someone is sending Grandma a message by killing people who wanted me dead. I need to find out who that someone is, and why they're doing what they're doing."

You won't find any clues at the dead guy's place. The killer is already gone.

"Probably you're right." He gave me a look that suggested he was right more often than he was wrong. "But humor me, please."

He humored me all the way into Volos.

~ ~ ~

Argonauton was the name of the coastal road. The way was lined with tavernas and other eateries on one side, and the gulf on the other. Boats hitched to the harbor-side sidewalk—a wide, flat grey ribbon, dotted every few feet with charming lamp posts, wooden bench seats with rust-chewed hardware, and the occasional garbage can—bobbed and swayed as the tide danced to the moon's silent dog whistle. Each of the eateries occupied the bottom floor of an apartment building. With these views the residences couldn't be anything more than high dollar, although the exterior walls were on the low end of fancy, and the awnings—Greeks loved their awnings—were a few decades newer than the Parthenon. Greeks who had money liked to pretend they didn't have money, the way people back home who lived in trailer parks liked to wear designer sunglasses and carry Louis Vuitton bags. Never let it be said that Americans don't know how to prioritize. Designer goods are our right.

Severed Penis Guy, whose real name turned out to be Petros Fridas, lived halfway down the city block in a pale yellow apartment building. The ground floor taverna was one giant washing machine that existed to clean grubby money. I knew this because Xander lobbed a text message into the backseat. He wouldn't allow me in the front, after an episode where I switched his music. Xander was hopelessly devoted to *Rembetika,* and I had declared the tinny screeching as noise pollution.

On the other side of midnight, Volos was slowly losing steam. Summer meant schools were out and tourists were still pouring into town. They were at least a month away from bubbling out of the airports, the train stations, the highways of their homelands, and trickling back into their houses. Tonight—well, this morning—they were stumbling to their hotel rooms, while Greeks straggled back to their cars in search of *bouzoukia* and discotheques. The main difference between the two was the music. The former featured live bands; the latter employed a DJ.

Anyway, they were bleeding away from the promenade, leaving Xander and I to figure out the best way into the Fridas apartment. The main door was stuck in the side of the building, but it required either a key or some benevolent soul to push the buzzer and unlock the sucker from inside. We didn't know anyone who lived here—

Xander pushed one of the lighted buttons on the panel.

A moment later a woman's static-speckled voice asked who was there. Xander said nothing. Laughter crackled out. The buzzer buzzed. Xander turned the handle and opened the door. From the way he was standing it was obvious he expected me to go first.

"Girlfriend?"

He shook his head.

"Lover? Paramour? Booty call?"

He shrugged. The light in his dark eyes suggested maybe, but he wasn't talking. Aunt Rita had told me there were no women—or men—and that as far as she knew he lived like a monk. I wasn't buying it. Men who looked like Xander didn't go without company for long.

Something unidentifiable skittered through me, leaving a small hollow feeling in its path. The word *Hmph*! sprang to mind.

"Let's go," I whispered, slapping biology aside. Not that I had any real clue where we were going or what we were looking for. I was relying on the old know-it-when-I-see-it.

We wended our way upstairs to the penthouse. It struck me that this was the second time I'd gone snooping through a dead man's home (although Cookie had only been faking death at the time, as an audition for when he became really dead a couple of days later). That, too, had been a penthouse apartment, although this one seemed higher dollar. The lack of garbage, hulking like paper spiders in the corners, suggested that either the inhabitants of this building were cleaner or they employed a janitor. When we came to the dead man's door, we discovered the police had marked it with a yellow tape X, one that told us we could not pass.

Xander did some kind of henchman spell on the door, involving a lock pick, and the door swung open. Not too many days ago I'd picked Melas's door, but it had taken me several more minutes and a YouTube video or two to figure it out. Xander had perfected the art of breaking and entering. Probably he had more experience.

We ducked into the apartment.

Fridas lived alone. Word on the street—okay, the Internet; I Googled on the way over—was that he was a bachelor and a mama's boy. He had a steady stream of girlfriends, but none of them had earned the privilege of moving in for more than a night or two at a time. Wherever the latest woman was grieving, it wasn't here.

Xander was part cat, part cat burglar. He moved silently through the dark apartment, without so much as catching his toe on a coffee table. Clearly he was some kind of supernatural being. Me, I hugged the wall and hoped it wouldn't let me down. When he realized I wasn't following him, he backtracked and grabbed my hand. Sparks flickered up my arm. He switched on a flashlight. Bits of the apartment revealed themselves in triangular-shaped pieces. Fancy digs. This much chrome and black Xander probably felt right at home. I reigned in a whistle when I saw the television. It took up most of the living room wall and curved inward, so that anyone sitting on the couch would be semi-surrounded by screen.

Good thing Takis wasn't with us. He'd find a way to make that television vanish.

After that, Xander kept the light down low. My brain was molasses; it didn't realize what he was doing until his back became a sudden obstacle. We weren't moving, and the place we weren't moving into was what I'd gathered was a bathroom, judging from the overwhelming scent of cologne wafting out in noxious, thready clouds. Beneath the cloud was another odor, darker, earthy, yet bright. Blood, I was learning, was complex and layered, like winter clothing.

I tried to push past him but I was going nowhere. It dawned on me that this was where Fridas had been killed and possibly dismembered before he'd been dumped in the undergrowth behind one of Mount Pelion's many water fountains.

Suddenly I was creeping backwards. Xander was on the move, but not into that room. Whatever was there he'd had enough and he was backing up.

We moved sideways, then forward, into the master bedroom, a room that was mostly bed with a mirrored ceiling. The word "pimp" sprang to mind, followed by "high class hooker," "blow," and, "Charlie Sheen." I gave the bed a poke. Water. It figured. Nobody outside of the 80s owned a waterbed unless they were shady.

Then my gaze snapped to the object sitting dead center on the bed.

"That's a feather," I said, stating the obvious, mostly because I had to carry this whole conversation on my own. "I bet it's an eagle's feather."

Xander reached for it. My hand jumped out, stopped him.

"Don't you think it's convenient that it's just sitting here, like it's waiting for us? Looking at it makes me wonder if it's a big chunk of cheese and we're the rats. If that's the case, this is one big trap."

He shook off my hand, scooped up the feather. As he did, the front door handle jiggled. On the other side someone female was muttering loudly about the police and their close proximity to pigs on the evolutionary tree. The tape ripped. The door opened. Whoever they were they had a key.

Xander pocketed his flashlight. His arm curled around me. All this darkness but, if memory served, there was nowhere to really hide except a walk-in closet on the far side of the room. We couldn't make it over there without creating some kind of ruckus. Under the bed was out, because there was no under the bed. The base sat flat on the floor, and on top of that, two hundred gallons of water.

Footsteps happened, all of them on the marble floors not too far from where we were dithering. They were moving closer. Eventually they'd be in here with us. Something told me they wouldn't be attached to anything we'd find warm and fuzzy.

Xander made a silent move. Unfortunately, his move was to flop back on the bed, pulling me on top of him.

I wasn't on top for long. He rolled us until I was pinned under him. Instinct, that silly cow, took over, wrapped my legs around him. Which wasn't easy. I was five-four, and five-four isn't a height that comes packaged with long legs. Xander was a lot of densely built man. Stocky, solid, broad. Not for the first time, I wondered if he was part Minotaur. Anyway, short legs, and a lot of man, meant my instincts had *really* worked to coil me around him—and prevailed.

"Who is there?" the voice accompanying the footsteps asked. Cool blue-white light pooled in the giant living room. Some of it spilled into the bedroom, but it was a big room, so we were still gift-wrapped in shadow. "I know there is someone in my Petros' house. I heard the floor squeak." She spoke with the kind of conviction that immediately told me she had pointed to her ear, even though no one could see her. "I told my son this apartment building was not a good one, but did he listen to me? No. Greek floors should not squeak. Everything is supposed to be made of concrete and steel, but I think the builder snuck some wood in there, so I will have to sue him. Concrete does not squeak, but wood, it squeaks. But maybe now I think the wood is not so bad because it tells me there is a burglar here. You should know I have a very big gun that I do not know how to use. Petros tried to get me to take lessons, but who has time for that? I think I am more dangerous if I do not know how to use a gun, eh? It could go off like that while I swing it around like this …"

BANG!

I yelped against Xander's very warm, very nice neck. A hint of chlorine lingered on his skin. It had mixed with his natural scent, creating a blend that was giving my hormones all kinds of instructions my common sense wouldn't let them follow. There wasn't going to be any grinding, kissing, nibbling, or anything else with an -ing on the end, unless it was mov-ing away from him.

BANG!

Holy cow, the woman was a nut!

Okay, yes, we had technically broken into her son's home, but what kind of sane person goes around randomly shooting guns in an enclosed space?

"Where are you hiding?" She said the words extra-loud, compensating for the temporary hearing loss that goes with firing a weapon twice in close proximity to the ears, without a pair of earmuffs. "I will find you."

The darkness went *POOF!* when she flicked on the bedroom light. My eyes squeezed shut. Slowly, as the pain faded, I opened them again.

Kyria Frida, I presumed, was taking a break from her bell tower. The S of her spine was on its way to becoming a C. Her serpentine eyes were unblinking under their wrinkled hoods. She had the face of a woman who only knew "please" as a word other people used out of weakness.

She stood there gaping at us.

It looked bad. It felt good. But it looked really, really bad. The only adjective I could pin to the position we were in was *compromising—a*nd I wasn't even being compromised.

The light flicked off. The woman stepped back out.

"I will wait out here until you put some clothes on your *putana*."

Wait—what? We were fully dressed! There was nothing going on except subterfuge. And a whore? Really? Who would pay for a woman dressed in cotton knit?

I opened my mouth to protest. Xander clamped his hand over my mouth. My pre-teen self rebelled by licking his palm. The man didn't so much as flinch; there was no way he was human.

He rolled off me. This time he didn't take me with him. His outline shoved its hand into his pocket. He was going to shoot her!

Oh. No. Never mind. Whatever he'd pulled out of his pocket it looked like a slim wallet.

With a flick of his wrist it opened, and he strode towards the light.

14

"What did you show her? Because I know you showed her something."

The old saying tells us we should let sleeping dogs lie. Xander wasn't a dog, and he was stalking through the night with me on his heels, back to the car, instead of sprawled on the ground with his legs in the air, twitching, which meant the old saying could go hang. Grandma's favorite henchman was cruising for an interrogation.

He ignored me. We dodged a couple of weaving tourists on the promenade. The night was thickening to a dense black that made other nights look a washed-out gray. Lights were dying faster now that the clock's little hand had scooted left. Xander walked with the confidence of a man convinced the sun was hanging overhead.

"What was it? Was it a nude picture? It was, wasn't it?"

I didn't think so, but I figured if I shot enough verbal arrows at him he'd give up and show me. Anything to shut me up.

He'd pulled whatever it was out of his pocket and gone forth into to the living room like he belonged. No apologies, no excuses. A moment later Fridas's mother had said, "When will you be finished with the *putana*? I need clothes to bury my son."

My heart had hurt for her. Yes, her son was a bottom-feeding scumbag who had probably wanted me dead, but to her he was a bouncy toddler with no regard for furniture, electronics, or personal space.

She had excused herself after that, leaving us to flee.

Xander kept walking. I hurried to keep up. We passed the University of Thessaly's seaside campus, a building that was perched right on the water's edge on a sturdy chunk of concrete. To the left was Saint Konstantine's Park, named after one half of the church that wasn't too far ahead of us. The church was Saints Konstantine *and* Helena, but only the guy got a park, which didn't seem fair.

"What did you show her?"

My thoughts zipped back to that day in the church, after Xander had rescued me by unloading a bullet in the Baptist's head. I'd found Xander in Saint Catherine's, doing what I thought at the time was praying. Afterward I wondered if he'd been talking to the Powers That Be. Not the religious ones, but the government agencies listening in. Grandma had, for her own reasons, allowed several agencies from God knows how many countries wire the church for sound. To what end, I didn't know.

That thought conjured up another, and it wasn't pretty.

"Are you … a … a *cop*?"

He stopped so abruptly I almost plowed into his back.

"Oh, God," I said. I might have been clutching my hair. "You're a cop. Grandma's right-hand man is a cop."

He was on me like syrup on baklava, like plates smashed on the floor at a Greek wedding, like a donkey on a bag of carrots. His hand circled my arm. He pulled me into the park.

Grandma's henchman-cop was going to kill me and heave my body into the gulf. I didn't want to die like this. I didn't want to die at all.

But for someone who wanted to kill me he wasn't being particularly violent. Someone trying to murder me probably would have banged me into a few trees, but he deftly steered me around them, until we were standing in its thickest shadow. I heard rather than saw him rustling around in his pocket, then he flicked on his flashlight and aimed the beam at the leather billfold. He shoved it into my hand.

I squinted at the rectangular identification card inside. It featured Xander's picture and full name: Alexander Dimou.

He worked for the National Intelligence Service. Greece's CIA. My hands shook as I thrust it back at him. They were icy chunks on the ends of my liquid arms.

"Holy crap," I said, trying not to upchuck. "Is that real?"

He lifted his head to indicate that it was indeed a fake, and pocketed the thing.

"Looks real," I said.

He shrugged.

"Does Grandma know you're a fake NIS agent during your time off?"

A single chin lift. *No.*

We had known each other for two weeks, but somehow he knew I wouldn't say a word to my grandmother. In a way, neither of us belonged. He was a foundling—or maybe a cuckoo—and I was the black sheep's lone lamb.

"The woman whose buzzer you pushed, who is she?"

He shrugged.

"Can I at least see the feather?"

He looked at me with a slightly constipated expression.

"Ha! You thought I forgot about it, didn't you?"

He flicked the feather out of his pocket, laid the quill across my open palm. The body of the feather was white, the tip a rich, dark brown.

"I don't know birds," I said. "Does it belong to an eagle?"

His mouth said nothing, but the downward tilt of his chin said, Yes.

~ ~ ~

Grandma was being difficult. She was difficult a lot. But I supposed she could say the same about me.

"What time are we leaving for the Fridas wake?"

We were baking. I didn't know what we were baking, only that I was up to my wrists in sugary goop. Who didn't own a stand mixer? Grandma, that's who.

"Never," Grandma said.

"But—"

"There is a difference between a Family and gangs. Gangs are promiscuous. They take anybody who wants to join. There is nothing holding them together except fear and greed. That man was the leader of a gang. It would not be right for me to attend his wake or funeral."

"You could send a representative."

"No. No one from this Family will be at his funeral. We are not the same people."

"Uh-huh."

"Katerina," she said, finger aimed at my nose. "Stay away from Fridas and his people. Nothing good can come from you being there."

"Okay."

"No. No 'okay.' You will not go. The end."

Oh, I was going. Melas had mentioned that Fridas was carrying my picture in his pocket. If Fridas had wanted to kill me, wouldn't he have hired his own assassin? He was a guy who could afford to outsource the job to one of his gang, or a third party—and had in the past. I was counting on somebody at the wake knowing what Fridas wanted with me.

"Okay."

Her eyes narrowed to dangerous slits. "Hmm …"

~ ~ ~

We were on our way to a wake. Marika was fiddling with the radio. She'd fixated on a euro-pop disaster that sought the potentially life-altering answer to a vital question: What does the fox say? Now we were negotiating volume.

As per usual, we had a lengthy tail—and was it my imagination or was there an extra vehicle tacked on today?

"I think we picked up another assassin," I said, eyeing the side mirror.

"*You* picked up another assassin. Nobody wants to kill me."

My gaze slid over to the huge black bag Marika had dumped on her lap. She was hugging it like an extra child. "Please tell me you didn't bring a gun. You didn't bring a gun, did you?"

"I did not bring a gun."

"Really?"

"No. You told me to tell you I did not bring a gun, so I did."

All this freedom was going to her head. She was getting downright mouthy.

"Are you okay?" I asked her.

"Low blood sugar. Normally I eat all the boys' leftover snacks, but now I am out with you my food intake is down."

"You want to stop and get something?"

"No, I brought supplies." She reached into the bag, pulled out the baby-sized submachine gun, dumped it in my lap so she could rifle through the contents.

"Yikes!" I yelped. "I don't want to touch your gun."

"It's just a gun. Here, hold these."

Two handguns fell into my lap. My immediate reaction was to slap them back to her.

Marika jumped. "*Ay-yi-yi*! Are you trying to kill us?"

"Don't they come with a safety?"

"How should I know? I took these from Takis. There were no instructions."

"How did you know how to shoot Cleopatra's car?"

"Improvisation. I watch television."

I was mildly impressed. She had handled it like a pro. "That's pretty clever."

"Any idiot can use a gun. Look at Takis."

Point taken. "You can't take those into a wake, especially not a gangster's wake. What if they search us?"

She looked at me like I'd grown an extra head. "If we go in there unarmed, we will be the only ones."

That sounded reasonable, which was another sign of how messed up my life was these days.

The wake was happening on the floor below the Fridas apartment, at his mother's place. I managed to score a parking spot closer this time, a couple of streets away. The assassins and the walking blowup doll were forced to park further up the street.

The three assassins left their vehicles, swaggered over to where Marika and I were preparing for our high stakes mission. As I suspected, they had a fourth guy. I did a double take when I got a good look at his face.

This one was Donk. He had dumped the wannabe homeboy costume for a black suit with a matching black shirt, tie, and sunglasses. I was sweating looking at him, and not in a good way.

"What the hell?"

He tugged at his tie. His smirk looked sweaty. One quirk of his lips and it would slide right off. "I'm moving up in the world. If I kill you I'll be able to cash in and impress my uncle."

"Baby Dimitri hired you to kill me?"

He glanced around nervously. "Uh, no. Don't tell him I'm doing this, okay? I want it to be a surprise."

I stuck between wanting to strangle him and rolling on the ground, laughing. What made up my mind was the cauterizing heat of the pavement.

"Who hired you?"

The smirk slid off. "Why do you have to say it like that, like I don't have skills? You know how many hours I've clocked playing *Call of Duty*? *Bow-coop*."

My gaze slid to Elias, Lefty, and Mo. "Keep an eye on him. Make sure he doesn't kill anybody—especially me."

Mo said, "Somebody tell the Yankee pig woman I would never let a child steal my money."

"Hey, I'm not a child," Donk snapped. He reached for his fly. "Show me your *poutsa*, we'll see who's a man around here and who's an interior decorator."

"An interior decorator?" Mo glanced around. "What is this silly child talking about? Somebody call his mama to take him back to kindergarten."

"Interior decorator, always carrying that rug around with you."

"This is a prayer rug! I carry it so my knees do not get dirty when I pray to Allah."

"If Allah made Persians," Donk said, "he doesn't care much about dirt."

Mo launched himself at Donk. The kid went splat, with a mad Persian atop him, slapping and pulling his hair. Arms folded, Elias and Lefty watched them catfight to the death.

"If I had a hose I could stop them like this." Marika clicked her fingers. "They are rolling around too fast for me to twist their ears."

Ugh. I pivoted on one high heel and marched away. Let the children fight. If professional killing didn't work out for them there was always pro wrestling—if there was such a thing in Greece. Although, knowing what I knew about Greek history, if there was wrestling it probably happened naked.

Marika jogged to keep up with me. It was a lot of work hauling that arsenal in her bag.

"Don't go waving those guns around," I told her. "No shooting unless they're shooting at us."

"Do you think they will shoot at us?"

"I hope not."

"Oh." The word was tinged with disappointment. "I have never been in a shootout before."

Yeah, the freedom was definitely getting to her. Marika was shaping up to be an adrenaline junkie stuffed in a stay-at-home mom's container.

"Me either," I said.

"Not even one? Americans have gunfights all over the place."

"Not even one. You went to Disney World, did you see any gunfights?"

"No, but Takis bought guns from a man under an overpass as soon as we left the airport."

I stopped to stare at her, openmouthed.

"He is very protective of us. He wanted to be prepared."

I blinked. She'd rendered me speechless.

"Do not worry, he sold them back before we left."

I shook my head. "I wasn't worried."

We took the elevator up. Last night Xander and I had taken the stairs. Only a masochist would climb five floors in heels. What if I needed to run later and my feet hurt?

The elevator hummed to the fourth floor. Like the floor above, there was only one apartment. The door hung open. People dressed in black were smoking in the dim hallway. Some of them seemed respectable; but who was I to judge? If there was anyone respectable in my family tree I hadn't shaken the branches hard enough to meet them yet. Inside the apartment someone was cooking up a feast fit for sending off a dismembered dead man.

I held my breath, lurched toward the open door, Marika on my heels.

People glanced at us but their interest didn't stick. I had done my best to make sure I didn't resemble the pictures in the newspaper. For starters, I wasn't black-and-white, although my dress was black. I'd picked up the black sheath in the Volos outpost of Marks & Spencer for Cookie's wake. It went perfectly with a pair of heels I could easily use to gouge out an eye—and possibly a heart—if necessary. My hair was slicked back into a bun, and I'd gone for my best no-makeup makeup. The me in the newspaper had been mostly barefaced, except for the dinner with Melas, when I'd dumped enough mascara on my lashes to sink a battleship. It hadn't escaped my notice that if Fridas was carrying around my picture then he probably wasn't the only one in his gang aware of my existence.

The apartment's floor plan was identical—as far as I could tell—to the one above. The awning was down; the light was arm-wrestling darkness, and so for now they'd settled on maintaining a dense gloom, the winner to be determined at a later date. The living room was thick with mourners, none of whom seemed to be outwardly too upset by the elephant in the middle of the room, which, in this case, was a coffin. The furniture had all been pushed to the walls to accommodate the hulking casket. Florists around the city probably wished gangsters like Fridas died more often; all their flowers were here, clumped together in this one newly built botanical garden.

Cleopatra sidled up to us. The heat had melted her into a snack-sized Robert Smith. Her dress was a black pillowcase.

"Can I stand with you two?" she asked me.

"Uh, no? Go away."

She glanced around like a small animal pushed into an unfriendly corner. "I don't know anybody here."

Interesting. I had figured her for a career criminal, like the rest of them.

"So go back to your car. Or mingle. Meet new people. Make friends."

"It's a wake, not a party."

"You're dressed for a party," I said.

Marika checked her out, her nose wrinkled. "What she is dressed for is a street corner."

Cleopatra didn't look happy. "I heard that."

"You were supposed to."

A thought popped into my head. "I guess you can stand with us, but you have to work for it."

She narrowed her eyes. With all the goop on her lids I wasn't sure she'd be able to open them fully again. It was some seriously risky behavior. "How?"

"Ask around, find out why Fridas had my photo in his pocket."

She glanced around at the wake's other attendees. We weren't exactly swimming in reputable waters. Too many shiny suits, too many women with dead eyes, who looked like they knew the most soluble brand of body glitter.

"Was he a criminal?"

"What do you think?" I asked her.

"I think I'm going to stand by this wall until you leave, then follow you."

"Thanks for nothing," I said.

She flashed her teeth. "Anytime."

Kyria Frida was over by the refreshment table, scanning the crowd for anomalies. I tried to look like I belonged, but I guess I'd gone too tasteful on the makeup because she lifted her arm, pointed her finger right at me.

"You!" she commanded.

Either she was a witch with very little power or people didn't care, because there was no parting of the sea as everyone stopped to gawp at me. They went on with the business of doing business. Funerals and wakes seemed like a good place to gather businessmen of a certain kind in one room. Melas had commented on the phenomenon at Cookie's wake.

Still, I froze in place. My feet were disobeying my head again—it was screaming at them to run fast, that a way.

"You," she said again. This time her voice seemed to be traveling from a shorter distance.

"Sweet Baby Jesus," I said. "She's coming over, isn't she?"

Marika looked her over. "Who is that?"

"The deceased's mother."

"She does not look happy to see you. What did you do?"

"Nothing," I squeaked.

"Uh-huh. I know what nothing looks like, and it does not look like something that would interest a charging bull. Don't worry, I have supplies, remember?"

I remembered. They were a last resort. As Kyria Frida cut her way between the bodies, like a battleship navigating the Panama Canal, I felt all the other resorts evaporate.

"You!" she said, planting herself in front of me. "The *putana* from my son's bed."

Marika opened her mouth to protest on my behalf, then the words sank in. "Bed? What bed?"

"There was no bed," I said.

"Lies!" Kyria Frida pointed to one of her Shar-Pei eyes. "I saw you myself. You had that man on top of you."

"Man? What man?" Marika asked me.

"There was no man." I tried to give Marika a tell-you-later look but I wasn't sure the message was penetrating.

The old woman squinted at me. I was a bug on a pin. "Now that I am seeing you, I know your face from somewhere else. Where have I seen it?"

"Nowhere," I said. "I've got one of those faces."

"How did you know my son, eh?"

There was a spot and I was standing on it. All that was missing was the bright light.

Hands on hips I said, "It's a secret, but I can tell you I've seen his penis." No point mentioning it was in a box at the time, nowhere near his body.

"Probably that is true. I bet you have seen a lot of them."

Marika threw her two cents in. "I have not seen his penis, but I heard about it."

Cleopatra materialized beside us. "I heard it was big enough to feed a whole family."

I raised my eyebrow and paired it with a stink-eye. She gave me a tiny shrug. Her face was serious but I wasn't fooled—she was grinning like Cheshire Cat on the inside.

The old woman shook her head. "He was not his father's son," she said sadly. Her face hardened again. It looked like a bag of decorative lava rocks. "Who are you?"

I pulled a name out of thin air. "Dina Manoli."

"The Manoli family in Kala Nera or the Manoli family in Agria?"

"Thessaloniki."

She tilted her chin up then down. "Never heard of them."

That's because they didn't exist—at least not with me dangling from their family tree. Moving right along … I was here for a reason, and that reason was fact-finding. So far I hadn't discovered a single useful fact.

"I'm sorry about your son," I said, putting on my best mourning face. "I can't imagine anyone wished him any harm."

Her serpentine eyes narrowed to dangerous slits. They had a lot of help from the heavy load of wrinkled laundry above them. "My boy was the head of a gang. Everybody wished him harm."

"So … no suspects?"

"Everybody is a suspect."

My body wanted to shuffle and squirm, but I gritted my teeth together and pressed on. "If you had to guess?"

"Everybody. Him." She nodded to the nearest black-clad back. "Him. Her. That man. His wife." She was nodding in a circle. "When you are important people want you to live or they want you to die—and that changes depending on how they will benefit. Maybe you killed him, eh? How do you benefit from his death?"

"She gets to live," Cleopatra said.

It was like watching a solar eclipse. As the moon slid between the sun (her) and the earth (me), her anger unpacked and pinned itself to her face.

"You are the American!" she hissed. "My son wanted you!"

A couple of mourners glanced over, but their interest evaporated fast. All the good drama was scheduled to happen tomorrow, graveside.

"Now would be a good time to go," I whispered to Marika.

"Do we need the supplies?"

"Not yet."

"Are you sure? Because the old woman does not look happy."

"No supplies," I said. "Not unless they flaunt their supplies first."

The old woman pulled a gun out of her black apron. She pointed it right at me. "My son had one last wish."

Yikes!

"Okay, now we need the supplies," I told Marika.

Marika opened her bag, began rifling through its contents. Metal and plastic clanked together. "Fully automatic or semi automatic?"

"What's the difference?"

She slapped a handgun on my chest. "Speed."

"Where I come from wishes are for sick kids, not criminals," I told Kyria Frida.

"My son was sick. Who else becomes a criminal?"

"Your son was a gangster who got his manhood chopped off."

"He did not!"

"Yes," I said, "he did."

Marika helped the situation by miming scissors chopping air.

"There is nothing wrong with my son's *poutsa*!" she screamed.

Instant cosmic mute button. Conversation died. Everyone stopped in their tracks. People in the hall shuffled in to check out the drama, and they, too, fell silent.

The four of us were standing off to the side, but we were the center of attention.

Suddenly, the room exploded with the sound of dozens of guns coming out of hiding. That mean girl inside me said, *Tag, you're it.* I hated to say it but she was right. Every last muzzle was homed in on me.

The lump in my throat was boulder-sized. It took a serious gulp to knock it aside. "Whoever killed him cut it off."

"Why would they do that?" she demanded. "What kind of monster does that?"

Probably her son had been the kind of monster who did that all the time.

A man pushed his way into our tense quartet. He had a face like the dead man, only not so dead. "What's wrong, Mama?"

"These *putanas*, they say your brother's murderer cut off his *poutsa*."

"Because it's true," I said.

"If that was true the police would have told us," he said. "Wait—I know you."

I wasn't about to tell them this case was linked to the murders of other heads of criminal organizations, or that they all tied back to my family in some way. If the cops hadn't shared that information I figured there was a good reason.

"I was in the newspaper," I said.

"He is right there," Marika said. "Go look. See for yourselves."

Our heads swiveled to check out the casket sitting serenely in the center of the room.

"It's not like the casket is closed," I said reluctantly, hoping Marika and I could glide out the front door before they unveiled the dead man's crotch. It wasn't that I disbelieved, but I knew a good mortician could work magic with putty and paint.

The room held its breath.

Kyria Frida waved her gun as us. "You, you, and you. The three cheap *putanas*. You first."

"Who are you calling cheap? She's cheap." I pointed to Cleopatra. "But we're high-end."

"She does look cheap," the old woman said.

"Hey," Cleopatra said.

The brother waggled his eyebrows at her. "You need a job? We can make you disappear from Greece and reappear on a rich man's yacht in the Mediterranean. We can even give you a new name. How do you feel about … Aurora?"

"How do you feel about snakes?" she asked him. The look on her face said that any second now she was going to shake her asp at him.

The crowd parted as we moved en masse to where Petros Fridas lay waiting on everyone in the room to show him respect. Greek Orthodox custom was to kiss the dead goodbye after they'd already hopped on the ferry to Hades.

Fridas had come a long way since yesterday morning, when he was chilling out at the morgue. No longer waxy and gray, he had a lifelike flush. His cheek was covered in lipstick. There was a lot of it in this room, most of it in non-standard mourning colors. There were places for fuchsia; a wake usually wasn't one of them. His suit was a severe gray with that criminal sheen. His shirt was black. His tie was a lesser black. Someone had fastened a gardenia to his lapel with a gold pin.

"Who is going to check?" the brother asked.

Everyone moved closer. At the same time, no one stepped up.

"You do it," his mother said.

He jerked his head up and down so violently that he could have been a Pez dispenser. "I don't want to look at his *poutsa*. What if it makes me gay?"

Yeah, that wasn't how it worked. "There isn't one to look at," I said.

"We will see," Kyria Frida said darkly.

"I'm not part of this, so I'm going—" Cleopatra started. Several guns turned to face her. "Never mind. I guess I will stand right here."

A bead of sweat squeezed itself out of a pore on my forehead. It went for a smooth roll down my nose before ski jumping off the tip. The Fridas family had money—illegally gained—but it hadn't invested in air conditioning.

My jaw clenched. There was nothing useful to be learned here—not now that the cats had all escaped the bag. Anyone who knows cats knows that if you want to keep them in you put them in a box, not a bag. Cats can't say no to boxes. It's a lesser law of the universe. "Somebody look."

Mother and son stared at me.

"No," I said. "Not a chance in hell."

"You have seen it before," the old woman said. "You said so."

In a box—but I didn't say that. There would be questions, and I wasn't in an answering mood. I wanted to go back to Grandma's and hit the shower, preferably with a hammer.

I turned to Marika. "You've got four sons and Takis. You could do it."

"I do not touch criminals," she said. "I mean, I do not touch criminals if I'm not married to them or related by marriage."

"Don't look at me," Cleopatra said. "I don't trust the things. They always go off when you least expect it."

I blinked. The movement was one of my brain's lesser processing mechanisms.

"We are in a room full of working girls," Marika said. "Get one of them do it."

Before the room had been silent. What it was now was devoid of breath. A great vacuum had sucked out all the air, and the person holding that vacuum was Marika. I had a sudden sinking feeling that the women I'd mistaken for hookers and strippers were girlfriends and wives.

My elbow nudged her elbow. "I don't think they work for anyone."

"What? Look at them! I know prostitutes when I see them. I am not judging," she said, hand on heart. "Times are hard right now, and maybe you have children to feed, and who knows where their fathers are? On a ship? In the army? Who knows? A woman has got to do what she has to do to survive."

"Marika," I said.

"What?"

"They're not what you think they are."

Her mouth formed a perfect O. "My mistake. It happens. My vision is not so good." She reached into her big bag. "Where are my glasses?"

"Forget about the glasses," I said.

"Good," she whispered. "Because I don't wear glasses. Imagine if I had to produce them."

"I will look," Kyria Frida said, ignoring her. Her gun traveled around the room in a wide arc. "You are all a bunch of sisters."

Which was the Greek was of saying we were effeminate men. Never mind that minutes ago she'd tried to foist the job off on someone else.

"Open the bottom half," she barked at her younger son.

He jumped to do her bidding, pushed up the lower section of the coffin. Whoever had dressed Petros Fridas had shunned formal footwear and shoved his feet into monster's foot slippers. They were big, they were fluffy, they were purple with black toenails.

His mother took a deep breath. She shoved the gun back into her apron pocket, hitched up her dead son's jacket before tackling the zipper. She peered inside. Zipped him back up. Rearranged his suit jacket. Dropped the lower half of the lid.

"Either someone chopped it off," she said, "or somewhere along the way my son became my daughter."

15

The boys were still fighting when we traipsed outside. The sun, not to be outdone, did its share of slapping me around. It was in cahoots with the pavement, which was pelting shimmering sheets of heat at me from ground level. Across the street, the water was quietly sloshing against the concrete wall. Even it looked tired of summer. We collapsed against the wall in a half-hearted patch of shade.

"That went well," Marika said. "All things considered."

"I told them."

"You did tell them. I heard you."

"People always want to disbelieve before they get to the believing."

"That is human nature. Believing is hard work. It requires faith." She poked me with her elbow. "Who were you on the bed with last night?"

"Nobody."

"But—"

"Xander," I said. "It was Xander."

"You and Xander?" she asked.

"No. No me and Xander. We were looking for clues."

She raised an eyebrow. "Okay, I won't tell anyone."

"There's nothing to tell."

"That's not what I heard."

"You heard it from a gangster's mother! We're not talking about a reliable witness here. There's no me and Xander."

"Okay. If you say so then I believe you."

Ack!

We slogged over to the cars, where Mo had Donk in a headlock.

"Let him go," I said.

"Let who go?" Mo glanced around, one hand shading his eyes. "I do not see anybody. I am standing here, thinking about how I will spend the money after I kill you."

The other three yelped, including Donk.

"Ugh," I said. "Get in your cars and let's go."

~ ~ ~

It was impossible to miss the flock of helicopters. They were big, black blowflies, hacking the air into buoyant chunks, moving in the direction of Mount Pelion.

"Looks like they are going to see someone important," Marika said.

Or closing in on the bad guys.

A horrible thought filled my head. There were a lot of bad guys on Mount Pelion, most of them concentrated in Grandma's compound.

"I have never been in a helicopter before," Marika was saying. "Do you think they would let me take ride? Would they let me jump out on one of those ropes?"

"Remember what happened at Meteora?"

"That was different. There was no rope."

"There was a rope ladder."

"Look," she said, changing the subject. "Sheep!"

There were sheep, a sea of lanolin tripping across the road, prodded periodically by a shepherd. Both ways, traffic had ground to a halt. Scads of tourists were leaning out a bus window, cell phones in hand. This was one Greek photo op they weren't going to miss. I jumped out of the car, snapped my own pictures, immediately sent them to everyone I knew who wasn't Greek. Before Takis and Stavros had drugged me and thrown me onto a plane I'd never been anywhere. Now I was somewhere, and I wanted to brag about it a teensy bit.

When we arrived at the compound, the helicopters were on Grandma's doorstep. Two had settled on ground outside the wall. My entourage, five cars strong now, crept along the dirt road behind the Beetle. They were probably wishing they'd signed up to kill someone with less baggage and fewer connections. The security guard was pacing back and forth in front of the open gates, muttering to a couple of brick-headed men in head-to-toe black. Black cargo pants, black boots, black T-shirts. There were white letters stenciled on the backs, but I wasn't down with Greek law enforcement acronyms. For all I knew they were an unimaginative circus troupe.

Melas's cop car was parked out front, too.

"Oh-la-la, Nikos is here," Marika said. "That man has the best *kolos* in Greece. Don't tell Takis I said that."

Didn't I know it? Still, his being here couldn't be a good thing, not with these helicopters in tow.

I followed Marika through the gates, glancing sideways at our security guy. He was talking a mile a minute, pushing his hands through his hair as he paced. The words were flying out so fast it was like trying to pick musical notes out of a blender's whizz.

Aunt Rita was standing by the fountain out front, hands on hips. She was deep in conversation with another couple of black-clad cops. The garage doors were down—unusual for daytime. Melas was leaning in the cool shade of the arch, unreadable behind dark sunglasses, watching my aunt and the men talk.

"Hey," I said to him. "What's up?"

One of the guys broke off the pair to look at me. "Who are you?"

"Nobody," Melas said, pushing away from the arch's smooth wall. "I know for a fact she's got nothing to do with any of this."

Fear flitted across Marika's face. "Takis?"

"He's fine," Melas said, in a low voice. "They're asking him some questions, that's all. They're talking to everyone." Marika hurried away. Melas curled his fingers around my elbow. "Come on, let's go for a drive."

"Is Baboulas okay?" I asked Aunt Rita, over my shoulder. Probably not a good idea to call her Grandma in front of the law enforcement goons. Someone in the family might need to bail everyone out—and that someone might be me.

"She's okay," Aunt Rita said. "These apes have questions, that's all."

My heart was going wild, and my adrenal gland was shooting streamers. What was happening? Was this about Dad or was the Family in deep doo-doo?

"Any hints?"

She pursed her lips, shook her head. The bricks glared at me.

"Let's go," Melas said, steering me away.

A wave of heat cut through the fear. My body was an idiot who didn't know when to save the lust for a more convenient time … and an appropriate target.

"I want to know what's going on."

"Drive first," he said, "then talk."

My bottom half gravitated toward the Beetle but my top half went the other way. Melas' fingers were strong.

"My car," he said, the big bossy boots.

The assassins, I noticed, had fled, probably because they killed people for money, which didn't go down well with law enforcement. Only Cleopatra was hanging around, buffing her nails behind the wheel of her bullet-ridden Renault.

I stuck out my tongue. She mimed turning a small handle and raised her middle finger. Some gestures are universal; this one happened to originate in Greece.

Melas yanked open the passenger door. "Get in."

"Where are we going? It better not be jail. You already tricked me once."

"It's not jail."

My eyes narrowed. "It better not be your mother's house, either."

He paused.

"Oh, God," I said. "You were going to take me back to your parents' house? Are you insane?"

"She likes you."

"She likes seeing me uncomfortable. There's a difference. You know what else does that? Cats. Right before they kill something."

"Mama's not that bad." There was a short pause during which I fired hate rays at his head. "Okay, she can be difficult."

It's possible I muttered, "Difficult is the least of the adjectives I'd nail to her forehead."

Melas shook his head, but there was a small smile hanging around his mouth, so at least he was aware his mother was a walking nightmare. The only thing more frightening than a monster is a monster with alleged powers of foresight.

There was movement by the arch. Several more law enforcement thugs had joined my aunt. None of them looked happy, or even capable of joy.

Melas swore under his breath. "You can get in the car or you can stay and answer questions."

I stared at him.

"Five … four … three …"

"What happens when you reach one?"

"I put you in the damn car myself."

I slid into the car, buckled the seatbelt, while my eyes combed the compound's exterior for … I don't know what. Melas kicked over the motor. He eased the cop car down the dirt road, out onto the main vein, threaded around this part of Mount Pelion. He took a left into the village of Makria and parked in the roadside parking lot, next to his parents' brown Peugeot.

He unlatched his seatbelt, leaned back in his seat. "They know your Grandmother busted Dogas out of prison."

My gut plunged into my feet. If they knew, Grandma was in major league trouble. But if it was a suspicion there was hope. Grandma wasn't a dummy.

"Know or suspect?"

"Know."

"Informant?"

He shrugged. "Every organization has someone willing to sing."

"Is it her?" *Her* being his former paramour.

"No. I don't know who it is. Whoever they are they aren't one of ours. These guys are from Thessaloniki. That's why they have fancier toys." His smile was wry. "They can't do too much unless they have proof—which is why they're there: to find proof."

"What about the video?"

"Too low quality to be definitive."

The mercury had to be closing in on a hundred, but my hands felt like they'd been plunged into a bucket of water, fresh off the plane from Antarctica.

"Will they find proof?" he asked gently.

Would they? I didn't know. Rabbit had been at the compound, but I wasn't privy to his itinerary. Maybe he was on the run in Turkey by now. Grandma had told me nothing—and now I understood why. A person who knows nothing doesn't have to lie. The trouble was, I didn't know nothing. I was in possession of enough knowledge to toss Grandma and Xander into a volcano if the Hellenic Police squeezed me the right way.

Not to mention—although here I was thinking about it—if the police had any smarts they'd be digging into the origin of the video floating around in the Internet. To say it had gone viral was like saying the Spanish flu gave a few people the sniffles.

For now, Melas had asked me a question, and I didn't know the right answer: the lie or the truth? How far could I trust him? More than he could probably trust me.

I took to my inner fence, and sat. "I don't know." It was partially true. Grandma had sprung Dogas out of prison, and she had harbored him at the compound, but for all I knew she'd scrubbed away every trace of him before shooting him off to wherever criminals go after they've been busted out of prison. Maybe Turkey, maybe Jamaica. I hadn't ruled out the possibility that he was in the dungeon that was apparently buried under the swimming pool.

"I was hoping for something more definitive, like a *no*."

"Look on the bright side," I said. "At least it wasn't a *yes*." That didn't inspire a vote of confidence, I could tell. The lines on his forehead were forming a bold V.

"I don't know what to do," Melas said, "and that bothers me."

"What do you mean?"

"Law enforcement is my life. I'm sworn to stop the bad guys, and your Family is the bad guys. But they're also decent people who've done good things around here. And then there's you …"

"Forget about me," I said. "I'll be gone as soon as I find Dad."

He nodded once. "Right." He didn't look happy.

"I went to the Fridas wake," I told him, attempting to change the subject.

He groaned, smacked his forehead. "What did I tell you?"

"Which time?" I flashed him a grin I didn't feel.

He shook his head. "Man … I bet you were one of those little kids, the ones who touch the stove even when their mother tells them it's hot, because they have to know for themselves if it's hot or not."

My turn to shake my head. I hadn't yet picked up the Greek affectation of jerking my head up to indicate a negative. How long would I be here before I did?

"I was a good kid."

"I didn't say it was bad."

"I wasn't one of those kids. It's a new thing. I didn't even know I had this … rebellious streak. I think it's different when everything is at stake."

"Your father?"

I nodded.

"We've had this conversation," he said. "Your father would want you to stay home, where it's safe."

The laugh blurted out of me. It was dry, painful, not a shred of humor in the thing. "He was taken from our *home*. The bad guys came to *where we live* and *took* him. Tell me, how is that safe?"

I didn't mention the secret stash behind the medicine cabinet in the master bathroom. That would complicate the situation. It wouldn't be long before men and women wearing TLAs like FBI, DHS, DEA, and maybe even CIA, descended upon Mom and Dad's house. If they tore apart my home, chances were they'd break something that mattered to *me* in an attempt to find something that mattered to *them*.

"It's not safe anywhere," I continued, since he wasn't picking up what I was putting down—as they used to say, back in the 'hood where I never lived.

"So whatever you say, there's a good chance I'm going to nod my head and agree until your back is turned. Then I'm going to do whatever I think can potentially lead me to my father. Nod once if you understand."

He stared at me.

I stared back.

"Was it worth it, going to the Fridas wake?"

"Undecided. We left empty-handed, but they let us live. I still don't know why Fridas had my picture in his pocket. His mother said he wanted me, but she didn't say why or how."

More staring. Then he said, "I need coffee."

"I could use some coffee."

"Not me—I *need* it. You're giving me a headache and a pain in the ass."

"You should see a doctor about that second one. I don't think coffee wields that much magic."

Words were failing him, I could tell by the arrow his eyebrows had formed. "You're going to drive me to the bottle."

We got out of the car. What should have been a thirty-second walk took five minutes because everyone stopped to greet and grill Melas. He was a local boy in law enforcement, which meant he was in possession of interesting stories and possibly gossip, which is the lifeblood of Greek villages. They had questions for me, too, mostly about how Grandma was doing, and whether or not my father had been found. Slowly, they were absorbing me into their tribe. Oregonians were friendly, but even in the suburbs everyone was aware they were part of a larger, city-sized whole. Inquiries were friendly but they weren't personal. Here they were personal, fact-finding missions, designed to dig up your secrets and analyze your character.

I wondered how long it would take Melas' mother to hear—

"Nikos! There is my boy."

Not long, apparently. The woman had hearing like a bionic dog. She was standing at the crossroads in a housedress, her hair a Spartan helmet. The only way to escape was to turn around and run, but she struck me as the kind of woman who had mastered the hunt.

"Mama," the mama's boy beside me said.

"Kyria Mela," I said, wishing I had the guts and wherewithal to yell, "Fire" and bolt. Unfortunately, she knew where I lived.

"Where are you going? What are you doing?"

"We were going to grab a coffee," Melas said.

"What for do you want to pay for coffee? You are wasting your money. Come home and drink coffee for free."

He was going to cave, wasn't he? Oh boy …

"The department is paying for it," he said. "Don't worry."

"But do they have homemade *finikia*? I do not think so. In fact, I suspect both the *kafeneios* here buy their pastries. I cannot prove it—yet—but I keep my eye on them."

"Can't the cup tell you?" I asked.

Her iron gaze stuck to my face. "The cup does not deal in trivia."

Oookay. Let me crawl back into my shell.

"Relax, Mama," Mela said. "This is business." His hand settled on the small of my back. Old eagle eye didn't miss a thing. Her eyes narrowed to vicious slits. I considered that she might be a supernatural creature, maybe a banshee; something that shot blue lasers from its eyes. Their current black-brown state was a disguise, an effort to blend in with normal society.

Next time I came to Makria I'd pack a stake.

"Business? Who does business with pretty women, unless they are prostitutes?"

I looked up at Melas. "The longer we stand here the more it's going to cost you."

His mother gasped.

"It was a joke," I said lamely. "Policemen from Thessaloniki are at the compound. They're trying to bust my grandmother."

Kyria Mela was living proof that it was possible to frown using one's entire body. She drew herself into a tight, angry column, her face pinched like a crab had been using it for claw-snapping practice. "I will go over there and tell them Katerina Makri has done nothing!"

"Mama," Melas said. "It's okay. It's under control."

But it wasn't, was it?

"What are they looking for?" she demanded.

"More like a whom," I told her. "A guy who broke out of prison."

"Yes, we saw him on the news." She patted my arm, moving from psycho banshee to empathetic human being so swiftly that I wondered if aliens had paused the world and swapped out her body for a kinder, gentler clone. "He will turn up eventually and your grandmother will be vindicated. Go. Enjoy your coffee. If you need me, I will be at home. Alone."

She turned and sped up the narrow, cobbled road, leading to most of Makria's residences. Straight ahead was Ayia Aikaterini—Saint Catherine's—and to the left was the village square, filled with souvenir stalls, *tavernas*, coffee shops. There was more mountain above and behind Makria, but from here it still seemed like I was standing on the world's roof. Melas steered me toward a table in the shade of a sprawling beech, its ropey roots punching up the cobblestones. Mother Nature was one pushy broad. He ordered two coffees, two waters, then asked if I wanted sweets. I shook my head, and the waiter moved off.

"Why didn't you leave me at the compound?" I asked Melas.

"I wanted to know what you knew before they got to you."

I chewed on my bottom lip for a moment, calculating what, and how much, I could say.

"I saw Rabbit."

"I know. Your name was in the sign-in book."

"No. At the compound."

"Shit." His expression turned several shades grimmer. "Shit. Why are you telling me this?"

"A problem shared is a problem halved?"

"What?"

"It's an expression."

"In America, maybe. Here it's a problem doubled, especially if you share it with a cop."

"Well excuse me," I said. "It just came out. You were being so nice to me and all, I thought I should share something."

He eyed me suspiciously. "What do you want?"

"Nothing."

"Uh-huh."

"Quit nagging me about going home. And stop getting in my way. I'm going to keep hunting for my father, with or without your help."

"I could put you in a cell and keep you there."

"You could try. I'd chew my way out."

He shook his head and laughed. "I believe you." His gaze slid left. "Jesus," he muttered. His mother was moving this way, cutting across the village square, a small plate in each hand. She sat both in the middle of the table and dusted her hands together. "You eat sweets, eat homemade." She shot death rays at the proprietor, a small, round man with a white apron and a friendly countenance. If pushed to it, I'd choose his sweets over hers; there was a high probability of poison or truth serum in her offering. To me she said, "Come back to see me again soon. We will have coffee, us women."

"Okay," I stammered. And I would, as soon as I wanted to self-flagellate, which would probably be soon.

She stamped a kiss on her son's head then hurried off again, headed toward the church.

Melas drove me back to the compound. The black metal birds were still outside the gates, pilots waiting on their cargo. There were no other signs of life, except the security guard, who was sitting in the guardhouse, biting his nails.

It was a bad habit—one I sometimes shared—but at least he wasn't spanking the Greek monkey, like his predecessor.

"What's happening?" I asked him. Melas was at my side. I had a feeling he wouldn't peel off until the other guys packed up their high-tech toys and buzzed away.

"They are searching the place."

"The whole place?"

He nodded. "They are talking to everybody."

"What did they ask you?"

"Katerina—" Melas started.

I shot him a not-now look.

"The wanted to know about a man called Dogas."

"What did you tell them?"

He shrugged, two palms up. "Nothing. I don't know any Dogas. They showed me a picture, but I have never seen him before."

If he was lying he was good at it. Probably it was genetic.

"And they asked if Baboulas has a helicopter. I said I know nothing about a helicopter. I stand at the gate all day, and all I see are cars, motorcycles, and sometimes farm animals. But no helicopters except these ones."

He went back to his post, leaving me to deal with Melas.

"Want me to come with you?" he asked.

I shook my head. "I can do this."

"Do what? Lie to the police?"

"Whatever it takes," I said.

Was that true, would I do whatever it took, even if it was wrong?

And who would be responsible for the measuring?

Grandma was sitting in a chair near the pool when I stomped into the courtyard. Her chin jerked up the moment she spotted me. The meathead cop swiveled his upper half to follow her line of sight.

He jumped up as I closed in on them. "Who are you? You the granddaughter?"

The courtyard was silent and still even though every corner seemed to be filled with small clusters of law enforcement and family. Takis was nearby with two cops. His arms were folded, his expression closed. He was mouthing off about steroids and their effects on male genitalia. From the looks on their faces he wasn't making friends. By the pool, Stavros was sweating as a three-man clump loomed over him. His mouth was moving, his expression playing dumb.

Xander was nowhere in sight. I wondered if Grandma had stashed him away somewhere as soon as trouble dropped out of the sky. Did they know about the underground hideaway and control room? What about the armory, such as it was? I mentally crossed my fingers that Grandma's secrets were safe. Somewhere along the way, the good guys had become the enemy. They were an impediment, cluttering the path between my and my goal. I never assumed, for ever a moment, that they could help me get to Dad—not these guys, at least.

"I'm Katerina Makris," I told the cop. I planted myself close to Grandma. "You okay?" I asked her.

"They are doing their jobs," she said. "Apparently they lost a prisoner."

"Stelios Dogas was not lost," the cop said. "Someone broke him out."

"It was probably aliens," I said. "It usually is."

The cop twitched. "It wasn't aliens."

"Are you sure? Because, man, aliens are pretty tricky with their spaceships and their beams of light."

He was looking at me like I should be the filling in a straitjacket burrito. That was kind of the idea. I wanted him to think I was an airhead, this side of nuts.

"That your yellow car out front, the VW?"

"I don't own it."

"You drive it?"

"Never on Sunday."

If he got the move reference it didn't show. "What about on the other days?"

"Only on some of them."

"You ever drive it to Larissa?"

"Not even once." That, at least, was true.

"Because a Katerina Makris signed into the Larissa prison on the day the prisoner escaped."

"I was there, but I didn't drive."

"Did you record a prison break while you were there?"

"No."

"Why were you at the prison?"

"I like convicts." I waggled my eyebrows suggestively.

"You're sick," he told me. "You should get help."

"I *know*," I said melodramatically. "That's what *everyone* says."

He cleared his throat. "Did you meet with Stelios Dogas while you were there?"

"This is going to go really slowly if you keep asking me questions when you already know the answers."

"There's more to asking questions than getting answers."

I did a ditzy head wag. "Like … what?"

"The truth."

Should I fluff my hair? I wasn't good at these things. Probably my hair was too sweaty for a real fluffing. "Sure, I met with Dogas."

He stared at me. I stared back. It looked like he was waiting on extra words to roll out of my mouth. Too bad. If he wanted words, he'd have to work for them. His whole body was tense. Any tighter and bits would start snapping off.

"What did you see him about?"

"Um … It's kind of embarrassing." God, gods, and the other deities would have to forgive me for the lie I was about to tell. Any other time I would tell the cops I was hunting down a lead on Dad, but if I told them the truth it would dunk Grandma in the boiling water. The last thing I wanted to do was give them a motive for her springing Dogas from the clink. "My plan was to make him fall in love with me so we could get married. Then when he died—and he's so old it's bound to be soon, am I right?—I'd have him stuffed and sell him to a crime museum."

Grandma was watching the sky, her face as unyielding as a brick.

He straightened up. "The crime museum?"

"Uh huh. I think it's in Kentucky or something. They're always looking to acquire new pieces. They pay big, too."

"My Virgin Mary," he said. "You Americans are sick."

I did a cutesy one-shouldered shrug. "It's culture."

There was movement at the arch. A gang of suited men—government suits, zero shine—strode into the courtyard as though their pockets were stuffed with bits of paper that gave them permission to do bad things. They were golems: take away their paper they'd be unarmed.

They stopped for a moment, scanned the courtyard, then one of them pointed and nodded in our direction.

My flight-or-fight kicked in, and then stood down when it realized I was screwed.

"Find the brother?" one of them asked the cop interrogating Grandma and me.

"Not yet."

Brother? Whose brother?

"Keep looking."

He reached into his coat then presented Grandma with a piece of paper. She looked it over, no expression to indicate whether it was good news or bad.

Then she stood, without so much as a groan. She was steel, and she wanted them to know they would crawl before she would bend. "Katerina," she said. "Tell your aunt to call my lawyers."

The men didn't cuff her, which was the best I could say. They formed a loose square around her and marched her toward the arch.

"You can't take her!" I yelled at them. "What right do you have? Where are you taking her?"

"It will be okay," Grandma said over her shoulder. But she didn't look okay to me. What she looked like was a little old lady. My grandmother.

"Police brutality," I said. I whipped out my phone and began filming. One of the meatheads broke off the pack and snatched the phone out of my hands. He flung it across the courtyard.

"You can't do that!" I shouted.

"Katerina, stay," Grandma said. "The family needs you here. Be here for them."

~ ~ ~

I stood watch in the courtyard, arms folded. I stood until the sun skulked away and the cops went chasing after it in their helicopters. Family came and went, all of them with questions and not nearly enough answers.

"Katerina," Marika said. "Come. Eat. There is nothing you can do right now."

"They said something about a brother. Rabbit's brother, I presume."

The night was warm but it was taking tiny cool bites. The answer popped in my head like a fragile bubble.

"Papou. He's the brother, isn't he?"

"Yes."

"Why didn't anyone tell me?"

"Probably, like me, they thought you knew."

I shook my head. "I didn't know."

"You are one of us, so sometimes we forget you don't know all the things we have always known."

That made sense. "What do I do now? Who's in charge?"

"I think you are."

Yikes. There was no way I could run the Family until Grandma's lawyers jimmied the door, greased the wheels of justice.

"Okay," I said. "I want to see Aunt Rita, Papou, Xander, Takis, and Stavros in the kitchen as soon as possible. "And anyone else Grandma would call during an emergency."

"Baboulas would not say as soon as possible. She would say right now."

"Right now, then."

"I will tell Takis to find them."

~ ~ ~

No Papou. No Xander. It was Aunt Rita, Takis, and Stavros gathered around Grandma's kitchen table.

"I have been doing this almost my whole life," Takis was saying, when I slouched into the kitchen and boosted my butt onto the kitchen counter. I didn't have the heart to fill Grandma's seat. "Being a mobster is what I do. This is my profession. So why do they treat me like I am going to talk if they ask a few uncomfortable questions? I know how to keep quiet. If you talk in this business you die. I don't want to die, I have a family. Okay, so sometimes my wife makes me wish I was dead, but not real death, more like vacation death. Go to an island, drink fruity drinks with little umbrellas and cherries, get a massage from a pretty girl, spear some fish. Maybe try sushi."

"I make sushi," Stavros said.

"You? Ha!"

"My sushi is good," he mumbled.

"Sushi," Aunt Rita said. "Who can eat raw fish?"

"You eat *taramasalata*," I said.

"That's different. It's eggs."

"Raw fish eggs," I pointed out.

She shrugged.

"I love sushi," I told Stavros.

He beamed. "I will make sushi for you."

I shot him a grateful smile before getting down to business. Arms folded I said, "Where are Papou and Xander?"

Takis looked at Stavros, who looked at Aunt Rita. They all shrugged.

"We don't know," Takis said.

"They're not in compound," my aunt said. "We checked everywhere after the police left."

"You called the lawyers?"

"Before Mama even left the grounds."

Aunt Rita was on top of things. She should be the one running this sketchy three-ring circus. Yet everyone was looking to me like I could perform magic.

Ask Tomas: I couldn't even belch the alphabet—any alphabet.

"Have we heard anything from them?" I asked.

"Not yet," she said. "They'll be contacting you as soon as they hear something."

"Me? Why me?"

"They know Mama expects you to take over if we can't find Michail."

"I'm not taking over anything." Everyone stared. They didn't believe me. Maybe something was getting lost in translation again, like, probably, my opinion. "I'm not! This is temporary. As soon as my father turns up I'm going home—with him. Thanks to Grandma I have to get a new job, and a new apartment. I don't know anything about running a crime syndicate—and I don't want to."

Stavros hung his head. "I thought you liked us."

Oh boy. "I do like you. You're all my family. But I'm not a criminal. I'm a Greek-American woman who wants a decent job, a great guy, and some kids, someday."

Takis made a sour face. "She thinks we're criminals."

"You're the mob," I said. "That's as criminal as it gets."

"No family is perfect," he said.

My aunt though, she was looking at me with sympathy. "I understand. I wanted to be Aliki Vougiouklaki, but she already had the job."

"Who?"

"She was Greece's National Star! Our Bardot and Julia Roberts!"

My eye twitched. "Why didn't you pursue an acting career?"

"My wife wanted me to be a businessman, and my mother wanted me to be a businessman for her. And now here I am, a businesswoman."

"I want to be a stay-at-home father," Stavros said.

Laughter blurted out of Takis. "Who wants to do that? Nobody, that's who. I have four sons and I would rather shove my *kolos* in a cactus than stay at home with them."

"I wouldn't mind," Stavros said.

"Okay, then I will tell Marika you are her new babysitter." He pointed at Stavros with his thumb. "This one cannot get a woman, and he's planning to stay at home with his children? Where is your *poutsa*? Did somebody cut it off?"

"You're kind of an asshole," I told Takis.

He shrugged. "Somebody has to do it."

Stavros bobbed his head like a sparrow. "He can be very useful during an interrogation, or when we need to hurt somebody."

This—this was exactly what I was talking about. I couldn't be in charge of anything where I needed a staff asshole.

"So what's the plan?" Takis asked.

What was the plan? If there was one no one had told me. And if they expected me to make one, I was too busy freaking out on the inside to plot. Someone else would have to do it.

I said the only thing that made sense to me. "First let's see what the lawyers say. In the meantime, we look for Papou and Xander." I pulled the shattered pieces of phone out of my pocket, dumped them on a heap on the table. "And I really need a new phone."

"What happened?" Aunt Rita asked.

"Police brutality." Then a thought popped into my head. "Where is Rabbit?"

16

"We don't know," Aunt Rita said. "If Mama sent him somewhere she didn't say where."

"Do you think she had him …?" I slashed my throat with one finger and hoped it translated.

Takis went *tst*. "Nobody gets whacked around here without me knowing about it."

I wondered if he was with Papou and Xander. That seemed like the most obvious answer. It made sense for Grandma to banish all three men with a single magic trick; one was an escapee prisoner, one was his brother, and the third man had busted him out of his cell.

"Okay," I said. "Put the word out that all three of them need to be found. They can stay in hiding if they want, but I want to know where they are."

The two men took off in different directions, but Aunt Rita hung back.

"You look like you've got a question."

My laugh was on the bitter side. "Dozens. But for tonight I need to know how to get into the cellar."

"What have you got in mind?"

I jumped off the countertop. "Nothing yet. But I need somewhere to go and think." And watch, while I was at it. If there was anything to see, I wanted to see it.

"Come, I will show you."

She led me into the front yard. We stood where the concrete varied almost imperceptibly from its surroundings. Aunt Rita grabbed the one of the knobs on top of the fence and twisted.

"You see it?"

"I see it," I told her. This spot in the yard was all but hidden from the rest of the compound. Grandma's garden was where the wild things lived, and most of them were leafy. For all I knew she had a triffid or two. So the odds that a random family member could spot Grandma—or us—taking a quick jaunt down to the control room were limited. Not that they'd talk if they knew … unless they were the Family leak.

The concrete pad sank slowly. The temperature dipped with it. Nature has its own air conditioning—in Greece it's called subterranean caves.

When it stopped we were standing in the Batcave.

There were no bats in Grandma's Batcave, but it had electronics out the wahzoo. Rows of computers, a wall of monitors, and a captain's chair with a big red button nearby, hunched under a plastic cover.

"These have Internet, right?" I said, referring to the computers.

"Of course. Down here the connection is private, so that nobody can monitor traffic."

In Grandma's case she wasn't paranoid—they really were out to get her.

"That's great," I said. "Thanks."

She put her arm around me, kissed my forehead. "You want company?"

"Thanks, but I could use some alone time."

"You need anything, you call me, okay?" She pointed out the complicated phone system. "Press number 2 and it will connect to my cell phone."

Then she patted me on the shoulder and went back out the way we had come in. Obviously the exit that led to Xander's room wasn't for everyone. Or maybe she respected his privacy while he wasn't around. For all I knew, the trapdoor locked somehow from the other side. The meathead cops hadn't found either of the entrances; I suspected there were other ways in around the property. Maybe one even led to the far side of the wall. It would be like Grandma to stash an extra contingency plan in her pocket.

I sat in the front row, where I had an excellent view of everything the cameras picked up. Life seemed calm in the compound. Everyone was picking up the pieces of their freshly tossed lives, but that was window dressing. Beneath the surface, they were tense. Their boss was gone—temporarily, I hoped—and some chit they barely knew was fumbling with the wheel. I was nobody. A mere twist of DNA was responsible for my current position. I hadn't done a thing to earn my place as second-in-command while Grandma was battling the forces of …

Argh. Well, the forces of good.

Funny how the good guys didn't seem so good from this side of the fence. What Grandma and Xander had done was monumentally wrong, but somehow in my head I felt like the police should at least have had the decency to knock on the door and ask politely if Rabbit was around, and could they maybe have a word with him if he was.

Without my phone I was dead in the water. I had no way to text Xander and ask where he was, and if Papou and Dogas were with him. Until the lawyers called all I could do was ferment.

I pulled up a browser window in private mode and surfed to the Crooked Noses forum, where news had already broken about Grandma's departure from the compound in police custody. They had gone out on several limbs, some of them surprisingly stable. They'd surmised that the police were hunting for Dogas and they believed Grandma had not only broken him out, but that she was also harboring a fugitive. Which was true—or had been. They'd analyzed the prison break footage, breaking it down frame by frame.

Someone else had jumped in with the information that Dogas and Grandma's advisor—Papou—were brothers. Then several other posters slapped him or her down for dishing up what was common knowledge.

Not so common; I hadn't known until tonight.

Greece was one giant Christmas tree with a bunch of boxes underneath, all wrapped with high quality paper and plush bows. Occasionally I was allowed to open one, but the rest were off limits. When I managed to snatch up one of the forbidden boxes and rattle the contents, it always sounded like rocks.

I planned my question carefully. Typed it in two-fingered.

If the police didn't find Dogas at the compound, where else could he be?

A smattering of replies came back almost instantly. *Dead. Alive, but in Turkey. Bulgaria. In Albania, disguised as a woman.* Someone made a crack about Aunt Rita and a handful of the chuckleheads joined in.

BangBang had something to say, but he or she did it in private.

He's probably close to the compound somewhere. If it were me looking I'd start in the village.

Makria?

The people there would do anything for Baboulas.

Including harboring a fugitive?

Which part of 'anything' is giving you a problem?

Ooooh, sarcasm, I typed.

Wasn't trying to be sarcastic. It's a real question. Something tells me you don't know how deep the ties go between Baboulas and Makria.

How deep?

Like I said: They would do anything for her.

Why? Because of the Regime of the Colonels?

In the late sixties a group of right-wing colonels staged a coup and seized control of Greece. When Greece emerged from the dark tunnel in 1974, they were missing a king and thousands of their own citizens. Grandma, the story goes, worked tirelessly to save the people of Makria—and the surrounding villages—from persecution and execution.

Because of that, because of a lot of things.

I typed: *They know she's a crime lord, right?*

Maybe they think there are worse things a person can be. Never underestimate the blindness that comes with loyalty.

Can I ask you something?

You can ask. Doesn't mean I'll answer.

Are you Yoda?

Xaxaxaxa! Not that green, short, or old.

('*Xaxaxaxa*!' is Greek for 'Hahahaha!')

So you're bigger than a breadbox?

What?

It's an American thing. A game. Twenty Questions.

I froze.

Holy cow. What had I done? I quickly clicked the X in the corner, closing the browser window. With an open palm I slapped my forehead, hoping to shake out the stupidity.

This is what I got for being tired and stressed. Now if I went back to the board I'd have to open a new account under a different name, and maybe try to not mess up by telling people I was American. God knows how much damage I had already done, all but revealing my identity to an avatar of a smoking gun.

I clonked my head on the table.

When I was done berating myself I pulled up a map of Makria. On the screen it looked even tinier, a lopsided spider's web radiating out from the crossroad.

Was BangBang right, had someone—or several someones—in Makria stashed Dogas away for safekeeping at Grandma's behest? If so, would I find Xander and Papou with him?

My mind traveled back to last night, to Xander and the moment we shared in the park. What if that ID card wasn't fake?

What if Xander really was the Greek equivalent of CIA?

~ ~ ~

Morning happened. When it came it was sudden, like the smashing of a plate on a hard, marble floor.

Officially, I hadn't slept. Unofficially, I was sporting an interesting drool stain on my chin.

When I returned to Grandma's kitchen, my new phone was on the table. It was the newest incarnation of my old phone, and a few quick swipes showed that someone had taken the time to set everything up as it had been. Perks of the job?

Whatever. I didn't want them. What I wanted was Grandma back in her kitchen, baking Greek cookies. What I also wanted was my father.

I wanted a lot of things I couldn't have right now.

First thing's first: Text Xander. I shot off a message, asking where they were, if they were okay, when they'd be back.

When I was done the new phone chirped. Aunt Rita.

"The lawyers are here," she said.

"At the compound? I thought they were going to call."

"Mama pays them enough to make house calls."

"Okay," I said. "I'll be waiting."

I ran into the bathroom, splashed water into my face until I resembled the newly undead, which was a major improvement. My hair I coiled into a neat bun on top of my head. Clothes ... ugh. Could I pass the wrinkles off as ironic? In Portland—probably. Grandma was loaded, so maybe the lawyers would consider me eccentric instead of a slob.

The gate squealed. Company was here. I smoothed down my shirt and hoped for the best.

There were two people on Grandma's doorstep, both men. One was a suit; the other was a rumpled suit. He hadn't mastered the difficult art of wearing too many clothes during a Greek summer. They both carried briefcases. They asked if I was Katerina, and when I confirmed that I was they said they had news and asked if they could come in.

I opened the door wide. "Be my guest."

If they thought someone of Grandma's position in life required a fancier abode it didn't show on their faces. They struck me as cardboard cutouts of real people—no expressions except the ones they came with straight out of the box.

They were, they told me, partners at Samaras, Samaras, and Samaras. I offered coffee but that seemed to make them uncomfortable so I didn't push the issue.

No Wrinkles said, "The police aren't holding Kyria Makri because she's guilty of a crime, but because they think she's guilty of a crime. They believe she's responsible for a prison break in Larissa. The prisoner is one Stelios Dogas."

"Let me guess, they can hold her for twenty-four hours unless they file charges?"

Disclaimer: All my knowledge about the law came from television.

They swapped glances.

"No ..."

Also, all my knowledge about the law was American, and sometimes British, and not even remotely Greek, on account of how there's no CSI: Athens. Yet.

"… They can hold her until they are tired of holding her. The crime is serious, and Kyria Makri is …"

"The head of a criminal organization?" I offered, thinking I should probably save them from having to say it.

"A businesswoman," Wrinkles said.

"A businesswoman," No Wrinkles agreed.

"Since when is it a crime to be in business?" Wrinkles asked. The question had a rhetorical hook, so I shut up.

They looked at me, two unblinking sets of eyes.

No Wrinkles moved the conversation onward. "In the event that Kyria Makri does not return home, she has requested that you replace her as the head of her business."

"No."

No Wrinkles blinked. "It wasn't a question."

"Doesn't matter. My 'No' stands."

He sat his briefcase on the table, flipped its lid, dumped a stack of paperwork on the kitchen table.

Grandma's kitchen was tiny at the best of times, but the walls suddenly jumped another foot closer. They wouldn't stop until I was squeezed into the captain's chair. Next thing I knew, I'd be wearing black and hobbling around in my garden, listening to people whine about their cheating husbands. I'd be the one baking baklava in this cloying kitchen, while my friends back home lived lives of not-crime.

How many ways were there to tell everyone I didn't want the job? Two languages—I spoke two languages and neither was delivering the message.

"That is not an option. Even when Kyria Makri is released …"

"I know she's sick," I said.

No Wrinkles exchanged glances with Wrinkles. "We weren't aware Kyria Makri had shared her health status with you," Wrinkles said.

"She didn't. A serial killer told me." I pushed back my chair and hoped they'd get the message. They didn't. I knew this because they stayed seated, when what I really wanted was for them to, as the British put it, bugger off.

Forget what Jesus would do; these bespoke clowns were used to Grandma, so the question was: What would Grandma do?

She wouldn't let them stomp her like ripe grapes, that's what.

"I need you both to leave. Call me when there's news. No news? Don't call."

I held the screen door open. As far as hints went it was a big one. Lucky for them they snatched up the opportunity to exit gracefully. The papers vanished into the leather case. The lawyers stood. They shuffled to the open door, stooping slightly to duck beneath it. The house was built back in the day when tall was something they did in other countries.

"Don't worry," I told Wrinkles, "I wasn't judging you on the suit."

He looked bewildered. "What's wrong with my suit?"

I shook my head. "Nothing."

He fidgeted all the way to the arch. Last I saw of him he was tugging at his tie, trying to figure out if the suit was a problem he needed to solve.

What they had told me was basically nothing I didn't already know, but they'd bill Grandma anyway. At least I'd saved her some money by booting them out the door as quickly as possible.

There was no way around it: I needed to find Rabbit. If I turned him in then maybe they'd let Grandma go, putting an end to this nonsense about me taking over.

Starting point: Makria. I had BangBang to thank for that flash of inspiration. He—or she—had said the roots were deep, which I interpreted to mean someone in the village knew something useful.

All I needed was a metaphorical shovel.

Okay, and an X. I really needed an X. You can't go digging without an X marking the spot. Ask any pirate—except those Somali guys. Everyone knows you can't be a real pirate without a parrot. Without a parrot you're a garden-variety terrorist and thief. I needed that X. And if I looked at a map of Makria carefully, it was shaped like one.

~ ~ ~

The crowd had grown by two outside the gates. Only one of the faces was unfamiliar—a thin, pale man with an achromatic goatee and eyes the color of blue Gatorade. He was leaning against a grubby white car from a cold war spy movie.

"Who are you?"

He said nothing, pulled out a knife, ran his thumb over the bright edge.

Elias rolled his eyes. "That's Vlad. He is a Russian poser."

The knife's tip pointed at Elias. "I have cut hundreds of men with blade."

"It does not count when they're already dead," Elias said.

"They were not dead until I kill them."

Okay, so another assassin. Great. "Who do you work for?"

"Boris the Bear."

"A bear hired you?" Even the wildlife wanted me dead. Fabulous.

"Boris the Bear imports heroin," Elias told me.

"The best," Vlad said.

Mo made a face. "The best. Ha!"

Vlad turned those cold eyes of his on the Persian. "Where is camel? Did you fuck camel to death?"

"Your sister is unclean. I threw her out after she asked for money. Did you know she is a Russian whore? Like your mother, I bet."

This was going to end in a disemboweling, or worse, so I stomped over to the other new arrival.

"Why didn't you come in?" I asked Melas. He was in plainclothes, which amounted to shorts and a T-shirt. By the looks of it he didn't skip leg day at the gym. That or he ran. Probably *away* from women like me.

"Can't," he said. "I'm supposed to be following you."

"You're not going to assassinate me, are you?"

"And ruin the view?" He grinned. "Wherever you go, those pinheads from Thessaloniki want me to go."

"Well, that's great."

"Where are you going?"

The idea came to me like an unexpected flash of lightning. "To visit your mother."

"Jesus," he said.

"I have a feeling she'd scare Him, too."

Cleopatra poked her head out the Renault's window. "I can't stay. Can one of you guys text me if anything exciting happens before I get back?"

Ugh.

"Sure," Lefty said.

"Katerina!"

I turned around, spotted Marika waving. She was hurrying over in a pair of sneakers and loose gym wear. Draped over her shoulder was her oversized bag, carrying, no doubt, her insurance collection.

"Wait for me," she said and picked up the pace. When she reached me she said, "Look, I dressed for adventure today. If we have to run, I can run." She looked me up and down. "Why the dress and sandals? Can you run in those?"

"I'm not planning on running today." Although the way my days went that could change at any moment. "I'm going visiting."

"Who are we visiting?"

"Kyria Mela."

She made a face. "Yeesh. That woman scares me." She looked at Melas. "I am not even sorry for saying that."

Melas's mother scared me, too. "Maybe you can wait outside? Someone has to keep an eye on the goons."

She scanned the newest arrival, made a small sniffing sound. "Who is the new guy?"

"Vlad. He's Russian. Apparently he likes stabbing dead people."

Hands on hips she fixed her attention on Vlad. "What is wrong with you, eh? What did the dead do to you?" She turned back to me. "Sick. I remember when Greece used to be civilized."

My car took a hit when she vaulted over the side, no door required. She slapped on a pair of dark sunglasses. "I am ready for anything. Let's ride."

"Okay, so maybe I am not ready for this. You said I could wait outside, yes?"

Kyria Mela was in her front yard, dousing the entire place with water. If it could stand still it was getting the hose. I jiggled in case she didn't realize I wasn't inanimate. The day was already hot—surprise, surprise—but the water sucked out of Pelion's springs was icy even in mid-summer.

Kyria Mela looked me over. "You are back."

"You asked me to come for coffee."

"I remember now. Who are these people?"

I lobbed out the introductions. "And you know Marika and your son."

"What are they doing here?"

"Marika's my friend."

"And sidekick," Marika said. "We go on adventures together."

Kyria Mela gave her the hairy eyeball. "Hmm," she said.

"And your son is following me because the policemen from Thessaloniki, who took away my grandmother, gave him orders." I laid it on thick, with a trowel.

Mama Mela wasn't impressed. "What is wrong with all of you? And you, Nikos? You follow this poor girl, too?"

"Orders, Mama."

"Orders! Did I give you orders? Did God give you orders? Did your father?"

I grinned at him behind her back. I would be dead meat when he got me alone, but it was so worth the minor gloat.

"Mama," he said in a quiet voice. "Police orders. It's my job."

"Always I am very proud of you, Nikos. But not today." She grabbed my hand, pulled me into the shade of her hallway. "All of you stay out there."

"I will stay out here, too," Marika said in a loud voice.

"Oh, good, because you were not invited," the older woman said.

When the front door slammed, I was on the inside, while freedom was on the other side. For a moment I wasn't sure I shouldn't make break for it.

"I suppose you want to see him," Kyria Mela said.

I stood there blinking in the dim light for several seconds. Who did she mean? With four missing men in my life, it could have been any of them.

"Yes?" I finally managed.

"Your grandmother needed a place to hide Rabbit. I volunteered, of course." She led me down the hall, to the room where Melas and I had sipped coffee the other day before she read my cup.

"Help me," she said. Together we moved the table aside, then peeled back the patterned rug. For a country built on rock, people sure had a lot of basements around here. "This is temporary. He is moving on soon."

"Away from Greece or away from life?" Because with Grandma's crowd you never knew.

"All I know is what Katerina told me. She said he was moving on, and I was to help you if anything happened to her."

Sure enough, Rabbit was in the ground, crouched in what was one small evolutionary step up from a spider hole. He was in sweatpants and a tank top that should have been a misdemeanor.

"Are we going now?" He squinted up at us. "Because this is worse than prison."

"All he does is complain," Kyria Melas said. "He is lucky to be alive and out of prison, and what does he do? Complain, complain, complain. I do not know how he got even one woman to sleep with him and have his child, let alone dozens."

"Charm." Dogas peered up at me. "My plane ready? You want some sausage before I go?"

"What plane?" I conveniently sidestepped his second question, the way one avoids cow patties, if they can possibly help it. "There's no plane that I know of."

"*Gamo ti Panayia mou*! Then what are you doing here?" He yelped when Kyria Mela clipped his ear with her shoe.

"I came for coffee."

"She came for coffee," he muttered. "I thought you came to move me."

"I didn't know you were here until now!"

"You did not know?" Kyria Mela asked me.

"I didn't know."

She patted me on the shoulder. "The cup knew, that is all that matters."

Rabbit cleared his throat. It took a while. When he'd finally cleared the sticky debris he said, "Get me the hell out of here."

"You shitweasel. I trotted out one of my favorite compound words. "My grandmother is in police custody because of you."

"Did I tell her to break me out of prison? No. She did it on her own."

"Yeah, because she believed you—or whoever commissioned that box—knew something about my father's kidnapping."

"Your father's kidnapping." He made a sour face. "He was a criminal. He is still a criminal. If someone kidnapped him it is because he did something to deserve it."

"My father drives trucks. He moves bubble wrap and packing peanuts."

That may or may not have been true, given that I'd discovered Dad was out of the country, posing as an Italian, on at least one of his alleged long hauls. But I wasn't about to tell that to this clown.

Laughter rolled out of the old man. "Packing peanuts. Ha!"

A minute later I'd hauled him out of his hidey-hole and dumped him on the rug. It took a while, okay? I'm five-four and on the pathetic end of fit.

"Talk."

He folded his arms. "What do you want me to tell you, eh?"

"What do you know about my father?"

"More than you will ever know."

"Start with who kidnapped him."

"That I don't know. Could be anyone."

"All that matters to me right now is who has him and how I can get him back."

"You? Ha! You are a child. You cannot do anything if the people who have him do not want him to be found."

"Sounds to me like you know them." I looked at Kyria Mela, who was now holding a metal box that resembled a military-issue footlocker. "Does it sound to you like he knows them?"

"I think you are right," she said.

He slapped the air with one hand. "I am old man and until a few days ago I was in prison."

"Which is like the information hub for crime. Crime moves through prisons. Pull a string inside and people dance outside. I've seen movies," I said. "I know these things."

Kyria Melas had something to say. "This one will not talk, not without encouragement. He is too stubborn, too old. You want to open an oyster, you have to force it to open."

"Huh?" That bit of eloquence was from me.

The old guy cackled. "Poor little Katerina, you are surrounded by crime. You do not even know what this woman is."

"Used to be," Kyria Mela said. "I left that life behind a very long time ago. But for you I could make an exception."

"Crime is in the blood. It never goes away." He nodded to me. "You are standing beside one of Greece's finest torturers. The soviets tried to recruit her but she was too loyal. A Makris dog."

"Huh?" None of this was making sense. Kyria Mela was in the crime game?

"It is true," she said casually. "But that was before Nikos came along."

He pointed at her with his thumb. "Biggest joke in history, this one's son is a policeman."

"We've met," I said. My knees began to wobble. They'd been doing that a lot lately. "I need to sit."

"On the floor—you cannot fall off the floor. Put your head between your knees," Kyria Mela said.

Funny, I'd given her son that same piece of advice the other day.

My bones shook. I looked up at Rabbit, who had helped himself to a chair. "Who sent the boxes?"

Two palms up. "You keep asking, I keep not knowing. You see the problem?"

"I could pull one of his nails," Kyria Mela said. "Or snap the little finger. Then he will sing."

"No," I said. "No singing." Or screaming. Sitting outside in the yard were too many people with guns. Last thing I wanted was all of them blasting their way in here. And I didn't want Melas to discover his mother's secret the hard way. If she wanted to tell him, that was one thing, but no one likes hearing from a virtual stranger that their mother is secretly the tooth, nail, and waterboarding fairy. "Give me a name."

"I gave you a name."

"The Eagle."

"And there was an eagle, yes?"

"There was an eagle with another box—one you said you didn't make." I chewed on a hangnail, until Kyria Mela pulled my hand away.

"I will put hot pepper on it. That is what I did to my children."

No wonder they fled Makria.

Once more, with feeling: "Who commissioned the box?"

He opened his mouth. I held up my hand, five-fingered, not giving a toss if I was insulting him or not. "The real name."

"A favor for a favor."

"No favors. Give me the name—the real name—and I'll see about getting you out of here. That's it."

Kyria Mela stepped forward with her metal box of what I suspected was mean tricks. "Go wait outside, Katerina. If it is important to you I will get you your name."

I tried the standing thing again and failed. Dizziness washed over me. "Who commissioned the box, Kyrios Dogas?"

"He will kill me if I tell you!" the old man hissed.

Kyria Mela grabbed my arm. "Katerina, go."

"There's a policeman outside," I told Rabbit. "If you don't give me the name I'll tell him where you are. The cops can have you."

"Oh-ho-ho, already defying your grandmother, eh? What will she say about that?" His words were bold but his smirk was on shaky ground.

"She's not here, thanks to you, and while she's away I'm in charge. I don't like it, but that's what she wanted. So I'll do things as I see fit, including giving you a one-way ticket back to jail."

"She broke me out of prison for a reason."

"Yes, and you didn't deliver, so she did it for nothing. As far as I'm concerned, back you go. We have no use for you. *I* have no use for you."

It was cold but it was true. If he knew nothing, he was worthless. I was okay with sticking him in a police car, sending him straight back to the hell he'd come from.

The problem was Detective Melas.

Rabbit was here in his family's home. If I steered Melas toward the escaped prisoner, there was no way not to involve his mother.

There would be questions from higher ups. Difficult, potentially career-destroying inquiries.

I couldn't do that to Melas. He was one of the good guys—the genuinely good guys. What kind of person would I be if I dragged him down with me? Not too many days ago he was part of a four-man team that had saved my life. No way was I about to thank him by ruining his career.

So basically my threats were emptier than the US vaults holding Germany's gold. But I didn't want Rabbit to know that.

My body unfolded as I stood. I was doing my best to tack an extra foot onto five-four.

"We're done here," I said. "The police can have you."

Poker wasn't my game. As far as I knew I didn't have a bluff face. But I tried, as I stalked out of the room, to move like I meant to leave him here for the police. My breath caught and held.

"Wait."

I exhaled, pivoted, strode back into the room. I said nothing, raised my eyebrows.

He leaned forward in the chair. His knuckles gleamed white as his fingers bit into his knees. The ravines in his skin deepened. "You have no idea what you are asking. He is … he is my son!"

"Your son?" I echoed.

Two palms up. "What is a man to do?"

"Ungh," I said. Whatever I'd been expecting, it wasn't that. I dropped into one of Kyria Mela's fancy chairs. "Your son." I gnawed on that a moment, then looked him square in the eyes. "Which one?"

"The craziest one."

Of course. Which other one would it be? The crazy one is always the obvious candidate.

"Why?"

"Who knows? He didn't say, I didn't ask. He demanded I make him a box, and that was all." Something in his voice rang trueish. My gaze slid to the woman holding the metal box. She nodded almost imperceptibly.

"He is telling the truth," she said. "I know when a man is lying."

Probably she did.

I rubbed my temples. I'd never had a full-blown migraine, but there was one lurking nearby, waiting to squeeze my brain.

"What about the other boxes?"

"Maybe he made them himself, I don't know."

"Does he have a name—a real name?"

"Katerina … You don't know the trouble you bring on yourself. Do you hear that sound? It's the water coming for you. You will drown in this world."

"Good thing I can swim. Tell me his name. Please."

"I have already given you too much rope. No more."

"His name."

"Would your father give up your name so easily?"

He had me there. For all his recently discovered flaws, I knew my father would die rather than give up my name to someone who might wish me harm. For now I'd stand down, find another way into the fortress.

"I don't know what Grandma had planned for you. She obviously wanted you out of jail and alive, otherwise you wouldn't be here. So I'm maintaining the status quo until I get different orders or I figure out something better. Which," I added, "doesn't seem likely, given that I'm winging it." I turned to Kyria Mela. "Is it okay with you if he stays until it's safe to bring him back to the compound?"

She nodded.

I had one more question for the man known as Rabbit. "Are you really Papou's brother?"

He scoffed. "Not anymore. It has been a long time since we were anything. Fifteen years ago the bastard put me in prison. Once a man sends you to prison he is not your brother."

The sun was clawing its way higher, heating up the small room, even with its shutters latched. Threads of gold peeked through the gaps.

"Who brought him here?" I asked Kyria Mela, as we gravitated to the front door.

"The quiet one."

Xander.

He and Papou were still unaccounted for, so they were next on my must-find list. Xander hadn't replied to my text.

"Are you going to …" She gave me a look loaded with meaning.

"Tell your son?"

"Yes."

"No."

"Are you sleeping with him?"

"Your son?"

"Yes."

"No. Not now, not ever." Unless I did. Which I wouldn't. Not while the Family was taking bets, and not while we were on opposite sides of the morality fence.

It was for his own protection.

~ ~ ~

Thirty-six hours after Grandma had been brutally hauled away by the Hellenic Police, my family was driving me to drink.

Katerina, should we kill a drug dealer? What if the drug dealer is stealing from us? What if the same drug dealer is stealing from us and calling us names? Katerina, what was the name of that tantric sex guy?

"Sting," I said.

"Stink," Stavros repeated. His thumbs worked like miniature pistons on his phone.

"Why?"

"Trivia game."

"The drug dealer isn't a stupid game," Takis said. "Or the stealing."

"What about the name-calling, is that real?" I asked.

"Sure, that could be real."

Marika snorted.

Takis turned on her. "Why are you here? I gave you four children and a house to clean—go clean them."

"The house is clean, no thanks to you, and your children are in the pool."

It was true, their kids were in the pool, not far away from where we were all sitting, under one of the courtyard's grapevine trellises. It was early afternoon and the boys were practicing their drowning techniques. Fortunately, none of them showed any talent in that direction; too buoyant.

"Rabbit's kids," I said, mulling over the morning. "Anyone here know any of them?"

"Sure," Stavros said, not looking up from his trivia game. "Rigas Dogas owns a *kafeneio* in Agria. It's on the promenade."

My left eyelid fluttered. "Why didn't anyone tell me?"

Takis busted out laughing. "Did you ask? No. How can anyone give you answers if you don't ask questions?"

"Why are you such an asshole?" I asked him

Marika had a smug look on her face. "Because I will not do a thing he wants me to do."

"*Skasmos*," her husband said, telling her to shut up.

"What thing?" I asked.

"Don't you tell her or I will—"

Marika's gaze landed on him with an almighty THUNK. It was like watching the space shuttle dock successfully at the International Space Station. "You will what?"

"Take away your allowance."

His wife sucked in her breath.

Stavros grabbed my arm. "We should leave before she explodes."

Marika shot up out of her chair. "No! You are not leaving—I am leaving. Katerina, let us go. Takis, you can watch the boys for once. It will do you good."

Like a summer squall, she moved off in search of a new piece of earth to rain upon. Unfortunately, she was pulling me along with her.

"Where are we going?"

"You are going to see a man. Me, I am coming along for the coffee."

~ ~ ~

It was 2 PM when I killed the Beetle's engine outside the *kafeneio*. Parking was easy pickings; the Greeks had scurried back home to their beds, along with the smarter tourists. Not the rest of them. They'd paid for sunshine and they meant to get their euros' worth of UVA and UVB.

Inside, a couple of baristas were wiping down tables. The manager was stooped over a small laptop, tapping numbers into the keypad. He didn't look up as Marika and I pushed through the door.

"You want a *frappe*?" she asked me. "Because I am getting a *frappe*."

"Make it two," I said.

I helped myself to the chair across from the manager.

"Rigas Dogas?"

"Who's asking?" He looked up at last, grunted. "You."

"Have we met?"

"I read the paper."

"I don't," I said. "It's full of rubbish and unflattering pictures."

He went back to his laptop. "What do you want?"

"I'm looking for your brother."

"I have a lot of brothers and sisters. I don't know where any of them are."

"The one with the eagle."

"Don't know him. Don't know most them."

"They say you do." *They* didn't say that, but *they* might have if I'd asked.

He slapped down the lid of his laptop. The table shook. "Then they are lying to you. Go away, I'm a busy man."

"I want to, believe me, but your brother keeps sending me gifts."

His eyes met mine. "What kind of gifts?"

"Body parts."

Horror skittered across his face, then vanished. "I don't know him, and now I don't want to know him."

"Your family is weird," I said. "If I had siblings out there I'd want to meet them."

"Not me." He tilted his chin up then down. "I know what my father is. I know what my brother is. Me, I live a quiet, honest life. I own this *kafeneio*. I sell coffee—good coffee."

Over by the counter, Marika was sucking on a straw. "It is good coffee," she agreed.

"Who is that?" he asked.

"Her unofficial sidekick," Marika said.

"So your brother is a criminal?" I asked Rigas.

For a split second he looked stricken. He'd stepped in doo-doo. "I don't know anything."

Yeah, right. "Do you know where I can find him?"

"Still in prison with our father? I don't know!"

Holy moly! More than one jailbird in the family?

"Your father isn't in prison. He broke out."

His eyes bugged out. "What?"

"I thought you read the paper."

"Mostly I look at the pictures," he said. "The news is too depressing."

He had a valid point. "Your father broke out and I don't think your crazy brother is in prison either. Not if he's sending me body parts. Do you have any idea where I can find him?"

"What is with women? You are crazy. You ask the same questions over and over, expecting different answers. How can I give you different answers if the questions are the same? I can't! How do you live with yourself, being so illogical? The only sane woman is my wife, and I have to say that, otherwise she will cut off my balls."

"Do you have issues with women?"

"Of course I have issues with women—you are women! You live to torture men. We are not tidy enough. We want too much sex. We don't want enough sex. If we don't bring flowers we don't love you. If we bring flowers it's because we have done something wrong. 'Take out the garbage. Bring in the garbage.' Sometimes you say it when it is not even garbage day, to see if we will jump."

"My father takes out the garbage, but it's always his idea."

He reopened his laptop and began jabbing at the numbers again. "No it's not—guaranteed. He's afraid of his wife."

"She's dead."

"Then he is afraid she will haunt him and nag about garbage from beyond the grave," he muttered without lifting his head. "Go away, now. I can't tell you anything else."

"Can't or won't?"

He lifted his head. His mouth opened to argue.

Then something went *BANG!* Glass shattered. Rigas slumped sideways, the laptop smashed as it belly-flopped on the marble-tiled floor. A red hole had appeared where his ear used to be. The ear itself had stuck to the tabletop. A bloody lake began to spread across the floor, its source on the other side of his head.

I hit the floor and scooted backwards, out of the line of sight.

My body shut down, but my brain couldn't quit staring down at the dead man. He'd gone from living, breathing human being to a corpse in under a second. How could that happen?

Nearby, the baristas were shrieking. My throat hurt, so it was possible I was screaming, too, but I'd mentally blocked it out. On the other side of the glass, across the street, the smattering of tourists were shouting and running. Obviously not their idea of a good time. I couldn't see them, but the sound of panicked shoes pelting blacktop and cement is universal. The two baristas fled through the front door, which struck me as ridiculous: they were bolting toward the origin of the gunshot. I peered through the window as best as I could without getting my head shot clean off my shoulders. Nobody else appeared to be hurt, and I couldn't see a shooter.

Marika pushed two *frappes* into my hands. She knelt beside the dead man.

"My Virgin Mary!" she said, wide-eyed. "I have never seen anyone shot before. Afterwards, yes, but never the shooting! She stared at him. "I would ask if you have a *servietta* but it is too late, he's dead."

Maxi pads. I remembered Melas mentioning the usefulness of sanitary products, when we were rifling through Dad's former best friend's apartment, only a handful or so days back. On shaky legs, I stumbled sideways, plopped down on a chair out of the red flood zone. I sat the two iced coffees down, pulled out my new phone, dialed Melas.

When I told him what had happened he swore. "Get down and stay where you are."

"I think the shooter's gone," I said.

"Stay down. Someone will be right there."

"Why aren't you following me?"

But he'd already hung up.

Huh. So much for tailing me. What had happened to scrape the hounds off my butt?

And where was my smallish mob of assassins? They'd melted away at the first—and only—gunshot, it looked like. I wondered if one of them was responsible.

I dismissed that theory immediately. If one of them had taken the shot the others would have pounded him into the concrete. No one wanted to miss out on their bounty. Still, when assassins flee it's eerily reminiscent of the way birds and animals take a long, fast hike before an earthquake strikes.

Less than a minute later, sirens began to wail in the distance. They were closing in on the *kafeneio* fast. Another minute and they were screeching to a stop, lights swirling, sirens howling. Two cops cars, with an ambulance riding their rear bumper. Melas wasn't among them.

Beside me, Marika hit the floor with a thud. It took a split second for the absence of gunfire to register, but that didn't stop my heart from freaking out.

I crouched down beside her. "Marika?"

She opened one eye. "I have never seen someone shot before."

"That's what you said."

"I realized my husband shoots people, like that shooter did."

Oh boy. Think fast. "I don't think he does it from far away like that."

"Do you think?"

Takis struck me as shoot-a-person-in-the-back-up-close kind of guy. "Shh, the police are coming. Don't say anything about Takis shooting people."

She closed her eye. "I can do that."

"*Gamo ti Panayia mou*," the first cop through the door said. He was a walking barrel that had rolled in a police uniform. There was a small, greasy *tzatziki* stain on his shirt. "I remember you," he said, pointing at me. "You're the one who kicked all that stuff off Melas's desk."

"Maybe I did, maybe I didn't."

"You did. I was there."

Now I remembered him. He'd hauled Penka away, that first day in the police station. He'd been wearing a *tzatziki* stain then, too.

"Okay, so that was me."

He scoped out dead Rigas on the floor. "You kill him?"

"No!"

The other cops were outside, separating witnesses and gawkers into separate piles. They seemed normal, not like gunmen, but what did I know? Marika looked like someone's mother—which she was—and yet she carried enough firepower on our adventures to sink a smallish submarine. So appearances could be dirty, rotten liars.

"You see my problem," Stained Shirt said. "I'm looking at a dead guy, then I'm looking at a mobster's grandkid and—" He looked at Marika. "Who are you?"

"Who am I? Nobody. I am a woman drinking *frappe*."

"You don't have a *frappe*."

"That is because she took them." She pointed to me.

Now wait a minute, I never took any—

I looked down at my hands. Sure enough, I was holding two *frappes*. That explained why my hands were cold. I'd figured it was shock. I shoved one at Marika, who began sucking on the straw with a '*See? I told you*' look on her face.

Stained Shirt shook his head, probably out of a desire to clear away the feeling that he'd stepped into the Twilight Zone. "Okay," he said. "Let's start from the beginning. What happened?"

I gave it to him from the top, minus the potentially incriminating details. Unfortunately that left me with a lopsided story. I had come in, talked briefly to Rigas Dogas, then a gunman shot him in the head. That sounded flimsier than plastic wrap, even to me.

Stained Shirt groaned and shoved his notepad back into his shirt pocket. "Tell you what," he said. "I'm going to hand you over to Detective Melas. You're more of a headache than I want or need."

"That seems fair," I told him.

Another cop car rolled up to the curb. Melas. He shot a glance at the shattered window, then moseyed over to the uniforms talking to witnesses. He was in plainclothes again today, flat-front trousers and a button-down shirt he hadn't bothered to tuck in. He'd rolled up the sleeves. Somehow he managed to blend dressy and casual and make it look like he fell off the cover of *Delicious Bad Boys Magazine*. Too bad ninety-nine percent of my brain was occupied by, oh, the dead guy on the ground.

Poor Rigas Dogas.

After a few moments, Melas broke away from his *compadres* and moseyed into the coffee shop. He looked down at the dead guy, then steered me outside.

"You okay?"

I shoved my sunglasses onto the bridge of my nose. "I want to puke on your shoes, does that answer your question?"

He gave me a funny look, inched out of the splash zone. "Witnesses are saying the shooter was some weirdo with a bird on his shoulder."

"An eagle?"

"How did you know?"

"Lucky guess."

He raised an eyebrow. "I'll get it out of you one way or another."

"What are my choices?"

He leaned in close. "*Now* you're flirting with me? Your timing is—"

"You wish," I said. "If I was flirting with you there'd be no mistaking it. I want to know what my options are, that's all." Because Melas had a history—well, not him, but his mother definitely had a history of using brute force methods of getting information out of people, and there was a good chance she'd passed the gene down to her son. So I thought it was fair to ask what my options were, before the torture started.

He stared at me. He did intensity almost as well as Xander. I wanted to crumple like a tin can.

"Kat …"

"Oh, all right. The guy with the eagle, I think his eagle was the one that delivered the second box."

"Why do I have a feeling you know who he is?"

"He's Rabbit's crazy son."

"Who's the guy in the coffee shop?"

"Also Rabbit's son."

"Tough family."

"Different mothers. Must run on the father's side"

"Do I want to know why you were in Rigas Dogas' coffee shop?"

"We were getting coffee."

He looked at me.

"Okay, Marika was getting coffee while I asked him questions."

"What questions?"

"Where his brother was, for starters. I had no idea they were … I'm not sure 'estranged' is the right word."

"What did Rigas say?"

"He denied any knowledge of his brother, beyond the basics. He even thought his brother might be in jail with their father."

"Stay there," he said. He walked over to the water's edge, made a phone call. He swaggered back a moment later.

"He was," Melas said. "Until a week ago."

"Did he break out, too?"

He shook his head. Very not-Greek of him. "He did his time so they let him go. Assault and battery."

"Let me guess, he was in Larissa's prison."

Nod. "Blood with blood."

"So he commissioned the box from his father before he got out, and he made the second one himself … why?"

"Maybe he likes you."

"I'd rather he pulled my pigtails or something."

"Pigtails?"

I bunched my hair into two fists. "Pigtails."

"Mmm," he said, in something dangerously close to a growl. "I like that."

I let my hair fall back into position. "Forget it." Too bad I didn't want to forget it. I'd conjure up that hunger on his face when I was alone, and relive it over and over. Stupid hormones.

"You're not the kind of woman a guy forgets without the help of amnesia." Then he flipped the switch and went back to business. "I'm guessing he sent the first box, too, since that's the one he commissioned."

"That seems like a safe bet. But why?"

We stood there for a moment, metaphorically scratching our heads. Melas in cop mode was intense, focused. He was granite and steel. Cold things. I couldn't help wanted to put my hands on him and warm him up.

"Nobody else has turned up missing a heart or … or …"

"Penis," I said.

He shot me a look. "Organ. So it's probably also a safe bet that he's responsible for the murders of three middle-ranking criminals. No sign of Harry Harry's eyes?"

I shook my head, clinging to my American body language. Then I remembered something. "I thought you were supposed to be following me."

"The guys from Thessaloniki called off the dogs. They found Rabbit."

Cold water poured through my veins. "Where?"

"Kala Nera."

Kala Nera—Good Waters—was one of the Pagasetic Gulf's coastal villages. It sat about a half hour's drive southeast of here, if you drove like a normal person. Greeks could shave the journey to fifteen minutes or fewer.

"Does that let Grandma off the hook?"

Some morsel of information was caught behind his teeth.

"What?" I asked him suspiciously.

"He's dead. He washed up on the beach. A bunch of kids had been using him as a raft."

My first reaction was to make a face. Greek kids did weird things for entertainment. Then my second reaction—the sensible one—kicked in. How could Rabbit be dead? Yesterday he'd been at the bottom of a hole in Melas's childhood home. How had he turned into a piece of driftwood so quickly? My stomach turned a shade more sour.

"Do you think it was his son?"

"I think a lot of people wanted Rabbit dead, but his son is top of the list."

"What's his name, the crazy son?"

"Periphas. Periphas Dogas." He was staring at me like he expected me to make an instant connection.

I didn't—at least not until I pulled out my phone and hit the Internet. The name was vaguely familiar.

"The king Zeus turned into an eagle," I said. "His mother must have been a hippy."

He nodded. "Apparently Periphas took the name personally. His records show he has an eagle tattooed on his back. The wings extend across his arms."

"The man takes his mythology seriously. So what now? Wait—they found Rabbit. Does this mean Grandma gets to come home?"

"She orchestrated and implemented a prison break. I don't think they'll be letting her go anytime soon, even without solid proof. I'm sorry." To his credit, he did look sorry. He liked Grandma, even if he didn't approve of her career choices. Good thing he didn't know about his mother's past.

Kyria Mela. Yikes. How had Rabbit managed to escape her care?

"I have to go," I said. "Things to do." Like checking on his mother.

"You okay?"

"*Frappe*," I said. "Busting to pee."

"Uh huh …"

Did he look like he believed me? That was a negative.

I decided to play the frail damsel card. Desperate times and all that. I was, after all, about to do a good deed. "I'm from Portland, not Detroit. I'm not used to all this death."

"They've picked up since you got here."

"Confirmation bias," I said in English, mostly because I didn't know the Greek words.

"What?"

"Confirmation bias." I spelled it out for him. "Google it. In the meantime I'm going to lie down." I stopped short of pressing the back of my hand to my forehead. I wanted to seem delicate, not crazy.

I trotted back to Marika, who was hammering Stained Shirt with stain removal advice. Poor guy, he looked dazed. Marika could be a human tornado. Good thing he didn't know what she was hauling around in that big bag over her shoulder.

"Ready for another adventure?" I asked her.

"Are we going to watch another murder?"

"Probably not."

She thought about it for a moment. "Everything is kind of a downer after you've seen a murder."

I thought that was a good thing, but then I didn't have four kids with a henchman, so what did I know?

She pointed at Stained Shirt. "Work the soap into the stain, then rinse with vinegar."

"Rinse with vinegar," he said tonelessly. "Work the soap."

We went out to the Beetle. Paramedics were loading the dead *kafeneio* owner into the back of the ambulance. There was still no sign of my assassins. I wondered what they'd seen—if anything. Not that it really mattered now that the identity of the gunman wasn't a secret.

"*Ay-yi-yi*!" Marika yelped.

I peered in. There was a wooden box on the driver's seat. This one was smaller than the others, about the right size to hold a couple of eyeballs.

"Okay," I said, thinking fast. "Don't squeal. Get into the car casually."

"But—"

"No 'but.' Not yet. I'm going to tell Melas about the box, but I need to go to Makria first, without him knowing." I shoved the box under my seat, trying not to think that I was probably sitting on Harry Harry's eyeballs.

"Okay. That sounds like a good plan." She threw back her head and fake laughed. "We could be Thelma and Louise. I am Thelma, you are Louise."

I couldn't remember which was which, so I wasn't sure if her comparison was on the planet of accurate. "You know they die at the end, right?"

"You don't know that. All you see is them driving off the cliff. They could have lived."

"Probably not."

"I want to believe they lived."

"That cliff was the Grand Canyon!"

She gave me a knowing smile. "We are arguing because we didn't touch red the other day."

~ ~ ~

We bickered all the way to Makria, until I cut the engine in the small parking lot outside the village. Surprisingly, apart from a tour bus and the Peugeot we had the lot to ourselves. Still no sign of my assassins. Or Cleopatra.

"Where are we going?" Marika wanted to know.

When I told her she wagged her finger. "No, no, no. You see her, I am going to have another *frappe*, and maybe a little cake."

She rushed off toward the village square, leaving me to face Kyria Mela by myself. I trudged up to her tidy cottage, but there was no answer when I knocked. So I tried it Greek-style, standing in her yard, calling her name.

A neighbor stuck her curler-speckled head over the fence. "She's at the church. Go and you will find her there."

If the village square or promenade is the heartbeat of a Greek village, then the church is its conscience. Although, I wasn't sure that was the case with Saint Catherine's. The priest, Father Harry, was firmly on Team Grandma, and he'd allowed her to have the church bugged. If Kyria Mela was in church, spilling her secrets aloud during prayer, then it wouldn't be long until the helicopters landed in Makria's village square and airlifted her away.

I hurried down the hill, on a mission to tighten her loose lips—if they were loose. This was a woman whose hair didn't dare move, in case she whacked it with a hairbrush. I turned right at the crossroads, rushed into Saint Catherine's, panting.

Kyria Mela was lighting candles, pressing their bottoms into the candle stand's shallow sand pit. Her mouth was moving a mile a minute. The ear on the other end of the conversation belonged to Father Harry.

Her mouth stopped when she saw me.

Father Harry whipped around. "Katerina!" he boomed.

Everything about the priest was jolly. He was Santa Claus in a black cassock and matching *skoufos*—the little black hat Greek priests wear. Could I trust him? Who knew? But I liked him anyway. Who doesn't like Santa Claus?

"What news, Katerina?" he asked. His voice dropped to a loud whisper. "What news of your grandmother?"

"The lawyers are doing what they can." I tried to give Kyria Mela a meaningful glance without Father Harry catching on. "Did you hear, the police found that escaped prisoner in Kala Nera this morning."

"Back to prison with that one, then, eh?" the priest said.

"Uh, not exactly. He's too busy being dead."

Only one of the two was surprised, and it was Kyria Mela. That I hadn't expected. A piece of me had suspected if Rabbit was dead then Kyria Melas could have been the person who made him that way. Not the dominant piece, but definitely a piece the size of a chocolate square.

"Dead!" she exclaimed. "How is that possible?"

"I don't know," I said. "This morning he washed up on the beach in Kala Nera." I gave her a look I hoped she'd interpret as *Don't say anything, the church is bugged*, and I think maybe she got the message because her lips tightened into thin white lines. Whatever her plan, whatever her orders, something had gone wrong, because in her mind Rabbit wasn't supposed to be dead. The last time she'd seen him he'd been alive, and she had every expectation that he'd remain that way until it was his time to go.

Father Harry made a small noise. "That man is God's problem now. He will face our Maker and our Maker will decide what is to be done with him."

He was wrong. Rabbit was my problem. He was supposed to be kept alive, but he died on my watch. And as long as they were holding Grandma, he'd continue to be my problem. Alive, there was a chance he could have been useful somehow. But now … there was no way they'd believe the Family had nothing to do with his death.

I wasn't entirely convinced of Team Grandma's innocence either.

"Kyria Mela," I said, giving her the *Let's get out of here* eyes. "Could you read my cup please?" It was a lie, of course. I didn't want her reading my cup again—ever. But I had to get her out of the church somehow.

Father Harry groaned. "What did I tell you about divining the future? It is against the church." It took me a moment to realize he wasn't speaking to me. "If God had meant us to know the future he would have given us the capability of foresight. Reading cups is the devil's work."

Kyria Mela grabbed my arm. "Yes, yes, and I remember a time when you came to me to ask if the church would take you. You did not say no to the cup then, eh?"

"It is a sin!"

"I read my cup this morning," she said to the priest. "It told me you would die. An accident. A fall from the dome while you were cleaning the cross."

"I do not clean the cross. The Greek Orthodox Church has a maintenance team."

"You fell from the cross. The cup never lies. I saw you splattered on the ground. Hundreds of tourists were taking photographs. Some were taking selfies with your corpse. And the video of your fall became the most-watched video in the YouTube history."

Father Harry scurried to the rear of his church, muttering the whole way. He vanished through the back door.

"Priests," she said. "They are worse than people on new diets. Everything is a sin, unless the Bible says otherwise. Even then they are picky about what they choose to believe."

"This is why I don't go to church."

It was part of the reason, anyway. My beef with God had more to do with my mother's premature death from cancer. I'd prayed and prayed and He was like, *Shh, I'm in Cancun, helping teenage girls go wild without their parents finding out.*

She smacked the back of my head. "You should always go to church. How else will you know what is going on in town?"

Like everyone else she had automatically assumed I was a new and permanent stick of furniture. No one seemed to understand that I'd jump the first plane out of here as soon as I had Dad back.

Dad. Somehow his kidnapping was all tangled up in this wad of criminal insanity. Funny, only last week I had assumed it would be easier to hunt for him with Grandma out of the way. Now she was someone else I was worried about.

Over Kyria Mela's shoulder I saw Marika sucking on a *frappe* straw while she chatted to a tangle of tourists. Whether they could understand her or not wasn't clear. If they couldn't, it wasn't slowing her down. She glanced over at me and went to wave, then snapped her hand back to her side when she realized whom I had for company.

"When did Rabbit leave the hole in your floor?" I asked Kyria Mela. "Did someone come to get him?"

"A man came to get him last night. Some creep with an eagle on his shoulder. It shit down his back and he did not care. What kind of man is this?"

Rabbit's son, that's who.

The sun was fierce but it couldn't stop the invisible yeti using me to wipe its feet. Goosebumps punched their way to the surface of my skin.

"Did Rabbit say anything?"

"Only that he was surprised the man had not come sooner. Dogas went peacefully. We did not know the man wished him harm. Even if there had been a problem, my husband and I are not equipped for any kind of battle. We keep a peaceful home, except for my old tools. My husband does not know I have them. I promised to give them up."

"Did he work for the Family, too?"

"No. He is a good man, like Nikos."

She took off in the direction of her house, leaving me at the crossroads. I wandered over to see what Marika was up to.

"Thank Zeus," she said. "I think these people are looking for sex. They keep asking for *poutsa*. The Family does not do prostitution so I don't know what to tell them. What do I know about prostitutes? Nothing." She frowned. "Or maybe they're asking about that dick in the box you got. Say, what happened to that?"

"*Kokoretsi*," I said.

Her mouth dropped open. She made a small whimpering sound, like somebody crushed their heel on her foot. Which gave me time to ask her three new friends if they needed help. Both men and the woman were paper white, with painful looking red patches where the sun had smacked them. They wore a similar uniform of loose T-shirts, baggy shorts, and what we called fanny packs back home. Their faces were the kind one saw in commercials advertising products that end with -wurst.

The woman of the trio, who spoke in thickened English, told me they were looking for a butcher's shop. I pointed her in the direction of a shop with animal carcasses swinging in the front window. It wasn't hygienic, but it was Greece. Their heads bobbed with gratitude and off they went in search of—much to Marika's relief—meat.

"Did you get the information you needed from the scary woman?"

"The son came for Rabbit last night."

"The one with the eagle?"

I nodded. We hoofed it back to the car and zipped back to the compound. It wasn't until I stopped outside massive garage that I remembered the box stowed under the driver's seat.

"Crap," I said. "I need to call Melas. I promised him I'd let him know if another box showed up." I fired off a text message and told him about the delivery.

My phone rang. "Where are you?" he asked.

"At the compound."

"Stay right there. And don't open the box."

As if I could. For that I needed Tomas, and I wasn't sure he was around.

Takis emerged from the arch's shadow. He didn't look happy.

Marika groaned. "I have to go—my baby needs his diaper changed. Let me know if you are going on more adventures, okay?"

~ ~ ~

Papou was in the kitchen when I carried the box back to Grandma's shack. Yes, Melas had told me to stay where I was, but didn't think it was a literal command. It would have been torture. The flagstones were engaged in a tennis game with the sun, and standing between them only meant I would wind up baked. Grandma's place had walls, but it also had shade.

"What's a guy got to do to get killed around here?" he said when I walked in.

"Join the Dogas family?" Argh! I slapped my forehead. "Sorry," I said. "That was insensitive. I'm sorry about your brother."

"What's insensitive about it? My brother was a prick. He lived like a prick, now he's dead like a prick."

"Kids were using him as a raft," I said.

"Huh. I didn't hear that part. They left out the best bit. What good are sources if they leave out the good parts?"

I sat the box on the kitchen counter, opened the refrigerator, poured a tall glass of chilled water. "Drink?" I asked him.

"Only if it is coffee. Do you know how to make Greek coffee?"

"Sure," I said. I'd never made it before, but how hard could it be?

Five minutes later, the old man was grimacing. "*Gamo ti mana sou*, what is this?"

"Coffee?"

"Weak. It's like a *mouni* without hair."

He was lucky I'd made him a cup of coffee at all, and now he was complaining?

"Is Xander back, too? Where have you guys been? Did you know the police took Grandma?"

"How do I know where Xander is, eh? What am I, his babysitter? He is a grown man. Probably he's with a woman. I wish I was with a woman. Give me the phone."

I passed him the house phone's receiver.

"Shit," he said. "I am so old I forgot all the phone numbers I used to know. Let's go get your car. You can take me for a drive."

"What for?"

"So I can look up some of my old flames, that's what. Some of them are dead, but a few are still kicking."

"You want me to drive you to a booty call?"

"Of course not. I already told you I can't remember the numbers. My plan is to show up uninvited and surprise them."

"Can't. Detective Melas is coming over."

"Bah!" He slapped the table. "Even that *malakas* can get laid, but me? I used to be a stallion!"

The conversation was taking a gross turn. Then the rest of his words sank in.

"I'm not sleeping with Melas," I yelped.

"Maybe not, but you will be."

"Will not."

"You have to! I put money on it! Don't tell your grandmother."

"Wait—there's a pool going?" Heads were going to roll, and in this Family that wasn't a metaphor. My eyes narrowed. "Who started it?"

But I already knew, and he confirmed it when he said, "Takis."

I called Marika. “Is it okay if I kill your husband?”

“Only if I can help,” she said. “I have never killed my husband before.”

Stavros came through the kitchen door. “Whose husband are you killing? If you need a henchman I can help.”

“Takis,” I said. “And probably I’m going to torture him first for being a little weasel.”

“I know torture. Only the basics, but I’m learning. Baboulas tells me I might be able to work my way up.”

“If anyone is getting killed around here, I’m first,” Papou said. “You want to practice your killing on me?” he asked Stavros.

Stavros made a face. “Baboulas would kill me.”

“All this killing …” Papou slapped his hands on the table. “What’s a man got to do?”

“You could join my cooking class,” Stavros told him. “We get a discount if we refer someone. We’re doing puffer fish in a few weeks. If someone screws up it could kill you.”

“I know a guy who tried that,” Papou said. “Didn’t work. Now he’s got superpowers.”

Melas was the next one through the door. “Is that Kyrios Bides? He doesn’t have superpowers. He just thinks he’s invisible. We keep picking him up for peeping through windows and flashing at widows.” He nodded to the counter. “That the box?”

Papou snickered. “He’s talking about you,” he told me.

17

Litsa wasn't home. Luckily for us, all four of her sons were. They were systematically working their way through the pantry. The eldest boy, the spitting image of his mother, minus the fake boobs, was hacking a boule loaf into chunks, using a cleaver. Tomas was at the kitchen table, head bent over a pile of uncooked macaroni. One-fingered, he was shifting them into patterns, making macaroni art. I wasn't an expert or anything, but the pattern looked mathematical.

The middle two boys howled like a pair of monkeys.

"Mama went out," said the eldest boy. "So we're cooking."

"Do you know how to cook?" I asked him.

"No, but the voices in my head know. They're giving me instructions." He swung at the loaf again. A piece jumped across the room. Tomas snapped out his hand and caught it, without so much as a blip in his pattern making.

"Voices?" I asked.

"They're people who live in my head. They've got nowhere else to go."

"Have they always been there?" Melas asked him.

"Have you tried electroshock therapy?" I said, trying to be helpful. "Sometimes the voices move out after you do that."

"He doesn't have voices in his head," one of the monkeys said. "He's a *skatofatsa*."

A shit face.

My mouth fell open. It would have hit the floor but it couldn't reach—not while I was standing. I held out the box to Tomas. Said, "Help."

He scrambled out of his chair and grabbed the box. "Oh boy, another one!" Fifteen seconds later he handed it back. "Whoever is making these, he needs to branch out. They're too easy. Periphas. He was a king, until Zeus turned him into an eagle. I don't know which I'd like more …"

"King," his older brother said.

"Eagles," the monkeys ooked. "Then we could peck people's eyes out."

Charming.

Melas and I fled in case the animals decided we were next on the menu. I threw a worried glance over my shoulder—I wasn't sure they wouldn't hunt us down.

I pushed Melas into Grandma's house, slammed the screen door and pressed my back against it, gasping. Maybe I'd take Jimmy Pants up on his offer. Not being fit was making me look bad.

"I am going to win," Papou crowed. "I can feel it. Look, she is already panting."

"This isn't a sex thing," I said. "We were almost chased by wild animals."

"Litsa's boys, eh? The eldest three are monsters, but the youngest one has potential to be a human being."

Melas' gaze bounded from Papou to me and back again. "Win what?"

"It's nothing," I said.

"The bet. We—"

I leaped across the room, clamped my hand over his mouth.

"Nothing. No bet. He's got late-stage syphilis. It's making him crazy."

Papou licked my hand. Argh! I wiped the old man goo on his face.

"See?" I said. "Crazy like a fox."

They both looked at me. "American foxes are crazy?" Melas asked.

Oh boy. I wasn't in the mood to explain that saying. So I said, "Only the old, crusty ones. Let's open the box."

Melas gave me a look like he wasn't done wanting to know about the bet, but he sat the box in the middle of the table. He took a deep breath. "Ready?"

Without waiting for an answer, he lifted the lid.

Inside, sitting in a red satin nest, was a pair of eyes. Dark brown, with a hint of too many years on the bottle. If only Eagle Boy had taken the Pontic Greek's liver instead; pickled products handled the heat better.

"Huh," Papou said.

We looked at him.

"It's a little bit anticlimactic when you can guess what's inside."

Anticlimactic? Ha! Tell that to my gag reflex. It was trying to grab ahold of my stomach contents, but apart from the *frappe* I was empty.

Harry Harry's, I presumed, eyeballs were staring at the ceiling. They didn't blink, didn't swivel. The pupils were cloudy and dull without life to animate them. My eyes began to water in solidarity. They weren't crying, per se, but they had a good imagination. They knew gouging had been involved.

"Okay," Melas said. Unlike the penis, the eyes didn't seem to be bothering him in the slightest. "I'm going to take these back to the station. Hopefully this time they won't end up in the *kokoretsi*."

The color bled out of Papou's cracks. "What?"

~ ~ ~

Melas asked me to walk him back to his car. We left a retching Papou in the kitchen.

"He took that well," I said.

"You went into a lot of detail. Are you sure that's how they make *kokoretsi*?"

"You don't know?"

"I'm an eater, not a cook."

"Then yeah, that's how they make it." Truth be told, I had no idea. I'd embellished for Papou's sake. He almost barfed when I mimed stretching and winding the organ onto the spit.

"Jesus," Melas said.

"Xander's still missing," I said.

"Xander's fine. He's that kind of man."

"What kind of man is that?"

"A survivor. Wherever he is, the other guy is losing."

"You know him well?"

"Nobody knows him well. But I know him enough. He'll turn up."

"But if you had to guess where he is?"

"Thessaloniki."

"Thessaloniki?" I thought about it. "He's with Grandma."

"My guess is he's up there in the shadows, making sure nobody hurts her."

I though about what she had told me about his past. "He's devoted to her, isn't he?"

"She raised him. He'll never forget that."

If Melas knew about the plastic card Xander carried on him, he didn't leak a word.

We'd already reached the driveway. Melas's car was parked between the fountain and arch. The front windows were down. He put the boxed eyes on the passenger-side floor, out of the sun.

"What are you going to do with them?"

"Check if they're Harry Harry's. Dust the box for prints. If we find any I won't be surprised if they match Periphas Dogas." He gave my body an approving look. "You going to tell me about that bet?"

"What bet? There's no bet."

"There's a bet." He slid behind the wheel, smirk firmly plastered on his lips, the delicious bastard.

"No bet. You're imagining things."

"There's a bet," he repeated, as he rolled away.

Damn him, there was a bet. But I wouldn't be telling him about it.

~ ~ ~

Night skulked in like a dog that had finished digging up the prized garden and was hoping you didn't notice its dirt-caked paws. The oncoming darkness didn't escape me, or the thickness of its shadows, but my brain was too busy vibrating in my head for me to get up and open the shutters to let the cooler air flood through.

Two men had died today—one of them inches away from where I'd been sitting. My memory kept hitting the rewind button, sometimes replaying the shooting in slow motion. There's no way to snatch the remote control away—not when your brain is the one mashing the buttons.

The house was an empty kind of quiet. On the kitchen counter the baklava steeping in its syrup looked as lonely as I felt, so I ate a piece, for solidarity.

I tapped out a Facebook status on my phone, attached a picture of the sheep tsunami from yesterday, and assured my friends and acquaintances, some of whom I'd even met, that Greece was amazing and I was in it.

My eye twitched. The little people-shaped blob at the top of the screen was red. People wanted to be my virtual friends. Lots of people. Fifty-three of them.

Who gets fifty-three friend requests in one hit?

A Makris, that's who. Which I discovered when I clicked on the blob and watched half my family's names scroll past. The Family wanted to claim me —online and off.

Not now. Not tonight. I clicked away, opened a browser window.

I didn't log on or in, whichever was correct, to the Crooked Noses Message Board. I didn't have to. Because my stupid phone remembered I'd been here before and gave the super-secret digital handshake before I had a chance to jab the button. And before I had a chance to hit the get-me-outta-here-I-want-to-be-anonymous button, my gaze hooked itself on the red envelope at the top of the screen. I had message. Or messages.

Tap.

Message. One single, lonely message. A bit like me.

Sender: BangBang.

Did you find what you were looking for?

My insides began to ice up, starting in my fingers. It spread quickly. In seconds my entire body was flash frozen. My mind skated back to our previous conversation, the one where I'd clicked away because I'd thrown a clue to my identity on the screen. Now here was BangBang asking if I'd found what I was looking for.

He or she knew I was Katerina Makris. I could feel it.

Several options fanned out in front of me.

Delete my account, sending these messages spiraling into the ether—or more likely, some database somewhere on a server, where, theoretically, anyone with a warrant or significant technological know-how could sift through my words and divine my identity.

Walk away; never go back.

Reply. Ask BangBang what they want. Promise riches, if need be.

Reply. Feign stupidity.

A smart woman would walk away, never to darken the board's virtual door again. So I fired off a message, because I'm the kind of person who can't resist squeezing a pimple until I'm left with a purple-red volcano where there used to be a humble zit.

But I compromised: I feigned stupidity.

Huh?

Succinct. Functional.

The light next to BangBang's name was green. He or she was online.

Dogas' hiding place. You seemed concerned about it last time.

Be cool, I told myself. Be casual. Pretend you're not a crime lord's granddaughter.

Oh, that? I'd already forgotten about it. Watch any good football lately?

No such thing as bad football.

Hahahaha. Got that right.

No. Got that wrong. Football sucked.

Which teams do you support?

Be enthusiastic. It's all part of the diversion. Remember, Kat, you want him to forget about the America flub.

All of them, I typed.

I held my breath.

Nobody supports all the teams. That's not how human nature works.

I do. So obviously that's exactly how it works.

I signed out. Closed the browser. Tossed my phone on the bedside table. Then I made a trip back to the kitchen counter for another diamond-shaped wedge of pastry, nuts, and syrup.

Solidarity.

I ate and tried not to miss Dad.

But what I really wanted was my mom. I would never be too old to wish she were here.

~ ~ ~

Dawn poked her nose through the shutters around 8 AM. Really it was almost mid-morning but I felt less lazy if I lied to myself and called it dawn. My bladder shot a flare. I needed to go and I needed to go now.

Barefooted, I dragged myself outside. Without Grandma here I could go barefoot without her disapproving and slapping slippers into my hands. Feeling like a rebel, I stretched my arms up over my head and yawned.

No sign of the morning's usual cool edge; I'd slept through it. Perfume flooded the air as the sun poked its fingers at the gardenias. Not far away, someone was splashing in the pool. Top 40 music trickled out of an open window.

For a moment this almost felt like college.

"Aunt Katerina?"

Argh! I whipped around, hand on heart, half expecting to get clubbed over the head by a maniac. What I got was little Tomas looking up at me, worry etched on his cute face. He'd made himself at home on the ground, where he'd been dissecting flowers. The parts were neatly separated into scientific piles.

Technically I wasn't his aunt, but in Greece respect often trumped biological accuracy.

"It's okay, I didn't pee my pants," I said, more to myself than him.

"My dentist appointment is tomorrow at ten," he said. "Can you still take me?"

"Want me to swing by and pick you up or do you want to meet by the fountain out front."

He giggled, reminding me that he was in fact a child and not a man in a boy suit. "By the fountain." Then he ran off, abandoning his flowers.

I was contemplating some downtime, maybe hanging with my goat, when Aunt Rita swung into Grandma's yard. She had topped a short denim jumpsuit with a curly blond wig. The fake hair was as big as hair got. Take her to a concert, people would hurl beer bottles at her head to knock down the skittle.

"It's party time," she said. "And by party time I mean business."

"Oh God. Hit me with it."

"You have meetings. People who want things."

"Do they want me to kill people? Because I won't kill people."

"No, some of them will expect you to hurt people."

"I can't do that either. Can I give them advice instead?"

"You can try," she said.

18

I wasn't a Grandma-level baker, and my thumb was more black than green, so I took Grandma's meetings under the umbrella near one of the courtyard's fountains. If I was lucky the running water would make the other parties want to pee, so hopefully they'd take their advice and shoo, without expecting me to hurt, kill, or con anyone.

I had armed myself with my new phone and a *frappe*, so I'd have an excuse to run away and pee, or take an imaginary call, if they expected me to kill someone.

My goat was chilling out nearby, crunching on a pool noodle.

"Jesus," I said. "Don't eat the pool noodle! I don't know if it's non-toxic!" He sort of rolled his eyes and shifted his attention—and teeth—to a deck chair.

Goats are the ultimate omnivores. If they can 'vore it they will.

Aunt Rita appeared in the archway with a sweaty man, his threadbare pants hitched under his belly. He was old enough to have fought in Vietnam —if the Vietnam War had been on Greece's radar—but young enough to never have been promoted past corporal. And he had a nose that could open cans. He stopped when he saw me, muttered something under his mustache I couldn't hear. He and my aunt exchanged words, some of them bordering on volatile, judging from the arm waving on both sides. Any more flapping and one of them was bound to take flight. Finally they seemed to reach an uncomfortable consensus. The man slouched toward me, following my aunt's clicking heels.

"This is George the Sheep Lover," she said.

"On account of how he …?"

"I love sheep," George said, glowering.

"As friends or …?"

The glare didn't dim. "Family."

Which answered none of my questions, and also brought to mind some of the worst places I'd been on the Internet.

"What can I do for you, Kyrios George?"

His scowl softened at my respectful addition of the Greek "Mr." to his name. How bad could I be if I understood respect?

"It is about my sheep."

I indicated for him to sit, but he chose to stand, his hat in hands. All this standing weirded me out, so I stood, too. Maybe Grandma wouldn't, but I wasn't Grandma.

"What's wrong with your sheep?"

"It's that *malakas* Yiannis the Sheep Fucker! He stole one of my sheep!"

My mind was officially boggled … and seriously grossed out. "Do you have proof?"

"He has my sheep."

"Did you ask him to return your sheep?"

"No, I did not think of that."

"Maybe you should try—" I started.

"Of course I asked for my sheep! That was sarcasm!"

Old George the Sheep Lover didn't strike me as the sharpest balloon, so I'd failed to catch his meaning. Mental note to self: old Greek men are snarky.

"Okay, so what other steps have you taken to recoup your lost sheep?"

"Not lost. Stolen."

"Your stolen sheep, then."

"I stole it back."

"And?"

"He took it again."

"Did he trespass on your property? Because I'm sure that's a crime." I looked at my aunt. "Is that a crime here?"

"Sure it's a crime. Is a crime the police care about? No. Not unless it's something old." She nodded at George. "He doesn't count."

"Hey," George said. "There was no trespassing. He lured my sheep with magic."

"Magic?" I leaned closer. "I suppose you're a muggle?"

"What is she talking about?" he implored my aunt. "I don't know what she is talking about. Where is Kyria Katerina? I want to speak with someone who can get my sheep back."

"Okay," I said. "I'll help you. But if this Yiannis is doing magic …"

"He gave my sheep a love potion and whispered sweet words to seduce her away from my flock."

"What kind of weirdo seduces a sheep?"

"It happens," my aunt said. "All kinds in this world."

Aunt Rita was a kind of her own, so I figured she knew what she was talking about.

What would any self-respecting problem-solver do? Grandma probably had her own way of dealing with this—club the thief, take back the slutty sheep—but I wasn't her. I was doing to do this old school.

"Where does he live? I want to talk to him."

"Good idea!" George boomed. "Break his legs."

"No, the leg-breaking isn't a metaphor. I'm going to *talk* to him."

"With a gun or a knife?"

"Uh, with my mouth?"

"And you think I am strange."

"I'm going to speak to the man. Using my mouth. And words. Maybe a few hand gestures, if necessary."

He looked at me. My meaning wasn't soaking in. The Family did crime. If there were words, eventually there would be bullets or lead pipes mashing kneecaps.

"Do I have time to talk with this guy?" I asked my aunt.

"There is someone else waiting, then you can go."

I pointed to George. "You're coming with me. But first could you wait? Maybe over there."

He wandered off to another shaded table, muttering.

The next person to ask for counsel was a familiar face. Kyria Koufo wore the same pinched mouth, the same stormy eyes. She didn't warm up as she approached. I could sympathize. Her husband had fallen into another woman's vagina. My ex fell facedown, repeatedly, on a dick. Although, as far as I knew, Todd hadn't made any plans to have me killed, unlike Mr. Koufos.

"Katerina is not back yet?" she demanded.

"Sorry," I said. "I'm the backup plan: Katerina 2.0."

She stared at me, blatantly unamused. "My husband is still fooling around with that she-dog. I want to know when he will be forced to stop. How long before he has me killed, eh?"

Oh boy, she was still fixated on my push-her-down-the-stairs plan, which hadn't been a plan at all. It hadn't even been a serving suggestion. It was me mouthing off, being a goof.

"Have you considered marriage counseling?"

"We are Greek. We do not do counseling."

I thought hard. "You go to church, don't you?"

"Of course. I am Greek."

"How about church counseling? Priests back home often guide couples through …" I hunted and pecked for an apt metaphor that had nothing to do with tossing people through windows, down stairs, or under buses. "… rocky waters. There's no shame in needing some help from time to time."

"You want me to speak with my priest," she said flatly.

"It's an idea." And a good one, I thought.

"About our private business."

I might have winced. Greeks didn't really seem to have much in the way of private business. The priest probably knew what was going on—or not going on—in the Koufo bedroom better than she did. And he probably knew about the affair.

For a moment I wondered if Father Harry was her priest. Grandma had never mentioned whether Kyria Koufo was a local woman or not.

"I'm not sending someone to push her down the stairs," I said. "That's crazy."

She reached out, slapped the back of my head. "Respect your elders."

I had respect for my elders, provided they weren't crazy. This one was crazy-cakes.

"No one is pushing anyone down any stairs while I'm in charge."

She stared at me until I fizzled like burning celluloid film.

"We will see."

Then she took to the skies on her broomstick.

Figuratively.

~ ~ ~

George the Sheep Lover and I piled into Aunt Rita's Pepto-mobile. Between the pink paint and the drop-top, I felt as if I were Barbie, with the wind tossing my hair like linguini.

Yes, the Beetle was a convertible, too, but this was *pink*.

Aunt Rita squealed out of the driveway and out onto the dirt road, blowing up a dust storm in my deadly entourage's faces. Guilt tweaked my nose. Elias didn't seem like a bad guy, and Donk was a kid who aspired to be an asshole when he grew up. The other two and Cleopatra, they could eat our dirt, as far as I was concerned. Aunt Rita honked the horn and we were gone.

Yiannis the Sheep Fucker lived in a hut on the mountain, at the end of a thin track of dubious stability. George the Sheep Lover lived in an adjacent hut. Both abodes were gray stone, cobbled together any which way and topped with red slate roofs. Between the two houses, a fence hugged the slope, but it was less wire and more air. Plenty of space for an ovine Casanova to lure through a sheep of easy virtue.

Yiannis was home. He was sitting on his porch rolling cigarettes. He had wild grey hair and a faded black shirt unbuttoned to his waist, revealing the wife-beater underneath.

He didn't look up as I picked my way across the chewed terrain. "What do you want, girl?"

"I'm here about a stolen sheep."

"There is no stolen sheep."

I stepped aside, pointed to George the Sheep Lover, who was hovering near Aunt Rita's car. "Did you or did you not take this man's sheep?"

"You cannot stop true love!" he yelled. He flung the cigarettes in my face, dived through his front door, and slammed it shut.

"That went well," I said to the others. "I like how mature you are about this," I told the man behind the door.

Silence.

I swung around, hand shielding my eyes. The sheep were in a fenced paddock chowing on sparse grass. Most of the time Greek shepherds and goatherds had to keep their animals on the move because the grass was so pathetic mid-summer and winter, but today both men had their flocks penned. George had told me more than I'd ever wanted to know about sheep on the drive over.

"Which one is yours?" I asked him. Because to me they were all the same sheep. Dirty, white-ish wool; sweet, docile, not-too-bright faces.

George squinted at the livestock. "That one."

Helpful guy, that George. "Which one?"

"Eh … one of them."

"You don't know which one of them is your sheep?"

"Of course I know! It is my sheep!"

Cripes. This was going to take some time. I could feel eternity butting into my day. "So, go get your sheep and take it home."

He stomped down to the paddock, jumped the fence, waded through the sea of sheep. When I had decided we'd be here forever, he crouched down and cupped a ewe's face and shouted, "I found her!"

"That is my sheep," came a voice from the hut behind us. "We are in love."

"You're a sick man," I said.

"You do not understand our love!"

He was wrong, I knew all about loving sheep … in souvlaki. Chunks of lamb smothered in *tzatziki*, topped with feta crumbles, onions, and tomatoes, all wrapped in a warm pita …

My stomach launched a protest. It was empty and it wasn't going to stand for that nonsense.

"You want to grab a souvlaki when we're done here?" I asked Aunt Rita.

"Sounds good," she said. "You buying?"

"I'm buying."

George scooped up his sheep—identical to the others—and deposited her on his side of the fence.

"And you call me sick," he said. "Who eats sheep?"

"Who is eating sheep?" the man in the house called out.

"These two," George said. "Can you believe it?"

The hut's door flew open. Yiannis poked his head into the sunshine. "You are a monster. Only monsters eat sheep. Sheep are not for eating."

"What do you do with your sheep if you don't eat them?" He opened his mouth. My hand shot up to stop him. "Forget it," I said. "I really don't want to know. You two should form a club or something."

"That's not a bad idea," George said. "We could have T-shirts."

~ ~ ~

We left the sickos to their sheep and got the souvlaki to go. I bought one extra.

"Hungry?" my aunt asked, eyeing the foil-wrapped roll.

"It's for a friend."

I had Aunt Rita drive us to Penka's stoop. The Bulgarian was counting change into a well-heeled woman's hand. The woman jumped when she saw us walking their way.

"Shame on you," my aunt said. "Why you buy your pills from Baby Dimitri?"

"Your guys are charging too much," the woman said. "These are tough times."

Aunt Rita rolled her eyes at me. "Don't listen to her, she's a millionaire."

"Yes, and I intend to stay one!" She stalked away in a swirl of skirts and the familiar tapping of high heels on concrete.

"What did she buy?" Aunt Rita asked Penka.

"Is confidential."

I couldn't stuff the laugh back down. "You know you're a drug dealer, not a doctor, right?"

"Bah! What do I care about who buys what? Fentanyl. She buy Fentanyl."

My aunt turned to me. "Now we have a problem because I know we did not raise our prices."

"Baboulas is away so the cats are playing?"

"I don't know what that means, but *I* think *they* think they can take advantage of Mama being locked up. Come, we have to go."

I handed Penka the souvlaki. "Lots of tomato and cheese."

"What is this for?"

"It's either a bribe or a payment."

"At least you are honest. For what?"

"I'm curious if you've seen a guy around with an eagle on his shoulder."

"Look at the beach. Every day I see men with eagles on shoulder, on back, on chest, on legs. Everybody has tattoo. Is tacky."

"I don't have one." My gaze slid to Aunt Rita, who had an anchor on her forearm. A remnant of her time in the army, back when she was a full-time man. She told me she'd joined because she dug sailors.

"Tattoo is not tacky. Is tacky that everybody has one. So common. Want to see mine?"

Before I could say "No" she'd bent over, flashing a mile of Cyrillic lettering, entwined with painful-looking thorns.

Aunt Rita winced.

I squinted at the letters. "What does it say?"

"Is Bulgarian saying. 'Big leek.' "

The sixth grade part of my brain translated the words into English, substituting that second 'e' for an 'a.' A tiny laugh bubbled out. I tried covering it up with a question. "What does it mean?"

"So what. Big deal. Nobody care. I have another one on the front." She jerked down the neck of her tank top, nearly knocking our eyes out. "This one says, 'My lighthouse hurts.' "

"You have a lighthouse back in Bulgaria?"

"No. It means I do not give fuck."

"The eagle," I said, remembering why I'd brought Penka souvlaki.

"What eagle?"

"The man with the eagle. It's a real eagle that sits on his shoulders."

"Greeks are crazy," she said. "Why would you want animal shitting down your back?"

"For what it's worth, I don't think he's completely sane."

"What he do?"

"Killed some people. His brother, father, a few others."

"Same-old story," she said. "People like him in Bulgaria, too."

"Have you seen him, heard of him, anything?"

"I would remember if I see man with eagle on shoulder."

That was true. Some things you don't forget.

She glanced around. "Okay," she said. "I see him now."

Everything froze except my mouth. "You see him … now? Where?"

"Behind you, on beach."

Aunt Rita and I swung around. Sure enough, Periphas Dogas was leaning against a streetlight, feeding his bird an ice cream. He was openly watching us.

"Is ice cream safe for birds?" I asked.

"Who knows?" my aunt said.

"Google. Google knows everything. I'm going to talk to him." He was a killer, yeah, but this was broad daylight and he was surrounded by sunbathers and other assorted tourists. "Call Melas and tell him Periphas is here."

I'd lost him before. I wasn't about to screw up a second time.

"You can't—" my aunt started, but her voice was lost behind the bored roar of an oncoming bus. I darted across the street between traffic.

When I got there, the man and the bird were gone. All that was left of them was ice cream melting in a warm puddle.

19

Not five minutes later, three cop cars screeched to a stop across from Penka's stoop. Melas, Stained Shirt, and two other uniforms.

"Where is he?" Melas asked. The wide expanse above his brows was creased like he'd taken up forehead origami. This particular piece was called *An American Pain in My Greek Butt*.

I tried not to look pathetic. I mean, the guy had been standing directly across the road from me, but somewhere between here and there—a whole twenty feet maybe—I'd lost him. How does that happen? Understandable if you're hunting, say, one of the Davids—Copperfield or Blaine—but Periphas was some criminal kook with an eagle. How could a guy disappear that quickly with a big bird on his shoulder? I had searched the beach, looked both ways along the road, then flitted back to roost with my aunt and Penka.

"Gone?"

"Yeah, I figured that. Where did he go?"

Ten seconds and he was already infuriating me. He was dangling bait and I bit.

"If I knew that I'd be there, wouldn't I?"

"Rita said you went to talk to him."

Aunt Rita looked at me and shrugged.

My hands knew the drill. They moved into position, on my hips. "Yeah, so?"

"Not a fast learner, are you? I figured the whole Baptist thing would have make you think." He thunked his knuckle on my forehead. I slapped his hand away.

"It's a public place. He was hanging out, watching us."

"What about your entourage? They see where he went?"

My mouth dropped open. I'd forgotten about them. Sure enough, they were all parked further down the road.

Melas pointed out the cars to the uniformed cops. They sauntered off in the direction of the parked assassins, who were casually slouched behind their steering wheels, trying to look as though they didn't kill for cash. Except Donk, who was hanging out car window watching everything, tongue lolling, hair waving. He reminded me of a big, goofy dog. He pulled his head in fast when he realized one of the cops was gunning for him.

"What was he doing?" Melas wanted to know.

"Periphas? Feeding ice cream to his eagle."

The V between his eyes deepened. "Is it safe to feed ice cream to a bird?"

"That's what I said! Aunt Rita was going to Google it for me."

He looked at my aunt.

"I'm still looking," she said. "I got distracted by an ad for fake nipples. Those things are amazing,"

"Jesus," Melas muttered. His gaze slid sideways, back to me. "So he was feeding his bird. What else? Was he armed?"

"I couldn't tell. He was leaning against that lamppost." I pointed to where Periphas and his bird had been a few minutes ago. "A bus cut in front of me, and by the time I reached the other side he was gone."

"You'd think a guy with an eagle on his shoulder wouldn't be easy to lose."

"Maybe he jumped into a car and zipped off while I was crossing the road. It's not exactly quiet here today. There's a lot of traffic."

"Any more questions, Nikos? You know where to find us," Aunt Rita said. "We've got somewhere to be."

Melas raised an eyebrow in my direction.

"Don't ask me," I said. "She drove. I'm along for the drive. Gotta love this freshly baked air."

"I know where you live if we've got questions," he told me.

"Not living there—staying. Temporarily. Like a hotel."

"Some people wind up living in hotels."

"Not me. I've got a perfectly nice home."

"Maybe you'll show me someday soon."

Was he serious? Pulling my leg? I couldn't tell. All this weirdness was messing with my radar. And I still didn't know if it was okay for birds to eat ice cream. I wanted to say they had problems with lactose, but maybe that was the Japanese.

I said goodbye to Penka, who was glaring at the cops, enough pressure behind her gaze to rips holes through them. Cops were bad for business, even when their attention was focused on someone else.

"Thank you," she said to me. "I love police. Next time bring more. Maybe they kill all my business."

~ ~ ~

Aunt Rita stopped three blocks up. Same stretch of beach, different crowd. No swimmers here—this was where the dedicated coffee drinkers hung out. And they were hanging out, enjoying the bleached starkness of the day, *frappes* close at hand, cigarettes poised between their fingers. Greece had the highest consumption of tobacco in the European Union. There were laws, sure, but they said nothing about smoking in public places if they weren't enclosed by at least two walls. Here there were no walls, but the umbrellas kept the low gray cloud in captivity.

"That is our dealer." Aunt Rita nodded to a table, where a woman was playing games on her phone. She had the requisite *frappe* and an ashtray, where a cigarette sat slowly dying. The woman lifted her head. A religious epithet formed on her glossed-up lips. She was my age, or within a stone's throw of it. Stick-straight hair that had chosen to lie flat after repeated threats with a straightening iron. She had one of those ombre dye jobs—dark brown at the roots, blond at the ends—that was trendy a couple of summers ago. She wasn't a fashion victim, but she was walking down a dark alley alone after midnight. It wouldn't be long before *Vogue* leaped out from behind a dumpster and clubbed her over the head.

"Rita," she called out, swapping the phone for the cigarette. She took a long drag then swapped again, adding her contribution to the cloud fund as she blew out a long plume of smoke. "You want Percocet? For you it's free." She laughed at her own h-i-l-a-r-i-o-u-s joke.

"Oh, to me you give it away? Because I heard prices went up."

Two palms up. "I sell the stuff, I don't set the prices. Got a problem with that, talk to Varvara."

"That louse. I am going to speak with her. In the meantime, prices go back to normal."

The dealer shrugged. "No problem." She looked up at me. "Are you on Facebook? I need more lives in *Candy Crush*. The *malakas* beat me again."

"Uh, I guess," I said. She looked at me expectantly. "Katerina Makris," I said. Ten seconds later I had another pending friend request. Her name was Tina Pappas and she was queen of the selfies. Seriously, the woman had over a thousand pictures saved to her albums, all of them self-inflicted, by the looks of it. Sometimes there were other victims with her, but hers was always the primary mug shot.

"Hit me with it," she said. I gave her another Candy Crush life, and she sighed the way I imagined a heroin addict did when they shot up. Then she grinned at my aunt. "How is Xander? I haven't seen him around lately."

Aunt Rita didn't say anything about his current status, which was missing. She sighed and said, "Gorgeous. I could eat that man on a spoon."

Tina's attention slid to me. "What about you?"

"I hadn't noticed."

Tina shook with laughter. "Really? You haven't noticed that Xander is a god? Are you human?" She clicked her fingers and leaned forward. She looked me straight in the eyes. "Are you a lesbian?"

"Busy is what she is," Aunt Rita said. "Baboulas has big plans for her and they do not include Xander."

"You and Xander?" I asked Tina. She shrugged, one-shouldered.

"I wish," she said. "Maybe someday."

~ ~ ~

This time we were headed inland. Aunt Rita was playing an old song from the 80s. Someone was going crazy in the Seychelles, and she was doing it with a voice like fingernails down a cheese grater. I suppose if a person had to go crazy tropical islands would be the place to do it.

Aunt Rita had given me the low-down on Varvara, who was one of the Family's suppliers. The pills went to Varvara, who dished them out to the dealers. Then the machine slipped into reverse to send the money back up the chain to the Family's pockets.

The assassins and Cleopatra were following. She must have had a life outside the stalking business, because she was never around in the mornings.

"Does my face look different to you?" Aunt Rita asked.

"Different how?"

"Different."

That covered a lot of territory, some of it hidden behind her Yoko Oh-no sunglasses. "Did you get something done?"

"Virgin Mary, no! I will never let a doctor cut up my face. What if they put the pieces back together wrong? What if they mix them up? It could happen. I know a woman who looks like Kyrios Patata Kefalas. Her eyes don't match, and now she has a mustache."

She was talking about Mr. Potato Head.

"I don't think you have to worry about the mustache, seeing as how you already shave."

"True. But what if they lose my nose? Remember Michael Jackson? *Ay-yi-yi.*" She patted me on the nose. "So do you see how I look different?"

I hated to admit defeat, but … "I'm an idiot, so you'll have to tell me."

"Botox!" she said proudly.

"Didn't you have to go to a doctor for that?"

"No! I did it myself. It falls off the back of a medical supply truck and we pick it up. So this time I took a little for myself, to freshen up."

"You stabbed your own face with a needle?" I felt my face shift into the 'horrified' position.

"Sure, why not?"

We stopped at a red light. She raised her glasses. Sure enough, the skin around her eyes was baby smooth. Her eyebrows were the sharp edges of a coffee table. Her forehead was where things went wrong. The flat half fell off a ledge, landing on four lanes of heavy traffic.

"Your forehead is uneven."

She dropped the glasses back into position. "I know. There wasn't enough Botox. Got to wait for another delivery. Until then, I'm going with hats and big sunglasses. What do you think?"

"That should work."

She didn't look too worried. Half of her couldn't. "Do you think so?"

"I didn't even notice until you took the glasses off."

"So, you're saying keep the glasses on? What about at night?"

"Can't you buy some more Botox?" Everything I knew about Botox came from the gossip columns. If someone looked unnaturally surprised, while maintaining a forehead flatter than my chest at thirteen, then chances were they'd been Botoxed.

"What for? I already get it for free."

"I thought you could even things up."

"Is it that bad?"

"No." Not that bad—but bad enough.

"Because I have some of those hats with the little veils."

"You're fine—honestly. Just …" I eyed her sideways. "… keep the glasses on for now."

Aunt Rita turned right, then right again. The Barbie car crept up a suburban street, a mixture of one and two-story houses. It looked middle class Greek, with its mature trees and shrubbery, and late model cars parked along the streets. The road was hardly cracked at all. At the front of each property was a fence. Or a wall. Really, it was more of a wall-fence. Three feet of stucco wall topped with two feet of iron fence. Almost nobody in Greece—at least in this area, it seemed like—had driveways. She pulled up to the curb. Cut the engine. The music died an instant death.

"Varvara is going to shit her pants." She reached over, popped the glove box. A handgun and silencer tumbled out.

"Are you going to shoot her?"

She screwed on the silencer, slapped it into my hand. "I'm not shooting anyone. You are. But only in the leg or something. You need to scare her, not kill her.

"What?" I squawked, shoving the gun back at her. "I'm not shooting anyone unless my life is in immediate danger."

"Okay, then I will shoot her."

"No!" My voice dropped to a loud whisper. I was trying—I really was—but my outrage was struggling against the restraints. "We can't go around shooting people!"

She shrugged. "Why not? That's the business. If you don't act they will think you are weak. There are people out there who already think the family is weakening with Baboulas away. You must show strength, flex your muscles."

She made it sound almost reasonable.

"Let's go talk to her before any shooting happens. Maybe we can avoid it."

"This is one of the many reasons I love you, Katerina: you are an optimist."

No, not an optimist. More like not a crazy criminal. I liked to think that I was a good person, and good people don't go around shooting people to make a point.

We got out of the car, planted ourselves by the front gate.

"Hey, Varvara!" my aunt hollered. "I know you're home, you dishonorable crook!"

There was movement inside. A voice floated between the shutters' brown slats. It was gravel and other small rocks.

"Who is it?"

"Rita."

"I'm on the toilet. Come back later."

Aunt Rita kicked the gate open with a combat boot. She was rocking this mullet-style: party above the waist (sparkly top, lots of makeup), shady business below the belt (cargo shorts and ass-kicker boots—likely steel-capped, judging from how promptly the gate leaped out of her way). She stormed up to the door, then stopped.

"Shit," she said. "New door." Not that I'd ever seen the old door, but I assumed it hadn't been made of steel bars, backed by one major weakness: glass.

"Can't you break the glass?"

"Knowing Varvara that is something stronger than glass." She glanced around the yard, marched over to where a fist-sized rock had been soaking up the sun, minding its own business. She gave it a fast, impromptu flying lesson. It exceeded all expectations when it sailed through the glass, decorating the marble floor inside with a mosaic of clear, shattered pieces.

"You broke my door," Varvara screamed from somewhere inside the house. "You will pay for this!" A toilet flushed, then a woman who looked like a bank manager shoved her face up against the bars. She was in a suit—pinstripe jacket and pencil skirt—with what was probably a Hermes scarf tied artfully around her neck. Not that I knew anything about Hermes other than its correct spelling—and that wasn't exactly rocket science. Her shoes were d'orsay pumps, and her favorite accessory was a freakin' flamethrower. "I want to shit in peace," she said and flung the door open. In that heartbeat between mistaking her for a successful businesswoman and realizing what she was toting, I recognized Varvara as Kyria Koufo, the woman who thought problems could be solved by shoving people down stairs.

Aunt Rita and I dived in different directions, both away from the flamethrower's path. Leaves crackled and steamed.

Varvara laughed. It was the cruel sound of mean girls laughing at the nerdy girl. I was never the nerdy girl but I didn't like mean girls. They traveled in packs, like geese. And there was nothing more frightening than geese.

"The family is getting weak," Varvara said. "Baboulas would take on the flamethrower like a man."

"She wouldn't have to," I said, making it up as I went along. This was one of those moments when a prior stint doing improv really paid off. Of course later, if I wasn't chilling in the burn unit, I'd think of a million other cooler, better things I could have said. But as far as comebacks went, the next thing out of my mouth wasn't so bad. "She'd have shot you in the face before you touched the trigger."

Varvara grunted. "Maybe once. But now she's getting old."

"A couple of weeks ago I watched her bearing down on an intruder with her shotgun in hand. I almost wet my pants, and I'm her granddaughter."

Her attention slid to my aunt, who was spit-polishing her gun. "What do you two want?"

"Ask her," Aunt Rita said casually, nodding to me. "While Mama is away everyone answers to Katerina."

"We've got a problem," I said. "Your dealers are raising their prices."

"So?"

"Grandma—we—are losing customers. No one authorized a price increase."

"I don't answer to a little girl. I have shoes older than you."

"Those ones?" I peered in at her shoes. They were gorgeous, but I wasn't about to let her know that.

"What?"

"They look secondhand to me," Aunt Rita said. "Did you get them from the Romani?"

Varvara Koufo sucked in her breath. Good thing she wasn't a dragon. Unfortunately, she was the next worst thing to a dragon: a woman with a portable fire machine.

"Look," I said. "Prices go back to what they were. If you can't handle that, we find someone else."

Was I saying the right things? Hard to say with my aunt behind me and zero visual cues. I tried to say it like non-compliance meant we'd send her to live on a farm.

She lowered the flamethrower's nozzle. "Fine. Then I want a bigger cut."

"No. No bigger cut," Aunt Rita said.

"Why do you want a bigger cut?" I asked.

"Because it's bigger. Bigger means more."

"I read the dictionary, too." I resisted the urge to scratch my head. "You … want more money?"

She glanced from side to side, as though inspecting her neighbors' houses. "I lost my job. How else am I going to pay for this place?"

"You've got another job?"

"*Had* another job. You think I can put drug supplier on my tax form?"

Yeah, actually. Greece was in enough financial trouble that I didn't think it mattered what you put down for an occupation, so long as you paid your taxes. Greeks had a long-standing habit of forgetting to pay Uncle Samopoulos. In the U.S. that scored you some prison time. Here they gave you a shrug and a "What are you gonna do?"

"I thought you were loaded."

"Was. Times are tough."

"So get another job," my aunt said from behind me. "You want a bigger cut? Forget it. You get what you get, same as everyone else."

"You're not the boss of me," Varvara screeched. She slammed the door.

"I bet I can guess what happened to her last door," I said.

"Story goes Varvara forgot to open it before she fired. The door burnt down."

"That's not what I was going to guess."

"People who live behind wood doors shouldn't use flamethrowers."

That I could agree with. "What now?"

"She will lower the prices, but to be sure we will leave her a message."

"What kind of message?"

"A scary one."

~ ~ ~

Aunt Rita wanted to dabble with arson. I wanted to leave a note suggesting prices had better return to normal by tomorrow morning, or else. There was nothing after the "or else," because that's where the power was: in the not knowing.

Ask Jack Woltz.

Or better yet, don't. Fictional characters don't answer questions, unless they've got Twitter accounts.

Old Jack received an "or else" and chose to ignore it. End result, he woke one morning, snuggled up to a horse's head.

Aunt Rita said blowing up Kyria Koufo's car would send a message. I said leaving a message would also send a message.

In the end we compromised. We left a message, but my aunt sketched a picture of a burning face on the bottom of the note.

~ ~ ~

Early evening, there was a knock at Grandma's door; the sort of tentative sound of a fist that doesn't know whether to knock on the screen itself or the frame. So it compromised and split the difference. On the other side was a middle-aged man in a white suit, white shoes, shirt unbuttoned halfway down to his waist. To his credit he wasn't wearing a gold medallion; the gold rope around his neck was probably heavy enough as it was. His chest was smoother than a baby's foot, but he had the whole George Michael thing going on above the neck.

"Yes?" I said.

"You are Katerina?"

"Depends. Who's asking?"

"Lazarus." He pointed to himself so that I got the message: he was Lazarus.

"Aren't you busy being dead?"

He laughed. "Good sense of humor. I like it." The laugh died abruptly, like a bird hitting glass. "No. Lazarus came back from the dead, like me."

This was getting weird fast.

"You've been dead?"

"Not for four days, but for minutes, yes."

"Was there a tunnel and white light?"

"Gold."

"Gold light?"

"Gold light, gold tunnel, mountains of gold. And God Himself was gold." His eyes flicked up and down my body. "Is that what you're wearing?"

I looked down at my cargo shorts and tank top. "Right now? It would appear so. Look," I said, "if you're here because you want me to kill, maim, or scare someone for you, the answer is no. If you're here for counsel, make an appointment like everyone else. If—"

"Relax, I have people who will do all that for me. Go put on a dress, something sexy, and don't skimp on the makeup because you look tired."

What was this guy's problem? He shows up at my door—well, Grandma's door—

An awful, terrible, heinous thought streaked through my head, buck-naked.

"Wait," I said. "Is this supposed to be … a *date*?"

"Why else would I be here in my favorite suit?"

Huh. I figured he was auditioning for the new Bee Gees. "Did Grandma do this?"

Two palms up. "She said you need a husband. I'm single. You're single. I want a family and you—" He looked me up and down like he was in the market for a horse. "—look like you've still got a few childbearing years left. Normally I like them younger, but you are well-connected."

"I'm twenty-eight!"

"That's thirty-eight in Greek dating years."

Unbelievable.

"Get out of here before I call the cops."

He laughed. "The cops. They won't do anything, not when they know who I am."

"Then I'll call the henchmen. This place is crawling with them."

I shoved him off the step, pulled the screen door shut.

"I can still see you," he said.

Easily fixed. I swung the front door into place. Yeah, it would have been more effective and satisfying to slam the thing, but I wasn't sure this place could take it. What would Grandma say if her house collapsed while she was away?

Away. Like she was on a vacation, instead of being held in captivity.

"I know you're in there."

"You could be a rocket surgeon with that brain."

There was a pause, then: "You think?"

I banged my head on the wall. "Go away. I'm not going anywhere with you."

Another long, pathetic silence. "Can I come inside?"

"No."

"Then I guess I'll be going now."

Good. Perfect. Excellent idea.

His footsteps moved away. Or rather, they grew softer. I twitched the curtain, saw he'd been faking it. He was standing next to Grandma's gardenias.

"I know you're still there!"

"No, I'm not. I'm leaving."

This time he left, swaggering away in his leather-soled shoes.

Too bad I forgot to get his last name. I wanted to put his name on a list of people to avoid. Also, maybe I wanted to Google him, because I'm nosy like that. Greek genes will out. I snatched up my phone, approved all those friend requests from the family, then starting picking through their friends lists to see if Loser Lazarus was one of them.

Not five minutes later, a single gunshot punctured the evening.

20

Then came the screech of metal trying to climb a tree. Up until then it had been silent, with a hint of Greek music wafting on the light breeze. Now, after the gunfire, the night was hemorrhaging sound. Footsteps, shouting, the sound of soldiers strapping on their battle duds.

Grandma owned a gun. A big one. She kept it—I discovered—under her bed, so I raced in now and helped myself to her double-barreled zombie slayer. I shoved my feet into boots and headed for the arch, shotgun muzzle pointed at the ground.

Was it loaded? Beats me, but I felt badass.

Almost everyone was moving in the same direction, except for the groups moving to the rear of the property, in case the shot out front was a diversionary tactic. I stormed through the arch, past the garage and fountain, through the gates. The swarm was moving toward a point beyond the gates, where a black Mercedes sedan had passed out, mid-drive, after convening with an olive tree. I raced to join them, elbowed my way to the front. Through the driver's side window the driver was visible, slumped over the steering wheel. The security guard glanced at me. Was I supposed to make the next move? What would Grandma do?

I nodded, and that must have been the magic gesture, because he jogged over to the Mercedes, checked for signs of life.

"Dead," he said. "Clean through the head, looks like."

Lazarus.

I knew it was his car because the vanity plate said so. The fourth Bee Gee wouldn't be returning from the dead this time. I wondered if the afterlife was as gold as he remembered.

I was about to call Melas when a cop car crunched up the road, a brown cloud on its tail. Melas was here. His timing was suspicious. He parked nose to butt with the Mercedes, got out of his car. Warm summer night, but he was in a leather jacket, black T-shirt, and jeans. He stalked over to the Mercedes, took in the shattered glass and the dead guy behind the wheel, then stood straight, shaking his head.

"Wow," he said. "Is this for me? You shouldn't have."

"We didn't do it!" At least, I didn't think we did.

"Yeah, I figured by the way your whole family is out here." He opened the car's door, didn't look up. "Who's this guy?"

"He said his name was Lazarus. No last name. The only other thing I know about him is that he's a chauvinistic ass."

"That describes a lot of Greek guys. Including me, sometimes." He zeroed in on the shotgun I forgot I was holding. "Nice gun," he said. "I suppose it's too much to ask if there were witnesses?"

I looked around. There was the guardhouse camera and the guard himself, but other than that there was nobody. Wait—what about my tagalongs? Elias had told me they were taking turns watching the compound—in pairs so someone didn't get clever and take me out on their own. Tonight it was the two newest guys, Donk and Vlad. Each of them was in his own car—probably both stolen. The Russian's car had German tags. Zeus only knew if it was legit or not.

I waved them over. Only Donk jumped to it. Vlad the Russian took his sweet time, and he did it while he huffed on a cigarette and eyeballed Melas.

Donk jogged over in his too-big suit. "What-sap?" he said in his try-hard English.

Melas indicated for him to take a look. "Did you see anything?"

"Like what?"

"Like a shooter."

Donk took a quick look. "Shit," he said. "That's my boss."

I stood there in disbelief for several seconds. "That bozo hired you to kill me? Some idiot in a white suit? I thought you were doing this solo, to impress your uncle."

"I was, but I was running low on funds, so I got a benefactor."

"A benefactor who wanted me dead?"

"Nobody is perfect." Then he fainted.

Boy, he was going to make one hell of an assassin someday.

My stomach was so tightly clenched I wasn't sure I'd be able to eat again. Even breathing was a challenge. How did my family live this way, where death and murder were a fact of life?

When my words came out they were trite, shallow clumps. I wanted to say something reverent, befitting the situation, but the signals switched on the way to my mouth. "I can't believe Grandma organized a blind date for me with this jerk. Who's next, Charles Manson?"

Melas tilted his head back and let the laughter rip. "He was here to take you out?"

"My life sucks, I know."

"It could be worse. But not by much."

He was wrong—it could be so much worse. For a couple of weeks now I'd been teetering on the edge of losing the person who mattered most to me. Fate could tip either way at any moment with one phone call, one delivery.

The same thought bopped him over the head. His face went to work rearranging itself in the stricken position. Not too far away, emergency vehicles were wending their way up the mountain, inbound from Volos.

"Sorry—" he started.

"How did you get here so quickly?" I asked him. "Did someone call?"

He shook his head, trying to catch up with the abrupt subject change.

"I was my parents' place when I got a call I figured you'd want to know about. We've got a lead on why all these gangsters want you dead. Turns out word is getting out that Baboulas has you earmarked to take her place when she dies. A lot of people don't like that. It's change. These guys don't like change unless they're doing the changing. They're worried you'll shake things up so they'll have to adapt—and adapting might cost them. The economy the way it is … the loss could be substantial. Fridas had a plan to sell you on the black market. Figured he'd get a good price on Baboulas' only granddaughter. There's a rumor he already had a buyer lined up."

"Who?"

"We don't know."

My stomach unclenched, twisted itself into new shapes, resumed clenching. "Do you think one of these clowns is responsible for Dad's abduction?"

"It's possible. The timing fits. Baboulas decides she's mortal after all and starts making preparations for a handover, and then your father goes missing? It's a safe bet they made him disappear so he couldn't take over. I guess no one figured your grandmother would rope you into the job sooner, or you'd probably be missing, right along with him."

I gave Donk a nudge with my foot. The poor kid was out. "So now they know, they figured they'd kill me instead of using me for leverage." I did some fast thinking, trying to swim my way between the sharks in my head. "Who's next in line?"

"Rita or Kostas, as far as I know. But they don't want the job, or Baboulas wouldn't have pinned it on you."

Uncle Kostas was a stranger. I'd never met him, never knew he existed until this month. I knew precisely nothing about him, except that he was about to become the head of his own Family in Germany.

And Aunt Rita was vocal about not wanting to sit in the captain's chair.

"Where is Aunt Rita?" I combed the crowd for that blip of fabulosity in the matrix. Just in time to be useful, Takis and Stavros slouched over.

"Cool shotgun," Takis said. "I don't think belongs to you."

"Finders keepers." Everyone looked at me, puzzled. "It's … an American thing. It means I found it, I get to keep it."

"At least until Baboulas gets back, eh?" Takis said.

I repeated my earlier question. "Where's Aunt Rita? I don't see her anywhere."

"How should I know?" Takis asked. "What do I look like, her babysitter?"

I managed to get a grip on my sudden urge to wrap my hands around his scrawny neck and shake. It seemed like bad business to strangle your unofficial sidekick's husband. Lucky for me, and for Takis, Stavros had something useful to say.

"She's visiting her children. The ex-wife only allows visitation once a month."

My heart broke a little for my aunt. I didn't know a thing about their situation, before or after the divorce, but I had an inkling how much Dad loved me … and how much my mother had loved me before cancer stuck its thumb in her. I could only imagine how it must feel not to have free access to your kids.

But maybe their mother was doing them a favor. This family …

"Thanks," I mouthed. Stavros gave me a small smile. His outer shell was a goober, but inside he was carrying around a heart of something better than gold.

"What's better than gold?" I asked.

"Cocaine," Takis said.

"Diamonds," Stavros said.

"Women," Melas said.

Takis scoffed at that. "You only say that because you're not married."

Whatever Stavros's heart was made of I didn't think it was women, although Takis would probably disagree, the little weasel.

Something caught on the edge of my senses. An anomaly. A sound that didn't fit into the evening. No one else noticed the call of the eagle overhead. Not until it swooped low, then soared away again, toward Makria.

"Ohmigod," I said. "That was an eagle! Follow the eagle."

Melas knew exactly what I was talking about. He leaped back into his cop car and blew up a Category 3 tornado of dirt and stones as he peeled away. The bird was headed toward the main road. Melas must have let the others know what was going on because the sirens split into two groups. The cops followed Melas's lead, and the ambulance eased on up Grandma's crude road.

The eagle dipped low, then vanished between the treetops. A moment later, the sirens died. I couldn't tell if the cars had stopped or a giant wormhole had opened and sucked them inside. Logic dictated the former, but Greece was weird.

Takis planted himself next to me, hands on hips. "What's with the bird?"

"It belongs to the guy who's sending us organs. The name is Periphas. Ring any bells?"

There was a long pause while we watched the paramedics load Lazarus onto a gurney.

"Dogas?" he asked.

I nodded. He threw back his head. Laughed. I was glad I gave good joke.

"First the Baptist, now Periphas Dogas? You are cursed."

Right then that felt true enough.

~ ~ ~

The moon was slowly emerging from its dark shell, and the stars were there to watch its coy act. Gardenias had pulled the green covers over their petals for the night. Now it was jasmine's turn to squirt perfume all over the night. In places it was like stumbling through the mosh pit that was the ground floor at Macy's. The paramedics had hauled Lazarus away a couple of hours ago; police had come and gone; the family had wandered back to their apartments and various corners of the courtyard. The mood was low-key, the air quiet apart from nature's bleating and the burble of the fountains.

I heard Melas pull up to the gates then crawl to a stop this side of them. My heart picked up its pace. It was a mash up of desire to hear Periphas was back in his crate and, well, desire.

The day had taken its toll on him. His broad shoulders were slightly stooped and he pushed a hand through his hair like he really wanted it out of his way. He looked more bad night than bad boy.

"Nothing," Melas said in response to what must have been my curious expression. He pulled out the chair beside me, dropped himself in it. "Sometimes an eagle is just an eagle."

"Except when it's not."

"There was no sign of Periphas or the bird."

I tugged on the Memories of TV Shows Past. "Not even tire tracks?"

"Too many tire tracks. It'd be like trying to untangle …" His mind wandered off to find a good metaphor but came back empty-handed. "There were a lot. The eagle was probably a coincidence."

No way was I buying that. "Come on, we both know Periphas Dogas shot Lazarus. Who else is following me around, killing people?"

"Lately? Could be anyone"

I slapped at his arm. He trapped my wrist in his hand. I was already warm, sluggish, but his was a different kind of heat—his made me come alive.

"Let go."

"Is that what you want?"

"Yes and no."

His manacle unlocked. His hand fell back to his side.

"The longer you stay the more complicated this gets," he said. "So what's the plan, are you taking over the Family? Because to me it looks like you are."

"Right now it's a temporary thing, until Grandma gets back."

"If she doesn't?"

It was a good question. Too bad I had no good answers. Say they kept Grandma indefinitely, with no one else in the immediate Family who wanted control, what could I do?

Nothing. I was stuck until the cops released Grandma and Dad was found.

I nibbled on a hangnail. What if someone else in the family did want to slide into Grandma's seat? All I had was her word, and her words were calculated with an engineer's skill and precision. She used them as levers to move the family into their rightful positions, according to her blueprints. The Makris Family was her pyramid; she was building it to endure. There was no room for error—or for truth, if a lie was the more efficient tool.

"I don't know."

~ ~ ~

Takis dropped out of the archway's shadow. He sauntered over to where I was standing, his face thoughtful, lips gripping a cigarette. We stood there in silence, watching the cop car's lights jiggle as Melas maneuvered the dirt road. When the lights vanished, he turned to me.

"I hear you are taking Litsa's boy to the dentist."

"He asked. I couldn't say no. What's with his mother? He said she had a thing."

"Litsa is Litsa," he said cryptically. "Baboulas would take me to the dentist, too, when I was small."

"Your mother didn't take you?"

Puff, puff, blow. "She died when I was a boy."

Guilt and sympathy stabbed me in the chest and gut. Here I was thinking Takis was an everyday dick. In reality, he was an everyday dick who had lost his mother, same as me. At least I'd had my whole childhood with Mom. Takis had been raised crooked by the mob.

"I'm sorry," I said. "What happened?"

"She died taking out the garbage."

"Drug dealers? Henchmen?"

"No," he said, looking at me like I was nuts. "She died taking out the garbage in winter. Whoosh! on the ice. Then she was hit by *tsiganes* selling watermelons. The pickup truck stopped quickly and watermelons crushed her head. I saw the whole thing while I was sitting on the front step, smoking."

"I thought you were a kid."

"I was a kid. I was seven."

"And you were smoking?"

Two palms up, cigarette trapped between his teeth. "What?"

I shook my head. "Never mind. I'm sorry about your mother."

"That's life," he said.

~ ~ ~

The dentist was in Volos. It was a neat, clean building in one of the nicer parts of the city, surrounded by upscale shops, businesses, and apartments with bold-colored awnings hunched over the windows. There was a grinning decal goat on the window, huge, sparkling teeth chewing a toothbrush.

The rest of the sign told me the dentist's name was Antonis Katsikas and he specialized in pediatric dentistry.

Tony Goats.

How about that, he really was a dentist. Take that, Detective Nikos Melas, oh ye of little-to-no faith. He'd tried to convince me that Dad's old gang was made up of dirt bags and criminals. When I'd spoken to them at the wake of Dad's former best friend, they'd all come across as mostly normal older guys with regular jobs.

I opened the door, scooted Tomas inside, tried to ignore the universal odor of dental clinics, a scent that, if pushed to describe it, I could only think of as synthetic mint green. As far as dental clinics went this one was swanky. Lots of toys for kids. A couple of widescreen TVs blasting Disney movies dubbed in Greek. *O Vasilis ton Liondarion*, I noted, didn't have the same ring as *The Lion King*.

The receptionist had one tiny smile and she gave it to Tomas. She was a low-key kind of pretty, hair in a sedate low ponytail that curled over one shoulder like a ferret. She was skating toward her mid-thirties, and she didn't look happy about the journey so far.

Dentists here did things differently. There was no mountain of paperwork or myopic scanning of the insurance card—there wasn't an insurance card, period. Yeah, Greece had private insurance for healthcare, but who needed it when good healthcare was free and they had God and folk medicine as backup plans?

The waiting room door opened. Tony Goats ushered out a girl and her mother. He beamed when he spotted me hovering near Tomas. Tony Goats was Dad's vintage. Like Dad, his hair was still black, except for a light frosting of gray at the temples. In his pristine, white coat he reminded me of an actor playing the role of Professional Dentist in a commercial hawking toothbrushes.

"Little Katerina Makris!" he cheered. "This handsome young man can't be yours!" He grabbed me by the shoulders, kissed both my cheeks.

Tomas giggled. "She's my friend and cousin."

"Litsa couldn't be here," I told the dentist.

"She never can," he mouthed over the boy's head. Then out loud he said, "Tell me, any news of your father?" He steered us both through the open doorway, down a short hallway, and into a consultation room. It was outfitted with a big chair, lots of lights, and an overabundance of cutesy animals on the walls.

It was like being assaulted by Disney.

"Not yet. I keep hoping …"

"Mikey's a survivor," he said. "He could eat his way out of an oubliette."

I tilted my head. My only frame of reference for oubliettes was *Labyrinth.* I was having trouble reconciling Dad with Hoggle. Or was I Hoggle?

More importantly, who was Jareth the Goblin King?

"One time, we buried your father and Cookie alive, did he tell you?"

Cookie was Dad's former best friend. He'd faked his death over and over, until the Baptist finally made it stick; the place he'd made it stick was in Grandma's swimming pool.

"No, he never said much about his life here, except when it was disguised as a fairy tale."

He pulled over the wheeled stool, perched on its edge, hands resting on his knees. The moment he started talking, they started moving with him, the way appendages always did with Greeks.

"We were boys … fourteen, maybe fifteen … and we had a test in school. History. Mikey and Cookie, they didn't want to take the test—and they said so in class. The teacher, he was an old goat. In hindsight a good man, but in those days he was one more nemesis, another person who wanted us to be children when we knew we were already men." He chuckled quietly. "Young people are stupid," he told Tomas. "I know because I remember being young. Our teacher, he told the guys that unless they were dead they had to take the test. Well, what do you think your father and Cookie did?"

"Faked their deaths?" I said.

His head bobbed with the enthusiasm of a parrot spying an oncoming cracker. "They faked their deaths. The rest of us, we helped them do it. But we were stupid—it was our first time staging a death. We forgot the part where there were supposed to be bodies, and a coroner, and all those things that come naturally with death."

Tomas was wide-eyed, the little sponge.

"Why don't you go into the waiting room and, uh, watch a movie or something," I suggested.

"No. This is more fun than cartoons."

I considered pressing the issue, but he was a Makris; the poor kid was doomed to a life of crime. He may as well learn how *not* to stage a death, which was where this conversation was headed.

Tony Goats patted him on the arm, then made a fist in the air. "You'll be fine, won't you, Tomas? You're strong like your father."

The boy's head bobbed. Tony continued where he'd left off.

"What we did was jump straight to the burial. We snuck into the cemetery in the middle of the night carrying two coffins we had stolen—"

Both of my brows took a fast hike north. "You stole coffins?"

"In those days we stole a lot of things. Those, at least, we intended to give back."

Oh. Well. That was different, wasn't it?

(No. No, it wasn't.)

"We took hose, drilled a hole in each coffin—"

That's exactly what I was meant. Secondhand coffins couldn't be a legitimate thing. Once you've put something—or someone—in one, there's no room for anyone else, no matter if it empties out along the way. No one wants death cooties, not even the dead. And not their living relatives. Maybe in other countries, if you hated your deceased family member, but not in Greece. It wouldn't be … done. The gossip would rub out every other act of benevolence for the rest of your life. *There goes the cheapskate who put their grandfather to rest in a refurbished coffin. Where is the respect? Nowhere, that is where.*

"—Then we dropped the coffins into holes that had already been excavated. And lucky for us, too, because we were lazy when it came to hard labor in those days. You wouldn't know it to look at Jimmy now—all he does is run, run, run. But back then? We were lazy kids. We only did physical things that were fun. So we lowered the coffins, and then Mikey and Cookie jumped down and slammed the lids on themselves. Then we covered them up.

"The next day—the day of the test—the rest of us went to school, and our teacher asked, 'Where is Mikey, where is Cookie?' and we told him they were dead. He didn't believe a word of it, probably because he knew us." Tony Goats chuckled. "He walked us from each one of our houses to the other—not everyone had a phone in those days—and asked if they heard about the very convenient deaths. Our parents had not, and to Baboulas and Cookie's parents it was a huge surprise. They made us eat wood—fourteen-year-old boys!—and made us take them to the cemetery to get Mikey and Cookie.

Eating wood sounded cruel, unless you're a beaver, until I remembered it meant getting corporal punishment of the spanking kind.

"We got there and they were gone! The graves were empty, the coffins lying at the bottom still with their breathing tubes." He leaned forward, whispered, "But there was no sign of Mikey and Cookie."

"Where did they go?" Tomas asked. The little guy was entranced. Okay, so I was, too.

"We didn't know it at first—not until after we found them—but it was that *malakas* Pistof—the man you knew—" He nodded to me. "—as the Baptist. He had followed us out there and saw what we did. So he blocked the breathing tubes with sticks and leaves. Mikey and Cookie had no choice but to dig their way out. It was that or die. And they weren't about to die, so they had to dig. When they got out, Pistof was gone and they were filthy, so they walked to the beach in Agria. They spent the day swimming, picking up girls, and then they ran into one of the girls we knew from school—"

"Was it Dina?" I asked.

He looked surprised. "Dina, yes. How did you guess?"

"We've met. She has issues."

His eyebrows rose. "Still?"

I was this close to telling him about the Dad shrine that was her entire house—minus the bathroom—when I decided Dina's quirks were her own private business. I didn't like her much, but she'd pulled through for me in a tough situation.

"Still," was all I said. His stare was loaded with expectation, his breath bated, but I wasn't spilling. Eventually he realized that I wasn't Greek all the way to the bone, so he moved on.

"Dina took them home, fed them, washed their clothes properly. Meanwhile everyone was looking for the boys." He hooked one foot on the stool's footrest, jiggled his knee. "When normal parents are looking for their children there is chaos. When mob families are searching for their children they take guns, hunt down their enemies, accuse them of kidnapping. The two families weakened the already-weak peace that day. I suspect that is why now Baboulas hasn't marched on her enemies and flattened them."

That did explain a lot. It was the whole boy-crying-wolf thing. If Grandma accused anyone of kidnapping her son, they'd say, '*Remember what happened last time? He was holed up with some piece of tail. Probably he's on an island somewhere with a mountain of blow and twenty hookers. Have you checked the Maldives? By the way, say "Yia sou" to our little friends—and our big ones, too.*'

"How did they find Dad and Cookie?"

"They went home that night, back to Baboulas' place. Went to bed, slept the night away while everybody was searching for them. The next morning they got up for coffee and cigarettes, like they always did."

"Coffee and cigarettes?"

"It was a typical Greek breakfast in those days." He wagged a finger at Tomas. "No smoking or coffee for you. Bad for your teeth."

"What about candy cigarettes?" Tomas asked.

"Bad."

"Which part is bad, the candy or the cigarettes?"

"Both."

Tomas hung his head. "Sometimes being a kid stinks. I can't wait to be —" He looked up at me. "How old are you?"

"Twenty-eight."

"—I can't wait to be twenty."

Tony Goats went on. "When Baboulas discovered the boys at the compound she had them locked up in the dungeon. You know about the dungeon?"

"Sure, but I haven't seen it."

"I saw it," Tomas said. "Sometimes my brothers sneak down there to poke sticks at the prisoners, when there are any."

Interesting …

"Are there prisoners down there now?" I asked him.

"No. Papou was down there but now he's not. But he wasn't really a prisoner. He yelled when my brothers poked him, then he chased them in his chair. He's fast."

So that's where the old stinker had been. Obviously the way down was well-hidden. "Where's the entrance?"

"I don't know if I'm supposed to tell you," Tomas said, his little face serious. "Baboulas might get angry."

"Don't look at me," Tony Goats said. "I don't know either. But what I do know is that somehow your father and Cookie broke out. It took them two days, but on the third morning Baboulas woke up to find them in her kitchen, smoking and drinking coffee."

"They never said how?"

His chin went up-down. "Never. We were all friends, but those two were tighter than—" He looked at Tomas, went hunting for a G-rated metaphor. "—than Greek plumbing. But mark my words, if there is a way out of wherever Mikey is, he will find it. If you can claw your way out of a grave and break out of Baboulas' dungeon, almost nothing can keep you in." He nodded to Tomas. "Ready?"

Tomas looked up at me. "Can you stay?"

"Wouldn't miss it."

He nodded solemnly and climbed into the chair.

~ ~ ~

Tomas's mouth was a cavity-free zone. Tony Goats gave us each a sticker. Tomas was a Star Patient and mine was a Special Award for Bravery. That seemed fitting. Dental equipment made me woozy.

The receptionist jotted down a new appointment date, six months from now. She smiled at Tomas, but me, I was a real pane: she looked right through me.

I tried not to stare at her on the way out. I had a feeling she had two faces, and this was only one of them.

~ ~ ~

Aunt Rita had more fun and games planned for me when we arrived back at the compound. She reminded me of one of the Apple Store "Geniuses" as she slid her finger around the iPhone's screen. "You have an appointment in five minutes. You've got enough time to pee and grab a *koulouraki*."

I spent thirty of those seconds debating which was more important: my bladder or my stomach. My bladder won, but I made it fast, that way I had time to snatch a couple of Grandma's cookies out of the container on the counter. I slid into home base—aka: the table under the grapevine trellis—as Aunt Rita was striding through the arch alongside a man who could have been George the Sheep Lover's brother.

"This is Spiros the Kreopolis."

Spiros the Butcher.

"Katerina," I said, offering him my hand. "Are you the *kreopolis* in Makria?"

His head bobbed. "Yes."

"Some tourists were looking for your shop the other day. I gave them directions."

"Thank you," he said. "I know, I remember them." He glanced around, his face pensive.

"Are you okay?" I asked him.

"Kyria Katerina and I usually do this in the garden."

"I don't do gardening," I said.

"What about baking? Sometimes she does that."

"I don't really bake either." His face fell. "But I'm working on it," I said in a hopeful voice.

"It's not the same."

I patted him on the shoulder. "I know. I'd rather she was here, too."

He sighed and perched on the edge of the chair, his leg jiggling to an inaudible beat. "Couldn't we …"

"Go into the kitchen?"

He nodded.

Why not? If he'd get to the point faster it was worth a shot. I was about to agree when I heard the sound of tires spitting dirt and pebbles. A moment later the driver cut the engine and a door slammed. Somebody was here and they weren't happy. A moment later Melas appeared through the arch. His face was a perfect storm. His fingers had a death grip on a manila envelope. Whatever he had to say it was bad news, not sad news; otherwise he wouldn't be wearing that mega-scowl.

"Uh oh," Aunt Rita said, scooting behind me. "Somebody peed on his baklava." She grabbed the butcher and they bolted, leaving me to deal with Melas and his mood.

"Katerina," he said, nodding curtly.

"Detective Melas."

He opened the envelope, slapped a couple of photos in front of me. "Ever see her before?"

For a moment, I mistook the photograph for a picture of a goat in frizzy black wig, then I realized that was no goat. She was bug-eyed, needle-nosed, and she was sprouting peach fuzz on her pointy chinny-chin-chin.

With one finger he pushed the second picture into my line of vision. Same woman, brand new bruises, including a couple of shiners that came close to fixing the bug-eyed problem.

"Holy cow," I said. "What happened to her?"

"Stairs. She says her boyfriend's wife pushed her. The wife has an alibi. So does the husband."

A little bell went *ding-a-ling* in my head. "Huh. That's some bad luck. I don't know her."

"A funny thing, the wife knows your grandmother. Her name is Varvara Koufo."

Oh boy …

"Everybody knows my grandmother."

"They're old friends."

"In case you hadn't noticed, Grandma is about as old as the Parthenon. All her friends are old."

"She's a middleman. A drug supplier. One of your grandmother's." He gave me a look loaded with meaning—and the meaning was that somewhere, somehow, by not too far of an imagination stretch, the Family was involved.

"You think Grandma pushed her down the stairs?" I asked.

"No."

I relaxed.

"I think Baboulas had somebody shove her."

Oh. Damn. He was probably right, but I wasn't going to say so.

"Sometimes bad things happen to bad people," I said. "If she was doing the horizontal mambo with a married man, it's not that much of a surprise. Karma can be like a bitchy schoolgirl."

"She said it was a man dressed in black."

"There you go," I said. "Lots of people wear black. It could have been anyone."

"She said he looked shady."

"*You* look shady when you're in a bad mood. You look shady right now."

There was a long pause while he scratched the back of his head.

"You think bad things should happen to people who cheat?"

Yes. No. I wasn't sure. I had, after all, caught my fiancé bobbing on another guy's knob, not long before our wedding. Had I wanted them to fall down the stairs?

No.

But I wouldn't have cried if they'd both tripped and fallen a terrible bonfire. And maybe I would have thrown a courtesy gallon of gasoline on them while they burned.

Then I remembered that Melas himself had been hiding the pepperoni in a married woman's drawers. And not any wife: she was Family. So he was probably sensitive about things like infidelity. Falling down the stairs would be the least of his worries if anyone found out about his affair and the secret baby that had resulted. It was more likely they'd cut him up into pieces and ferry his parts to the corners of the world. And when they reached shore, that's when they'd set his chunks on fire.

That, I figured, was the best-case scenario.

"I don't know," I mumbled. "I'm not really qualified to judge."

He chewed on that a moment before speaking again. "You want to hear the funny part?"

I glanced at the woman's *After* portrait again. "There's a funny part?"

"You know who the husband is?"

"Kyrios Koufos?" Mr. Koufos.

"A Greek woman doesn't always take her husband's name. Things have changed. Her husband's name is Katsikas." He waited for the penny, the cent, the drachma to drop.

Katsikas. Goat. "Tony Goats." I groaned internally. "Please don't tell me the husband is Tony Goats."

Two palms up. "Greece is a small country."

"She's got ten years on him—easy."

"Trophy husband."

"But he's a dentist."

"She funded his new clinic, at first. But turns out he's a good dentist, so now he's doing okay."

"Tomas does love him."

"Kids love the guy. Parents do, too." He hung his head, rubbed the back of his neck, looked up at me through his unruly hair. "When I was kid, Mama used to take me to this old man who also doubled as the town's blacksmith. If you had a bad tooth he'd yank it out between shoeing donkeys."

"They shoe donkeys?"

He nodded.

"Huh," I said. I figured that was only a horse thing. Live and learn.

"Used to be little Greek kids got a lot of rotten teeth. Too many sweets, like vanilla submarines. That stuff eats teeth."

"Vanilla submarines?"

"It's a spoon sweet. They mix mastic resin with sugar. Scoop up a spoonful. Drop the spoon in a glass of ice water. It hardens the mastic, then you slowly suck and lick it off the spoon." He looked at my mouth as he said it. I wondered if he was thinking what I was thinking.

Probably not. I was thinking I'd really like to try one of those vanilla submarines.

"Look," I said. "Grandma's locked up, so I know she didn't authorize anything. And I … I wouldn't."

"Kyria Koufo said it was your idea."

"What?" I shouted.

He pulled out his notepad, flipped through the pages. "She said pushing her husband's *putana* down the stairs was your idea, and that you maybe took it upon yourself to carry out your plan to impress your grandmother and prove you're part of the Family."

"Of all the stupid things I've ever heard, that's definitely one of them."

He shoved the notepad back into his pants pocket. "I don't think you did it. But somebody did."

"You said Kyria Koufo has an alibi. Who is it?"

"Her girlfriend."

The laugh sort of fell out. "She's a lesbian? Then why does she care who her husband sleeps with?"

"Appearances," he said. "You know what it's like here."

"I'm getting the picture. Who's the girlfriend?"

"You're going to love this," he said. "It's her husband's receptionist."

A small flame began guttering in my head, and the shadows on the walls turned ugly. Witches—the warty-nosed kind—and demons danced. I remembered now where I had seen the snooty receptionist before. Behind me. Following me everywhere, except during the mornings when she was working for Tony Goats.

The receptionist was Cleopatra.

Cleopatra was the receptionist.

Once that particular penny dropped I felt stupid. I'm one of those people who screams, "How can you not know Clark Kent is Superman?" at the TV screen. Bad makeup and big hair was Cleopatra's nerdy glasses.

"I met her," I said slowly, trying not to give away the current location of my brain wanderings. "She's sour."

"Sour or not, she swore up and down that she was with Kyria Koufo when the victim had her accident."

"Maybe they were together." I raised my eyebrows, gave him a meaningful stare. "Maybe they pushed her together."

"We're considering all the angles," he said. "I wanted to know where you fit into this."

"Nowhere," I said. "I made one joke about pushing her down the stairs, because she was spinning some story about how her husband and his girlfriend were going to kill her for her fortune. I even said it was a joke."

His eyebrows shot up. "So you *did* tell her to do it?"

"No. I cut into a conversation that was none of my business and made a stupid joke, then followed it up with a legal disclaimer. I live in a litigation-obsessed country, so I covered my ass."

"That doesn't work here. We know not to shower with our hairdryers."

"When you shower," I said, remembering how Dad used to talk about how they got a bath on Saturday, one after the other, all in the same bathwater. As the eldest he got to go last. The cleanest water was for the littlest.

"I shower every day. Want to join me?"

Yes. "No. Don't even try and pin this on me. Ask Grandma—she heard me say it was a joke. It's not my fault Kyria Koufo is a nut."

"You keep calling people nuts. That an American thing?"

"Nuts. Crazy. *Trelos*. You don't have that saying here?"

"No. We put serious muscle into our insults."

"So I've noticed." They put muscle, and everything else they could fit, into insults—the more offensive the better. It was a wonder the Greek Orthodox Church didn't pack its gold and abandon ship.

"Backing up … you said she claimed her husband and his girlfriend were trying to kill her?"

"That's what she said."

"Did she say anything else?"

I shook my head. "That was it. My mind was on other things. Where is Kyria Koufo now?"

He shrugged. "At home, I guess. Why?"

"No reason."

"Katerina …"

"I want to talk to her, that's all. She dumped me in the shit and I want to know why."

We were going to have words. Big ones. And if she brought out the flamethrower I was going to break it over her head.

"I can't stop you, but—"

"You're right," I said. "You can't. I don't know if this a free country, but I'm going to act like it is until someone tells me otherwise."

~ ~ ~

Aunt Rita was out front, sliding through a gallery on her phone. She waved goodbye to Melas, then pulled me into the shade with her.

"Look." She handed me her phone, pointed with a shiny fingernail. Today it was a French manicure. "Those are my boys—your cousins."

They were teenagers. Good-looking kids with the family nose and our dark coloring. "I can't wait to meet them," I said.

"One night a month, that's all she gives me with them. I tried to get more but the courts … They know what I do—what we do. The papers say I get every other weekend, but they won't enforce it when she refuses to honor the decree. What can I do? I take whatever I can get. It's better than nothing."

"Is there anything Grandma can do about it?"

"There are very few people in this country who want nothing from Mama. I am one of those few. I will never ask her for anything. I'm not much of a man—but this is my business and I handle it like a man."

"Maybe you're not much of a man, but you're one heck of a woman."

She tipped back her head and laughed. She put her arm around my shoulders. "The circumstances of you coming here are the worst. But I'm glad you came."

My nose began to clog as tears gathered behind my eyes. But before they could roll out I remembered something.

"Where's Kyrios Spiros?"

"He had to go. Meat delivery."

~ ~ ~

I had a bone to pick, and the person I had to pick it with was Kyria Koufo. But first I needed to cover my butt. Somebody had pushed that woman down the stairs, and I wanted to make sure it wasn't Team Makris, before I went in swinging.

Who was I kidding? I was going to ask politely why she had knifed me in the back. Then I'd swing. Maybe. So I sent word out for the entire family—husbands, wives, kids, employees—to assemble in the courtyard. It took about ten minutes for the slow pour to stop. Then we stood there, all of us slowly baking under the Greek sun.

"This is a lot of family," I said to Aunt Rita. "Do we have a megaphone or something?"

She looked puzzled. "What's wrong with your voice?"

"Not Greek enough, I expect."

"You are plenty Greek. All you need is a husband and children to practice your yelling."

It was true: the Family's women knew how to screech. Their blood-curdling cries could slap birds out of the sky, peel paint, shatter glass.

My aunt squeezed my shoulder. She had big hands, didn't realize her own strength, so I came this close to wincing. "I will do it for you. Tell me what you want me to say."

I told her I wanted to know if anyone was responsible for carrying out Kyria Koufo's wishes by pushing a woman down some steps.

"Varvara," she muttered. "That woman … We should have set a fire."

"You might get your chance," I said. She brightened at the thought, then did my yelling for me.

Mid-crowd a hand waved an invisible banner. Aunt Rita ushered its owner closer. It was my cousin (second cousin, third cousin, who knew?) whose name I couldn't for the life of me remember.

He worked his way to the front. I flipped a small wave. He flipped one back.

"What's the story?" I asked him. "Did you do it?"

"Baboulas said she would have a task for me soon, involving Kyria Koufo, but it didn't involve pushing anyone down any steps."

Curiouser and curiouser. "What was the task?"

"She didn't say. But I had the feeling it was a hit on Kyria Koufo herself."

That couldn't be right, could it? The women were friends. What possible reason could Grandma have to wipe her off Greece's face? It couldn't be the rising pharmaceutical prices. They were a new development, a direct result of Grandma's absence.

I needed to speak with Grandma. Now. Or, as close to now as possible.

"Okay," I said, not really sure if anything would ever be okay again. I felt like I was blindfolded at a circus, and occasionally I managed to sneak a glimpse, a swirl of colors, flashes of scenery and cheering crowds, but never enough to form a solid picture. Sands were shifting beneath my feet. And I was drowning myself in metaphors and descriptions of things that didn't matter.

I dialed Grandma's lawyers, asked if there was any way they could finagle a visit. They made all kinds of "Gee, we don't know noises" until I snapped.

"I'm driving up there now. Get me in." Then I felt bad and tacked on a soft "Please."

Google gave me two options for the drive north. The three-hour or two-hour option. No prizes for guessing which one I'd take.

Marika jiggled over to hug me. "That was a good effort, but next time you do the talking. That is what Baboulas would do."

Takis followed her over. "Next time. Ha!"

His wife delivered a crushing glare. He was unfazed.

"You ready to saddle up?" I asked her. "We're going on another road trip."

Her eyes lit up like a monochromatic Christmas tree. "Do I have time to get my bag?"

"Make it quick."

"What about my lunch?" Takis cried.

"You have two hands," Marika told him.

"But that's your job!"

Her hands planted themselves on her substantial hips. "My job, eh? When do I get paid? Never, that is when."

"I give you all my money. Okay, not all of it, but most of it."

She stared at him the way one stares at a strange new bug, if they're not the squeamish type.

"Maybe you should sit this one out," I said, not wanting to come between husband and wife, especially when one of them was out for blood, and the other one was a henchman.

"No. I am coming with you. Takis can watch the children and cook for once." She shook a finger at him. "This is what you get for refusing to take me anywhere—ever!"

"We went to Disney World!"

"With our children! When we did we have time, eh?"

"We had time," he muttered.

"When?"

"There was that time in the bathroom."

"In the bathroom!" She turned to me. "Do you know what he means?"

It was pure self-preservation the way my hands flew up to cover my ears. "No, and I don't want to."

My "No" must have been silent, because her mouth kept moving and words kept bubbling out.

"He couldn't find the wastebasket to put his dirty toilet paper inside! In America! He wanted me to get for him the wastebasket under the bathroom sink. So he called me into the bathroom for that because he was too lazy to cross the room himself. I was in there for five minutes while he ranted and raved because he did not want to flush the paper." She turned back to her husband. "You are a peasant!"

Greek plumbing was notorious for gagging on toilet paper. So most places kept a small wastebasket next to the toilet. If you were lucky it had a lid.

"You are a *strigla*!" Takis said.

Hag. Witch. Banshee. Succubus. The word encompassed a multitude of female sins. It was a fighting word.

Marika sucked in her breath, pulled back her shoulders, puffed herself up for battle. The match was on. Which meant I was going solo. No way did I want to stand here and watch Takis curl up into the fetal position and cry.

I slipped away, leaving them to their domestic battle.

"Wait—" Takis called out. "Where are you going? Don't leave me alone with this *strigla*!"

Marika cuffed him.

"Ow!"

"Thessaloniki," I shouted.

"How will you get there?"

"Car."

He laughed. "What for do you want to go in the car? We have a plane."

I'd been in the family plane twice. My memory banks only retained part of the first trip because Takis drugged me. Then Grandma drugged me, so

I'd missed the second one entirely. Both times I had Takis and Stavros for company. The puny worm was a pilot.

"I'd rather take my chances with the car."

"Take the plane," Marika said. Her eyes were bright. Already I could see where this was going. "I have never been on a private plane."

"And you won't be going this time, either," Takis said. "This is Family business."

"She can come," I said, trying not to laugh at his scowl. "Marika's my sidekick."

She gave him a "*See?*" look.

He ignored her. "If you drive you will have company."

He was right, damn him. Where I went, the assassins followed. They couldn't follow if I hopped on a plane to an unknown—to them—location.

~ ~ ~

Takis had called ahead so the plane was gassed up and waiting on the tarmac when we arrived. Unfortunately, we had company, and a lot of it. I felt like the prettiest girl at the party.

Lefty was the first to object to me bailing on a jet. "What if someone assassinates her while she's away?"

"They won't," Takis said. "Nobody in this family has been killed on my watch." He made a face. "Nobody who was standing with me. I am quick, like a cobra."

"I don't trust him." Lefty glanced at the others. "Does anyone trust him?"

The rest of the crew shook their heads, jerked their chins up, spat on the ground. Basically, it was a negative all around. I got it, I really did. Takis was a weasel. But Grandma trusted him, and the man could fly a plane.

"I trust nobody who is not me," Vlad said.

Mo gave him the hairy eyeball. "I would not trust myself if I was you."

"Russia shits on Persia," Vlad said.

"Everybody shits on Persia," Lefty said.

I shook my head, to clear out the nonsense, mostly. "Why are any of you here? Your bosses are getting picked off one at a time. Chances are if you manage to kill me you won't get paid."

"Death is its own reward," Vlad said, fingering his knife.

I rolled my eyes. "Somebody get him a black cloak and guyliner."

Snickering all around, from everyone except Vlad, who glowered. Then: "What is guyliner?"

That was Donk.

"Nobody is getting on the plane," I said, "except Takis, Stavros, Marika, and me. That's it. I have somewhere I need to be and I can't have all of you tagging along."

Cleopatra, I noticed, wasn't with them. But I knew where she was: manning the phones at Tony Goats' clinic.

"But we never get to go anywhere," Donk said.

"You've been following me around for days!"

"Yes, and you are boring. This is the first fun thing you've done."

"I took you to Meteora," I said.

He snorted. "That was before I was an assassin."

Marika flicked his ear, made him yelp.

"You're not an assassin," I told him. "You're a kid who should be at summer camp."

"Maybe you are not so bad," Mo told me. "Still unclean and a Yankee pig, but not completely stupid …"

High praise, indeed. It was a wonder I didn't faint.

" … But I agree with the small boy," he went on. "You are not leaving the ground without us."

"I never said that," Donk said. He looked faintly alarmed.

Mo ran to the plane, whipped out a pair of handcuffs and fastened himself to the landing gear.

"*Gamo ton keratas*!" Takis swore. He hurled his keys at the ground, stomped his feet. Only the gravity of the situation squelched my laugh. Any other time I'd be roaring at the ridiculousness of it all.

"What did I say?" Marika said.

"I don't know," Takis yelled, waving his hands. "You say too many things. How can I pick one?"

"Your language! We have children!"

"Yes, but are they here? I don't see any children. Because they are at home, where you are supposed to be."

She swung her bag at him, caught him behind the knees. He stumbled forward.

"*Keratas*?" I asked. That was one I hadn't heard before.

Stavros to the rescue. "It is when another man sleeps with your wife."

Oh. A cuckold. I thanked him and stuffed the word in my head, hoping I wouldn't forget it. You never know when a word like that could be useful.

Time was ticking onwards. I was getting tired of these butt-heads and their petty power struggles. I wanted to go, and I wanted to go now.

"Can you fly this thing with him on the wheel?" I asked Takis.

"Only if I drive it around first and break him into little pieces." Takis didn't look too unhappy about that idea. "I will do that."

"Murderer!" Mo screeched, hugging the wheel.

"Hey!" I pointed at him. "You're an assassin. You don't get to decide what's murder. But you've got a point. We have to find another way," I told Takis.

"No problem," he said. "I brought my axe. I will chop off his hand."

"Then my people will think I am a thief!" Mo protested.

I crouched down beside him. "So unlock the cuffs."

"Never!"

"Okay." I looked up at the others. "Time to bring in the big guns."

21

Stavros was back. Under one arm he was carrying a large package wrapped in brown paper. He'd volunteered for the "Free Mo" mission, and went into Volos for supplies.

I eyeballed the package. "What is that?"

He tore the paper, showed me the contents. "Secret weapon."

No, not really a weapon, except in the war against obesity. More like a breakfast food.

"I meant bolt cutters! Or a lock pick!"

"You told me to get something to get him out of the cuffs. This will work and it will save the handcuffs."

For the most part I was a live-and-let-live person. Whoever you worshipped, that was cool with me, as long as you didn't rub my nose in it or blow up my people. Go crazy, find yourself a fictional ancient deity from outer space, find a flying spaghetti monster, wear a colander on your head. But if you cuffed yourself to the landing gear of a private plane, causing a major delay in my life-or-death plans, I'd be okay with using what I had against you.

Normally.

Unfortunately, using bacon against someone whose religion prohibited the delicious meat violated my moral code. Also, it was a waste of bacon.

"If you don't want to do this I could get cats," Stavros said in a hopeful tone. "I know a woman who breeds cats."

"Cats?"

"A big cage full of cats. I will throw his rug inside."

"I don't think we'll need the cats," I said. Getting between someone and their God didn't seem like a good idea.

"What is that?" Mo asked, craning his neck.

"Bacon," I told him. "Not my idea. I really don't want to use it."

He scooted backwards. "Unclean pigs! Keep the sin food away from me!"

"Uncuff yourself and the bacon goes away."

"Kat," Stavros whispered in my ear, "it is turkey bacon."

I pulled him to one side, away from Mo. "What?"

"It's healthier!"

"Not a word," I said. He pressed his lips together in an imitation of silence.

"You want me to do it?"

"No, I'll take the heat." Getting someone else to do the dirty work didn't sit right with me, even if theirs was the hand that bought the bacon. I tore a bigger hole in the paper, pulled out a wannabe rasher and laid it across Mo's forehead like it was an ice pack.

"Ahhhhhh! It burns!"

"It's raw bacon," I said.

"Allah is trying to burn it out of me!"

"It's not in you. It's on your face."

"Arrrrggggghhhh," he howled. "Get it off me!"

"Get it off yourself. All you have to do is unlock the cuffs."

"I cannot do that!"

"Sure you can. Get the key, unlocked the cuffs, and get away from my grandmother's plane. Then the bacon will stop."

"Never!"

"More bacon for you!" I laid another strip across the assassin's forehead.

"I do not have the key!" he howled.

I crouched beside him. "Where's the key?"

"I do not know, I swear it. I found them. And by found them I mean I stole them from that policeman."

"From Detective Melas?"

He shrugged. "Who knows? Greeks all look the same to me."

My teeth began to grind like sweaty strangers in a club. Melas was the last person on earth I wanted to talk to right now. But I stomped to the far end of the plane, where there was a patch of shade, and made the call.

He picked up on the second ring. "Melas," he said. "Come."

I thunked my head on the side of the jet. "You missing a pair of handcuffs?"

"You mean besides the ones you stole?"

He'd cuffed me to the fireman's pole in his house after I broke in. I managed to pop the cuffs, with Aunt Rita's help, and kept them as a souvenir.

"You basically threw them away. It's your own fault."

He blew out a sigh of exasperation. Things must be tense at work if I was punching his buttons this quickly. "Yeah, I'm missing a pair." His tone turned suggestive fast. "Wasn't one pair enough for you? If you wanted more you could have asked."

"Wasn't me. It was Mo." I gave him a quick rundown, including the part about the turkey bacon."

"Jesus," he said. I pictured him banging his head on the nearest hard surface. "I wouldn't blame the guy if he killed you now. I'd probably testify on his behalf."

I cut him off mid-character assassination. "I could use the keys."

His laugh was more like a bark. He asked where we were, so I told him.

"I'll be right there. I wouldn't miss this for anything."

~ ~ ~

It was five minutes later. We were all maintaining our positions.

"Get it out of my face," Mo pleaded. His eyes were shut but all his whining was keeping his mouth more open than not. A rasher of the pretend bacon worked its way down his cheek. The more he talked, the closer it got to his lips, until finally he got an accidental mouthful.

"Argh!" he wailed. "Allah will never forgive this!" He tried flicking it away with his tongue. "This is bacon?" His face scrunched up. "I thought it would taste better. Infidels are obsessed with bacon, so my expectations were very high."

"It's turkey bacon," I said. "It's nowhere near close to the real deal."

He sniffed. "You tried to trick me, infidel, but it did not work! Now I will kill you, for certain."

I was about to unload a serious chunk of my mind, but then the cop car rolled up to the airstrip.

"I can't wait to see what you come up with next," Melas said when he got out of the car and joined us on the runway. He stood there looking cool in his dark glasses, arms folded, legs apart.

"You say that like I'm the one who cuffed him to the landing gear."

"Somebody get my rug," Mo said. "It is time for me to pray."

"No," I said. "No rug for you. Get it yourself."

Melas produced the key, unlocked the cuffs, pocketed them once he had freed the Persian assassin. Mo stomped back to his car, snatched up his rug. Then he faced Mecca and apologized for coming this close to eating forbidden meat.

"Going somewhere?" Melas asked.

"Not really. I like hanging out at airstrips."

"Looks to me like you're going somewhere. Why else would that one—" He nodded to Mo who was groveling to Allah. "—cuff himself to a plane?"

"He's crazy. Crazy people do crazy stuff."

"Does he know Harry Harry is dead?"

Mo quit praying. "What?"

"Harry Harry is dead," Melas told him. "Been dead a few days now."

"Impossible," Mo said. He went back to praying.

"You heard the man," I said. "It's impossible. We're going on a shopping trip to Athens." I was,making it up as I went. "Takis is flying us there."

Melas gave me a look like he wasn't buying what I was trying desperately to sell.

"You don't strike me as the shopping trip kind."

"How would you know?" My body forgot that I was lying and went straight into indignation mode. Hands on hips. Chin jutting forward.

"Shopping is my life. It's my favorite hobby. I spent over six hundred hours shopping last year. And that doesn't include online shopping."

"I know enough about you to know you're part hound dog, especially when it comes to your family. I'm guessing you're following a tip about your father, or …" He rubbed his temples as though he was downloading information from the psychic hotline. "… You're going to visit Baboulas. Probably the second one."

I golf clapped. "And this is why you made Detective." I turned back to Takis. "Let's get this bird off the ground." He saluted sarcastically and opened up the plane.

"It's going to become the *putanas*," Melas said.

"What? I understood the individual words, but I have no idea what you said."

"It's a Greek saying. Get on that plane and it's going to be a big mess." He tilted his head toward my undesirable entourage. "Those guys don't look like they want you going anywhere without them."

"Can't you do some kind of cop thing?"

"I could—"

"So do that then."

"—But I won't. I'm outnumbered. And I'm guessing they're all armed."

I pulled him aside. "Look, you're right, I'm going to see Grandma. I can't tell you why. I won't tell you why. But I need to go." In fact, I could have driven there with all the time I was wasting here.

He focused on some point past my shoulder. Nodded. "How many does the plane hold?"

The groan slid out of me.

Stavros piped up. "There are enough seats for all these assholes."

"What about me?" Melas asked.

"You're not coming," I yelped.

"Why not? Flying is fun."

"This is business. Family business."

Two palms up. "So take care of your business. I'm tagging along." He grinned. He'd gotten one over on and me, and he knew it. "For fun."

Fine. Anything to get off the ground sometime soon.

I trotted over to tell the assassins what was up.

"We're not getting on a plane with a cop," Lefty said. "What if he arrests us?"

I swung back around to look at Melas. "Promise not to arrest anyone?"

"If they promise not to do anything that gets them arrested."

"Promise?" I asked them.

Lefty glanced at the others. They all shrugged, except Vlad, who didn't seem like shrugging was his thing. "Okay, we promise."

"Promise?" I asked Melas.

"Sure, why not."

"Okay. Everybody saddle up!"

~ ~ ~

I was stuck between a window and Melas. He'd planted himself next to me, ejecting Stavros from the aisle seat first. From the air, Greece was brown and an exhausted shade of green.

Melas nudged me with his elbow. "You going to tell me why we're going to Thessaloniki?"

"We're not—I am. And no, I'm not telling you."

"Okay," he said. "I was curious. Have they given you permission to see her?"

"The lawyers were trying."

"I might be able to get you in if they can't."

"Really?"

"I can't promise they'll go for it, but they will if they want my cooperation again."

The plane dipped. Almost time to land. We'd been in the air fewer than ten minutes.

"Thanks," I said. "I'll take any help I can get."

"Katerina," he said. "What ever you do, don't say anything that could incriminate you in any way or get Baboulas into more trouble. They're looking for an excuse to throw away the key."

My eyes misted. A lump wedged itself good and hard in my throat. The words couldn't push past.

He took my hand, and I let him.

~ ~ ~

Grandma wasn't in the lockup facility at the Thessaloniki Police Headquarters. She was gone. My heart squeezed all the juice out, then relaxed when I realized they didn't mean the dead kind of gone. I tried to process what the boys in black were telling me, in the brightly lit interrogation room. The periodic, and almost imperceptible, flicker of the gas-filled tubes kept me hovering on the edge between nervous and nuts.

But I played it cool; hard not to when the air-conditioning is set to late October. There was no austerity in this building. Even the coffee was the good stuff, served American-style.

"What do you mean she's not here?"

The guy slouching against the wall, arms folded to keep away the criminal cooties, was the same guy who'd hauled Grandma away. He'd witnessed my dumb act; now he was getting the real dumb deal.

"We had to let her go. Look, we *know* she sprang Dogas out of prison, but she had too many alibis who swore otherwise."

"Who?"

He looked pissed. Not a man used to losing to a woman—or anyone else. "A whole village. Every one of them claimed she was at a church thing at the village square at the time. They all saw your grandmother there. I couldn't crack a one of them."

Well, well, well. Makria had come through for her, for better or worse, for lawful or not. Mostly not. Completely not. But they had come through for her.

I measured and cut my words carefully. “If they say she was there, she was there.”

“The hell she was. I know it, they know it, you know it.”

The door opened. A suit stepped in. I recognized him from the compound on the day of the raid. He had a face like a stack of unfinished paperwork: smooth, line-free, and completely without character or little doodles in the margins.

“I don’t know anything except that my grandmother isn’t here. How did she leave? Did you put her on a bus or what?”

“She had a ride,” the cop told me. “One of her men. An Alexander Dimou.”

Was it my imagination or did he press a subtle emphasis upon *her*? He flicked a glance at the suit. Repulsion skittered across his face, and then it was gone, leaving him about as readable as the Voynich manuscript.

“All yours,” he muttered. Through the door he went, leaving me with the guy in the suit.

I shivered. He didn’t. But then one of us was wearing fewer clothes.

“So you’re the granddaughter,” he said.

I said nothing. He had made an observation, that’s all. There was no hook at the end of his comment to suggest a question had taken place.

“How is the search for your father coming along?”

Okay, so that was a question.

“Things would be moving faster if law enforcement would cooperate.”

Not so much as a twitch. “Not our jurisdiction.”

“What is your jurisdiction?”

“Greece.”

“Are you Hellenic Police?”

“Yes.”

He was good; I’d give him that. The lie rolled out without a squeak. But his eyes darted left for a fraction of a second before reattaching themselves to mine. Probably he was cursing himself internally for that glitch. Men like him did training to rid themselves of tiny tells. They wound up excellent at poker, but not at life.

"We can help you—we want to. But you have to help us."

"How?"

"You're in a unique situation. You're closer to Baboulas than anyone."

"I'm living in her house. There's a difference between physical closeness and intimacy. She doesn't share anything with me."

"Then get her to share. Your father's life could depend on it."

He wanted me to betray Grandma. Be the leak in her trireme and sink the Family. And here I was, the woman who said she'd do *anything* to get Dad back. Was that true, would I do anything? Or did my *anything* have edges like any other box?

"Think about it," he said, shunting the decision-making to one side, for now. "I'll be in touch. He pushed the door outward, held it open with one flat palm. "If you stay on this road, you'll discover uphill and downhill are the same direction."

"I've studied the great philosophers," I said. "You're not one of them."

Then I left while I could.

~ ~ ~

"She's gone," I told Melas. He was waiting downstairs, firing birds at smirking pigs on his phone. He shot me a surprised glance.

"What?"

"They say it takes a village to raise a child. Apparently a village can also yank a crime lord's feet out of the fire. She has alibis." I told him what Thessaloniki's finest had told me.

He pocketed his phone, stood with his hands on hips while he stared off into the distance, somewhere over my shoulder. I waved my hand in front of his eyes.

"Xander picked her up," I said.

"Yeah, I figured he was here. He goes where she goes, unless she tells him otherwise. You okay?"

"Relieved. Worried. This isn't over." It felt like someone had popped the lid on a tube of Pringles. There would be no stopping until the last chip was eaten, and so far the cops had only licked the powdery flavoring on top. "Also, I realized you're beating me in Angry Birds."

Melas molded his hand around the curve of my nape. My hormones shot hot glitter and streamers. But beneath the hormonal fanfare was a warm, reassuring glow. He wanted to get a better look down my front, yes, but he also had my back.

"I don't mind that you're a loser," he said.

He reeled me in, pecked me on both cheeks, then gave me a quick hug.

Afternoon traffic was light in Greece's second biggest city. That's the power of the siesta. I leaned back in the rental car's seat, closed my eyes. And when I opened them again we were at the airport where Grandma's jet was waiting.

Takis and Marika were arguing off to one side in the shade. The assassins were slumped against the small terminal building, smoking. But not Mo. He was swinging his Aladdin sword, making swishing noises with his mouth.

Oh, God, he was pretending to be a Jedi, wasn't he?

"Is he pretending to be a Jedi?" Melas asked me.

Great and terrible minds.

"I think so."

"You keep some weird company."

I looked him up and down. "Tell me about it."

He grinned. "Just so you know, I want to kiss you right now." Then he smacked me on the butt and swaggered off toward the plane, leaving me to cool off in the sun.

Takis and Stavros didn't ask questions. They knew the business meant knowing when to keep quiet. They'd pounce on me when we shed the assassins and cop.

Not Marika. She began to fire questions as soon as we boarded the plane. I tried to answer using an array of creative grunts and hums, but she had four kids and Takis; noises weren't going to satisfy a Greek wife and mother.

Finally Takis stomped back from the cockpit. "Shut up so I can concentrate!"

The jet dipped.

"Who's flying this thing?" I asked.

Two palms up. "The autopilot."

"*Po-po*," Marika said. "You have one job on this plane, and even that you can't do."

Takis pointed at his wife, then the finger swung toward me like I was due North.

"No more, you two. No more spending time together, having women's adventures. You go home and cook. You," he told me, "learn to cook."

"I'll tell Grandma you said that."

"Heh. Maybe I spoke too hastily. I have to go land the plane." He hurried back to the cockpit.

"Being married to Takis is a life sentence," Marika told me.

The jet swooped lower.

"*Gamo ta pethamena sou*!" Takis muttered from up front, threatening to sexually violate someone's dead bodies. "Some *malakas* is parked on the runway. Who parks a car on the runway?"

"In India sometimes they have cows on the runway," Stavros said.

"Cows on the runway …" Takis snickered. "Nobody listen to Stavros, he is an idiot."

"It's true," Stavros said in a low voice. "The planes have to fly around until the cows move."

Mo stuck his head over the seat. "The moron is right, they have cows."

"Nobody asked you," Takis yelled from the front. "Why are you here? Your employer is dead!"

"I wanted to ride on the plane," Mo said. "It's the same as a Persian plane." He sounded disappointed.

"Why don't they put a horn on jets?" Takis went on. "Leather seats they have, plush carpet they have, but no horn."

"The jet engine noise is usually warning enough," I told him. "You can't really miss it."

"Except this *malakas* missed it." There was a short pause. "Definitely a *malakas*. It's Xander."

"Is Grandma with him?"

"Hard to say."

I got out of my seat, worked my way to the cockpit.

Takis shot me a dirty look over one shoulder. "What are you doing? Get back there. Nobody is allowed in the front except me."

I scuttled backwards.

"If you are going to stand there, be useful, send Xander a text message and tell him to move his *kolos* off the runway."

~ ~ ~

Xander moved the SUV. Takis landed the plane and we all piled out. My gaze cut through the bodies, hunting for Grandma.

"Where is she?" I asked Xander.

He tilted his head toward the SUV. The windows were up, the engine running. I beelined for it. I yanked the driver's side door open, boosted myself into the driver's seat, turned sideways to look at Grandma.

To hug or not hug, that was the question.

Grandma's fingers were busy with a crochet hook and smooth white yarn. Her eyes were bright, alert, and completely focused on me. How she could crochet without watching her hands was beyond me. Sometimes I glanced down to make sure I was nailing the whole walking thing—and I'd had nearly twenty-eight years of practice.

She hitched an eyebrow into the sardonic position. "Are you catching flies with your mouth?"

No hug.

"Nuh-uh. Are you okay?"

She made a vague noise, waved her hand as though slapping away my inquiry. "Where did you go with my plane?"

"Thessaloniki."

"Rescue mission?"

"I had questions."

"Questions." She laughed. "Go ahead, ask." Her head went back to bending over the hook and yarn.

"Are you planning to assassinate Kyria Koufo?"

"No."

The knots in my shoulders fell into loose skeins.

"Did Tony Goats really try to hire someone to kill her?"

"No. Roll down your window."

I did as she asked. She leaned over me, called out to Xander.

"Katerina is coming with us."

~ ~ ~

Greece was two countries, the new superimposed over the old. Except, the new was smaller, and like a midriff top it had a hard time covering Greece's ancient underbelly. It yanked, pulled, tugged, but old bits kept popping out.

Tony Goats' office was new, shiny, where well-off people sent their children to get their teeth inspected and drilled. But behind the building was a grimy alley that had been here since long before an architect thought up the structure out front. The alley contained all the elements present in every alley throughout history, across the globe: dumpster, fried rice, stray dog, screeching cats, and a corpse. The dead man had been clubbed over the head with a twelve-inch statue of Athena, an item found in every souvenir shop in Greece. Now the goddess of war, wisdom, and lots of things a feminist would be proud of, was taking a dip in the red pool around Tony Goats' head.

"Katsikas," Grandma said. "Katerina, call the police."

I called Melas. My voice crackled as I debriefed him.

"Jesus," he said. "Who fries rice?"

"Never mind the rice. It's the universal law of alleys, there's always fried rice."

"I'll be right there. Don't go anywhere."

I turned to Grandma. "He'll be right here. He said not to go anywhere."

~ ~ ~

We were going somewhere. Grandma told Xander to wait for the police, while we went to take care of business.

I launched a minor protest. "Melas said not to go anywhere."

"I heard you the first time," she said. "And we are not going somewhere—you are. I am coming along for the ride."

Inwardly, I sighed. "Where am I going?"

"To Varvara Koufo's house." She tapped on the GPS. The talking map immediately began interrogating me, demanding to know where I wanted to go, in a sterile, saccharine voice designed for maximum condescension. "Tell it to go to Varvara's house," she said.

"Why me? Can't I press a button or something?"

Not only did I not like the talking map's passive-aggressive personality, but I also wasn't one of those people who socialized with Siri—not when I could type stuff and get a silent, accurate result.

"No. Tell her where you want to go."

Her. Like the tin woman had a job and feelings.

"No."

"Tell the map where you want to go."

"Disney World," I said clearly.

"*Do you mean Walt Disney World, Orlando, Florida, U.S.A.; Disneyland, Anaheim, California, U.S.A.; or Disneyland Paris, Marne-la-Valée, France?*"

"Florida," I said.

"*Calculating distance and route.*" The tin woman wandered off to play with her calculator. A moment later she was back. "*Unable to calculate distance and route. Please choose an alternate destination. Preferably someplace realistic.*"

Sarcasm from a machine. What a world.

"Varvara Koufo's house," Grandma said, flicking her gaze sideways at me. The map adjusted itself to accommodate her command. No sass, no sarcasm this time.

"Why did we go to Tony Goats' office?"

"To give him an alibi," she said. "Now I will go to see Varvara Koufo, to let her know her husband is dead."

"Are you going to kill her?"

"With what, Katerina? Do you see a gun? I have my crochet, that is all."

I had a feeling a crochet hook was a deadly weapon in Grandma's hands. Not that I knew much about killing people, but I was sure you could make a decent garrote using yarn and a hook.

"Why would Tony need an alibi?"

"He was Michail's friend. A good boy. I did not want a good boy to go to jail for a crime he did not commit."

"What crime?" I repeated my earlier question. "Are you going to kill her?"

"Only if talk fails—and I do not believe it will. We are old friends who do not always face the same direction when it comes to business. This is one of those times."

~ ~ ~

Half an hour meandered by.

You're not supposed to leave pets, kids, or adult grandchildren in the car with the windows up, so I had rolled everything down twenty-nine minutes ago. Greece was being uncharitable today: no breeze, no flirtatious hint of rain in the near future. There was shade sulking here and there, but it seemed to shift whenever one of Kyria Koufo's neighbors tried to hide in its lower temperatures.

A little fishwife had set up shop in my head. She was yelling at me to quit being a moron. Grandma should have been back by now, and even the voice in my head knew it. Cold sparklers waved inside my gut, making pretty, icy patterns in my last cup of coffee.

Grandma wasn't one to walk into a dangerous situation unprepared. It was in her nature to be the one with the upper hand, the trump card, the secret weapon. Me, it was in my nature to be the one spouting tired metaphors. I'd watched her knock on Kyria Koufo's door and vanish inside when it opened. There hadn't been any switcheroos between here and the house.

Had she given me the slip, going through one door, escaping through another? Maybe. But why would she do that?

I jumped out of the SUV, slammed the door behind me. I dropped my bag's long strap over my head, so that it sat across my body. No weapons inside except my slingshot, which lived in there with a bag of marbles that had been a loaded gift from Baby Dimitri. The gun someone had left on my bedside table, before my confrontation with the Baptist, had quietly vanished, somewhere between it not firing when I squeezed the trigger, and me shaking like a Chihuahua on meth as my rescuers ferried me back to the compound in this exact same SUV.

The gate squealed as I pushed through. I walked up to the door, which had been repaired since Aunt Rita lobbed a rock at it. Listened. This was Greece—no one walking past would think my eavesdropping was weird. Chances were they'd done the same thing themselves. Around me, boy cicadas wheezed love songs to girl cicadas. Not too far away, a rapper was spitting out Greek words. There was a steady hissing from further down the street where one of the neighbors was spraying her yard with the hose.

But from inside this house? Nothing that I could hear.

I knocked. "Kyria Koufo?" I called out. "Is Grandma still here?"

There was a small sound on the other side of the door, then it opened. Kyria Koufo was wiping her hands on a calico apron.

"Katerina! She was here and then she left."

Rats! It looked like I had inherited a few genes from Grandma after all, including the escapee allele. "Did she say where she was going?"

"Your grandmother is not a woman who shares her plans. All I know is that she went out the back door. She looked like she was in a hurry."

I thanked her and trotted back to the SUV. The plan I was cobbling together involved driving around the neighborhood until I saw an old woman in black ambling down the street. Which would narrow my search parameters by pretty much nothing. You couldn't throw a crust of stale bread in a Greek village without hitting an elderly widow. Sometimes I suspected Greece had a quota to fill. One-point-two black-clad fossils per square meter.

I pulled out my phone, dialed Aunt Rita.

"Is Grandma at the compound?"

"No, she's with you and Xander."

"Not anymore. Somebody killed Tony Goats. We left Xander there to talk to the police."

Not with words. Possibly with Charades. Probably he was going to be there a long time while they guessed at words.

"Where are you now?" she asked.

When I told her, my aunt unleashed a string of curse words that, when mashed together, made no physiological sense whatsoever. Some of them flew right over my head. But they were colorful.

"Wait there. Don't go in."

I made vague promises I had no intention of keeping. Kyria Koufo had an overabundance of bones for me to pick, and I meant to pick them while they were in one neat pile on the other side of the fence. She had chosen me to be her scapegoat, hiked prices on prescription drugs, and now she'd made Grandma vanish. Now I was starting to wonder if she'd killed her husband, too.

I pushed through the gate, trotted up to rap on the door again.

Kyria Koufo poked her head out. She looked harried. Given the nature of her non-relationship with her husband, I wasn't all that surprised at the lack of a river rolling down the dry bedrock of her cheeks. Something told me her drought was permanent.

"What now?"

"I couldn't find Grandma. She's nowhere in the neighborhood."

"Look harder."

"There's a limit to how hard I can look without a team of bloodhounds."

"You didn't even start the car."

"X-ray vision," I said.

She shrugged and went to close the door.

I jammed my foot in the gap. "I want to look in here."

"For what? She is not here."

"Your word isn't exactly reliable. You told the police it was my idea to push your husband's girlfriend down the steps. You even suggested I did it as some kind of hazing ritual."

"It *was* your idea."

"It was a joke! So when you tell me Grandma isn't here, I'm not sure I believe you."

I put on my best imitation of Grandma's intense stare. But either she was immune to Grandma or I was a lousy mimic, because she didn't cave.

"Look at that," she said, shaking her head. "It's a travesty!"

"What?" I threw a glance over one shoulder, half expecting Grandma to have circled around to steal the SUV from under my nose. But the car was still there, snugged up to the curb.

When my head swiveled back around, there was a gun butted up to my nose.

22

She goosed the tip with the metal stub, pulled me indoors. Somehow she managed to make my forward progress feel like I was talking a step backward. The Koufo-Katsikas home was Greek chic … from the seventies. I was standing inside a fruit bowl where only orange-colored fruit was allowed. Tangerine walls. Clementine couch. Persimmon cushions. The wax in the lava lamp was a blobby papaya. But the pieces looked high dollar, chosen and placed with precision by someone who'd been paid for their terrible taste.

"You stupid child," she said.

I reached for my handbag but she jabbed me with the gun again.

"Take it off slowly. Drop it on the floor."

"Did Grandma tell you your husband is dead?"

"How very sad. Excuse me if I do not cry. I plan to save my tears for the funeral."

"Did you kill him?"

Because it looked to me like she could have killed him. He was having an affair, she was having an affair …

Her expression said I was a world-class moron, which validated how I felt. "Of course I did. He was using her!"

Two things dawned on me. *Her* was Cleopatra, aka: Tony Goats' receptionist. And now that Kyria Koufo had admitted to committing murder she probably wouldn't stop at one. Murder seemed like it had a lot in common with potato chips: you couldn't kill just one person. One death lead to another, lead to another, until you'd killed the whole pack, and then flopped on the couch in a fit of self-loathing, telling yourself that tomorrow you wouldn't kill anyone at all.

"Were he and the girlfriend planning to kill you, or was that bullshit?"

"One way or another, I wanted Katerina gone. Prison, death, it's all the same to me. Sometimes, in this world, you have to lie to get the outcome you want. It's too bad she refused to arrange their murders."

"Where's Grandma?"

She kicked the door shut, sealing me off from the sounds and light of the outside world. The shutters were drawn, the windows closed. An unnatural twilight. My nerves fired warning shots. In response, my hands clenched, but there was nothing for them to snap. Deeper in the house, something moved.

The gun prodded my cheek. "Walk. Go down the hall."

"Where are we going?"

"Walk."

My heart was going *wiggity wack*. Great. I was in danger, and the organ responsible for keeping me alive was pounding in time with a one-hit wonder.

"Jump," I said, without thinking.

Kyria Koufo smacked my ear with the gun. "Walk."

Yeah, yeah, she was real bossy with a weapon to underline her words. I wasn't that scared of her.

In all fairness, it wasn't a bravery thing. Under normal circumstances—pre-Greece—I would have been a weeping, wailing mess if someone pointed a gun at me. I'd have a mouthful of "Yes m'am, no m'am," and I'd be asking precisely how fast she wanted to me to walk, lest she shoot. But after my ordeal with the Baptist, Kyria Koufo wasn't all that scary.

Which was stupid of me. A person pointing the business end of a gun at you is scary. Even if the piece isn't loaded, they're still trying to frighten you.

But it was backfiring on her. Any residual fear I felt was slowly dissolving in the cauldron of anger bubbling in my head.

"Last door on the left."

I took it slowly, one small step for woman at a time.

"Women are supposed to stick together," I said.

"Says who?"

"Women."

Somewhere behind me, a door opened and closed. The gun gave me a temporary reprieve, a few inches worth.

"Honey, where are you?"

I knew that voice. Cleopatra.

"In the hall," the woman at my back said. "I'm taking care of a problem."

"You haven't even begun to take care of it," I said. "Hurt Grandma, I give you a day. That's if the Family decides to go easy on you."

"I have a plan," she said.

Footsteps stopped somewhere behind us. I felt Kyria Koufo turn around. "Why have you still got all that mess on your face. Go wash it off. You know I hate all that makeup."

Cleopatra hesitated.

"You going to let her talk to you like that?" I called out. "I don't like you, but I thought you had guts."

"My Virgin Mary," the woman who had been tailing me said. "What is she doing here?" She sounded surprised—and not in a good way. Her words were embossed with a watered-down fear.

"Looking for Grandma. Hey," I called over my shoulder, "did you know your boss is dead?"

There was a short, shocked pause. "Antonis is dead?"

"It's for the best," Kyria Koufo said.

"What happened to him?"

"I did it for you." A thin whine had wiggled its way into the older woman's voice. "He was using you."

"I was working *for* him," Cleopatra said. "Good, honest work. In return he gave me money—money I *need*."

"What for do you need his money? I have money."

"Yes, but his money didn't have strings."

"Christ on a cracker," I said in English, then switched back to Greek. I slowly turned around. "What does any of this have to do with Grandma and me?"

"Nothing," Cleopatra said, but she wasn't looking at me. She was staring at Kyria Koufo as though her lover was dog poop smeared on her shoe.

Varvara Koufo's head swiveled from me to Cleopatra and back again.

"Your grandmother is stealing from me!" Her words were damp, hard pebbles. "I want to raise prices, she says 'No.' I want to diversify, bring in some sisa, she says 'No.' I know an excellent sisa cook who could make us all a fortune, but Katerina says she won't be responsible for Greece's destruction. So high and mighty. Sometimes I think she believes she is a better class of criminal."

I wanted to high five Grandma for saying "No" to sisa. The 'cocaine of the poor' was ripping the country apart, now that regular drugs were increasingly unaffordable.

Ungh! What was I thinking? Drugs were bad. Prescriptions drugs could be a controlled kind of bad; they often came with warning labels longer than the Magna Carta. Pop a pill to stop smoking, you could wind up in the kitchen contemplating the merits of knife juggling. Got psoriasis? Say goodbye to patchy skin, say hello to oily gas. In some ways, the pharmaceutical industry was Ursula from *The Little Mermaid*. So me sitting here hooraying Grandma's stance on sisa wasn't really a victory for the War Against Drugs.

They're getting to you, the mean girl inside me said. *Soon you won't be* like *them—you will* be *them*. The bad thing about an inner mean girl is that you can't kick sand in her face and put laxatives in her brownies.

"I hope you can run," I said, "because the Family won't stop hunting you. And if you kill me, too, it will be that much worse."

Tell me Grandma's still alive. Tell me …

"I won't kill you. Only her."

Relief mingled with anger. Grandma was alive—for now.

"What are you going to do with me?"

"That's up to you. You have two choices. You let me kill the old woman, then you go back to the Family, where things will change. You will be in control. Everyone will follow your commands …"

Phenomenal local power … in an itty bitty fiefdom.

"… and together we will make an even bigger fortune selling sisa. You will be rich beyond anything you have ever imagined. Powerful. Young. The world will kneel in front of you. Or—" She made a face. "I will do a deal with the next head of the Makris family, if there is one."

"You want me to betray Grandma?" It was the second time today I'd been encouraged to sell out.

"What's the problem? You barely know her or the Family, and she's trying to force you to take her place. What kind of loving grandmother is that?"

"Aren't you trying to force me to take over?"

"No!" she cried out. "I am offering you a choice. What choice has she offered you? None. She rolls over you like she rolls over everyone. I give you choices. She takes them away. You could take the sisa deal, then walk away if you want. Hand the Family to someone else. Go live your life in America, doing whatever it was you did before." She looked at me expectantly.

"Bill collector."

"Was that a job or a hobby?"

"Job."

"Not bad," she said. "You could go back to that."

"Can't. Grandma burned down my workplace."

"See?" She leaned close, as if we were sharing a secret. "You could be free of all that," she whispered. "You could be your own woman. But first, Katerina has to die."

"Or we both die?"

"No. If it were up to me I'd kill you, too. If you don't take the deal I'm giving you away, as a good faith gift."

"Huh?" Eloquent, I know. But gifts were things, not people.

"He came here to kill me, you know, because I offered a bounty to have you assassinated. He is killing everyone who wishes you harm. But we made an agreement, the Dogas boy and I. But if you and I make our own agreement, then I will be happy to kill him."

"You and Periphas Dogas?

She did a tiny, but affirmative, shrug.

My bravado rolled over and played dead. Varvara Koufo was one of the freaks who had wanted me dead, and now she was in cahoots with a bird-loving psychopath.

"Which assassin was yours?"

"The Russian."

Vlad. The meanest of the bunch. "What's the agreement?"

"I get rid of your grandmother, the Dogas boy gets to keep you."

"Why didn't he get rid of her himself."

She shrugged. "Nobody else has the balls to take on the infamous Katerina Makri, except me. It was a good deal for both of us."

"What do you say, will we be in business together?"

"I don't know," I said. "I'm trying to think of a polite way to tell you where to shove it."

There was a soft, malignant chuckle.

Cleopatra glanced backwards and gasped. A shadow appeared at her elbow. It stepped out of the gloom, into the slightly lesser gloom. He wasn't wearing mirrored shades but I recognized the man as Periphas Dogas. Mostly because of the big freakin' eagle on his left shoulder.

"Shh," he crooned. "Don't move. Don't move and everything will be okay."

Holy cow, was that meant for me? This guy was several musicians short of an orchestra.

"What are you doing here? We agreed you wouldn't come until later." Kyria Koufo sounded pissed off.

"Doing time made me impatient. You move too slow."

"We have a timetable here, Dogas."

"You have a timetable. Me, I want to be sure everything is being done right. I don't want anything happening to my prize."

"We made a deal. I promised not to hurt her."

"And look, here you are with a gun in her face."

"I had to get her inside somehow," Kyria Koufo hissed.

Now that I was seeing him without the mirrored shades, Periphas Dogas was his old man, with an easy forty years shaved off the crevasses, crags plastered over with acne scars. Prison had stolen his body fat and shoved some gym-built muscles under his skin. The effect was lumpy and mean. He was a junkyard dog in a man's skin.

"What, you never heard of an invitation? You are a coarse woman, Koufo. A peasant. Even amongst peasants you are rough, unpolished."

Her face twisted into unhappy shapes. "Who are you calling a peasant? Look at your family. Your mother is a *putana,* who lay down with a dog that stuck his *poutsa* in everything with a pulse. They were not even husband and wife."

The bird lurched as he gave a carefree shrug. He was creeping closer. "Maybe that's true, but I rose above that. Self-improvement, that's what I strive for every day. I refuse to rot in a village like a peasant. What is life for if not for the pursuit of perfection?"

She scoffed at that. "You are a genius. Where did prison fit into your plan?"

"It was an opportunity to meet new people, make contacts that can't be made anywhere else."

Kyria Koufo rolled her eyes. "Only an idiot would look at prison as a career move," she told Cleopatra and me.

"I can see why the old man didn't stick around all those years ago …" Periphas stuck his head through the open living room door, glanced around. He pulled back and made a face. "You've got no ambition beyond the accumulation of wealth. For two minutes I have been listening to you and I'm so bored I'm thinking about sticking this gun in my mouth to get away from you. Good thing you've got my girl there or I might be tempted."

The old man? Did he mean old Rabbit boned this nut with the gun on me? Yikes. He really did get around.

"You are indiscreet," Kyria Koufo said. "Now that I have thought about it, I do not think I need you. I can kill the girl, kill Katerina, and kill you for being annoying."

"I can shoot faster. Also, I have this cool eagle. Do you like my eagle, Katerina?"

Kyria Koufo nudged me with the muzzle. "Quiet."

"I want her to answer," Periphas said.

I was shooting for bold, but my words came out sticky and tentative. "Does it have a name?"

"Sam Eagle." His skin pinkened. "I liked *The Muppet Show*."

"What are you going to do with me?" I asked.

"We're going to disappear together, for a while. Then when you realize you love me, we will come back so you can claim your Family for me."

Kyria Koufo coughed up a small, bitter laugh. "You are deluded if you think the Makris family will submit to you. To her, yes. But never to an outsider."

"A woman will do anything for a man she loves. And she will love me."

"I do not care what you do with her. She is another obstacle, as far as I am concerned."

"Why did you run away from me when I tried to talk to you?" I asked him.

"It wasn't time for us to meet." Periphas held out his hand—the one that wasn't aiming a gun. He flipped a 'come here' wave. "Give her to me and we can go about our business."

My captor shoved me toward him.

"This won't work," I said. "The Family will be looking for us."

Aunt Rita knew where we were. Someone was already on the way.

"Then we have to go now," Periphas said. "I've got a van out back. Did you get my gifts?"

"Gifts," I said flatly.

"The heart, the eyes …" His voice dipped to a seductive level. "…the other thing."

Oh my God, gifts? There weren't enough exclamation points in the world to express myself right now.

"Dude, are you high?"

He looked at me like I'd forgotten to bring my sandwiches to the picnic, and I realized I'd blurted in English. There wasn't a Greek equivalent of "dude." It was singular in its awesomeness. So I translated to Greek and lost most of my oomph. It's the price you paid when you were bilingual but not completely versed in slang and the current cool lingo.

"I never take drugs. Even when I was in prison I was clean." He looked mildly offended. "My body is a temple."

A temple of crazy.

"Most guys send flowers. Or they let you know they're interested via the age-old art of conversation."

"That's not how I do things. Not when it's destiny."

"Destiny?" I squeaked. "This isn't destiny, it's stalking!"

"It's not stalking to kill for the woman you love, it's romantic."

"We have very different ideas about romance!"

He looked miffed. "You are the first woman I've killed for. I never loved anyone this much."

"Love me? We've never even met! You don't know anything about me." My voice was beginning to climb the decibels. At the rate this was going I'd be able to shatter his skull a few sentences from now. "Anyway, if they were for me, why did you address them to Grandma?"

"I didn't. Katerina Makri, that's your name, yes?"

"Yes, but with an S on the end."

He looked baffled. "Why would you have an S on the end of Makri? You're a woman."

"Well, I have an S. Deal with it."

He glanced from Kyria Koufo back to me. "Nobody told me about the S."

"Who cares?" she said. Her face said she definitely didn't give a rat's hiney. She wanted us dead, gone, out of her way.

Then I heard a *clang* from somewhere behind one of the doors. It was muffled and distant, the kind of *clang* that says, '*Help! I can't quite reach the saw to cut these ropes*.' I crossed my fingers, hoped it was Grandma. I'd do anything to spring her out of this nut house. Kook One and Kook Two were welcome to shoot each other, or whatever fate suited them.

"Go see what's happening down there," Kyria Koufo told Cleopatra, who had been quiet all this time. "Use more gas if you have to."

Panic was beginning to snowball inside me. "Gas? What kind of gas?"

Cleopatra squeezed past us. She had the nerve to look slightly sorry, but not sorry enough to whack her lover over the head, grab her gun, and shoot Periphas in something non-vital, yet excruciating and crippling. The older woman watched her sway toward the door, which meant she missed the shadow moving past the living room shutters.

My heart stuttered. Someone else was here. Hopefully a rescue team.

Something primeval inside me—something that knew about things like prolonging a confrontation so that the cavalry has time to show up and slay the bad guys—said, "Your plan stinks, Varvara."

Forget God's laws: I had committed a Greek mortal law. Nobody calls a person an easy thirty years their senior by their first name. It's a 'ban-able from all good society' offense

Kyria Koufo jabbed me with her gun. "Shut your mouth. You have no respect."

"Sure I have respect … for people who deserve it. You've done nothing to deserve it. You're a … a … drug dealer."

"I am a businesswoman!"

I scoffed with a nonchalance I didn't feel. "You're a middleman. Not smart or rich enough to acquire the product, and not personable enough to sell it. You sit in between the important people like a leech." I made slurping noises.

Periphas' grin was on the far side of crazy. "My future wife is clever. A warrior! A woman fit for the Eagle."

"And you." I turned on him. "You're this close to being a date rapist."

"Not even once. I have been saving it for my wife."

"Ugh! What's wrong with you?" I yelled at him.

"Okay, honey, now we are leaving," he said. "You talk too much, but I can fix that."

"This is nothing," I said. "Normally I talk so much more than this. I never stop—ask anyone." I nodded to the shadow at his back. "Ask him."

Periphas whirled around in time for Xander's fist to smash his jaw. I snatched the gun out of Kyria Koufo's outstretched hand, shoved her into the wall, with zero regrets or apologizes, and ran toward the door through which Cleopatra had vanished.

I was teetering at the mouth of a basement, wooden steps vanishing into the gloom. There was light but it was off to the side, almost entirely bled out before it reached the bottom of the steps. A small hissing sound was coming from the same direction. Then I heard a laugh, the disconcerting tittering of a drunkard.

Grandma.

"Who paints your face?" she was saying. "A monkey? It looks like a baboon wiped his rainbow-colored *kolos* on your face."

No prizes for guessing who she was talking to. Couldn't be anyone but Cleopatra. Was the faux Queen of the Nile armed? I didn't think so, but I couldn't be sure. Good thing I had a gun now, even if there was an excellent chance I'd be too scared to use it. Last time I'd gotten lucky—or unlucky—and the gun hadn't fired. Still, never underestimate the terror of knowing you're standing at the wrong end of a gun. Just because it's broken or unloaded, doesn't mean it can't kill you.

I took the steps slowly, lowering my weight in the next best thing to silence. On the other side of the door there was a fight happening. But Periphas and Kyria Koufo didn't stand a chance against Xander.

At least I hoped they didn't.

"Shut up, old woman!" Cleopatra said.

"You put the mask on my face, idiot. My Virgin Mary, Varvara always picks the stupid ones."

"I know what to do," Cleopatra snapped. "I work for a dentist!"

"Not anymore. Wee … you are unemployed like the rest of Greece!" Grandma was higher than a runaway balloon. "Want to see me do a cartwheel?"

"No!"

"*Pfffft*. You are no fun. Clowns are supposed to be funny."

I didn't think so. Clowns were freaky as hell. Even before Stephen King dreamed up Pennywise, clowns were on my 'Hell No' list. To me the ultimate monster would be a clown wasp. Or a wasp clown. Imagine one of those bearing down on you, rictus grin oil-painted on its face.

Slowly, I turned to face the puddle of light. It was overflowing from an old bulb dangling overhead, the bulk of its aura contained by a flimsy metal shade that looked a lot like a cheesy UFO prop from a 1950s B-movie. Beneath it was an old-fashioned dentist's chair, and reclining was Grandma, nebulizer mask over her mouth and nose. Cleopatra was standing to her left, wielding … nothing?

What kind of bad guy was she, anyway?

Grandma cackled. She pulled her mask to one side, said, "Ha-ha. I know something you do not know."

Nitrous oxide was a partial time machine. It had shunted Grandma's mentality back to those awkward and obnoxious tween years, when her mouth was busy scribbling checks her body and current position—in the present, strapped to a dentist's chair—couldn't afford.

"What?" Cleopatra asked in a bored voice.

"BANG!" Grandma dropped the mask back into place, took a deep breath.

Was that my cue? I couldn't tell if it was a cue, or an inside joke, or a random flapping of my grandmother's juvenile tongue.

Just in case …

I felt up the gun. Damn it, this was a handgun, not a pistol. There was no hammer to cock, no loud click to strike fear into Cleopatra's heart—if she had one.

So I whistled and said, "Yoo-hoo, I'll make ya famous," in English. *Young Guns 2*'s best line didn't sound nearly as cool in Greek.

Cleopatra whirled around to face me. I stepped into the light. Her gaze dropped to take in the gun in my hand. She rolled her eyes. "You're not going to shoot me, you spineless cow."

"I have a spine. It's straighter than yours." I put on my concerned face. "Have you been checked for scoliosis?"

"What?" Her mouth was all protest, but her back was trying to snap itself into a straight line.

"Step away from my grandmother."

"I was trying to free her."

"Yeah right."

She sighed like I was major pain in her ass—probably not the first—and flicked open the straps around Grandma's ankles. Grandma's foot shot up, nailing Cleopatra in the chest.

"Careful of her implants!" I yelled.

"These are real!"

I tilted my head. "Both of them?"

While Cleopatra was busy trying to think up a lethal comeback, Grandma clipped her ear with a shoe.

"Stop it," Cleopatra squealed. "I'm trying to help you."

"Some help you are," Grandma said. "You cut the gas."

"Grandma!"

The door at the top of the stairs swung open with an audible creak. Something stumbled through. I whipped around, but staring into the light had temporarily zapped my bat skills.

Curse words rolled toward us, a tumbleweed of insults and suggestions about what we should do in hell, and with what and whom. I didn't fancy the bull, the goat, the Romani, or the rolling pin, but as little as we knew each other, Kyria Koufo had no way of knowing my preference for attractive human males.

As she landed at the bottom of the stairs, I realized I now had a problem: two targets, one gun. Given that Grandma seemed to be kicking around like a donkey, I went with Kyria Koufo and swung the gun in her direction.

"Freeze," I said.

"My baby," she said, "what are you doing?"

Huh? Oh. That wasn't meant for me. In the dark it was hard to tell. Given the spontaneous declaration of love Periphas had tossed my way there was no knowing if it was contagious or not. But no, as she shuffled closer it became obvious her attention was on the walking Makeup Gone Wild advertisement.

Cleopatra straightened up. "It's not right keeping an old woman tied up in the basement."

"That's not an old lady, it's the devil."

"I have been called worse and by better people," Grandma said. Then she giggled—giggled!

Giggling usually has an age limit. After that it's a sanity problem.

Or, in Grandma's case, a nitrous oxide problem.

"She would kill us both if she could," Kyria Koufo said. "That's why she came here—to kill us."

"Not her." Grandma nodded to Cleopatra. "You. You went behind my back and betrayed me. It had to be done."

The world tilted. I couldn't get off so I leaned against the wall to wait it out.

"Because you are a fool," Kyria Koufo hissed. "I handed you the keys to a vault of gold but you turned it down, snatched the keys away, and threw them in the ocean."

"Listen to all the drama," Grandma said. "You should have been on the stage!"

Kyria Koufo reached for the gun I was holding. "No," I yelped and slapped her fingers. I channeled my inner crab, scooting sideways until I was free of her, then I switched animal spirit guides and launched into a leopard crawl.

BANG!

We all jumped. Everyone was looking at me.

"It wasn't me," I said. "Upstairs."

BANG!

Then silence.

I scurried toward Grandma.

Something clanked overhead. I jumped up and began unbuckling the rest of Grandma's restraints. Kyria Koufo lunged at me and managed to miss, colliding with the tank of nitrous. I jerked Grandma out of the chair. She got a nice, soft landing, courtesy of my body, but at least she didn't break a hip. Cleopatra wrestled Kyria Koufo to the ground.

"Shoot the tank!" Cleopatra said.

Shoot a person? I couldn't do that. But I was pretty sure I had the guts to shoot a tank of nitrous oxide.

I pulled the trigger. There was a loud boom, followed by ringing in my ears as the gunshot's sound waves raced across the room and buried themselves in the underground wall.

As I stood up, I saw the jagged little hole in the tank, accompanied by a loud hissing. But no fireball.

"Nitrous oxide isn't flammable," I said to no one in particular, mostly because they couldn't hear me after the gun's roar. High school science told me it wasn't flammable, but panic has a way of kicking perfectly good knowledge aside so that it has room to show off.

I grabbed Grandma, steered her toward the stairs.

"Xander's up there," I yelled. "Maybe the police now, too."

In that same moment the basement door opened. A man-shape loomed over us, and because there wasn't much light visible around his edges, I knew we were safe.

"Take her," I told Xander. "And don't take anything she says personally. They loaded her up on happy gas." He scooped Grandma up into his arms, and vanished up the stairs.

Which left me alone with Cleopatra and Kyria Koufo, who were giggling like a pair of idiots, slapping at each other, pulling hair. Throw in some Jell-O and I'd have a pay-per-view event. Hopefully it wouldn't be long until the police arrived. They could sort these two nuts into separate piles. But until then I was staying put.

Suddenly, another shape filled the doorway at the top of the steps. This one was smaller, more slightly cut than Xander.

Periphas was still alive.

My breath caught. I held it captive in its bone cage.

He limped down the stairs and dropped his backside on the bottom step. The eagle was gone. He had a red, flooding hole in his left shoulder. His breathing was shallow, ragged. He glanced over at the women, but he couldn't see me. The thin light was like cornstarch, thickening the shadows.

He swayed on his makeshift seat. Xander must have mistaken him for dead or incapacitated, which was the only reason he was sitting here now. He pushed up off the step and shuffled toward the tussling, giggling women.

"Where is she?" he rasped.

The two hens cackled.

"Where?"

Any other member of my family might have stepped forward, tapped him on the shoulder with the stolen gun, said "Peek-a-boo."

Not me. I was less Makris, more chicken.

Behind him, I inched toward the steps. The plan was to bolt up the steps, slam the door, and wait for someone bigger and tougher than me to take care of this three-person mess in the basement—hopefully someone with a shiny badge and the law on their side.

The steps had other plans. The first one sang out as I lowered my weight onto its head, the little crybaby. I crunched down on my lip to keep the curse words in the paddock.

Too late. Periphas' head swiveled first, followed by the rest of him. His gaze latched onto mine, and for a moment we stood there, each of us a deer, watching an oncoming train.

We both lunged: me up the stairs, him toward me. My chin slammed one of the higher steps as he grabbed my ankle and pulled.

I went mule, kicking and bucking, desperately trying to land an incapacitating blow. The gun was still in my hand but I was facedown and in danger of shooting myself in the ass, literally, if I reached back and fired.

The hyenas laughed harder. They'd stopped tussling to enjoy the death match.

Some match. I was a former bill collector, whose hobbies included television, eating, and naps. His interests lay with the ancient arts of murder and organ removal. There was no "match" about it.

How do you fight batshit crazy?

I couldn't do anything on my belly. I had to roll, so that's what I did. As I twisted I trapped his head between my knees and squeezed. He grabbed my shins and jerked, but his left arm was weaker, which gave me an opening. I pulled my knee high and tight against my stomach, then kicked the snot out of his shoulder.

He gasped. Stumbled backwards.

When he recovered a split second later my other foot was waiting for his face. Something made a satisfying and gross *crunch.* I was too frightened to gloat. Like a four-legged spider, I attempted to scramble up the stairs.

"Run and I'll kill you, *mouni*!" he shouted behind me, because using the Greek equivalent of the c-word is always the way to attract a woman.

He grabbed both my ankles, yanked me back down the steps, obliterating what little progress I'd made. Then his right hand circled my neck. The left gripped my ponytail and pulled until hot tears flooded my eyes. I lifted my hand to shoot. He let go of my hair to slap it away. The gun clattered on the basement floor.

My mouth formed a word. "Help!"

I meant for it to be less croak, more primal yell.

There was one more tool in my arsenal. It required cozying up to the enemy. My arm curled around his neck and lured him closer. His grip on my neck loosened. He thought I was submitting to his loony fantasy. My mouth bypassed his lips. I sank my teeth into the tip of his nose.

Periphas Dogas shrieked, flailed. His feet scrambled on the basement floor but couldn't get a grip. I didn't let go.

The women laughed harder.

I wasn't letting go—ever, if that's what it took to survive.

Then I felt hands on my shoulders that didn't belong to the crazy guy.

"Jesus," Melas said. "It's okay, we've got it from here."

"What's she biting?" a voice I didn't recognize asked.

"His nose, I think," someone else said.

"Harsh."

But they both sounded mildly impressed.

Finally, I let go. I looked up to see Melas, Stained Shirt, and a cop I didn't know crowding the steps.

"If you think I will marry you now, you're crazy!" Periphas howled.

Melas raised an eyebrow. "Something you're not telling me?"

"The organs. They were love offerings."

"Jesus."

23

The other puzzles pieces fell into place during questioning, but I didn't hear about them until long after I'd buried myself under a pile of Grandma's pastries and attempted to eat my way out. Now that she was home, she'd taken up baking with a vengeance. Xander and I sat in the kitchen, quietly watching her empty sacks of flour and sugar into mixing bowls. Every so often Xander glanced at me, a silent question in his eyes.

What do you think, is she okay?

I gave him a tiny shrug, because I couldn't tell. She was my grandmother but he knew her better than I did. What toll does it take being locked away, losing a long-term friend to greed?

~ ~ ~

After I'd eaten my weight in Greek cookies and Grandma had gone to bed, I wandered out to the courtyard. I couldn't sleep. My mind was too cluttered. I dragged myself to the pool, sat on its tiled edge, swished my purpling legs through its cool water. Yeah, I could throw on a swimsuit, but I didn't want to commit. This was all I needed, to know that the water was there. A couple of the resident dogs loped over, tongues lolling as I petted them. When I stopped, they flopped on the ground nearby, in case I needed something to hug.

I wasn't the only one ground down to a dense powder by the day. It wasn't long before I heard the familiar hum of Melas's car, followed by his footsteps. They were slow, even, economical. He stopped somewhere behind me, shucked his shoes, and when he sat down beside me he'd rolled his jeans up to his knees. The dogs lifted their heads briefly before resuming their snooze.

"Long day," he said, after a while.

"You got your man, your woman, and your other woman."

"Triple bonus." He nudged me with his elbow. "You okay?"

"It's not every day a lunatic declares his love for you with severed body parts." I put on a fake-excited teen girl voice. "I can't wait to tell all my friends!"

Melas chuckled. It was a warm, comforting sound.

"He sang like a bird once we got him to the hospital. Wouldn't shut up about how much he'd loved you and how you'd betrayed him."

"Betrayed him. Ha!"

"He admitted that he'd been planning to kill Kyria Koufo anyway, despite their deal. Said he was going to box up her tongue for you as a wedding gift."

"Wow, does he know how to charm the ladies or what?"

He laughed. "We're letting the other woman go."

"Cleopatra? Why?"

"Her name's Cleopatra Katsika."

My head jerked up. "Wife, daughter, distant cousin?"

"She's Tony's niece."

"Incestuous bunch."

He nodded. "She told us she was following you as a favor to her uncle. Tony believed your father hadn't been kidnapped. He thought it was a game your father cooked up."

"Why?"

But I knew why—because that's what Dad and Cookie did when someone wanted them to take a test. Tony had believed there was test in play, a game afoot. My brain boxed up that thought and carried it to a dark corner for closer inspection some other time.

"Apart from following you around and sleeping with a drug distributor and killer, she didn't commit any crime," Melas explained. "She claimed she was trying to free your grandmother in that basement." He looked to me for confirmation.

"I guess," I muttered.

"We can't get a word out of Varvara Koufo. She won't say who pushed her husband's girlfriend down the stairs, or who killed her husband."

I raised my hand. "She told me she killed her husband. The Russian assassin, Vlad, he was on her payroll. Probably he pushed the girlfriend down the stairs."

"We'll round him up. Your entourage seems to have dissipated."

I nodded. "All except Elias. Grandma is hiring him for protective detail. She's impressed with the way he stopped the others from killing me. I'm surprised they didn't follow me to Kyria Koufo's place."

"You can blame me for that," he said. "I know I do. At the airstrip, I told them if they followed I'd lock them up."

A door opened. Then was the scuffing sound of slippers on concrete. Grandma was making a midnight trip to the outhouse. There was a pause, then: "Katerina, my love, why are your feet bare? Put on some shoes. You, too, Nikos. And keep your hands where the sniper can see them."

"Sniper?" He sounded worried.

"There's no sniper." I thought about it for a moment. "Okay, maybe there's a sniper, but you should be fine. You being here isn't going to help with the bet, though, that's for sure."

"I knew there was a bet! What are they betting on?"

I groaned. "The Family is betting on us sleeping together."

He tilted his head back, laughed. When he stopped laughing his face was stained with a wicked grin. "Is that right? Who's running the book?"

"Why?"

"Maybe I want to place a bet."

"You wouldn't!"

"Sure I would." He winked. "I've got inside information."

I jumped up, shoved my wet feet back into the sandals I'd kicked off. "Don't you have a home to go to?"

He laughed. "Come on, I've got something for you in the car."

"What is it?" I asked suspiciously.

"A surprise."

~ ~ ~

There are always casualties in war. Fallen soldiers who leave behind orphans, widows, and other hearts that bleed for them.

Periphas Dogas left his eagle. Maybe the bird missed him—who could tell? It was an eagle, for crying out loud. They're known for patriotism and performing feats of dog snatching in urban legends.

Anyway, Periphas Dogas had a bird, and now the bird didn't have Periphas Dogas. Melas was giving me a look like I knew what to do with an abandoned eagle.

"Forget it," I said. "I already have a goat."

"And now you have an eagle. You're like Dr. Doolittle."

"Can't Periphas take it to prison with him?"

"No. It was a problem last time. Kept eating the rats."

I didn't see how that was a problem until I squinted between the lines. The eagle had been stealing potential food from hungry men, in a country that didn't have the cash to feed its prisoners properly.

"Fine," I said, rolling my eyes so he knew it was a major hardship. "I'll take the damn bird."

He hooked his finger into the top of my dress. "Want me to tell you how I'm going to win that bet?"

"You're not winning anything. I'm going to make sure you lose."

He grinned. "Honey, if I win, we both win."

~ ~ ~

Offloading the eagle turned out to be easy. Papou took one look at the eagle the next morning and claimed Sam Eagle for himself.

"I will love him and squeeze him and call him Yiorgos." He looked sideways at the caged bird, which was glaring at Grandma's potted saplings. "Okay, maybe not squeeze him or he will tear out my throat." He nodded to me. "Where are you going?"

My body had taking a beating on the basement steps, but I didn't care enough to cover them up. Battle bruises. I'd pulled on a sundress, flats, and sunglasses. Now, I was Makria-bound.

I dropped my bag over my head, pulled it into position. "I have to see a man about some meat."

"Get some for the bird, eh? What do eagles eat?"

"Mice. Vermin." Not something in large supply at the compound. The family kept cats. Or, more accurately, the cats kept the family around so they'd have servants. The way things had worked out, I never did get to chat to the local bird nerd. Maybe I'd have to now that there was an eagle in the family. Sam Eagle had to eat. Eventually, he'd need healthcare.

"See if they have some lamb, eh?"

One lone car waited on the dirt outside the compound's gates. On the hood sat Lefty, gun in hand, looking his normal, bland self. He was everyman. He was nobody.

"We've still got a problem, you and I," he called out. "A conflict of interest."

Behind me, Elias tensed. Cotton whispered to nylon polymer as he eased his gun from its hidden holster. The security guard stepped out the guardhouse, rifle raised.

My voice wobbled out. "You planning to shoot me?"

The beige man made a face. "You seem like a nice girl." He patted his flat belly. "But I like to eat."

"Your employer is still alive?"

He chuckled at the punch line of an inaudible joke. "I'm still here."

Surprise yanked my eyebrows northwards. "Working for yourself?"

The bullet stepped out of the sky, buried itself in Lefty's forehead, the way a projectile does when flung by an accurate pitcher.

Lefty slumped right. His gun tumbled onto the dirt road, followed by his body.

"Meep," I said, heart flailing its hands Kermit-style in my chest.

I whirled around, hand shading my eyes. The sniper on the main building's roof waved. Naturally, as it was around here, he was one of my second or third cousins.

"Too soon?" he yelled.

"Too soon!"

"I'm working on my timing!"

I gave him a thumbs-up, out of shock, mostly. My feelings were gloppy and a messy sort of mixed. Lefty had wanted to kill me. I wanted to live. But I was the kind of deranged optimist who wanted to live without other people dying.

Apparently I couldn't always have both. Somehow, for now, I had to make peace with that so I wouldn't completely lose my shit and wind up in the psych ward.

Once I found Dad, I could safely crack.

Footsteps came to check on the dead man. And in the distance, sirens began their approach.

I didn't stick around; I had somewhere to be.

~ ~ ~

The sun flogged me half-heartedly as I walked to Makria. Despite its name it wasn't even close to being Far, Far Away. Elias followed at a discreet distance. Behind the wheel of a black Mini Cooper he was bound to attract more attention than me. Greeks didn't drive slow, and Elias was crawling. A huffing, puffing bus on the brink of extinction overtook him. The driver waved the second, smaller, less well-known Greek flag: a raised middle digit.

When I arrived at the village, the former assassin parked and followed me on foot. I didn't mind so much. Grandma paid him, but he was new to the Family, like me. We were muddling along, figuring things out.

Spiros the Butcher was hacking the head off a pig when I stepped through his open door. A blowfly was doing laps, working up an appetite before it settled on a cut of meat.

"*Despinida* Katerina!" he said, beaming. Miss Katerina.

"Just Katerina is fine, I promise."

He jerked his head up. "It would not be proper. How can I help you today? You need meat?"

I told him about the eagle and he suggested lamb. He got to work with his cleaver, making chunks out of what had once been a perfectly serviceable leg.

"What did you come to see me about yesterday? We were interrupted and I never got a chance to find out."

He didn't look up, but there was a funny expression on his face, as if he wasn't sure whether to go on or not. Finally, he must have decided I was okay, because he said, "Those people who came here, the tourists, do you remember?"

The Germans who had asked about a butcher's shop. "I remember."

"There was something strange about their money."

"How do you mean?"

"Wait, I will show you." He wiped his hands on his apron, then from beneath the counter he rustled up a lockbox, which he opened with a key he kept on a string around his neck. He plucked a handful of euro bills from inside, dumped them on the counter in front of me.

I picked them up one at a time. This wasn't my money; I wasn't familiar enough with it yet to know its quirks and secrets.

"I don't know what I'm looking for," I admitted.

"That money feels wrong," he said. "And I know money. First I knew drachmas, now I know euros, and these are not real euros."

"They look real enough."

He shrugged. "They are very good copies. Whoever did this was a master because he fooled even me at first." He tapped a thick finger on the side of his head. "But I am not stupid. As soon as I counted the money for the day, I knew it. When I took the money from them I had gloves on. But with bare hands?" He picked up one of the notes, rubbed the corner between his fingers. "This is fake."

"Counterfeit …" I murmured.

Was counterfeiting something the Family did? No idea. Nobody had given me a cheat sheet.

"Let me think for a second," I said. "Have you told anyone else?"

"Who am I going to tell? The police?" He laughed. "This is why I came to Kyria Katerina. She knows what to do about these things."

Someone came to this village—Grandma's village—and passed counterfeit money off as the real thing. Even if that were the Family's bailiwick, she wouldn't do that to her people. She and Makria, they had each other's backs.

I poked around in my bag, pulled out my purse, counted out an equivalent number of notes. "Here. I'll swap you real money for your fake money."

"Are you sure?"

"Absolutely."

"You are a generous girl." He beamed. "You have much of your grandmother in you."

He meant it as a blessing, but I couldn't see it as anything but mixed.

~ ~ ~

Grandma was still baking, with Xander for company. He wasn't letting her out of his sight, except for trips to the outhouse. I didn't want to mess with her coping mechanism, so I sat at the kitchen table quietly and sought out the occasionally misguided wisdom of the Crooked Noses. Counterfeiting was a widespread problem, the board's archives told me, but success stories were rare. The euro was difficult to duplicate, yet in a small Italian town named Giuliano, an organization called the Napoli Group had developed a reputation for producing almost flawless copies. In the Naples area counterfeiting was an art form passed from father to son. Scam artists from all over the world gravitated to Giuliano to beg for moneymaking lessons. There was a strong rumor that Kostas Makris, a Greek-German crime lord had sent one of his own to Italy to bone up on counterfeiting skills.

My blood chilled. My hands suddenly had all the rigidity of a rubber chicken. I suspected the rest of my body was in a similar state, which was why I maintained the sitting position. If I moved I'd wind up in an untidy heap on the kitchen floor.

Kostas Makris was my father's brother. My uncle in Germany. And inside my childhood—and adulthood—home there was a safe stashed full of cash and alternate identities, one of which was Italian. I dredged my memory for entry and exit stamps, clues about where Dad had been and when. But all I could recall were tales he had told me about long-distance truck trips he'd had to take for work. When I'd taken that brief, unwanted, jaunt back home, only the most recent date in one of the passports had stood out.

I needed to see the rest.

"I need to go home," I said, clicking off my phone. "There's some business I need to take care of. Then I'll be back."

I could have told her—maybe *should* have told her. But my uncle was her son. Loyalty passed to sons before granddaughters. When I delivered the news about the counterfeit money, it would be with proof in hand.

Assuming she didn't already know.

Distrust bubbled in my midsection …

Grandma's hands quit kneading. When her eyes met mine I realized that somewhere along the way they'd warmed from flint to chocolate chips. In half a month we'd come a long way together. Where would we be another month from now? A year? Would she still be here in this kitchen, baking her worries away?

"Takis will take you in the jet," she said. "Stavros and Elias can go, too."

I shook my head. "No henchmen. No bodyguards. I want to go on a regular airline. No private plane."

"Katerina—"

"I'm doing this my way. It's important to me that it be all above-board. But I'll be back."

She nodded. "Okay."

I'd saved Grandma's life, and now I was standing up to her. Things were slowly changing.

And now I was going home.

Home. Mom and Dad's house.

Where there was a safe full of money, and passports with Dad's face and other men's names. Where there was a gun I hadn't known he had.

"You did well while I was … away," Grandma said. "I knew that strength was in you."

"There was no choice. Sink or swim."

"There is always choice."

The phone came on again. I was fiddling, the way I did when my mind was chewing cud. "I thought that puzzle box would be a clue."

"We both thought the same thing. We are optimists, you and I."

"You?" The word blurted out.

She nodded, went back to the kneading. "Even after all I have seen in my life, I want to believe in good things. I wanted to believe Rabbit had an answer for us, a clue about Michail. He owed me big. But …" She shrugged.

Rabbit had let her down.

But if I could help it, I wouldn't.

If there was a correlation between Dad and the counterfeiting I was going to find it. And there was one. I could feel it lounging in my gut, lazily waiting on me to make a connection.

The End

Author's Note

Thank you for reading *Trueish Crime*, the second of Kat Makris' adventures! Want to be notified when my next book is released? Sign up for my mailing list: http://eepurl.com/ZSeuL. Or like my Facebook page at: https://www.facebook.com/alexkingbooks. You can also stop by alexkingbooks.com to see what's new and what's coming soon.

Reviews can help other readers fall in love … or avoid a terrible mistake. All reviews are greatly appreciated!

Thank you, again.
All my best,
Alex A. King

Made in the USA
San Bernardino, CA
07 September 2017